USE ONCE
THEN DESTROY

Previous Books by Conrad Williams include:

London Revenant
Game
Nearly People
Head Injuries

USE ONCE
THEN DESTROY

STORIES BY CONRAD WILLIAMS

NIGHT SHADE BOOKS
SAN FRANCISCO & PORTLAND

"The Machine" © 2002 by Conrad Williams. First published in *The 3rd Alternative* #31
"Supple Bodies" © 1993 by Conrad Williams. First published in *The 3rd Alternative* #1
"The Light that Passes Through You" © 1997 by Conrad Williams. First published in
    Sirens & Other Daemon Lovers
"Nest of Salt" © 2004 by Conrad Williams
"City in Aspic" © 2001 by Conrad Williams. First published in *Phantoms of Venice*
"Other Skins" © 1993 by Conrad Williams. First published in *Panurge* #20
"The Windmill" © 1998 by Conrad Williams. First published in *Dark Terrors 3*
"Wire" © 2001 by Conrad Williams. First published in *The Museum of Horrors* as
    "Imbroglio"
"The Burn" © 1994 by Conrad Williams. First published in *Blue Motel: Narrow Houses 3*
"The Owl" © 2004 by Conrad Williams
"The Night Before" © 2004 by Conrad Williams
"Edge" © 1995 by Conrad Williams. First Published in *ABeSea*
"MacCreadle's Bike" © 1992 by Conrad Williams First Published in *Darklands 2*
"Known" © 2000 by Conrad Williams. First published in *The Time Out Book of London
    Short Stories 2*
"The Suicide Pit" © 1999 by Conrad Williams. First published in *Dark Terrors 4*
"Excuse the Unusual Approach" © 1999 by Conrad Williams. First published in *The 3rd
    Alternative* #25
"Nearly People" © 2001 by Conrad Williams. First published by PS Publishing

First Edition

ISBN
1-892389-67-3 (Hardcover)
1-892389-68-1 (Limited Edition)

Night Shade Books
http://www.nightshadebooks.com

For Ric Coady

Many thanks go to the editors who originally selected these stories: Andy Cox, Peter Crowther, Ellen Datlow, Dennis Etchison, Stephen Jones, John Murray, Nicholas Royle, David Sutton, and the late Karl Edward Wagner. Thanks also to the following for their interest in my work and their encouragement and assistance over the years: the British Fantasy Society, the Horror Writers' Association, Ramsey Campbell, Mike Chinn, Peter Coleborn, David Cowperthwaite, Jeff Dempsey, James Frenkel, Claire Herschell, David Howe, Glyn Hughes, Maxim Jakubowski, Graham Joyce, Christopher Kenworthy, Joel Lane, Jeremy Lassen, Paul Miller, Mark Morris, Robert Morrish, Chris Reed, Michèle Roberts, Michael Marshall Smith, Jason Williams, and Rhonda Carrier.

CONTENTS

THE MACHINE

When he asked her, she said: "A car, wasn't it? Or was it a bus?" There was a little smear of mayonnaise on her mouth and her hair was scrunched like dead spiders' legs at the back, where she had not been able to see it to comb in the mirror. Graham had parked the car by a pub, The Britannia, that overlooked the flat, greasy edge of sea. Inside he had bought them halves of bitter. The barmaid seemed preoccupied, unable to look them in the eye when he ordered. The only other couple were sitting at a table inspecting a camera.

"Don't you remember resting your hand on mine? On the gear lever?"

Julia looked at him as if he had asked her to perform an indecent act. Maybe, in asking her to remember, he had. He watched her as she moved her glass on the table, spreading rings of moisture across the cracked varnish. He could smell beef and onion crisps, smoke from the little train that traveled between Hythe and Dungeness, and an underlying tang; the faint whiff of seawater.

"Can you—" he began, but stopped himself. Her answers didn't matter anymore. He didn't know how long they should stay here. He didn't know how long it would take.

Three months ago, he didn't need to mash her food for her or accompany her up and down the stairs. She wouldn't slur his name or regard him with a lazy eye. "Where are we?" she said, one Sunday morning as he re-entered the bedroom with a tray of tea and toast. "I don't know where we are."

He sipped his beer. It tasted sour, as if what had filled it previously had not been properly purged from the glass. The symptoms of brain cancer—or *gioblastoma mutiforme* as the specialist revealed to them (with an unwelcome flourish, as if he were introducing an unusual item on a menu)—are headaches and lethargy, seizures, weakness and motor dysfunction, behavior changes and unorthodox thought processes. This form of cancer, the specialist said, was particularly aggressive. If it were a dog, it would be a *toza inu*.

"I don't want the rost of is," she said, pushing her drink to one side. "In bastes faddy."

He rubbed her knuckles, white and papery, and tried to smile. "It's okay," he said. "Come on."

Outside they headed towards the sea, compelled by an unspoken mutual need. She was not to know that he had been here before, many years ago. She just wanted to see the ocean one more time before her sight deteriorated. He allowed her to lean on him and they went slowly over the uneven shingle; it didn't matter. Time had lost its meaning. Time was nothing anymore other than now and the next thing. "Next week" was as alien to his vocabulary as a phrase of Russian.

The tide was a long way out, visible only as a seam of pale gray that stitched the lead of the sky to the dun of the beach. Fishing boats trapped on the shingle faced the sea, their bows raised as if impatient to return. Explosions of static from their communication radios made her start. She moved into the collapsed light as though immersing herself. The air was thick here. It seemed to coat the beach. Her footsteps in the shingle beat at the friable crust of his mind and in the shape of her progress, the delicacy of her step, he saw how near the end was.

The sea was affecting the light in some subtle way that he had not recognized before. It erased an area above the horizon, a band of vague ochre that she would stare at during the moments when she stopped to rest, as if it might contain words, or the barest outline of them, some code to unpick. An explanation. Around them, the beach slowly buried its secrets. Great knots of steel cable, an anchor that had lost its shape through the accretion of oxidant, cogs so large they might well drive the Earth's movement. All of it was slowly sinking into the endless shingle.

Us too, he thought, blithely. *If we don't keep moving.*

"He isn't here," she said, panic creeping into her voice.

"He'll come," I insisted. "He'll come. He always does."

"You saib he would be fere."

She wasn't going to be pacified. He was tiring, and sat back against one of the drifts of shingle, watched her move away from him, a gently wailing wraith in black clothes that were now too big for her. He lost her for moment, against the distant flutter of black flags on the boats, and when she re-emerged, it was to drop, exhausted, to the stones. He hoped she would be able to sleep, at least for a little while.

A wind was rising, drawing white flecks to the crest of the waves. It was getting rough out there. Small fishing boats tipped and waggled on the surf, bright and tiny against the huge expanses of cobalt pressing in all around them. Behind him, urgent bursts of white noise from the radios wrapped voices that nobody received. The deserted boats looked too blasted by salt and wind to be up to the task of setting sail for dab, pout and whiting.

An elderly couple picked their way through the shingle, hunting for sponges perhaps, or other similarly useless booty. All he remembered seeing on these beaches were rotting fish-heads and surgical gloves, thin, mateless affairs flapping in the stones like milky, viscous sea-creatures that had been marooned by the quick tides. The couple reached Julia, then passed her by, giving her a wide berth.

He hauled himself out of the shingle, noticing how the flinty chips had crept over the toes of his shoes; always the beach was in the process of sucking under, of burying. He tried to understand the motivation for building on something so insubstantial: the sheds and houses dotting the beach were grim little affairs, colorless, uninviting, utilitarian in the extreme.

He caught up with Julia; she looked withdrawn to the point of translucence. Her skin was a taut, gray thing that shone where her bones emerged. Salt formed white brackets around her mouth. The shingle had shifted across her boots, completely concealing her feet. He gently drew her upright and picked the strands of hair away from her eyes. Her scalp gleamed palely through a scant matting that had once been thick, black and silky. When she opened her eyes though, everything else became superfluous. He felt scorched by her gaze, as he had for the past twenty years. Even with her flesh failing so quickly, she could not be anything other than beautiful if she had strength enough to open her eyes and look around her.

"Are you hungry?"

She shook her head. "Where is he?"

He smiled. "You've always been impatient, haven't you? I told you he doesn't come till dark. We've got an hour yet. At least."

"I want to walk," she said, looking around her as if assessing the landscape for the first time.

"You sure you aren't too tired?" he said. "Okay. Come on."

They trudged up the beach, the strange, stunted vegetation like hunks of dried sponge or stained blotting paper trapped between the stones: sea campion, kale, Babington's orache. Angling towards the row of weatherboard cottages that lined the Dungeness Road he looked back to the great hulk of the gas-cooled reactors of the power station. Maybe they were causing the sizzle in the air, or perhaps it was the taut lines of the fishermen, buzzing with tension as lugworm and razor clam were cast far beyond the creaming tides. He told Julia that special grilles had been constructed over the cold water intake pipes for the reactors because seals kept being drawn into them. She nodded and shook her head. One eye was squeezed shut, her lank hair swung about her lowered face. A vein in her temple reminded him of mold in strong blue cheese. The color of decay. Nature consuming itself. He reached for her hand but she snatched it away as if burnt.

They toured the strange, attractive garden at Prospect Cottage where he took a picture of her standing by a circular pattern of stones that were adorned with pieces of colored glass and a single, brilliant white crab's claw. A rusting, battered trumpet had been nailed to the back door but it was so deteriorated, he couldn't tell if it was the right way up. Though the day was overcast, it had a dry, scorched smell and the air was unpleasantly metallic in his mouth, as if he had pressed a spoon against his fillings.

The previous time he had been here—the only other time—had been with his school on a field trip as part of his geography course. The teacher who accompanied them, Mr. Wilson, spoke with what Fudgey, his best mate, had said was an "X-rated lisp." His sibilants weren't so much softened as slurred. He always sounded drunk and though the boys had suspected he might be, they never smelled any booze on him; only the musty depth of the tweed that he wore or stale pipe smoke. Mint imperials.

"It's because he's missing a few teeth on his top set," one of the more liberal teachers explained, when Fudgey had been overheard mimicking him. "You should see him trying to eat a banana. I have to leave the staff room."

Mr. Wilson was more interested in birdspotting than the shape and behavior of the land. At lunch one day, he had taken some of the more interested boys with him—squeezed into his beige Rover—to the reservation and passed around binoculars that smelled of the clothes he wore. He pointed out garganey and greenshank and Balearic shearwater. On the way back, he allowed the boys half an hour on the beach while he went to post some letters and make a phone call. "You can take off your ties but leave your blazers on. This isn't a holiday. You are still representing your school."

"You are shhhhtill represhhhhenting your shhhhhchool," Fudgey intoned, spot on. "Represhhhenting my arshhe, more like."

They kicked about in the shingle and threw stones at the half-submerged gears and cogs and bolts. They agreed that this is what the world would be like after America and the Soviets swapped H-bombs. Merce found a fish-head and forced it onto the end of a stick, then chased Bebbo around—"Snog it! Snog it Bebbo! Snog the fish, you fishy-faced piss-pant!"—until he was crying. Fudgey and Graham broke away from the other three boys and headed towards the water. A naturally formed ledge gave way to a steep slope of shingle. At the edge, they could not see what had been concealed from them until two or three feet away from where the land sank towards the water.

The woman was on her knees, her jacket and blouse discarded. Her bra was lost for a moment against the shocking white of her flesh. She was weeping, trying to cut into the skin of her forearms with a piece of shingle. To her right, his back to her desperation, a man in a panama hat was sitting cross-legged in a deck chair, smoking a cigarette as he watched the horizon. All the boys could see of him was a fat, neatly barbered nape bulging over a collar; the merest edge of brow.

"Lovely view," Fudgey said, a little queasily. "Let's get back to the car."

"Wait," Graham said, but he couldn't explain what it was he wanted them to wait for. After a while, Fudgey's insistent tugging at his elbow broke through his fascination and he allowed himself to be led away.

The following day, the final day of their week in Dungeness, Mr Wilson gave them another period of free time. Fudgey wanted to play football, but Graham declined, explaining that he had a headache and just wanted to go for a walk on his own, to clear his mind. He made his way back to the spot on the beach where they had seen the woman. The deck chair was still there. Where she had been kneeling, he found a smooth, glistening curve of steel buried in the shingle. He dug at it a little, moving away the stones from each side until he had unearthed a disc as large as a train's wheel. What looked like caterpillar tracks, clean and freshly oiled, snaked around the wheel and deep into the ground. As hard as he pulled, Graham couldn't budge it. He saw too, once he rocked back onto his heels, breathing hard with the exertion, how some of the stones were spattered with black spots of blood.

He stopped at a hot dog stall on his way back to the bed-and-break-fast and ordered a Coke and a packet of ready-salted crisps. It was only as he was handing over the money to the woman that he recognized her.

"Hello," he said, and his voice cracked on the second syllable like a recording on perished tape. The woman regarded him as if he were a retard; rightly so, he realized. Hellos were gambits, usually, not something you said when you were about to be on your way.

"Sorry," he explained. "I saw you on the beach yesterday. You were—"

"I *know* what I was doing," she hissed, her eyes flicking away from his to scan their immediate surroundings. She came down the few steps at the rear of the van and grabbed him by the collar. Her cuff slid away from her wrist a little as she dragged him inside and he saw a pinkish bandage pinned tightly around her forearm. She closed the door and bolted it, unclasped the latch that kept the serving hatch opened. It was very hot inside, and heavy with the smells of enthusiastically recycled cooking oil and raw onions. Graham fed crisps into his mouth, trying hard not to appear frightened.

"Would you like some Coke?" he asked, offering her the unopened tin. She slapped it from his hands. He stopped eating and neatly closed the bag with a few twists.

"I'm sorry," she said, her voice gusting from her collapsed mouth like heat from an oven. She tousled his hair and sat on her stool, pinching the bridge of her nose between her fingers. "He said that I would have an answer before nightfall tonight. The wheels had been greased, he said. He said that the technology, though old, was of a perfection you would not find anywhere else. Ancient technology. He told me that it wasn't certain if it had been made by man or not."

She snorted, a sudden, bitter sound that was devoid of any laughter she might have meant for it. "Anyway, I don't care about that. As long as it brings him back to me." She stared intently at Graham. "My husband," she said, spicily, as if it were obvious. "A sweet, sweet man. He would help anybody. Stupid, lovely man."

Her left hand had moved to her forearm and worried at the bandage. The pinkness at its core deepened. Graham stared at the bolt on the door. He retrieved his can of Coke and pulled the ring opener. Beige froth fizzed out over his hand. The woman didn't pay him any attention. It was as if the memory of what had happened to her husband numbed her to extraneous sensation.

"There was a car on a dual carriageway. The A12 going north, towards Ipswich. A nasty bitch of a night. Wind. Rain. So hard it was coming at you side on. The car hit the central reservation and went out of control. End over end job. Came to a stop in the middle of the road. Eddie, my husband, and me, we were about a hundred yards behind. He pulled over and put his hazard lights on, ran over to help. I sat there because we were on our way to a party and I didn't want to get my hair wet. I'd just had it done, especially.

"Seconds later he was hit by a Ford Mondeo doing ninety miles an hour. Do you know… the force of the impact knocked him out of his shoes. Lace-ups. And they pinched him a little, those shoes. He was always going on about them, how he ought to get another pair."

Graham rubbed the back of his hand across his mouth. The saltiness of the crisps had made his lips sore. "What happened on the beach?" he asked.

The woman closed her eyes and then clenched them even tighter, as if the darkness behind them was not deep enough. "You don't need to know anything. I'm sorry you saw it. I didn't mean to upset you."

"Who was that man?"

By degrees she relaxed. Her eyes reopening, she reached behind her to unbolt the door. "You can go," she said, and her voice was soft and likeable now.

"Was he your boyfriend?" Graham asked.

The trace of a smile. She shook her head and then she frowned. "Yes," she said. "I suppose he was, after a fashion."

"I don't remember how I got back to the bed-and-breakfast."

"Sorry?"

They were sitting on a bench watching the colors in the sky warp as the sun ground itself out against the black mass of the power station. Julia's skin was stippled from the cold; what color it had enjoyed now thinned to that of cooked chicken, but she refused Graham's jacket when he offered it to her.

"I was just remembering," he said, turning his face away from hers, "the first time I came here. With the school."

"Where was I?"

"I didn't know you then. We didn't meet for another fifteen years."

"Where you seeing someone else?"

Graham watched the edge of the sun slip behind the reactors. Parts of the sky were green. The sunsets here were always spectacular.

"No, Jules. I was only fourteen."

She giggled. "You were neber fourteej."

The last three of the day-trippers that had come to Dungeness for a dose of stinging surreality got into their Ford Focus and backed out of the pub car park. They all turned to look out of their windows as they trundled past the bench, their faces partially eclipsed by the oily flash of weak streetlamps on the glass.

"How are you feeling?" he asked.

"It could be workse," she said. "I mean, God, I could have a brain tuzour."

He drew Julia gently upright and kissed the top of her head. Sometimes, when she slept, he would nuzzle her hair, enjoying the clean, warm smell of her scalp. He endured a second or two of real panic when he thought of her gone, her and her unique smell, and it seemed more unspeakable, for a moment, that he might not be able to recall her scent rather than the way she spoke or talked or touched him.

"We should go now," he said. "He might be here."

The strange buzzing noise persisted, though it was not so much in his ears anymore as deep within him, like the thrum one feels in the chest at a rock concert. It was as if the vibrations were rising from the stones themselves and, if he trained his view on the trembling shoreline, they appeared to writhe in the gloaming, pretending to be the leading edge of a tide long retreated.

He makes things perfect she had said, all those years ago. He had come across her one more time, on the morning of their departure. She was sitting in a bus shelter and the gin was coming off her in sharp waves, like the poisonous veils of a deep sea fish repelling unwanted attention. *Well, not so much him as the beach he tends, and what lies beneath it. Even before him, before there was that stretch of Kent, before the stones and the sea, even, there was something that moved and rotated and ticked off the seconds, and all the while it was rusting and seizing up. Like an old person. Exactly like an old person.*

Her eyes, when she looked up at him, were clownishly large, filmed with tears. *But it won't die. My husband came back to me last night. The tears in his body, they were all gone, like he had zipped them up, as easy as that. He's... he's perfect. But I'm scared of what perfection means.*

He had gone back to the bus, his mind burning with her words. How, as a child, she had watched two girls playing in the surf. And one had been sucked out by a surge of water. And the other girl had been crying and somehow, minutes later, managed to grasp hold of her limp, outstretched arm and pull her from the water. They had lain together on the stones, one of them heaving and wailing, the other as still as the beached fishing boats that gathered shadows beneath their cracked, peeling bows.

She had stared at them for an age, while everything surrounding the girls, everything beyond her focus, seethed and blurred and warped. And she had blinked and the girls had risen and walked away up the beach, their hands linked, laughing, laughing, with wet hair and the white impressions of the stones on their legs and arms. She found a highly polished lever, brassy with oil, sticking out of the stones where they had lain. When she tried to move it, she felt a deep ratcheting under her toes and the lever sank out of sight.

There was a deckchair on the beach now, the alternating white stripes of its ballooned fabric like ghostly ribs floating above the ground. Graham smelled cigarette smoke and thought he could see a pulsing coal hovering a little way to the right of the chair.

"I'm tired, Gray," Julia said. He removed his jacket and pressed her back into the pebbles, cushioning her head, which looked tiny and white and punched in with two many dark holes and shadows. There was a moon low in the sky, like an albino's eyelash. What light there was came from the stars, or the ineffectual blocks of orange in the pub windows. A great arm of rusted steel reached out of the stones further up the beach, the hinges where its elbow might had long been gritted up with salt and time. Perhaps it was a crane, or a digger, a model of which he had enthusiastically played with as a boy. He had seen other heavy plants around the beach at Dungeness, silent, slowly being subsumed by the stones, like mammoths caught in tar. Nothing moved here, but change was constant.

Graham approached the figure. "Do you look after the beach?" he asked. The man looked no different, despite the intervening years. When he turned around, Graham could not meet his eyes. The mouth wore a sweet smile and he inclined his head towards the chair. Graham went to sit down, but saw that the man intended for him to take what was lying there. He picked the stone up and moved away. Behind him, the creak of the deck chair and the rasp of a match.

"Here?" he called. "Is here okay?" There was no reply. The sound of the sea was almost lost to distance now. There was the barest whisper, but that might well have been his own breath, hurrying on his lips as he bared his arm to a beach that suddenly seemed to whiten, as if the moisture on the pebbles had evaporated in an instant.

The stone in his fingers felt warm and familiar. It had been honed, and he pressed the edge against his skin. Beneath him ran a tremor, from the north end of the beach to the south. The pebbles chuckled as they realigned themselves. When the blood came, Graham looked up at the night sky and waited. Despite the wheeling areas of nothing at his shoulders, he had never felt so smothered. After a little while he was able to return his attention to the wound. Blood tigered his arm. It had drizzled the patch of stones by his foot. From somewhere, what looked like spark plugs and the teeth of a partially concealed cog had emerged. They gleamed in the subtle light, shop fresh, it seemed, oiled, primed for use. Infinitesimally, the cog turned. He heard Julia shift in the stones, a couple of meters away but he could not see any detail in the black shape she made.

He thought of the woman, and her failed attempts to perfect her husband. Unlike the girl she had witnessed on the beach, he was too far removed from what it was to be human. All that had happened was that his injuries had been bettered, had reached a sublime point that could not be bested by the crude materials that had served him previously.

Perfection, he could see now, never had to mean something good.

The man in the deckchair had gone. The pebbles shifted again. Graham's feet were buried in them. He felt something mesh with the leather of his shoes. A metallic taste filled his mouth. A chain had wound itself around his hand and was binding the muscles of his arm. Blood coursed along the links, oil-black in the night. Where was the difference here? He was soft and it was hard, but they were both machines, in the end. Machines needed other people in order to work properly. An hour, two hours later, his body hardened by fatigue and the attentions of the machine, Graham, by degrees, felt himself being released.

He remembered how he had thought the machinery was slowly being buried. How he had attributed its sounds to other things. He had been wrong in so many other aspects of his life that to be mistaken now was hardly unexpected. He trudged over to the shockingly small shape of his wife. He held her close to him, feeling her bones through the twill of his jacket. When he heard Julia's breath leave her body, the tired echo of the surf collapsing on the stones, that too came as no surprise. He watched the sky at the horizon slowly flood with color. The sun would rise before long but he didn't need it to be able to see the shining grid of machinery pumping and gyrating across the beach. For a little while it seemed rejuvenated, super-real like an image manipulated by computers. He watched until spent, it grew still. The stones shifted and soon there were just the occasional glimpses of gears and pistons, as it was when he had arrived many years ago.

Like Julia, the beach was striving for perfection. Unlike her, it had yet to attain it. She was real to him and yes, even beautiful in the dawn. The smell of her was deep in him, *of* him. He would not forget. A part of her, at least, was perfect now.

Supple Bodies

Traveling north, Beverley's reflection in the black window fed the panic already fixed in her eyes. She appeared haunted, and in a way she was, though by ghosts she felt she ought to have better control over, coming as they did from within. She pushed her focus beyond the ashen tilt of her face to the shapeless mass of England streaming beside her. It was cold in the carriage; static disguised as a voice had apologized for faulty circuits and hoped she enjoyed her journey. Her body was indifferent to the chill now, having suffered the tunneled gusts of winter at New Street Station where her connection had been late. Even her breath lacked the warmth necessary to mist the glass.

She guessed Warrington was near; they'd pulled out of Crewe fifteen minutes previously. It unsettled her that there lay such vast tracts of unlit land between towns. It was as if the dark were humoring man's petty attempts to stave off its gloom, knowing it could encroach at any minute. She peered into its depths now, trying to discern the shape of Runcorn's water tower against the sky on her left. She looked back across the cabin. A young man met her gaze, attracted by her sudden movement. When he saw she wasn't aiming her glance at him he returned to his book. On that side Daresbury laboratory should be visible by now. Her stomach muscles bunched; she must have boarded the wrong train, but that was stupid. The sticker proclaiming this train's schedule was above her head. There: Stafford, Crewe, Warrington Bank Quay....

She relaxed, blaming the darkness and her doubts about the wisdom of this visit for her nervousness. Typically, thoughts of home seized her as soon as she allowed herself to loosen. Back there, the compulsion to atone had led to self-abuse; her legs were a mess of bruises where she'd driven the wooden handle of a knife into them. Knowledge that such punishment was empty, born of a need for redemption, saved her from turning the knife around and opening herself to the world.

She looked down; restless ghosts had drawn her hands to a belly now flat and hard. Still, four months on, its hollowness keened at her. Looking back she'd been pathetic, moping around, feeling sorry for herself, though it had been the right decision, the only choice. She couldn't be mother to a child forced upon her. Nobody in London knew what she'd done. Presumably with this visit that would change. The voice crackled into life just as the train noticeably slowed. They rounded on a blaze of silver that must be the station. Beverley gathered her luggage and stepped into the aisle, where her attention was snatched towards a man sleeping a few rows away. His mouth was open; she could see deep into it: fillings, trembling ligaments of spit, an intermittent squirm of tongue. Something about the raw, red color of it disturbed her. She hurried to the doors.

At least she'd missed the rain. Clearly Helen had refused to wait, though the delay had not been long. She walked the glistening platform carefully, taking the steps down to the exit. She considered a taxi but the pub wasn't that far and anyway, it was time she made a stand against her fear—she'd not let it rule her life forever. Crossing the busy road, she paused in front of a hotel, trying to remember directions she'd neglected to write down during their phone conversation that morning. Her breath was a helix of white threatening to congeal into faces she might recognize. To avoid them she squinted ahead at the town center, a good enough target should she lose her way. As she walked the rain returned, keener than she'd known it for some time, urged on by a bitter wind. They'd joked at college that she must visit the Land of Snow and Ice for a reunion and now she was here it seemed the joke was grounded in some truth. She couldn't help feeling she was here for the wrong reasons, though, trying to escape an atmosphere at home that lent itself to introspection. At best, the days here would alleviate that unhealthy practice; at worst, she'd return home having infected her friends with melancholy, to begin the cycle afresh.

Up ahead the road dissolved in a wet mêlée of color: the orange of streetlights merged with the red and white glare of cars, making it hard to see beyond. When she returned her gaze to the pavement, their blur lingered in her eyes. Blinking this and the rain away, she stopped to hoist a bag further onto her shoulder, aware that there were shapes approaching from the light, coalescing one moment, separating the next, till it became clear there were three of them. With little conviction she hoped it was Helen and the others. She could always go back to the taxi rank, but as she thought this she strode forward, her flesh eager for the test even if her heart wasn't. Of course, they passed by with barely a glimpse in her direction, three men deep in conversation about a recent soccer match. Beverley breathed out and promised herself not to fret again over such confrontations, which must become commonplace if she wished to have her old life back. Her old life. That was a joke. Didn't part of the reason for this trip hinge on the possibility of it becoming a permanent uprooting? Her bedsit in the city was little more than a beacon for bad feelings: the stench, the whoop of sirens, the obscenities that echoed through the night all seemed to gravitate towards her, bunched in blankets by the window each evening. When the rotting skyline grew too depressing, there was always her reflection to ponder, duplicated by some flaw in the glass, like a double negative. Often she'd search her twin's jarred face minutely, convinced it was different to her own, that something was amiss in the hollowed eyes, the pallid flesh, till she doubted its identity, ruing the absence of any wit and warmth that might have saved any generosity in the face. The coldness of her room would seem to seep into her at times such as these, making the concept of death almost attractive. And why shouldn't it be? How distant was the step between passing judgment on a fingernail of warm flesh, a beating shred of potential, and terminating her own life, which so far was a wretched, unfulfilled span?

She squeezed the handle of her suitcase till its plastic ground against bone, freeing her of thoughts she was determined to repel. A cluster of derelict buildings clung to the pool of black between streetlights like an embodiment of her fears. One had been a shop of some kind. A peeled awning struggled to state its name among rot and the attack of time. It seemed like a sore in the midst of so many other healthy buildings, as though a disease had sprung from the ground on which they lay. Beverley shivered, rushing into the arc of light that ringed the town center. Soon she spotted The Postern Gate, recalling it from her chat with Helen.

Its warmth flew to her as she swung open the doors. She saw Helen's red hair a second before she was recognized in return. They embraced by the bar, watched by the few who had come out to begin their binges early. The girls carried drinks to a quiet corner, complimenting each other's appearance, bemoaning the fact they saw so little of each other these days; the usual inroads to conversation. When she'd caught up with everybody's progress, or lack of it—Helen was the only one to boast a job, and that because her father ran the company—Beverley asked about Paul. Helen seemed to stiffen; the smile she offered was a few teeth short of the dazzler for which she was famed.

"He's probably a little quieter than you remember him," she confided, swirling the ice in her glass. Beverley didn't care much for the intimacy contained in those words. But perhaps she was becoming too paranoid.

"He was never that loud to begin with," she countered. "But he's got a good sense of humor. He used to have me in stitches." The barb had found Helen; her smile shrank further. Beverley wondered if she should tell her of the night she and Paul had spent with a couple of bottles of wine in their second year at Bristol. In the morning, their mouths had been chapped from so much kissing, but nobody had noticed. Suddenly she felt sorry for her quiet attack. Helen had invited her; Helen it would be, if anyone, to whom she would reveal her secrets. If she had a thing for Paul, then Beverley ought not intrude. Friendship, and the prohibitive distance of two hundred miles, said so.

"How long are you staying?" Probably the question wasn't meant to come out so curtly but that was how Beverley heard it.

"Till you turf me out," she smiled. "I don't know. The weekend, I suppose. I'd like to stay longer but...." She reached out and squeezed Helen's hand. "I'm so glad you asked me to come. I've missed you."

Helen's look softened. "It's only been six months, silly."

"I know," said Beverley. "But London's been pretty hard. I haven't made many friends down there. God, I can't believe college is finished. We were good together, weren't we?"

"Still are," dazzled Helen, before emptying her glass.

Approaching ten o'clock they strolled home through back streets cluttered with bin sacks and the echo of their footsteps. Once more they'd escaped the rain; clouds were spreading across the sky, chased by a wind they could no longer feel. Black polythene sagged with the weight of small puddles that glistened like silver mouths: they resembled drunks collapsed against the wall. Beverley had to keep looking down to make sure nothing had taken hold of her hand since it had grown numb with the cold. The persuasion of a presence by her side was great indeed; it was frightening to think the rumor in her womb was moving beyond the confines of her flesh and pervading the air with its essence. Towards the end of this alley she could see a couple in silhouette kissing, but they looked as if they were devouring each other's faces. Thankfully, Helen drew her to a halt before the pair were disturbed.

"Home," she said, needlessly, though Beverley was glad for her voice. They squeezed through a buckled gate and stepped through the back yard's rubbish. A cold lump shifted in Beverley's midriff, causing her to wince. For a lunatic second she thought the abortionist's tools had failed, but once that was quashed, hunger remained the only alternative. A yeasty, sick smell assailed her as the back door was pushed open, accompanied by a damp heat that instantly filmed her with sweat. They tiptoed around sports holdalls brimming with dirty football kit. More of it trailed up the stairs and was draped over radiators.

"Brings back memories of college, doesn't it?" Helen said, leading the way. It didn't, but Beverley nodded anyway. She couldn't remember hygiene dwindling to such levels during the years they'd spent together. Maybe it had, and she had become immune to it until she left. There was a dim memory of unwashed plates, but the smells were unfamiliar. Now Helen was gesturing limply in the poor light with hands like dead spiders.

"You'll sleep in there," she said, jutting her jaw in the direction of the living room. "There's Paul's room, no don't knock, he's asleep. Mine's next door and Daniel's next to the bathroom."

She'd almost forgotten about Daniel. They'd been pretty distant and spoke only fleetingly but then, as she recalled, he'd always preferred his own company.

"Is he still writing his scary stories?"

"God yes. I think he won an award for one of them recently. I'm sure he'll tell you all about it, if you ask him. Providing he can drag himself out of his pit at some point."

In the kitchen Helen flicked on the radio and turned the volume down. Meaningless, metallic pop chittered from the speakers. Helen cooked an omelette that was far too salty, but Beverley's stomach accepted it readily enough. The boys drifted into the kitchen, perhaps attracted by the smell of food. Beverley sensed a change in the room, as if the light or temperature had been lowered slightly. Darkness piled against the windows.

"Too late, gentlemen," Helen sang. "Beverley's gobbled the lot." Beverley blushed, despite her familiarity with everyone. Perhaps she was blushing because of Paul. He loosely clasped her around the neck and kissed the top of her head.

"Our little gang is complete once more," he whispered, sitting on the table's edge.

Daniel hovered by the sink, rubbing his unshaved jowls. He looked as though he'd not seen sunlight for weeks. A silence fell, and Beverley felt it expedient she should break it, not wanting any awkwardness to develop while they attempted to renew friendships that had had half a year in which to cool off.

"How's Billy Shakespeare? Written any bestsellers lately?" As soon as she'd said them, she regretted the words; they were glib, disrespectful, and Daniel wasn't one to respond well to smart talk. His face proved it, his smile pained, as though he were trying to dry swallow a pill.

"Trying my best," he said, lamely.

"You'll have to let me see some of your stuff," she said, giving him her best smile. He nodded and sloped off, explaining that he had to meet a friend. His movements were jerky as he fumbled with the door, as if he were stricken with rheumatism.

Was Helen tight-lipped because of Daniel's lack of warmth or was it because Paul had kissed her? Beverley could almost see the room filling with tripwires. She wouldn't have come if she knew she'd have to consider every word or action with care.

"Right, now I've been fed, would anyone like to catch last orders?"

Helen consulted her watch. "It's a bit late for that now. This isn't vibrant London, you know."

Beverley didn't know whether this was another jibe, but she was too tired to care. "Anyway," Helen continued, "I'm up early tomorrow. I've got to open up at the office."

"That sounds vaguely rude, Hel," Paul growled. "Can we come and watch?"

Helen tutted, though with a humor in her face to which Beverley hadn't yet been treated. "You've a busy day tomorrow too, haven't you?" Her raised eyebrows seemed a cue for Paul to say goodnight but instead he leaned over and opened the fridge.

"Beverley, I give you Paul's Late Bar. Let's go to the living room." He pulled out a clutch of beer bottles and kicked the fridge door shut. Helen looked for a moment as if she'd follow them but she'd already pre-empted and no doubt her pride was too great to allow her to renege. She mumbled what may have been "Sleep tight" and disappeared into her room.

They drank beer in front of a subdued TV that flickered colors over them in lieu of a light. From here, Beverley could see beyond curtain-shy windows into the streets below. The smell of curry from the Indian restaurant beneath the flat drifted up through the floor. She could see buildings against the night like so many shades of black limned by a chalkiness shed by the moon. It appeared beautiful out there now the clouds had been swept away, though she guessed the cold would fall on the town in earnest now, freezing the water that had soaked Warrington throughout the day. Again she felt as though the dark was pressing against the glass, though suddenly she was reluctant to confirm this suspicion with a closer look in case she glimpsed something other than the sky. At one point, a distant shattering made her flinch, thinking it had broken into the flat, but it was just the TV trying to impinge on their conversation, which was comfortingly banal, consisting of recollections of nights out in Bristol where they had all studied Humanities, or Inhumanities, as Paul called it. For the first time in a long while she found she was enjoying herself, able to relax and take pleasure from beer, banter and an absence of malice. She thought she heard footsteps creeping about outside the living room so, buoyed by the drink, she moved closer to Paul. It would serve Helen right if she were spying on them.

"Have you and Hel got a thing going?" she asked, as a car exploded on screen.

"At the risk of sounding big-headed, she'd like to think so. Not my type, though. Too prissy. Too bloody stifling." He burped and patted her leg.

"So why don't you put her off?" His eyes were dancing with vivid TV color: there was nothing in there to focus upon. It was like staring at polished glass, or ice.

"I've tried," he said, "but there's no harm done as long as she doesn't go all *Fatal Attraction* on me."

The chill was returning to her stomach. Cancer, she thought, before gritting her teeth until the notion left her. It must be the beer. The idea that she would be alone in this room before too long petrified her but she thought it unfair to re-open old wounds with Paul for the sake of a bed and some company. All that was cast away when he leaned over and kissed her.

The room beyond his head swayed unpleasantly. She was put in mind of the smell of sour breath forced between her lips in the park while hands ripped and beat at her below. A stain of cold crept around her innards swift as ink on blotting paper. She tried to block the memory but it was too recent, too brightly tattooed on her mind. She lunged her head forward, turning the kiss into something savage, almost desperate, taking his tongue so deeply into her mouth that it seemed it must choke her. Her hand went for his waist, tugged at his shirt. In the unreal light, his skin seemed blue and powdery; at such close proximity it appeared there were tiny cracks worming across his flesh, but how could she trust her eyes now? Halting her assault, he led her, breathless, to his room. He neglected the light switch so she was aware only of a few vague lumps that might have been furniture or piled clothes. An odor rose, thick and sweetish, but she managed to ignore that too. Only the passion mattered; she could feel it uncoiling from deep within, reigniting her extremities to the pleasures of touch she'd believed long dead. He paused to put on a condom and in that hiatus, phantoms reached for her, trying to achieve substance in her thoughts, but she managed to bear down until Paul glided into her.

"Make me warm," she murmured, turning her head away from his, unsettled by the play of his dark features over hers. She was aware of the clapping of their bodies and, after a few minutes, his nails, shockingly long, gouging tracks in the bedside table as his control dwindled. Beneath the veneer she thought she saw something squirm. She rolled her head away once more and closed her eyes. The freezing knot inside her shifted, seeming to drift out and coat Paul, make him chill and solid; even his mouth felt brittle as it tried to meet with hers. Their ardor was triggering thoughts of that night in the park rather than help eclipse them; she pushed him away, conscious of a frigid umbilicus stretching between them. It must have snapped, for the cold channeled back inside her, releasing them to sleep. She guessed he'd climaxed because he didn't question her withdrawal from their lovemaking.

Oddly, as darkness grew absolute behind her eyes, the images of violence lessened, despite her vulnerability. They were soon replaced by the stock visions she believed she'd left at home. Her dreams had followed her north, it seemed. Increasingly, they were turning to death, or some bastardized form of it, too cryptic to be recognized as such but no less harrowing for that. She no longer believed it was simply winter lending itself to such black thoughts. In sleep she felt herself hardening, her flesh infected by the bone till her entire body was ossified, save for a liquid core that moved in slow, cold pulses.

She recognized the caravan from ten summers before. Her parents had left her, sickly and tired in bed, while they spent a few hours on the beach before lunch. Boredom had worked where medicine failed, inspiring her from the mattress to limp outside into sunshine that felt tangible on her sallow face. The spider's web in the hedge drew her eye at once, probably because it was so perfect, glittering in the light like a mandala of frost. She couldn't see its architect; presumably it was hiding, waiting for a fly. Without thinking, she went back inside and stunned one with a newspaper as it butted at the windows. Delicately, she transported it by a wing to the web, where she let it fall, The fly vibrated ineffectually, its head swiveling as though attached by a thread. When the spider skated out, she gasped at its size. She watched its jaws working as it pumped venom into the fly's carapace. After a couple of minutes, the fly was still; soon it would be cocooned. But no, its back end was shivering. A reflex action, then? She felt her gorge rise as white commas—eggs birthed in extremis—slid from the fly to become trapped on the web. She had counted fourteen before nausea dragged her back to her sick bed.

Waking, Beverley heard Paul's clotted breath at her side. She was appalled by her senses, the way they presented everything with a sinister alternative. She had to get away from the ambiguity, it was beginning to grind her down: Warrington, if anything, was augmenting the imprecision of her thoughts rather than helping to hone them, and bring her rationality. She dressed as quickly as the ache in her back and buttocks would allow, wrinkling her nose to the smell of rubber and come. As much as needing to be free for a while, she was loath to let Helen know where she'd spent the night—not that she wouldn't have a fair idea. Her breasts tingled, though whether from Paul's enthusiastic mouth, or the invisible need of her womb's memory, she was unsure.

Night held sway outside, but only just; a slow, thin blue was rising behind a factory whose roof resembled a row of books slumped to one side. She'd guessed correctly about the frost. The bin bag grins had crystallized; the cobbled back streets were treacherous. She fared little better on the main roads, slipping every dozen steps or so. The only other thing she saw was a stray dog licking at a puddle filmed with oily rainbows that the frost hadn't been able to infect. Tree stumps punctuated the bare strips of pavement, their surfaces tinged with fungus. What grass there was existed as weeds clenched in the joins between buildings and paving stones. Litter muttered in gutters or fluttered, trapped by the ice. Lifeless, bleak avenues spliced from the arterial road snaked into darkness. She wished she could escape the encroaching brickwork like her whitish breath, which fled skyward. Everything around her was angular and solid; the only curves belonged to her, yet even they had been spoiled by stiffness brought on by the cold and the previous night's exertions. Even sex was hard; she supposed it had to be if it was to work. Tenderness gave way to thrashing, muscles grew tensed and strained. The solidity of his cock, bolting her to the bed. God, what she'd give for something pliant, something soft.

The rush of cold inside her brought her to a stop. Suddenly dizzy, she leaned against a wall and waited for its passing, but when she resumed her journey, her light-headedness translated itself as hallucination: she thought a Beverley clone was matching her stride on the other side of the street, or something slight and pink was. Gritting her teeth against this determined paranoia, she refused to look or acknowledge the tell-tale pangs in her gut any further. She'd heard of amputees who could still feel the limbs that had been severed and, though she'd suffered a similar experience, she mustn't let it continue. Her grief was misplaced and she didn't want to relive that awful night each time she needed reassurance.

Light ahead drew her like a magnet. Condensation on the café's windows blocked her view of its interior: a smear of red passed to and fro, then disappeared. She opened the door to a blast of heat and the smell of coffee, of burned toast.

"With you in a minute," came a voice. Beverley took a seat by the window, comforted by the softening mist. Outside was dream-like now, the building's edges blurred, touched with blue leaves of ice. She thought she could hear a child crying somewhere but it was so distant it could be anything, a cat maybe.

"What would you like, love?" He'd popped up from behind the counter and was unwrapping tins of coffee from stiff plastic. His red jumper seemed out of place in the midst of this drab dawn.

"Just tea, please." Her voice sounded scratchy; perhaps she'd caught a chill off Paul. She tried to smile but the cold had turned her muscles sluggish; it felt as though her mouth might crack. She rubbed her cheeks until the tightness retreated and leaned back in her chair as the heat began to work its way into her body. Faded posters clung to the grimy walls, reminding her of her childhood: Cresta, Texan, Spangles. She smiled, almost remembering their flavors.

Her tea tasted gritty but it rid her mouth of staleness and helped combat the chill within. Staring into the liquid, which swirled from the movement of her spoon, she felt sleep trying to return. Warmth was helping her forget the tension. Happy to doze, she rested her head in a hand and followed the patterns of steam as it curled towards her. She saw herself lifting a baby in her arms, letting it meld to the curve of her skin as she offered her nipple. Even as he became an unyielding mass, his mouth rictal, she cooed, inciting him to suckle. As his mouth touched her, his rigidity spread, lips and breast crumbling like fragile casts of sand.

When she sat up, she noticed she was weeping. The heat had turned unpleasant. Her sweat smelled sweet, sickening her. She didn't know what was worse: the blunt, cheesy truth of Paul's room or her own deodorized lie. She left a small hill of coppers on the saucer and hurried out, ignoring the man's questions about what was wrong. Her eye yearned for something sinuous but it was all just stone and glass, enameled by winter. The sky was similarly uncharitable, steel-colored and bereft of any cloud that might have brought equilibrium. She felt like a transparent sac filled with rot that people stared at and avoided. The street remained conspicuously still; she imagined faces at windows, hiding behind curtains, waiting for her to pass before venturing outside. She would tell Paul when she got back. Yes, she'd confess everything originally meant for Helen's ears but that she'd destroyed with her gainsaying. The knowledge that at last she'd be sharing some of her poison was liberating. Merely the thought of it was helping her to feel purged.

Daniel was up; she could see him drinking from a mug as he looked out on the morning from his window, so at least she wouldn't have to wake everyone up by ringing the doorbell. She recalled Paul's warmth and a murmur inside spread tingles through her body. She would slip into bed and press against him, tickle him awake with her tongue. The memory of the rape winked like an ember but could not bloom; she'd do her best to staunch it till they talked.

Daniel let her in a moment later, gesturing with his mug. "Can I make you a coffee, Bev?" he asked, brightly. He didn't seem fazed by her dawn movements; no doubt this was the best time of his day—he certainly appeared perky enough.

"No thanks, Daniel," she whispered, squeezing his arm. "A bit later. I have to see Paul." She slipped by him up the stairs and opened the door to Paul's room. A loop of cold air wound itself around her but she didn't remember leaving a window open. Dull light seeped through the grimy window. Paul's shape seemed to writhe on the bed as if he was in pain but it was only the grainy darkness tricking her. She moved closer, realizing she'd halted her breath. The blankets had been shucked off, perhaps during his convulsions. His back was impossibly arched; his hands flung almost coquettishly to his sides. His muscles could be clearly defined, embossed against the skin. She couldn't see his eyes, they were hidden where he'd buried his head in the pillow. His mouth was stretched too wide: threads of blood at its corners showed where the tension had been too much. A great white column stretched from between his lips to the ceiling, seeming to skewer him to the bed. She touched him; her fingers fused to his skin. It hurt to pull free. Pressing her fingers to the column brought the same result. It was as if the ice that filled him had overflowed, burst from his mouth.

Beverley staggered out. She could hear Daniel typing in his room. A radio played softly somewhere, perhaps by Helen's bed. Would she be awake yet? Before she could move to find out, something stirred inside her. It felt as though her innards were fossilizing by the second, beginning to fracture like ancient, parched stone. A dry trickle began at her core. Her spine became an involuntary arc, cracking like splintered wood. Mouth agape, still as a discarded puppet, she waited for whatever it was to crawl from her.

THE LIGHT THAT PASSES THROUGH YOU

I was on my way to work when Louise appeared, seeming to peel away from the gray cement walls of the block of flats opposite. She drifted into my arms. I could feel her bones, thin and febrile, poking through the shredded leather of her jacket. As I drew her inside, I noticed it was a jacket I'd given her, five years ago—the last time I'd seen her. She made sticky, glottal noises into the crook of my arm as I led her upstairs. Her hair was matted with dog shit; her mouth pinched and blue.

"What are you on?" I asked, but the question could have been directed at myself. I should have been taking her to the hospital. She didn't answer.

I sat her down in the hallway while I ran a bath. My face dissolved in the mirror.

"Can you...?" Clearly, she couldn't, so I undressed her myself, trying to keep my eyes off the breasts I'd once caressed. Unbidden, a memory of me rubbing olive oil into them on a hot beach somewhere made my cheeks burn. "Let's get you into this bath. Come on Louise." She'd lost weight. The skin around her navel was purpuric and slightly raised, like that of an orange. I hoped her condition was due to vitamin deficiency and exhaustion. I wished I hadn't written to her.

She revived a little when the suds enveloped her. She found some kind of focus, frowning as I no doubt looped in and out of view. Her slight overbite rested upon her bottom lip: something I'd once found irresistible. Now she just looked afraid.

"It's been like—" she began, and coughed a thick comma of mucus onto her chin, "—like I've been drowning. All this time. Just as I thought I was leaving, going out like a candle, you rescued me." She collapsed slowly into the water; her ribs, for a moment, seemed like huge denuded fingers pressing against the flesh from inside, trying to punch their way out.

There was nothing particularly unusual about our relationship to warrant my attempt to contact her. At the time, I was nineteen, she eighteen. We said we loved each other. Although we had no money and still lived with our parents, we believed we were independent, different from anyone else because we were intelligent; we were mature about sex.

We were stupid. We were children.

We holidayed in Wales one summer, borrowing a caravan that belonged to a friend of my father's. We buried each other in the sand and lost sleep, fucking with impunity. It was exciting, hearing her approach an orgasm without fear of a parent barging in on us. She missed a period.

I wanted to go with her on the day she aborted. I'd traveled to Stockport with her to make the appointment, sitting in a waiting room trying to avoid the female faces around me, watching faded vehicles slew across wet, wasted dual carriageways which reached into the dun fog over Manchester. Louise's mother went with her when the time came because she paid for the operation. The private clinic was picketed by pro-lifers that day. Louise told me they pleaded with her to re-consider, that they would help to bring up the baby. It fluttered in her womb. Ink blot eye. Fingernails.

When I saw Louise again, she'd gained something which made me nervous for a while, something which shone dully in her eyes as if the surgeons had implanted some strange, ancient wisdom at the time of termination. We talked about it and grew very close; smiles and kisses drew a frosting over the bad area, like icing decorates the mold in a cake. I suppose we believed we were richer for the experience. Louise became clinging; I thought it was love. I never believed that we would be together forever but she didn't doubt it, as if this trauma provided a bond we must never break. Sometimes I'd lie awake at night feeling like the carcass of a sheep; she, a dark scavenger of emotions, burrowing ever deeper into the heart of me. That I felt guilty for entertaining such thoughts shouldn't have brought me comfort but it did.

It was like laying down a bundle of kindling when I tucked her into my bed. I left a window open and glanced at London's center. It seemed strange that I would be working in that glut of noise down there while she slept, a Rapunzel in her tower. I left a note with my number by the bed, in case she should wake up. I had to lean over and smell her mouth.

On the Northern Line, I tried to spot other faces which bore the same kind of expression as Louise. A fusion of vulnerability and assuredness. The look of someone who knows they will be protected and cared for. I couldn't find anything like it here. Maybe it was London which prescribed a countenance of stone; to progress here, you oughtn't allow any emotion to slip.

It was a photograph which did it. A black and white shot of Louise staring out of my bedroom window, one breast free of a voluminous cardigan, her body painted white with morning sunshine. She wore a sleepy, gluttonous expression: we'd just made love. I'd placed some crumpled cellophane over the lens to soften her image. When the picture fell out of a book, I wondered what she was doing now. It pained me to think that the partners we felt so deeply for can be allowed to drift out of our lives. We were both five years older than the time it had ended. Old enough, responsible enough to face each other on a new footing and be friends...

... Ha.

I thought about her all day. I even tried calling her but all I got was my Duo plus: "*Hi, this is Sean, all calls gratefully received, except those from Jeffrey Archer or Noel Edmonds...*"

"Lou? Are you there? Pick up the phone."

I left the office as early as I could and caught the tube back to Belsize Park, having to wait an agonizing time at Camden for the Edgware connection, which was late due to I don't fucking know—litter on the line, driver claustrophobia, lack of application.

She was still in bed when I got back. I heated a bowl of celery soup in the microwave and fed it to her, remembering too late that she despised celery. And what else? Beetroot? She didn't seem to mind now though, her belly grateful for anything to mop up the misery in which it was dissolving. The early February sky shuttered out the light in gray grades across my wall; she became more beautiful as darkness mired her features.

She sat up against the headboard, the duvet slipping away from her body. She didn't attempt to cover herself. I gave her a tee-shirt.

"What happened?" I asked, lighting a candle—she wouldn't have appreciated the harshness of a bare bulb.

"I don't know," she said. "It's like I described earlier. I feel as if I've been gnawed away from the inside. For a while, I thought it was cancer."

I bit down on my suggestion that it still might be; the candle's uncertain light sucked the gaunt angles of her face and shoulders into chiaroscuro.

"Lie with me," she said.

My sleep was fitful; I was expecting her to murmur something that would shape the formless panic I was barely managing to fasten inside. I lay awake listening to the horses stroll up Primrose Hill Road at 5 a.m., trying to delve for conversations we had, or pregnant pauses stuffed with meaning. All I could remember was the sound of her crying.

I nipped outside at around seven, when she was stirring, to the baker's for croissants. I picked up a pot of jam and the newspaper, a pint of milk and headed back to the flat. Only gone five minutes, it was some surprise to find her showered and dressed, painting her nails and listening to one of my Sting albums.

"We'll go out after brekkie," she said, slackly pursing her lips and blowing the varnish across their wake. For a moment, it seemed she was miming a blow-job. You can show me around Camden."

"How are you feeling?" I asked, unwrapping the croissants and offering her a knife.

"Better." She broke off a corner of bread and chewed it, dipping her next bit into the virgin surface of the jam, getting crumbs in there. That was something that pissed me off no end when we were together. It didn't bother me now. Maturity, I suppose. She looked at me slyly, as if she were testing me; I ignored it.

"It's good to see you, Louise," I said. "Really."

"It was a beautiful letter. How could I not answer it?"

"I didn't necessarily expect to see you on my doorstep… you know, a letter, a phone call or something, to let me know how you were."

"It was an invocation, Sean."

"A what?"

"I said, it was an invitation. You called to me, I was on the brink. Your timing was immaculate." She raised an eyebrow. "It always was."

Camden was pinned down under a grimy, stifling sheet of cellophane. Drawing breath was like sucking exhaust fumes through a burning electric blanket. She leaned against me as we threaded through its unfriendly streets, funneled into passageways and alleys pumping with sound and people.

"This is wild!" she laughed, the plum gash of her mouth halving the pallid remains of her face, once so fleshy and pinkish; at once she looked both like the most alive and the most enervated person and in Camden that was saying something. She looked synthetic, the skin too tight, as if it might split and waft the smell of plastic toys over me. But her eyes had lost their initial vagueness, fastening on individual blurs of color as it all streamed past us, like a hawk tracking its dinner. The whites were so clear they were almost blue.

We tooled up and down the main drag, trying on sunglasses and hats. She fingered jewelry and squeezed the arms of thick jumpers, which made me feel even hotter. I pointed out the egg-tipped folly of GM-TV and she scoffed when I told her it was a listed building. I showed her where I'd seen Adam Ant handing over some coins to a charity collector as we crossed the walkway over the Grand Union Canal into a tight knot of stalls and alcoves. The heat was building up here; candles were sagging on their displays and the drifts of antiques shone dully in a solid mass of bronzed light. Every time Louise brushed against me or held on to my arm, I sagged, as if she were transmitting weight through her touch. At such moments, she would perk up and become animated, trying on hats or mugging in smeared mirrors, laughing as my face grew greasy and pale.

The stream of people was endless. The pavements were so obstructed, pedestrians spilled into the road, slowing the traffic which began to trail back towards Mornington Crescent Tube. The crowds seemed to be swelling, like a single bloated body, inflated by sore tempers and the ceaseless, airless heat. I pulled Louise into a café, worried by a mild panic that had transmitted itself into an hallucination of us crushed beneath a stampede of bodies as they attempted to escape their stifling skins. I bought cappuccini, hoping I could relax sufficiently at the counter before she noticed my discomfort.

When I turned round, Louise was bathed in sunshine. Because of the angle of her chair and the way the sunlight was blocked by the weirdly squashed conglomeration of buildings, only she was favored by its color. It invaded the thick pile of her hair, seeming to imbue each filament, like one of those carbon fiber lamps. It moved across her face like thick fluid. A comma of wet sunshine touched her lower lip and I found myself wishing I could kiss it away. I still wanted her, even after such a long time had passed. No time at all. Everyone around her seemed to diminish, shadows on the wane, growing sluggish like figures trapped in tar. And then she looked at me. For a moment, I wasn't sure what kind of fire it was that filled her eyes, certain only that it wasn't human but then the moment passed, and she smiled and everyone was a component of a greater animation once more. She just seemed like a willowy girl, lost in the scrum. Unremarkable.

"Get this down you," I said, pushing across her coffee. "It'll put hair on your chest."

"This place reminds me of my last few years," Louise said, furring her top lip with the froth of her cappuccino. I don't know why, really. Something about the way everything feels sad and unreal but is all disguised by movement. I bet this place seems more like its true self when the shops close and everyone pisses off."

"What have you been up to these last few years?" I asked that, when all I wanted to know was how she'd turned up in such a state on my doorstep. Now she looked in some semblance of control, I was finding it hard to believe that I'd seen her like that, *in extremis*.

"It felt like I was being followed. No, that's not right, it felt like I was being hunted. I had to keep moving or I felt I'd be consumed by something so big I couldn't even see it. Just an aspect of it, I saw, usually in sleep, moving furiously, like an engine part well-oiled, pistoning and thrashing around. It belonged to something that was vast and after me. Hungry for me." She took another drink of coffee, then reached over and tapped a man in a vest and combat trousers on the shoulder. Asked him for a cigarette. After he'd lit it for her, she turned back to me and spoke around a mouthful of bluish smoke.

"I left Warrington just after we finished… after you finished with me. I got a job with a waste disposal firm in Keighley."

"Keighley? Why Keighley, of all places? Middle of nowhere."

"No, *I* was the middle of nowhere. Anywhere, everywhere else was a grip on something real. I was on Temezepam by this time, for my depression and insomnia but it wasn't working. The doctor gave me Prozac, and that was better, for a while, until I wanted to do nothing other than sit in front of my window and watch the litter being blown across the street. I kicked all that but it was like the feeling had settled into me and wouldn't go away. I slept late, ate less, became constipated. I began to appreciate a particular kind of darkness I found in the loft. There was a cat, Marlon, his name was, that would sleep up there. Made his way over the roofs and climbed in through a hole in the eaves. We'd curl up together, flinching whenever a bird's claws rattled on the tiles. It was almost magical. I felt safe; that thing that was looking for me wouldn't have me here. It was just me and Marlon and the dark. Holding on to Marlon's fur kept me real and sane. If he wasn't there, I think I would have just… well…."

"How long were you in Keighley for?" I asked, sensing a dangerous moment of self-disclosure if I let her carry on.

"Not long. I hitched a lift to Scarborough and did some work at one of the hotels. Cleaning rooms in the daytime, serving behind the bar at night. I liked it. Days off, I'd walk along the beach up to the amusement arcades. I met boys there. When it got dark we'd go behind the generators and I'd just let them do what they wanted to me. I went with this really gaunt, ill-looking boy called Felix. He was half Croatian. I sucked him off and when he came—"

"Jesus, Lou—"

"—when he came, there was blood in his semen. He blamed it on me, said I'd infected him—some nonsense like that—and he tried to strangle me. I didn't fight him off. I was struck by how beautiful he looked in the thin light rising from the harbor behind us. I think he got scared when I started smiling at him. He left me alone. I like to believe you were thinking of me at that very moment. My Guardian Angel, rescued me with some attention."

I laughed nervously. I didn't like anything she was telling me. I was jealous and I was resentful of her for keeping a hold onto me. My letter hadn't been a cry for reunion, it had been a friendly endeavor to find out what was happening to someone I cared about. But I found myself hooked on her story. "And then?" I asked, my voice dead, resigned.

"I stayed in Scarborough for some time. A year or so. Things changed. I found that I seemed to be waking into thick air. Walking, blinking, breathing—it was all such an effort. Things weren't right while somehow keeping a surface of normality. I'd see something odd, but everybody else's reaction would be non-existent and it might be hours or days before I told myself that no, it was not right but by then I'd suspect that it hadn't happened at all."

"What kind of things? What are you talking about, Louise?"

"I'm talking about the skeletons of fish on the beach flopping around, trying to get back into the water. I'm talking about sandcastles that didn't dissolve when the tide touched them. A couple kissing under a streetlamp whose heads melted into each other."

"Tcha!" I said, rocking back on my seat and attracting a few glances from the punters sitting nearby. She'd drawn me into her story so effectively that this nonsense had spat me out, like a newborn, unable to cope with the sudden influx of normal sensations. I sighed and rubbed my eyes. She wouldn't give up on it though.

"A dog smoking a pipe. A parrot on a smiling tramp's shoulder picking his brains from a bleeding eye socket. Burning children playing leapfrog on a lawn."

"Stop it, Louise."

"I was there. I saw this happening."

"In Scarborough? I've been to Scarborough. The strangest thing they have there is a ghost train that squirts water at you."

"Yes. But, although it was Scarborough, it could have been anywhere. I was drawing these things to me. I was in some kind of midway. A lost soul."

I necked my coffee. I could feel myself bristling under her expectant gaze. She'd always been like this, pushing the envelope of provocation and gauging my reaction till I exploded. "If you're trying to make me feel guilty for finishing with you, you're doing fine. Not that you're one to hold a grudge."

"I don't blame you for this, Sean. I did at first. I spent all my time thinking of you. Thinking of how our child would have been two, three, four, five. You laughing and having a good time. Fucking lots of women. I played the whole victim thing. I wanted you and hated you in equal measure. I needed you. But then I realized all my misery was externalized too. It got so bad very quickly that I didn't even notice things had changed until I started paying attention to the outside world rather than my puffy face in the mirror.

"The coming of daylight seemed to take longer than it ought to in the mornings. I'd see weather forecasts predicting rain or shine but there was a constant haze, like the sun trying to force its way through mist. It never changed. I'd visit my parents and they appeared to talk through me, looking at my face but somehow misdirecting their focus as if they were talking to someone standing behind me. And then this awful sense of something coming, gravitating towards me..."

I noticed that I was holding her hand but I couldn't recall reaching for her. Her casual referral to her pregnancy had shamed me. I couldn't say anything.

"And you wrote to me. It was salvation. There was no longer a sense of me being consigned to limbo. Does this sound silly to you? Because there are others. I saw one or two, drifting like me, pale and withdrawn like flames that can't quite catch upon what they're supposed to be burning. People who were dismissed from somebody's life. People who had an umbilicus disconnected. God knows what would have happened to me if you hadn't written. I think I'd have faded away. Winked out. There's still something missing. Something I need in order to give me a sense of being complete but I'm buggered if I know what it is."

It was a lot to take in. I wasn't convinced by a great deal of what she'd imparted but I had a handle on her dislocation. I'd been gearing up to ask her how long she planned on staying but it didn't really matter if she stayed a few more days, if it meant she'd get back to full speed.

"A party," I said, lightly, trying to dispel the intensity that had drawn in around us. "There's a party tonight. Why don't you come? It will do you good to kick back and relax."

She appeared briefly reticent but agreed, her eyes hankering after some morsel of encouragement as we held each other's gaze for longer than necessary. It was a look I'd once suffixed with a kiss or a touch of my finger against her neck. *Don't get back into that*, I thought, pushing away from the table. I couldn't understand why she'd want to get involved with me again if there was even the shred of threat she might return to the dire illusions of her mind.

The party was at a friend's place in Hammersmith; we were to meet by the bridge at one of the pubs which snuggled up to the Thames. Benjie was there to greet us, a tall affable lad who didn't care if he was thinning on top as long as there was a beer in front of him. One of those people who needs only the most rudimentary of introductions before getting on well with anyone, Benjie soon had Louise feeling comfortable and interesting; she soon relaxed into the evening. A fine evening it was, the sun losing itself to the strata of colour banding the horizon. Great jets would lower into it as they nosed towards Heathrow. We stood and watched them halve the sky till it grew dark and cold.

For my part, I felt better now that Louise was being shared around a dozen or so other people. I could allow my anxieties to shrink within alcohol's massage and see Louise as someone more than a chipped and faded signpost to my past.

Benjie lived in a first floor flat on a wide avenue behind King Street. When we arrived, stopping off en route to buy beer from a 24 hour inconvenience store that didn't sell Beck's or Toohey's, there were already around thirty people stuffed into the kitchen and living room. Overspill meant that the landing and stairs were occupied too, by flaky looking individuals wadded into sheepskin coats with excessively furred collars. They probably looked furtive because they'd crashed the gig; not that it mattered: Benjie was hospitable to all. I followed him into his room where a hill of coats and plastic bags swamped his bed. A couple were leaned across them, kissing each other with such fervour that it seemed his mouth must engulf the entirety of her lower jaw. His left hand violently kneaded the pliant spread of her right breast. She could have been dead. I sensed Louise stiffen beside me and squeezed her hand, understanding her revulsion. The unison was void of any tenderness. Perhaps Benjie noticed it too, because there was a needle in his voice when he asked them to move over. They simply stopped kissing and staggered from the room, lobotomized expressions all round. The woman was wearing six inch rubber platforms and a black cat suit. An exterior white leather corset battled to keep her chest in situ. She hadn't even bothered to take off her heart-shaped satchel with its blunt rubber spines.

"Kids, eh?" said Benjie, plonking his sweater on the pile. I followed suit but Louise refused to take her coat off. "Actually," Benjie continued, gesturing after the zombies, "that was Simon. Top bloke. Known him since school. Spacecat. Does a bit too much of the wacky baccy to keep him compos mentis but you can't hold that against him."

So, the party. Which was as punishing as any party I'd been to before. We drank. And then there was a spot of serious drinking. And a post drink drinking session and then a long stretch of complete and utter drinking. Benjie's windows in the living room had been sealed shut by whoever had last painted the flat. It grew so stifling that the ceiling eventually shed a thin, bitter rain of nicotine moisture. I ranged around the room, trying to find the door so that I might lose some of my own fluids but it appeared that someone had painted that in too. I started laughing till panic hovered but rescued myself by simply pissing my pants. It proved an excellent sobering technique. I poured what was left of my Budweiser on to my jeans and made like I was the clumsiest arse ever but nobody cared a toss. I found the door where I'd left it and spilled on to the landing. Someone was playing Nirvana - *Drain You* - with the volume turned all the way up to eleven. I yelled a line from the chorus and dived for the toilet only to find a queue which, in all probability, was the longest toilet queue in the history of clenched bladders. I had the last laugh, though, when my brain caught up with the fact that I'd already been.

Simon's disembodied head loomed in front of mine. "Where the fuck is the rest of you?" I almost shrieked, but it was all there, just slow in arriving. God, I was spannered. He grinned, showing off a gold pre-molar. He smelled of beer, smoke and CKOne but then, so did everybody else. His skin possessed a greasy olive hue; up close I could see that his lips were rugose and discolored. His rubberised partner, I guessed, was being trampolined elsewhere.

"Highayemsimon," he said. "Hooeyoo?"

"Me no speaka your language," I replied, suddenly cottoning on to his flighty Scots burr. I barked laughter and slapped him on the arm. "Sorry. I thought... I thought... oh cocks to it. I'm Shhhhhuh... Sean. Benj told me you were Simon but it's good to have it confirmed."

"Hoowazatlassyacuminwi?"

"Her name's Louise." I came right back with that one, getting into the swing of it.

"Shizaspankinlassamtellinyi."

"Too right." I sensed he was waiting for me to continue. "She's not with me, if that's what you're wondering." If I'd had my brains in properly, I'd have asked him to be tame on her; she wasn't ready for some fast talking shagmeister bundling her into his bed. Talking about Louise reminded me that she was here. I caught sight of her standing on the edge of an intense circle, watching the interplay. She looked - God, strange word to use but it summed up her appearance - she looked *ripe*.

Her face was jutting and beautiful, her eyes hungry on everyone. Having finally divested herself of the coat, her breasts hugged the deep collar of her blouse like loaves in an oven besting their tins. No longer the ingénue I'd staggered into adulthood alongside, she appeared confident and armed with secrets, like a soldier returned from a killing field.

But that could have just been the alcohol, twatting around with my head.

I started towards her, eager to let loose some of the thoughts with which I'd been so circumspect that afternoon. I wanted to draw her into the crook of my arm and tell her I'd missed her. Tell her I was sorry.

But then Simon was locked on to her, their bodies flush with each other as they traded words. I watched them flirt, dipping heads against ears so that lips brushed lobes. Yoked together, I watched the tethered jewel at Louise's throat move with each undulation they created. Violence spread through me. I wish I could have let it come. Louise's capitulation and Benjie's hand on my shoulder prevented me. In that moment, Simon was condemned.

Black out.

I surfaced from a terrible dream in which I'd been kissing a woman whose lips were sticky, whose tongue, whenever it emerged to roil against mine, was coated in a clear membrane. She worked my mouth with spidery endeavor, knitting it closed with her adhesive spit. Black eyes burning into mine. When she wrestled with her clothing, to reveal that yawning part of her which would dissolve and ingest me, I lurched away, opening my eyes to dawn as it drizzled the curtains. Bodies were sprawled around me. I hauled myself upright, shuddering with cold and the mother and father of all hangovers. The Fear unzipped its dark little bag and teased me with its contents but I couldn't remember anything beyond Benjie, me and a bottle of vodka. My jeans felt stiff against my legs. There was a smear of lipstick on the back of my hand.

I negotiated the snoring corpses till I was on the landing. Benjie's door was shut. I remembered. Some time in the night I'd gone for a glass of water, opened his bedroom, mistaking it for the kitchen. Louise was straddling Simon in the bed; the hill of coats had slid to the floor. The first thing I saw was the last thing to follow me back to sleep. Her breastbone, slick with sweat, or his saliva, overlaid with a lozenge of pure white light which pulsed with every languid stroke of their lovemaking. There was light elsewhere on her, solidifying in clusters and then dispersing like minute shoals of fish only to coalesce once more on her thigh, her mons, her navel. But it was that oval of light on her sternum which transfixed me, even as her eyes met with mine and she flew towards a climax that terrified me for its intensity. Simon was paling beneath her, jerking around: a rabbit mauled by a stoat. His hand reached out, almost desperately. Froth concealed his mouth. Louise was keening, slamming down upon him and baring her teeth, eyes rolled back till I could see their whites. The light inside her intensified and gathered at her core, retreating from the surface of her skin till it was but a milky suggestion deep inside her. Then it sank to where he must have been embedded in her. I couldn't watch any more, not when she drove her fingers into his mouth to allay his scream.

Was that really how it had happened? My sozzled brain painted a detailed picture, but my dream had seemed equally alive. If it had happened, how could I have been so calm as to close the door on them and get back among the dead in the living room? How could I have returned to sleep?

I thought of the first words Louise had mumbled to me after her abortion all those years ago. She'd said: "I was so close to darkness, it felt like I could never again be close to the light."

She'd been chasing it ever since. I'd taken it from her and something as simple as a letter had given it back. A letter that had been as much a cry for help as an olive branch. I thought of the places she'd passed through over the years, alternate lands that had claimed her as she drifted, loveless. I thought of how easy it could be to consign someone to such torment. I tried to imagine the hunger that needed to be sated in order to forge a way back.

My hand on the door. It swung inwards. The pile of coats was still there. Beneath them, the bed appeared not to have been slept in. The room was still, its occupants gone. I was happy to leave it that way but found myself entering the room. There was a scorched smell. A cigarette burn, probably. I dragged the covers off the bed. A thin plug of mucus, streaked with blood, stained the undersheet.

"Simon?" I said to it.

A sound drew me to the window. She was standing by the streetlamp, which died at that moment. Subtle light crept through the avenue. I heard a milk float play its glassy tunes far away. She was smiling as she waited, holding her coat closed on whatever it was that burned inside her. I sniffed and dug my jumper out of the pile, went down to hold her hand and send her a plea through my lips when I kissed her.

Nest of Salt

In order to find the most shocking parts of London, she said, *you have to go back to being a child. You have to see things simply, as a matter of good and bad. You need to rediscover that innocence.* She went on:—*There is a place, one of many blackspots in the capital, that sucks death to it as fiercely as a hungry baby at the tit. And I know where this one is.*

Egan hurried along Edgware Road as if trying to shrug the voice from him. It hung in his thoughts like sour odors in sick rooms. He resented the way she had gravitated towards him at the party, latching onto him and falling into conversation as if she were in the middle of a heart-to-heart with an old friend. As the rain arrowed into him, he couldn't help but wonder that she had sought him out, that he would have been no safer from her attentions if he were hiding under a box in the utility room. But he had been swigging Kronenbourg from the bottle, propped against the kitchen sink, waiting for the alcohol to overtake him enough to be able to initiate something with the dirty-blonde girl in the jogging top at the other side of the room. He never felt so old, other than when he was invited to parties. Especially parties where everybody else seemed so much younger than him.

"What are you, thirty years old? Thirty-five? And shy as fuck." Her breath carried meat and spice on it, her eyes were surrounded with papery skin, gray as coley flesh. "Well I'll tell you something. You're not shy. You're infected. We all are. Scarred too."

He kept drinking, but the lager failed to dissolve either the restraints that kept him from talking to the blonde, or the guts to tell this strange, tiny girl to fuck off and leave him alone. When the blonde finally went off with a guy in a rugby top (tucked into his belt-less Wranglers; collars turned up) Egan found his irritation wasn't as great as it might have been. The girl's voice was soporific, attractive even, despite the bile that it was couched in.

"I saw a guy in Great Portland Street getting his teeth kicked in to fuck and back," she was saying. "The kid doing the kicking couldn't have been older than fourteen. He actually yawned while he was doing it."

Later, in a dark, anonymous room at the top of the house, she sucked his cock but he couldn't come, mainly because the room was too hot and he could see commas of light in her eyes, upturned to watch his reaction, but also just because he couldn't, he didn't. Not these days. But he felt the need to find other things to blame. He was too conscious of his paunch; his breath might not be at its best. Something in her spit, it seemed, was astringent. It stung the peeled head of his penis. He heard her lift her skirt and rub at herself. But the sound was all wrong: she was too dry, even if she wasn't turned on at all. It sounded like someone scouring a callous with the sandpapered strip on a matchbox. She sounded powdery, unstable.

He left soon after, when she was in the bathroom. He showered when he got home, but he couldn't get rid of the slimy feel of her mouth writhing on him. He fell asleep as soon as he got under the blankets, but when he awoke, he felt anything but refreshed.

A car horn split the frangible air two feet in front of him as he trotted across Praed Street. The driver's face contorted as it accelerated past, though Egan couldn't tell, as he rocked back on his heels, whether it was down to his rage at having to brake for Egan's foolishness, or the shapes the rain made on the windscreen.

Office workers were pouring out onto the street for their poorly packed sandwiches and over-milked coffees. Yet it felt much later than lunchtime. A layer of slate-colored cloud had slid across the sky. Only the thinnest edge of light trembled above the staggered horizon, like hope receding. Egan felt pressed upon, his sinuses tight, trying to build a bridge to a headache unfolding in his crown.

Titchard was where he said he would be, lurking under the Westway, his trademark beanie rammed down over his ears, the ends of his jeans gathering a deeper blue where they scuffed against the floor. He was wild-eyed, shivering with cold, or whatever it was racing through his head; probably nothing more powerful than caffeine. Titchard was tissue-thin, his cheeks so hollow they were almost transparent. November had bruised his face, turned the tips of his fingers blue.

"Like fucking lolly sticks," he said, rapping them with his knuckles. "I've got Raynaud's disease, me. I couldn't get warm on a fucking kebab spit. And you keep me waiting."

Egan apologized and ushered him across the road. He bought them mugs of tea in the Regent Milk Bar. "And I'll have an ice cream," Titchard said.

"You were complaining about the cold a minute ago."

"Yeah, well I'm a contrary fuck, aren't I?"

"Circus Street," Egan said.

"Look at her," Titchard said, ignoring him. A woman in combat trousers and a fur-lined suede jacket had wedged herself into a corner of the cafe and was hunched over a mobile phone, texting feverishly.

"Receptionist," Titchard said. "You can tell, look. Long fingernails, except for the forefinger, right hand. For dialing."

The surface of Egan's coffee seemed too pretty to spoil. He stared at it while Titchard got it out of his system.

"Just look at her. No straight parts on her body. She's a fucking walking chicane that one. Big lips, big eyes, big tits. Jesus. Do they have any idea, what they do to us? Succulent. Fucking succulent. All give. All yield, innit? Push your finger in anywhere and it's all soft. All succulent. Not just her mouth that's pouting. Her whole fucking body."

"Christ, Stu, give it a rest."

He took a large swallow of his tea and sat back in the chair. "Sorry mate, I'm trying to pack up the fags. I'm all over the place at the minute."

"Circus Street," Egan said again, more urgently. "Do you *know* it?"

"You'll find it in Circus Street," she had said, as he pushed through the crowd of people between him and the way out. "This nexus of filth. This crack of doom house. How badly to you want it? Nearest tube, Edgware Road." As if she was inviting him to a party, or arranging a lunch date.

When he got back to his flat in Kentish Town he listened to records on his cheap Bush turntable and tried to forget about her. The only alcohol in the flat was an ancient bottle of Boa Vitória that he and his ex had bought on a day-trip to Wimereux six years previously. There were no limes, no brown sugar with which he might make *caipirinhas*, so he tried it with orange juice instead. Vile, but it would have to do.

An hour later, Shelley, his flatmate, reeled in from a pub crawl in Archway. A youthful, forty-something archivist for a terrestrial TV company who always seemed to smell of paper glue and rubber bands. She kissed both his cheeks and regarded him in a fond, maternal way that reminded Egan of an old woman watching puppies in a pet shop window. Moving away, her heel caught in the loops of headphone cable and tore the jack free.

"Gosh, I'm sorry," she said, and stumbled over to retrieve it.

"It's okay," Egan snapped, snatching the jack up before she could reach it. His cheeks burned; he had always been self-conscious about his music, not liking others to hear what he was playing, hating the way some people interpreted your tastes and judged you upon them. But Shelley seemed not to notice, or maybe didn't care, even though the volume was right up, drowning out what she was trying to say to him. He punched the power switch, killing the plea as it shrieked from the speakers:

I wish I could eat your cancer…

The stillness of the flat seemed to inflate between them. He had to fill it before she did, or before the panic instilled by the girl at the party got there first.

"Do you have an *A-Z*?" he asked.

"No," she said, and caught hold of his cardigan sleeve as if to prevent her drunkenness from getting the better of her. "But you can use Streetmap." She led him into her bedroom and gestured at the laptop on her desk, its screen waxing with smears of color. He sat down and called the website up, trying to ignore Shelley as she undressed behind him.

"There is no Circus Street."

"What's that?"

"Circus Street. There isn't one. Not near Edgware Road. There's a Circus Street in Greenwich. What the fuck is she on about?"

"What are *you* on about, more like?"

"I'm trying to find Circus Street, isn't it obvious?"

Shelley unhooked her bra and sat down on the edge of her bed. She pressed her arms together and turned her face to the window. Her paper-white breasts seemed to overflow the narrow gap they had been forced into, as if they might spill over and slide to the floor. "There's no need to shout at me," she said.

"I'm sorry," Egan spat, rising, irritated by her lack of circumspection. They were flatmates, no more. At the door he said it more softly, but either she didn't hear or she chose to ignore him. He went out.

He walked for an age, through the rain, his hands deep in his pockets, playing with, in one, a conker he had rescued from the side of the road a few years before and, in the other, a pair of baby's socks: *his* socks, to be accurate, something his father had given to him when he was much younger. After a few miles, his head was clear of the Brazilian spirit, and he felt in need of coffee. He bought one—and a new mini *A-Z*—from a petrol station on Hampstead Road, but the coffee was gritty, watered down and so hot that it possessed no flavor. He ditched it and flagged down the cab before he'd even thought about what he was doing.

"No," said the driver, as Egan leaned into his window, "I don't know a Circus Street in Marylebone. You sure?"

Egan got him to drive there anyway, and outside Westminster Register Office, the rain backing off now, but still bitterly cold, he consulted his *A-Z*. He saw how the area was segmented between Baker Street and Edgware Road and decided to sweep each zone methodically, until he had ticked off every square inch of the maps. Either the publishers, or the girl, had made a mistake and as much as it niggled him that she, surely, must be in the wrong, a tight, frightened speck of him believed that Circus Street did exist. This shadow zone of the capital. This blackspot, as she described it. As he trudged up and down the grids described in his pocket maps, he believed he could almost feel it, as a tremor in the ground, a throb as of something sore that draws heat and blood towards it, in order to nourish itself and make itself well again.

He slunk through narrow mews that were nestled in shadow as well as the more exposed squares, in which he felt relentlessly scoured by the silent occupants, as he hurried along to the next corner, and the next set of white place-names. It seemed as though the rat-runs and alleyways and arterial roads could only conceal Circus Street from him for so long. His conviction that he would stumble upon the thoroughfare burned more fiercely for every street name that ought to have crushed his belief. Seymour Place, Nutford Place, Forset Street, Harrowby Street, Brendon Street, Crawford Place, Molyneux Street, Shouldham Street, Homer Row, Homer Street… it got so that he was certain he had found what he was looking for even though the letters and the post codes told him otherwise.

He had to admit defeat a little before midnight. Tiredness and cold had crept through his legs and settled in the pit of his stomach, pulling at his extremities, wanting him to curl up into a ball and recover. He walked back towards Baker Street along York Street, thinking about the hot, buttered toast and the tea he would make when he got back to the flat. The steaming bath. Bed.

The cold was so brutal, it had caused his nose to run. He wiped it with the back of his hand and then stopped when he saw blood.

"Fuck," he said, sniffing hard and rooting in his pockets for a tissue. He didn't have one, and in the end he had to reluctantly use one of the baby socks to stem the flow, which was increasing by the second. He turned so quickly when he heard the female laughter that he cricked his neck. A woman was standing at a bus stop leaning over a mobile phone, trying to protect herself from the blasts of wind streaming along Baker Street. He stalked past her, dabbing at his nose. As he drew abreast, the corner of his eye picked out a silvery flash and he recoiled, thinking that he was about to be struck by some kind of blade. But it was the reflected headlights from a taxi as it powered by, rioting across the remains of a shattered pane on the bus shelter. People were heading home from nights out. Some moved reluctantly, as if saddened that their evenings were over; some hurried, desperate for bed.

For the first time in an age, Egan found himself thinking of his childhood; specifically, the procession of bedtimes that filled his infancy.

His bed had been large for a child, a cast-off from his parents, who had bought a new one for themselves. It had dominated his small room, lying along the wall opposite his window. From here, he could see the plastic model King Kong on his desk, which glowed in the dark, and the Junkers being chased by the Spitfire, badly painted Airfix models depending from the ceiling on lengths of cotton. There were no trees or nearby buildings to spoil his view of the night sky. He preferred it without curtains. The landing light on, spilling a soft orange parallelogram across his books and the poster on the wall of Lee Majors as The Six Million Dollar Man. The skies packed with cloud or clear as a sponged blackboard. He remembered theme tunes from TV programs that his parents liked to watch, drifting up the stairs: *M*A*S*H**, *The Sweeney*, *Kojak*.

He touched his nose. The blood had stopped. And then another image, a flash, no more, as if someone had broadcast a subliminal message to him: another room, another night at the window and his shadow spoiling its color against another wall. The shape in another bed. An arm curled around a small, bedraggled bear.

Troubled by this, but in a vague, amorphous way, Egan caught a night bus home, drank a liter of water and fell asleep, fully clothed, expecting every and any sort of dream to shuffle through the frantic vacuum of his mind, but none came. None, at least, that he was aware of.

A week of this. A week of trudging north to south, south to north along streets that at any other time would be anonymous to him, occasional routes almost instantly forgotten the moment he left them behind, bland conduits between the As and Bs of his daily existence.

Circus Street.

The name itself seemed a mockery, a Big Top joke designed only to make a clown of him.

Frost crusted the pavements and curbs of some of the lesser traveled avenues today. He had retrieved his greatcoat from the back of his wardrobe that morning, faintly appalled by its musty smell as he dragged it across his back. Breakfast was forsaken, despite the spread that Shelley had laid on for him. He barely heard her voicing her concern as he slammed outside. He had been trying to call Titchard the past few days, irritated that he had failed to get in touch over the whereabouts of this mystery street. Which meant that his phone had been cut off, or he'd drawn a blank at the library, where he worked. Or he'd forgotten to look into it for him, which was just as likely.

Annoyed at having to break off from his hounding of Marylebone, Egan caught a tube to Seven Sisters and walked the mile to Avenue Road. Titchard lived in a studio flat at the top of a purpose built block. He had shelves filled with professionally folded shop-fresh T-shirts which he never wore because he couldn't refold them in that special way. His bookcases were stuffed with garish horror volumes in every combination of black and gold and red. His refrigerator usually had a bag of coriander in it, a couple of packets of Viscount biscuits, a potato or two. Nothing else. On his walls were framed letters he wrote to TV magazines praising his favorite programs. He had a nice stereo, separates, with a pair of Quad speakers. His Mac was constantly plugged in to the net, downloading photographs of Heidi Klum which he printed off and glued to the ceiling. It was a bright flat, very clean, and depressing as hell.

He wasn't answering the doorbell. Sunday, shy of noon. No library in the world opened on a Sunday. Titchard, up before lunch on a weekend? Never. A neighbor buzzed Egan in without question and he took the stairs two at a time to the top floor. He could hear music in Titchard's flat. Four Tet, the kind of stuff he liked to listen to while he was browsing supermodels or buying expensive bits of kit from Arcam and Nad.

Egan tapped lightly at the door. It was unlocked. He went in. The place was a shambles. The far wall had been cleared of bookshelves and the word NO had been written on it, in what looked like indelible marker pen, maybe a thousand times, in varying sizes. Empty takeaway food cartons were strewn across a heavily stained carpet. Dog shit was smeared over the sofa and clung to the cleats of a pair of discarded running shoes. Images from a bukkake website were plastered all over the windows, shutting out the light. Badges of blood were stuck to items of clothing that lay around as if thrown during a fit. Titchard was sitting in the kitchen scooping the dregs from a tin of Heinz Soup for One. His left hand was crudely bandaged and blood had seeped through the gauze, drying to a tan glaze. He dropped the tin and scooted away on his backside when he saw Egan. Egan stopped where he was and held up a placatory hand.

"Stu, calm it, okay? Just take it slow."

Titchard scrabbled for a knife from the draining board and brought down half a dozen plates while he was at it. They smashed and rattled around him. One of them must have dealt him a glancing blow, for a tick of blood, like a Nike logo, swooped suddenly across his forehead and began leaking into his eyes.

"What are you taking, Stu?"

"Fuck off," Titchard said. "Just get the fuck away from me, you fucking freak. You psycho."

"What are you talking about?"

Titchard stabbed the air between them with the knife, even though Egan was a good six feet away and coming no closer. The smell of a sink that has known nothing but grease and decomposing food for a number of weeks slowly erupted around them.

"Get the fuck —"

"Stu."

"—*away from me!*"

Egan stepped back, alarmed by the sudden turn in Titchard's voice. Ligaments stood out on his neck. His face was turning the same color as the blood turned dry on his hand.

He was about to say something else, but Titchard was crying now, and turning the knife around, threatening to drag its edge across his throat. The look in his eye said he would do it, no trouble at all.

"Okay, okay, I'm going," Egan said, backing off further. His foot slid across something soft, but he didn't look down. Titchard was as sprung as an over-wound clock. He might unleash himself at Egan at any moment. He might do anything. "One thing," he said. "Just one. Did you find Circus Street? Do you know it?"

The tears came freely now. Titchard's mouth opened in a silent scream that Egan believed he heard, at some rarefied level. His nape leapt. Lines of spit across Titchard's mouth caught the ambient light. They looked like bars, shutting in what he might otherwise have shared. He began tearing at his clothes, not caring where the knife went. When the blade slashed against his biceps, Egan left, his heart skipping like a flat stone across a cold, still lake. He sank with it to the street, where he called an ambulance on his mobile phone and gave them Titchard's address. He was hurrying away in the direction of the tube when he heard glass breaking behind him. He turned to find Titchard leaning through the frame, blood having turned his hair into a sopping cap. Red lashed off him. The jags of glass remaining in the putty were dangerously close to his throat.

"How could you leave her like that?" he yelled. People in the local shops came out to watch. Someone said: *I'm calling the police.*

"Pictures. How could someone take pictures? How could you leave her for me to find? *Like that?*"

He screamed again, an unthinkably deep cry of rage and pain, and then he let his head drop onto the teeth of the window.

Somehow he was still screaming. How could that be, Egan thought, as he ran away. How can a dead man scream? But then he realized it was he himself making all the noise. Dead men, well, they can scream plenty.

Shelley didn't ask him where he'd been. She dropped her keys on the table, pulled off her jacket and knelt by him as he shivered in the armchair. She eased off his shoes and placed them outside the door, then she opened the windows to allow the smell of dog shit to escape. She cleaned up the carpet as best she could, drew a hot bath, and shooed him into it.

He didn't say anything. He didn't ask her to leave. She soaped his back, shampooed his hair. She kissed his cheek, then his mouth. She didn't seem to mind that he didn't reciprocate. He looked at her only once, as the bathwater was turning cold, and beads of sweat were rising on her forehead. He put out a hand to spoil her rhythm, and she relaxed her grip on him.

He said, "It's not you."

He said, "I'm sorry."

He could tell she wanted to talk afterwards, but he needed to get outside again. Titchard had been on the local news that evening. They referred to him as a crazed loner who had taken a hostage but who had committed suicide when the hostage managed to get away. Police wanted to interview the man who had escaped.

"I was no hostage," Egan yelled at the screen. He sensed Shelley stiffen on the sofa beside him. He turned to her but couldn't say anything. They were no longer flatmates, but he needed to finish what he was doing to have any chance of giving her the kind of attention she craved. He held her hand briefly, apologized, then hurried out into the night.

A taxi. A hunt through the creased, heavily annotated pages of his A-Z. Legwork. Tons of legwork. The girl from the party seemed distant now, as if he had fictionalized her, as if she existed in a dusty chapter of a long ago part of his life. Something, almost, that might not have happened.

Harewood Avenue. Boston Place. Balcombe Street. Linhope Street. Huntsworth Mews. Chagford Street. Glentworth Street. Siddons Lane.

No joy. Night fell on him without him noticing. A police car drew up alongside him while he was standing in the middle of Cabbell Street, gazing up at the flats. He was asked if he was all right. He was asked if he had been drinking. He was asked if he might leave the vicinity because he was making the residents nervous, him standing there, stock still, for nearly half an hour.

Egan headed back towards Baker Street, deciding for one last sweep of the roads off Crawford Street before calling it a day. Titchard walked with him, memories of the two of them drunk on home brew one Christmas in a shared flat where there had been no money, no other booze. One of the best Christmases. Simple, with a good friend. Not a shred of tinsel in sight.

How could you leave her for me to find. Like that?

He rubbed his face, and found it cold and unmoving, like dough gone stale at the back of a fridge. His coat was too old to be effective against the chill. One winter too many, maybe. Him too, he felt, thinking bitterly of the way Titchard had slackened on the fangs of the window, like a tired baby with a pacifier folding instantly into sleep.

He thought of his bedroom back home, and the sounds of his parents having a late meal, something by Vesta, some dried thing in a packet that was rehydrated with boiling water. Ravi Shankar on the stereo. The sound of a cork being pulled on a bottle of Black Tower. Perfume and aftershave clashing. Tweed and Denim.

Rising from bed. Looking out of the window. The garden, a black hole, sucking attention into it. Somewhere down there were a dozen tennis balls. A water pistol. Goal posts. Comics—*The Dandy, The Beano, Whizzer and Chips, 2000 AD*. A bag of jawbreakers. A bag of Salt 'n' Shake. Summer, there might as well be nowhere else on the planet. Six weeks of school holidays. Kicking a ball around with Dad. Being allowed to stay up to watch James Bond, *Match of the Day* and *The Abominable Dr Phibes*. Pancakes for tea.

You left her. Like that.

He remembered playing in the garden, happily lost with his toys, wondering if Steve Austin would come to the rescue before Maskatron drove his Tonka lorry over Action Man. He remembered shadows moving across him, and his father saying: "This is Joanne. She's going to play with you for a bit. I have to take your mother to see grandma in hospital. Be nice with her. Be good."

And the girl, Joanne, didn't have a face. She was always positioned with her back to the sun, and the sun was so high and bright that her face couldn't release itself of the shadow that clung to it. She said, *Put away those toys. Let's go on an adventure.*

She took his hand and they moved deeper into the garden. The black hole, sucking them both in. Impossible to return.

She showed him forgotten lettuces growing in a row, savaged by the sun, their leaves punched through with so many tears they looked more like small nets.

Slugs, she said. *Do you know that slugs have four noses?*

She was picking one up. She was *picking one up*. He regarded her with a mixture of fear and admiration.

You can kill them with beer. They love beer. They fall in and drown in it. What a way to die. But there's a better way.

She took a glass cruet of salt from her pocket, the type he had seen in motorway service stations and roadside cafés whenever he had been on holiday with his mum and dad. He was thinking of beer. How his dad loved to drink it straight from the can. He had been allowed to try a swig once, and he had spat it out immediately. He was thinking how much he would hate to die, drowning in beer.

I love doing this, she said. *This is like a hobby to me. Slugs. I hate slugs.*

"What have they ever done to you?" he asked, but she was deep into what she was doing now, holding the slug on the palm of her hand, tipping the spout of the cruet towards it. When the salt began to pour, he reflexively shifted away, shaking his head.

"That's not... I don't like it," he said.

What's not to like?

The thing in her hand, once so fat and shiny, now resembled a cooked slice of mushroom: black, twisted in on itself, slowly exploding into foam. He almost shared its suffering, the excruciating pain. Salt had once become trapped in the red raw edge of a hangnail that he had been worrying for hours. He knew what salt could do to open flesh, and that was all that a slug was.

She stared at him, her hand outstretched, the slug dying, twisting like something spinning in the wind. *How to kill a slug*, she said.

He pushed through the doors of the Europa mini-market and made his way, blinking, to the shelves. He grabbed a loaf, a jar of cut-price beetroot, a box of crackers and a half bottle of vodka. Standing in front of a wooden-faced cashier, in the act of riffling through the receipts and shopping lists in his wallet for the correct note, he saw her, the girl from the party, at the next till along, bagging something before ducking out into the howling street.

"Hey?" he called, but she had turned the corner into York Street and was hurrying along towards Gloucester Road, a smear of dark intent momentarily outlined in pools of smoky orange sodium. He followed, biting his lip whenever she sank again into the stretches of gloom between the streetlamps. The way she diminished called to something inside him, a memory, or a doubt. Seeds of light clung to the tail of her coat—maybe it was edged with a reflective strip—leaving a trail for him to follow.

He felt he must catch up with her soon—he was eating up the ground with great strides compared to the bird-like steps she took—but if anything, the distance between them was increasing. He lost her by the time he reached the top of York Street, but no, a shadow was arcing across the wall, following the curve of the road in Harcourt Street, much larger than the subject that cast it. Egan ran now, pulling in breath to call her name, when he realized he couldn't remember it; maybe it hadn't been offered to him in the first place.

"Hey!" he called again, but the sound was ripped apart by the wind and the traffic lowing along the Old Marylebone Road. By the time he had crossed that, impossibly she was a hundred meters or more at his head. He saw her pause for a moment, then her posture altered subtly—

was she casting a glance back towards him?—before she moved to her right and vanished from view.

Egan felt panic fastening the top few buttons of his shirt. He pushed himself to a sprint, not able to understand why he needed to catch up with the girl. But he feared that if he lost her now he would never discover her— or for that matter, his—connection to Circus Street, if one, or it, existed. The tube station was still open, although the barriers were half closed and a guard was standing by, checking his watch and chewing what looked like three packs of gum.

"Last Circle Line train via Liverpool Street's just pulling in," he said. "You'd better get a wiggle on."

Egan could hear the brakes of the train as it drew up to the platform. Feverishly he fed coins to the ticket machine. He crashed through the barrier and hurried down the stone steps but he was too late. He saw the driver give him a wave as he piloted the train out of the station. The first few carriages were empty, but the train had gathered pace by then, to such an extent that he could not discern any detail in the figures populating the rear coaches. It was only when the sound of the rattling train had dissipated and the lights of the platform were doused—one by one, slowly, darkness approaching him as an almost solid thing from the far end of the station—that he realized he wasn't the only one who had missed its departure.

The figure, her figure, dawdled after the darkness as it came his way, but never so quickly as to outstrip it. While her legs were temporarily striped with the color from the bulbs, her face remained banded with night. She held before her a battered, scuffed handbag, a hand pinching each lip. He heard the snap of it opening like a gunshot. The silence around it was an assault. Christ no, he thought, and couldn't fathom why. He must not allow her to show him what was inside that.

Another bank of lights cut out, shriveling the distance between them. He smelled her: sour and metallic, like blood, like the bright taste of a coin. She opened her mouth and what looked like bleached sand fell from it, schussing across the platform, pounds of the stuff. The incongruity of the vision drew him out of his torpor: he bolted.

He ran so far, so hard, without any thought other than the panic of flight, that by the time he came to his senses, for a short while he no longer knew where he was. The madness of his predicament fell around him, with his freezing sweat, like so many dead leaves. He was convinced, somewhere between there and here—wherever here was—he had used Circus Street. Maybe it could only ever be used in extremis, a hidden byway of his own creation, a forgotten path in the A-Z of his mind. Maybe this was why he had been unable to find it. She had returned to show him how simple it was.

He glanced back the way he had come but already he was unsure where that insidious territory lay. Normal sounds were returning, as were the landmarks that fastened him down to the real, true London he thought he had escaped from, so great were his speed and desperation. The girls' school, Francis Holland C of E, at the top of Ivor Place was wreathed in shadow, its great oak door teasing him with a promise of security that he would not find, at least until he got home. He crossed the A41 and followed the Outer Circle around Regent's Park, tempted only momentarily to traverse the locked gates and cut through its center. The street and the lights were more reassuring. On the eastern edge of the park, as he was approaching the Royal College of Physicians, a black taxi slowed for him, its driver raising his eyebrows. Egan climbed gratefully in, the warmth enfolding him. The smell of the driver's cheap aftershave and his gruff voice—"I thought you needed a lift. You look all done in."—were welcome, for once. Egan gave his address, but as they were cruising through Camden, its empty streets still seeming somehow busy, he felt Titchard shifting closer to him on the leatherette, and smelled the blood in his hair as it dried to a crisp. To avoid looking at him, Egan leaned forward and told the driver to take the Kentish Town Road. A mile or so along it, Egan terminated the ride and reluctantly stepped out into the cold.

He had never broken into a building before. He almost walked past the library. It looked less like a municipal building than a front for some kind of bargain basement furniture shop. The window was filled with sun-bleached leaflets about family benefits. There were old photographs of Kentish Town too, that could be purchased inside, along with reproduction maps of NW5 from as far back as the mid-nineteenth century.

Occasional cars and buses swept by behind him, twisting the cold air at his back that suggested a presence, ready to tap him on the shoulder. He shrugged off the unpleasant feeling and tried the door. It was locked, of course. He wondered how long it would be before the police arrived if he were to smash the window in and set off the alarms if, indeed, there were any. How valuable could well-thumbed library copies be?

He was still considering this as he put a half-brick through the flimsy glass.

He kicked out the remains in the frame, wincing as he did so as he thought of Titchard's pale neck. An alarm *was* sounding, although it was difficult to hear above the thump in his own chest. Inside, Egan stumbled through the dark to the reception desk. Behind it he saw a row of returned books in protective plastic sleeves. A cardigan was slung over the back of a chair. Light from the street picked out a pair of frameless spectacles that for a moment made the shadows and wood they rested on something potentially human, observing him. He headed to the back of the library and a room with a sign that read *Staff Only* on the door. A poky kitchen with spilled sugar on the top of a fridge that had hardened into miniature Alps. A kettle, a toaster, both of which were blackened by time and spillages. A plant in a pot that needed watering. A copy of the *Sunday Telegraph*.

Sirens.

Egan hurried back to the window and, bypassing the reception desk from this new direction, his eye fell upon a ring binder as stuttering blue light mottled its cover.

No. No. No. No. No. No. No. No. No. No. No. No. No. No. No.

He was too tired, too scared to trust himself to return to his flat without opening the folder and losing himself in front of his fellow passengers. He did not know what he might do if he were enclosed in a bus or a Tube, with the madness that existed within these cardboard covers. Shelley was waiting. And despite himself, that almost decided him. He could do with some warmth, some yield in his life at the moment, instead of all these angles and edges, cement and stone. But in the same breath he knew it was unfair to draw her into what was fast stripping him of his sanity.

Nexus of filth. Blackspots. I know where they are. I can show them to you.

He suspected that he knew where they lay, too. Open him up here and now and there'd be one.

"Here and now!" he shouted. The other people along Kentish Town Road melted from his path.

Egan ran until he could no longer be sure if the sirens were still whooping, or it was merely his own labored breath. Rain was adding to the vicious tilting of the wind now, producing squalls that felt as bitter and as stinging as slaps across the face. He stopped at the foot of Hampstead Road. Warren Street Tube would have him home within five minutes. But west was Edgware Road. He felt so close to some kind of resolution that he collapsed against the railings overlooking the Euston Underpass and scrabbled with his nails at the binding on Titchard's file. Inside were several pieces of paper. One was a map of Marylebone, and parts of Paddington, such as they were, from 1865. The others were bad photocopies of newspaper clippings from—Egan squinting to read the dates—1952, 1965, 1978. He studied the 1952 paper, a front page from the *St Marylebone & Paddington Record*. Lots of dense text. One small photograph, of a woman leaving a sober-looking building of gray stone, her hand outstretched to try to deny the cameraman. He couldn't read the text because of the poor reproduction, and the ungenerous lighting, the unswerving assaults of the weather. He could only make out some of the headlines on the page, banal space-fillers for the most part, with unimaginative headlines: *TRAPPED IN LIFT*; *FURNITURE BURNT*; *PORTER DIES*; along with adverts for the Hastings and Thanet building society and Handjoy cream ("No vegetable peeling stains on *my* fingers!").

Frustrated, he tucked the file back under his arm and hurried along the Marylebone Road. He felt Circus Street within his grasp; it winked at him, like an ember in the ashes, every time he closed his eyes.

Miraculously, depressingly, there were no buses or empty cabs piling along the A501, when usually there might be a convoy. Every taxi that roared past was occupied. Rain drummed against his scalp. He could no longer feel his toes or fingers.

Titchard's fingers, like lolly sticks. All of him now, like that.

Egan pushed on. When he reached Baker Street he took a right on to Crawford Street, and ran until he found himself in familiar surroundings: squares, avenues and mews he had poked along during better days, quieter days, when his bid to unearth Circus Street had been little more than a bone thrown to his curiosity. Something to pass the time. He heard a bell ringing for last orders a moment before the smell of the pub hit him, a mix of sour ale and mushrooming ashtrays, the desperation in the high tang of after-shave. He pushed through the doors into a chamber filled with smoke and a hubbub he couldn't begin to unravel into constituent words. At the bar he ordered a half pint of Guinness and took the drink to a corner occupied by a woman with a platinum helmet of hair and a deep scowl. Dark veins exploded through the pale wastelands of her cheeks like the patterns in a geranium leaf. She smoked cigarettes through a plastic filter as she played patience with a pack of pornographic cards. He nodded at her and then forgot her as he returned again to Titchard's folder. His fingers, as he released the hasp on the cover, seemed almost cartoonishly blue in the soft light of the pub. But even this wasn't sufficient for him to read the text without bringing the paper closer to his eyes, and squinting, as if he were long-sighted.

More adverts: *ARE YOU BORED on Sunday afternoon? Join our Sunday Club—Dance and Make Friends in a Pleasant Atmosphere. 3.30—6.30, 2/6, inc. Refreshments.*

Rita Hayworth in *Affair in Trinidad* at the Gaumont, Edgware Road.

Don't make a MOVE without considering Jelks for PRICE, SERVICE and CONVENIENCE.

He wanted to reach through the photograph and move the hand that shielded the woman's face.

The movement of cards. Lurid spreads. Butchers' shop window shots of young women bent into unlikely positions. The snap and flutter of the hand being reduced one by one on the scratched, stained table. The randomness of a clutch of cards that might or might not play out, depending on the whim of chance, the journey their shuffling took. Raw, red, glistening images. The women appeared sore. Used. Overused.

MURDERESS! Court Hears How She "Peeled Girl Like a Potato."

But he couldn't get beyond that headline. The words were a mush of ink, the toner not reduced enough to compensate for such poorly printed text. The original must still be in the library somewhere. The thought of returning filled him with a fatigue that made him moan. It was impossible. There would be police. And even if there weren't, it would take him an age to find the relevant article. Titchard might not even have replaced it properly.

He consulted the map. Elegant, cursive script identified each street. The shape of the neighborhood that he had scoured in the A-Z was more simple in this representation, it seemed. Fewer buildings. Fewer streets, perhaps. A lack of complexity in any and all ways. A less complicated era.

And there it was. Circus Street. It leapt out at him as though it had been waiting for his eye alone to fall upon the paper after years of hiding among dusty old volumes. It seemed to burn with intent.

Egan tore at his *A-Z* to find its modern correspondent. Here: Enford Street, a street he had walked by on countless occasions. A street he had traveled along, his nose buried in his maps. Shaking his head. He almost laughed out loud.

He drained his glass and made for the door. Outside, the wind and rain had intensified, but he didn't feel it anymore. His tiredness too could not impinge. He turned left and began to run, but not before he caught sight of the woman in the pub, licking her lips at him, slapping a card against the window for him to see. A woman jacknifed across a bed, yawning at him in a snapshot of scrupulous carnage.

It wasn't the woman on the card though, or the neat way in which she seemed opened, that clung to his thoughts. It was the bedspread that had tugged at a memory. A peppermint stripe that he had known on duvet covers of his own, back in childhood.

The posters curling away from his wall, the Sellotape not taking: Steve Austin touching his toes. Murmurs from downstairs. Bottles of beer popped open. Fish and chips sweating in a paper cone. The scent of vinegar and pickled onions made his jaw ache. The crackle of a stylus finding a groove. Joan Baez. *Diamonds and Rust.* Laughter. A tender admonishment: *Quiet, you'll wake the kids.*

Rising from his bed. Treading softly on the landing, his shadow rearing up against the bathroom door. Avoiding the creaks in the floor. Another room. Another bed pushed up against the wall. Looking down at his sister, on her knees, her face pushed into the pillow as if trying to burrow away from something that chased her through her dreams. The way she moved, captured by the sheets and her childish exhaustion: slow, cumbersome. Sluggish. He despised her. He felt weighed down by her. He despised her. He despised her.

A sister. "I had a sister." The words came in a rush, unbidden, and wind filled the vacuum of his mouth, slapping him back to the here and now. Chairs were being piled onto tables inside the Marylebone Bar & Kitchen, where he had lunched on a number of occasions, sometimes with Titchard, once with Shelley. He liked it. It made him feel at home. Circus Street fell away from its corner like a bloodless wound. He looked up at the street sign and now he could just make out the shadow of Enford Street's predecessor, lurking behind the fresh white plastic.

He moved into the street and felt himself diminish under its immensity. A dozen steps, and the shadows of himself that grew as he bypassed the streetlamps were suddenly joined by another.

She said, "It doesn't look much, but this street has a purity that goes beyond, almost, what purity means."

She said, "Do you remember this place?"

He answered quickly, honestly, even as the question was dying on her lips.

"Yes," he said. "No. Yes. No." Tears came and he couldn't understand why.

"You weren't you, then," she said. "They took you away. They sat you in white rooms and looked inside your head. You wore jumpers, even in the summer. You made layers for yourself and hid deep within them."

He knew the school on his left, and the Western Eye Hospital at Circus Street's end, where the Marylebone Road beheaded it. On the right, houses partially toppled by the demolition ball tried their best to retain a fundamental shape. He stopped in front of one of the shells and peered in through its shattered façade. Stepping across the doorless threshold, he paused in what had once been a hallway, and shut the door behind him, the brass knob in his hand feeling smooth and warm to the touch, as it always had. His father's sheepskin coat was hanging on a hook on the wall, next to his mother's scarf, which shed perfume like a flower on a drowsy summer evening. He heard them somewhere deep inside the house, a soft clash of crockery: her washing plates, him drying them. The radio in the background. *Walk in Love*, by The Manhattan Transfer, a song that they laughed about at school because of the line *We take our clothes off.*

He moved through the house, and he felt her at his elbow, something there, but not there, like a stain in the air, an odor. Through the back door, into the garden they went. A large fence acted as a windbreak. Silence filled the space.

"Go on," she said. "Go on." Her eyes were wide, as bright as freshly minted pennies. "I'll take the blame for you. Blame is all wrapped up in this. Blame and pain. It tastes no different." She gave him the camera, and told him to take lots of nice pictures for her.

He had led his sister along this path while Joanna waited inside. His parents were in the hospital, at the side of his grandmother, who was not expected to last the night. Down to the place where the lettuces were stunted, scorched by that infinite summer, what existed of their leaves chewed into lattices by the slugs. Down to the area of bracken and shadow. These places, they are always down.

His sister had talked nonsense to him. A baby still, on the cusp of real talk, practicing with her lips and tongue the sounds she could make. *Diggol. Gok.* He gave her cherry brandy to drink. She screwed her face up at the taste, but opened her mouth every time he offered the bottle. Trust takes a long time to die.

The way the babysitter, Joanne, had showed him: He took the knife from his pocket when his sister was drowsy, on the point of collapse. He tore at her skin as best he could, being careful not to cut too deeply, and then dragged her to another part of the garden, where he had emptied three sacks of salt into a scarred tin bath. Pain was dragging her out of her befuddled state. Before she could scream, he filled her mouth with salt and rolled her in the bath. The salt became wet, discolored. He almost lost her under it. She tried to cry. It seemed, before death leapt at her, that crying must be the apogee of her ambition.

"Slug," he had called her, when she could no longer hear a thing.

He sank to his knees in ashes and rubble. A sheaf of Polaroids lay on the floor, strewn like a bad hand of cards strewn by a disgusted player. It seemed as if the earth had vomited them up, unable to stomach their contents. She looked like something boiled in a pan, a hot pink, like a prawn. Shining, swelling, the exposed flesh of her face puffing up to blind her.

She said, "This place, and the others like it in this bad, old city, they need to be sustained, just like you or I. Nourishment sounds so very comforting, doesn't it? Well, it can be anything but. Especially here. Back in the bosom of family. Such houses never want anything else, really."

He looked up at her and she held out her hand to shield herself from the damaging heat of his gaze. He saw the curl of her lip. The salt encrusted into the brackets at the corners of her mouth. The black hole of Circus Street seemed ringed with teeth. He collapsed back under the weight of its obscene appetite. She shut up then, concentrating, and flensed him so quickly that he thought it was just his clothes that she'd shed. Then the pain caught up, the pain that was too great to survive, the pain that shocked you to death. A pain so pure, so extreme, so different that he felt himself climax, even as he was trying to drag himself away.

CITY IN ASPIC

It was a place that needed people in order for it to come alive. In winter, the streets whispered with uncollected litter and nervous pigeons. The air grew so thick with cold that it became hard to walk anywhere. When night came, the water that was slowly drowning the city turned the darkness into an uncertain quantity. There was astonishing beauty here too, though, even where there oughtn't be any. The crumbling structures, the occasional bodies dragged from the waterways, the bleach of winter that pocketed the city's color for months on end: all of it had a poetry, a comeliness. Massimo understood this skewed charm. Where others saw moles, he saw beauty spots.

Many times Massimo had wished he could simply drift away like the tourists at the tail end of the season, or the leaves that blew from the trees. It would be nice to spend the coldest months of the year further south, perhaps with his cousins in Palermo. But now that was not possible. He and Venice were stuck with each other until March.

He stood on the balcony of the honeymoon suite, smoking his last cigarette and enjoying the garlicky smells of *chicheti* that wafted up from the *osterie* on the Riva degli Schiavoni. One of Venice's interminable mists had risen from the Canale di San Marco and clung to the façades like great sheets hung out to dry. Behind him, from deep within the hotel, the sound of the vacuum cleaners on the stairs competed for a short while with the toots of the *vaporetto* and the bell of San Nicoló dei Mendicoli. The last of the guests had checked out that morning and in a little while, Maria, the cleaner, would be finished and he could lock the great doors of the Hotel Europa until next year.

He could have his dinner here, on this balcony, every evening if he so wished. The corridors would be his alone to patrol. A different bed to sleep in whenever he liked, though such a choice disturbed him perhaps more than it ought. Deaths had occurred in some of the Europa's rooms; children and divorces had their origins on a number of those mattresses.

He flicked his cigarette end in the direction of the canal and returned to the room where he smoothed the bedspread before taking the stairs down to the ground floor. His father, Leopoldo, had told him this was a job of great responsibility; if he went about it with professionalism, then he would be considered for the post of reception clerk. He was under no illusions. He was a security guard, no more. In the seventies, his father had run the Europa with a touch of élan and much warmth. Tourists who stayed at the Europa came back the next year and the year after that. And then the hotel had been taken over by men in suits with large bellies and eyes that gleamed when they assessed his father's profits. They paid a hefty sum to take over the hotel. Massimo's father was tired. A stroke had robbed him of his personable nature. Though the hotel was Massimo's birthright, he agreed with his father that they should take the money in order that it should fund his senescence. But his father, though crippled by the stroke, clung to life and the money was running out.

Maria, who had been a cleaner here for as long as he could remember, patted his arm before she left and told him that spring would be here before he was aware. "Take advantage of the rest," she advised him. "You'll be busy again too soon." Perhaps seeing the bitterness in his eyes, she smiled at him. "Your father would be proud of you."

And now, alone. The magazines had been read and the puzzle books completed. The evening stretched before him like the interminable carpets on the five floors above. He took a cursory stroll of the ground floor, checking the window catches in each room and the locks on the doors. The furniture was shrouded with dust sheets that reduced everything to the same, lumpen shape.

He was about to return to the lobby and rewatch an old football video when he saw the single glove draped across the newel post. The stairwell reached up into darkness, those risers beyond the sixth step lost to a night that had fallen on the city as stealthily as snow. It was a lady's glove for the left hand, made from black leather and scuffed with age. The interior smelled of perfume. Maria must have come across it while she was preparing the rooms for the winter. He pocketed it and drew the curtains across the front entrance but not before noticing that the street was empty. He didn't like the way that Venice was abandoned each year. It was as if sunshine and long days were the only things of interest to visitors. Newly married couples ran the gamut of clichés before returning to their homes; the way the tourists clung to St Mark's square or were punted around in boats suggested that Venice had nothing else to offer.

Irritated by this train of thought, Massimo turned off the television and went out into his city, a place where he could still get lost in the dark, a place that thrilled and comforted him like no other. The somnolent lap of the water against the gondolas was the beat of a mother's heart. It was not merely a comfort. It justified him. It fastened him like a bolt to the earth and gave him substance.

He stopped for coffee and *grappa* at the *Trattoria al Canastrello* and watched from the window the black water as it ribboned beneath the Ponte di Rialto. One of his favorite occupations was observing people, but at this time of the year the only people around were the old and infirm. They drifted through the streets as if the weight of their experience was shoring Venice up, as much a support for the ancient city as the countless larch poles that cradled it beneath the waves. Venice, during the winter, seemed to run down like an old clock. Its streets and façades could still play a backdrop for anybody from any time over the last fifteen hundred years without them seeming anachronistic. He would not have been surprised to see Marco Polo himself hurrying along the Fondamenta del Vin. The people fastened Venice to the here and now. But when there were no people, it was as if the city were immune to history. Venice had the quality of an eternal ghost.

A woman with one hand paused at the apex of the bridge to look into the water, but then he saw how the light was absorbed by the dark glove on the limb that he thought had been missing, which made it seem invisible. She was moving away from the bridge, in the direction of the San Polo district, when Massimo remembered the glove in his pocket. He cast a handful of lire on to the table and burst out of the trattoria into the cold. The air was damp and settled heavily in his lungs.

By the time he was under the grand arch at the top of the bridge the woman was nowhere to be seen; she could have taken any one of the half dozen exits away from the canal. Frustration bled through him. He glanced back to the warmth of the trattoria and saw that somebody had already taken his place at the window, was hunched over a newspaper. Angry, he stalked in the direction she had taken, rubbing at the glove in his pocket. It was an old thing. Tomorrow, no doubt, she would buy herself a new pair, thus rendering pointless this little chase of his.

Massimo walked for twenty minutes, until the fog had drawn an ugly, persistent cough from his chest. He tugged at the collars of his coat but the damp was in him and around him now, settling on the thick black twill like dew. He heard a brief snatch of music from one of the *pensiones* but it was stolen away before he had the chance to place it. The absence of people disarmed him. During the day, this area was a hive of activity filled with *erberia* and *pescheria*, along with jewelers' shops and clothes stalls. Now it was lonely and its voice was any number of echoes. The lack of physicality, of motion, had taken away his confidence. The street names were made indistinct by the quickening mist. He had grown up in this city, and understood that part of its charm was its complication of alleyways, but never before had he felt so lost. His home had turned its back on him.

Shutters closed noisily on the night. Venice was sealing itself against the hour.

He stumbled gratefully upon the Campo San Polo where he was able to reorient himself. Eager to return to the hotel, he lingered as he heard the skitter of heels clatter through the arches towards him. She was still nearby, or somebody else was. He bit down on his compulsion to find her and hurried back to the Europa. Once there, he locked the glass doors and threw on the lobby lights.

He placed the glove behind the reception desk and checked the phone messages. There was just one, from his father, who felt well enough to take lunch with his son the following day, if the weather was fair.

In bed, Massimo allowed the creaks and sighs of the old hotel to lull him. At least here, among these well-known and much-loved sounds he could feel at home, even if his city had shown him its inaccessible side tonight. He slept and dreamt of hands reaching out from the sacrament-black waters. They would not rest until they touched him. And where they touched him, a little part of his happiness, his warmth inside, was switched off for ever.

He wakened feeling hollow and feverish. He knew it was his blood sugar levels in need of a boost, but could not resist blaming the dream on his skittishness. He wished, as was so often the case with other dreams, that he had been unable to remember it.

He took breakfast in another of the suites, white dust sheets covering the furniture and brightening the room, while also making it cold through its lack of definition. The mist had disappeared. Feeble sunlight splashed across the roofs and turned the surface of the canal into the color of watered-down milk. Feeling better, he set the timer on the central heating to ensure that each room would be warmed for a few hours, and switched on the television.

In the night, a murder had been committed in Venice, at the *campanile* near the church of San Polo. According to the reporter, who was standing by the Palazzo Soranzo in the square, his nose red from the cold, the woman had been found just after midnight by a man walking his dog. The camera switched angles to show the crime scene, which was dominated by a white tent erected by the *carabinieri*, a number of whom were standing around with machine guns hanging loose over their arms. Bystanders watched as a stretcher was shunted into an ambulance, a crimson blanket covering the body.

Shaken, Massimo switched off the bulletin and showered. He had picked up a sniffle after last night's adventure and he felt too ropy to go out. He considered calling his father to cancel lunch, but the old man did not take the air much these days; he would be looking forward to spending a little time in the sunshine with his boy.

Massimo toured the hotel, desultorily checking windows and locks. He flapped ineffectually at the pigeons that had settled on the terraces and made a mental note to buy some disinfectant and talk to Franco, the handyman, about getting some netting to drape from the roof, to prevent them nesting. With a heavy heart, he locked the hotel doors behind him. It was not so much the emptiness of the old building that got to him, but its silences. Coming back to a quiet place, that over the years had known so much bluster and happiness, was saddening in the extreme. It was a different hotel to the one his father had run. It was as if, at the time of Leopoldo's departing, its spirit had left too, perhaps clogged up with the gears of the old-fashioned fob watch he wore in his waistcoat, or bunched in a pocket like one of his maroon silk handkerchiefs.

Massimo spotted his father easily. His beard was a white strap for his chin and he wore the only tie he owned, a dark blue knot against a badly ironed white shirt.

"Hi Pop," he said, bending slightly to kiss the top of the old man's head. The beard was not clipped as neatly as it once had been; his hair was haphazardly oiled. He smelled of burnt toast.

"*Buon giorno,*" Leopoldo said, formally. "*Come sta?*"

Massimo ordered another glass of Prosecco for his father, despite his protestations, and a *grappa* for himself.

"You heard of the killing?" Leopoldo said, through the slewed mess of his mouth. He dabbed at the corner of it with a handkerchief every ten seconds or so. The left side of his face seemed to be sliding away from his head. It gave him a dismissive air that, Massimo suspected, pleased his father no end. He seemed distressed by the news, though.

"This morning, yes," he replied. He could not help feeling guilty. His father's stare still had the capacity to find some speck of fault in him, even when there was none.

"A woman, they say."

Massimo grunted.

"They say her left hand was skinned, like a rabbit."

"I didn't know that." Reaching for the glove in his pocket that, of course, was not there, Massimo betrayed more of his nervousness than even he expected of himself.

Leopoldo had noticed also. "Are you all right, son?" He tried to reach out the withered nonsense of his own left hand but he could do no more than waggle it in Massimo's direction.

"I'm fine. It's the hotel. Strange to be there with nobody else around."

"It is a good hotel. She will protect you."

"I know Pop. I know."

They were halfway through lunch when Massimo thought of something.

"How did you know about the hand?" he asked. "You said it was skinned."

"So they say."

"Who are 'they'?"

Leopoldo wiped his lips. His plate was littered with splinters of chicken bone. Much of the sauce patterned his shirt; he was having a good lunch.

"I have my friends," he said. "Friends all over Venice. They stay in my hotel sometimes. Maybe when they need a little help. Polizia. I have friends there too. You don't think your papa has his contacts?"

Sadly, Massimo understood that, like his father, the only friends he could lay claim to were friends of the hotel first. They were friends by extension.

"It's nice to see you again, Pop."

"You too. We should do this more often. You should come visit me."

"I will. I will."

Massimo walked his father to the *vaporetto* and waved him off before deciding to investigate the murder site for himself. The crowd had dispersed since the body had been taken away, but the white tent remained, as did the *carabinieri*. Police tape sealed off the area. By day, the *campo* did not seem capable of possessing the menace it had exuded the previous night. All of its shadows had been washed clean by the sunlight.

He wanted to ask one of the policemen, or perhaps one of the louche reporters leaning against the wall smoking cigarettes, if they knew anything more about the death and whether or not Leopoldo's nugget of gossip bore any truth. Instead, he walked away. To say anything might be to incriminate himself. He could not help feeling in some small way responsible for the woman's death. If he had caught up with her, he might have been able to give her her glove; his presence alone might have been enough to dissuade her pursuer from attacking.

On the Ponte di Rialto he saw a dark cat withdrawn into the shade. His father had loved cats and had kept many at the Europa over the years. Massimo beckoned it to him but it did not come. It was only as he drew nearer that he realized it was not a cat at all. It was another glove.

Massimo did not go out that evening. He ate his dinner in the hotel kitchen and played patience in the lobby while the television murmured.

He paid it no attention, but its burble was of some comfort. He thought about calling some of his old friends, people he had not seen for many years, and asking them round for drinks but he did not possess the courage. It would be too much to find that they had moved away from Venice or worse, that they had remained but did not remember him. The hotel had nailed him to this city. He might be taking care of it at the moment, but he saw now how it had more than taken care of him. He stopped dealing cards and looked up at the paintings on the walls, the worn carpet leading from the door to the reception area, the sofas under their dustsheets, the ashtrays on the fake marble tables. He suddenly despised the hotel, and the way his father had shackled him to it. He envied the old man's freedom. All of Massimo's formative years had been poured into the hotel and while it had remained robust, fashionable even, he had found himself at the doorway to his forties, his promise, his potential dwindling like the hair at his temples. Venice was like an ill-matched spouse that one gets used to, that one learns to if not love, then abide. Its waters lapped slowly at one's resolve; Massimo had been worn down by it. He had capitulated.

Evening had lost its ripe colors to the night. Faint drifts of cloud were scrapes at the bottom of a bowl of dark chocolate. A cold wind, a taste of winter, was coming in from the north, inspiring shapes among the twists of litter. Massimo sat back in his chair and reached for the bottle beneath the desk. His hand brushed against the gloves. He took two quick shots of *grappa* and picked up the telephone. His fingers remembered the number before he had fully mustered it in his thoughts. He was surprised by the readiness of this memory. *She can't still live there*, he thought, as the line burred with the ringing tone. The lights in the hotel dimmed and then grew very bright. He was about to hang up, embarrassed by this asinine plot, but was startled into saying something when a voice suddenly leapt down the receiver at him: "Pronto!"

Adelina Gaggio remembered him. How could she not, she had argued? Though it had been thirty years since they had last spoken at length, when they were both at school, their conversation had been spiced and easy, as if they had never lost touch. Her voice had been a soft hand enclosing his, bringing him in from the cold.

Yes, she had eaten, but she was at a loose end tonight and would be thrilled to come and see him. She too lived in the Sestiere Castello, in Calle Dietro te Deum, and would be with him within the hour.

Massimo hurried around the lobby, stripping back the sheets to try to rouse some color and warmth from the old building. He changed into clothes that were not so tired-looking and relieved the wine cellar of a few bottles of Bardolino. It was as he was wiping them clean and trying to remember which bunch contained the key for the dining room, where the glasses were stored, that he heard two very loud thumps above his head, as if somebody struggling to remove his shoes had managed to kick them across the room.

The spit vanished from his mouth. He had nothing in the way of a weapon, other than a broken snooker cue from the games room that had been waiting months for a repair that would never happen. He took the lower half of it, tight in his fist, and padded along the corridor to the stairs. Throwing the switches to illuminate the upper floors might scare the intruder off but the coward in Massimo could not bear to ascend in darkness. He was half way up the second flight, the suite of rooms where the sound had come from in view, when the lights went out again, staggered, as though a finger was deliberately flicking off each set. Massimo's hand would not settle on the butt of the cue. He paused, his breath coming harder than this simple exertion ought to inspire, while his eyes accustomed to the fresh dark.

A pair of pigeons had flown into a window, confused by the reflections in the glass. The electrics, old and unreliable in such a building, had fused. Hadn't they suggested their unpredictability to him downstairs just now? He clung to the possibilities like a child at the tit. But if the circuits had fused, shouldn't the lights go out as one?

There were different sets of switches. The ones he had thrown at the foot of the stairs and separate consoles for each floor. If there was an intruder up here, then he was still up here. Where was the sense in breaking in, dashing downstairs and then killing the lights after the caretaker had gone to investigate? Massimo removed his attention from the inked-out column behind him and forced his focus to gel on the shadows ahead. Nothing moved up there that he could see, but now he could hear the slam of a window in its frame as the wind increased.

He swept up the final flight and stood at the end of the corridor. The door to room 29 was ajar. Biting down on his fear, he approached it. He would swing first and ask questions later. The thought of violence encouraged his heart to beat faster. Six feet shy of the door a moan slipped out of him as the gap in the doorway shrank and the door snicked softly shut.

Downstairs, the entry buzzer rasped.

The torpor of fear fell away from him like a chrysalis. Refreshed by the promise of an ally, he hurried back down the stairs and unlocked the doors. Adelina was standing hunched against the wind, a smile fading. She had taken off one of her gloves to press the buzzer. Her eyes went from his own to the makeshift cosh he brandished.

"Come in," he said, grabbing her arm roughly.

She stiffened under his fingers. He apologized quickly and told her what was wrong.

"Call the police," she said, as if she were explaining something simple to a child.

"I can't. I'm not sure."

She rolled her eyes, the first expression she had shown him that he remembered from their youth. Time had bracketed her face with a kind heaviness that nevertheless had fogged his recollections of her until now. She marched past him and took the stairs two at a time. He noticed that the lights had come back on.

"Wait," he said, and hurried after her. Despite his anger at himself, he stopped in the same place as before and watched her open the door. He saw the shadows spring back as the light went on and then the counterpane on the bed diminishing, the narrowing of the watercolor on the far wall as the door swung slowly shut. He waited for her to cry out. A minute passed that felt the length of a season. If he went downstairs now, the frost would be gone from the car roofs and spring would have lent its freshness to the canals.

Adelina emerged, wiping her hands off against each other. She looked bored, as a person waiting for a bus in the rain might.

"A window had come loose," she said simply, and brushed past him. "Do you have something to drink?"

His attention kept returning to those hands, even after the first bottle had been consumed, when his body had relaxed into itself and his earlier panic seemed distant and foolish. They were slimmer than the rest of her body, as if they had once belonged to another woman. She used them to help shape her words, which had loosened with the drink, and were accompanied with frequent laughter. It bothered him slightly that she refused to take off the left glove, but the wine was numbing him to his insecurities. It didn't matter. It didn't matter at all.

It seemed absurd to Massimo that their paths had not crossed, even by accident, in the three decades since they shared classes at school. Since then, she had stayed in Venice for all but one of the following years, and had worked as a saleswoman for the Murano Glass Company since the mid 1990s. She had never married, but she had a teenage son, Bruno, who was currently traveling in England. "My life now, I want to devote to animals. And then find myself a good husband. Have some happiness before they put me in my pretty little plot on San Michele."

Towards midnight, the two bottles drained, they suddenly became aware of the passage of time. The wind had become a constant howl but

Adelina declined Massimo's offer to take one of the rooms, gratis. She left with his telephone number, and promises that they would keep in touch now; that they had no excuses not to. Her kiss on his cheek stayed with him, like a line of poetry, or a new song that feels like an old favorite by the time it ends. He fell asleep in the chair.

When he wakened, he thought it was morning, but the light was the artificial spill coming from the brackets on the walls. His mouth was sticky with wine. He saw from his watch that he had been asleep a matter of two hours. It was cold, the heating having turned itself off, but that was not what had roused him.

Somebody had screamed. The wind was dead, so he couldn't blame the sound on that. He rose from his seat and switched off the lights in order to see better when he pressed his face to the window. Two hours was more than enough time for Adelina to have arrived home safely; nevertheless, unease spread like indigestion through his chest.

On the ground six feet away from the doors, a suede glove the color of the cement it rested on flapped at him, as if agitating for help. There were no blocks of light in any of the other buildings he could see, which suggested that he had imagined it after all, but another scream, this one deeper and somehow more liquid, stitched by frantic gasps, cut through his doubt. He closed his eyes and pressed his forehead against the cold glass, as if its chill might numb the distressed part of his mind. What could he do to help? The scream had been severed and originated from the maze of streets off the main drag. He could spend half an hour looking for its author, enough time for a body to be dumped in the canal and a killer to become a ghost. He might have opened the doors anyway, and tried his best, if it weren't for the grate of heels on the pavement. He moved back from the window into the sanctity of shadow and watched as a shadow lengthened in the frame afforded by the Europa's entrance. Something in its deportment rattled him. The shadow seemed too stiff, too jerky, as if the joints of the owner's body had been fused together. It became, in the second or two when he realized the figure was going to pass into view, dreadfully important that he did not look at who it was, regardless of the fact that the other would not be able to see him in the gloom. He turned away, like a child from a bad dream, and sensed eyes burn into him, scorching him away layer by layer. He felt raped by their awful scrutiny.

An age later, he craned his neck and saw that the figure had gone. The glove, though, remained on the ground, fingers curled skyward, like a dead animal that had withdrawn and hardened. Was it the woman he had seen the day before? He could almost believe that her presence had given the glove that solidified, bereft appearance and was grateful that he had lost her on the bridge that night. Because for the first time, he suspected that *she* had been tracking *him*.

Signorina Sinistra. He heard the name a dozen times the next morning in the marketplace as he shopped for vegetables and fruit. "She takes the skin from the left hand," a voice at his shoulder said as he was testing the ripeness of an avocado. Another, queuing behind him while he took coffee in a bar, confided: "They found another body this morning. Near the Arsenale. A man this time. His hand, oh my Lord, his hand!"

Another body. That made two. A little premature, he thought, to start giving the killer a moniker, providing a myth before its time. And how could they be certain it was a female murderer? But then he thought of the footsteps outside the hotel and he shuddered. He must hurry back and burn the gloves that he was keeping under the desk. God only knew why he had bothered to collect them in the first place. They had brought him nothing but trouble. He suspected his complicity in the murders had begun with the recovery of the first one, as if that simple act had been some kind of secret signal, a green light of sorts.

A police car was parked outside the hotel when he returned. A somber-faced man with doughy jowls standing by the passenger door tried to smile at him but the curve of his lips only served to turn his mouth into a flat line. Massimo's heart lurched when he saw that the entrance doors to the hotel were open. Two policemen were standing inside.

Massimo said, "I'm sure I locked that this morning."

The somber-faced man, who introduced himself as Inspector Scarpa, shrugged. "It was for the best we stay until you returned. You are Leopoldo's son, yes?"

Massimo nodded. Inspector Scarpa aped him. "My first job," he said, "when I joined the police, was here, at the Europa."

"Oh?" Massimo moved away from the other man, into the warmth of the lobby. The two policemen looked at him as if he were trespassing. He saw a third policeman now, standing behind the reception desk with his hands clasped behind his back, watching the television screen. A football match was playing.

"Yes," said the inspector, following Massimo into the hotel. "A most terrible case. Your father must remember it. Some people staying here. Two men. They tortured a woman, a young girl in fact, in one of the rooms. But they escaped."

"I don't believe you," Massimo spat, horrified that his hotel could be guilty of such a secret. His father had never mentioned such a thing to him.

"You must have been no more than a boy. It was in all the newspapers.

Twenty-eight years ago. A big, big story. The girl died as I recall. A complication. She developed infections. Nasty business." He shrugged again, as if it were a game.

The policeman had grown bored of the football match and was picking through the coffee cups and notepads on the desk.

"Do you have a search warrant?" Massimo barked, and then smiled awkwardly at the inspector, hoping he would take the outburst as a joke. Inspector Scarpa's eyebrows had raised.

Now the policeman had seen something; Massimo could tell from his expression what it was.

"Well thank you, for looking after my hotel. I'm grateful to you. I'll make sure I'm more careful in future."

"Careful in what way?" Inspector Scarpa said as the officer lifted the gloves into view and all eyes turned on Massimo.

He asked for a glass of *grappa* and they brought him one. The inspector looked like an indulgent uncle who has caught his nephew watching a pornographic film. The face seemed born to police work. *Tell me all about it,* was its message. It was big enough and friendly enough to absorb lots of information. The inspector was a sponge.

Massimo told them everything, right up until the previous night when he had seen the woman in the street. The only details he changed concerned the checking of the second floor room: he could not admit to Adelina searching it for him. The inspector had made a barely imperceptible gesture with his hand when he mentioned Adelina's name and thereafter his concentration was qualified with a slight frown, as if he couldn't quite understand Massimo's dialect.

When he was finished, Inspector Scarpa said, "Can we see the room?"

Massimo swallowed the last drops of the *grappa*; his "Sorry?" was strangled slightly by its fire.

"The room you checked. Where you heard the intruder."

"There was no intruder. Just a window that wasn't locked properly."

"Can we see it?"

"I don't see why this is so—"

Inspector Scarpa held up his hand. In a soporific voice, he said: "*Per favore,* Signore Poerio. Please. Indulge us. We shan't take up too much more of your precious time."

The first sting of sarcasm. It hit home more acutely, coming from Inspector Scarpa's affable mouth. They suspected him of something. Well let them.

"This way," he said, brusquely, and set off for the stairs without waiting for them to gather. On the second floor he slipped the bunch of keys from his waistband and hunted for the relevant master. As he did so, the inspector ran his fingers along the slender knuckles of his opposing hand, eliciting cracks from the joints with little tweaks and twists. The sounds were unbearably loud in the corridor. Massimo dropped his keys. Nobody seemed to mind.

"Adelina, you say?" muttered the inspector, in a far-away voice. "Adelina?"

"Yes. What of it?"

Another shrug. "It's familiar. It's familiar to me."

Massimo opened the door and stood back to let the other four men into the room. In the mirror, before he could enter, he saw them looking down at a body. The crimson rug that it lay on had once been white. He reacted more quickly than he believed himself possible, closing the door and locking it before the police had a chance to stop him. Fists pounded the door yet still there was no rage in Scarpa's voice. He sounded saddened. Perhaps he and his father had been closer than he let on. What was it Pop had said? *You don't think your papa has his contacts?*

Massimo hurried downstairs and pulled on his coat. His mind would not stand still for long enough to be able to formulate a plan. He should pack a suitcase. He should contact Adelina. Perhaps he should steal the police car.

Instead, he locked the hotel doors behind him and scurried west along the canal. Once past the Piazza San Marco he paused on the Calle Vallaresso, listening for sirens. In Harry's Bar, he pushed past the lunchtime gathering and found a telephone. He dialed and let it ring for a full three minutes but his father did not answer. Then he tried Adelina's number. An Englishman answered.

"Adelina," Massimo said. "I need to speak to Adelina."

"Non capisco, amico." His Italian was frustratingly poor.

"Adelina Gaggio. She lives there. Can you get her for me?"

"Non. Nobody here by that name."

Massimo had punched in the correct number. There was no doubt. "Please. You have to—"

"Hey? You deaf? I said nobody here called Adelina. *Testa di cazzo.*"

Massimo slammed the receiver down. He could go there, to the street Adelina had mentioned, but without an address it could take hours to find her and even then she might not be in. She might be at work.

The glass company.

Excitedly, he dialed 12 and obtained the number from directory services. When he got through to the receptionist at Murano her contact list did not contain any reference to Adelina Gaggio.

"Has she been with us long?" the receptionist tried. "She might not be on our list if she joined us recently."

"Five years," Massimo said. A white, abject face stared at him from behind the bar. He was about to order a bellini from it when he realized it was his own, reflected in a mirror. "At least five years."

"I'm sorry."

"She must—"

"Very sorry, sir."

What now? He struggled to keep himself from crying out. He had nobody to go to, other than the police, and they would not be patient with a man who had locked some of their colleagues in a room with a woman he had ostensibly murdered. But surely they would see that his panic was inspired by innocence. If he had killed somebody in his own hotel, would he not take pains to dispose of the body, rather than blithely stroll around Venice having left the main entrance unlocked?

How could Adelina have lied to him? The coolness of the woman as she came out of the room. How could it be that he had called her after twenty years only to find that he had invited a deranged killer on to the premises? The police would not believe him if he told them this, but it was all he had to offer.

He dialed 112 and was patched through. He tried to explain but every time he finished a sentence, the police operator would ask him to expand on every iota of information or ask him to spell the names he mentioned. Then the operator would fudge the spelling and get him to repeat it.

"Adelina," the voice buzzed. "What's that? A-D-A...?"

It dawned on him then, and he gently replaced the receiver. He glanced out of the front windows but how could he chance it? Then again, they would have any rear exit covered too. They would not expect him to leave by the front door.

He saw a group of suits standing to return to the office and he hurried after them, catching up with them, and purposefully barging into a middle-aged woman. He put on a big smile and apologized profusely as they filtered on to the street. He put his hand on her arm. There was wine in her. She was happy and forgiving. She covered his hand with her own and said it was perfectly all right. He asked her what she had had for lunch. He asked her the name of the perfume she was wearing. In this manner he passed along the street with his new friends. He didn't look back until he was in sight of a safe alleyway he could move down. Only now were the police cars drawing up outside Harry's Bar. He ran.

This time his father did pick up the phone. But he heard a click, as soft as a pair of dentures nestling together, and he understood that what ought to have been the safest house of all was now the most dangerous.

"I'm okay, Pop," he said. "I'm all right."

"Massimo," his father said. "I'm sorry."

Massimo killed the connection hoping that even those few seconds had not been enough to expose him to the authorities a second time. He had been running for days, it seemed, but it could only have been a matter of hours. The sunlight was failing now. The light on the canals was turning the color of overripe peaches. From the east, a wedge of flat, gray sky was closing upon Venice like the metal lid to a box of secrets. Freezing air ran before it, as though the weather too was trying to escape the city's confused sprawl.

His thoughts turned to the inspector, who had seemed so understanding, yet had contained an edge as hard as the coming cold snap. His past seemed as caught up in the Europa as his own. He wished he had had the time to ask his father about the incident that Scarpa had mentioned. He would have been a ten-year-old when the hotel had provided a torture chamber for some of its guests. He couldn't remember a thing about it, but then he would have been shielded from such an appalling event. He thought of the way his father had said sorry and did not like what his mind came up with.

With no better task to turn to, Massimo caught a *vaporetto* to San Tomà and hurried the two hundred meters or so to the Campo dei Frari. The woman at the reception desk of the Archivio di Stato looked as impenetrable as a bad clam but she was sympathetic to his needs, even if the five hour window for requesting materials had lapsed.

It didn't take long. Once he had been shown how to access the microfiches and blow them up on the viewer, it was simply a matter of trawling through the front pages of *Il Gazzettino* from 1973. A photograph of the Europa's exterior halted him before any of the words. The headline took up much of the page but this had no impact on him once he had noticed the small photograph at the foot of the page, the victim of the torture who had died. He didn't need to read the caption to know it was the woman he had entertained in his hotel the previous night.

It was there, in black and white, and his brain had sucked it in even though he had averted his eyes, fearful of an image decades old. Yet he wasn't happy. They could have got it wrong. They could have mixed up her picture. They *must* have got it wrong. The alternatives were too outlandish to swallow.

Everywhere he looked, there were gloves lying companionless. In the canal, sitting on windowsills, hunched on the floor near lampposts and benches. His panic mounted as he counted them. Nothing looked quite so dismal as a discarded glove. Did each one signify a terrible death in the city? Just because two bodies… three bodies had been found didn't mean that more were lying in wait, stretching back to a time when the killer had set out on her spree.

Snow had begun to fall on the city. Already the narrow streets and uneven roofs were dusted with white while the canal absorbed the flakes and remained black. In some areas, where the light was poor, the canals escaped from view completely. They became plumbless moats that one could look into without hope of ever finding an end.

At Fondamente Nuove he persuaded a *vaporetto* pilot preparing to go home to take him to San Michele. The promise of ten thousand lire if he waited to bring him back was enough of a lure. On the short journey, Massimo watched the waters creaming at the bow while Venice fell behind them. A series of lights came on around the Sacca della Misericordia, as though people had opened their windows to watch his journey.

The island loomed out of the dark. More and more, his father had made references to this place, with its pretty cypress trees. It would be expensive to find him a plot here, but it seemed, even through Leopoldo's oblique language, that his heart was set upon it.

Even from here, in such unsociable weather, Massimo could smell the perfume of cut flowers on the graves. As the *vaporetto* drew up alongside, the white stone of the Convento di San Michele seemed lambent in the murk.

"You know the cemetery is closed, *Signor*?"

"Just wait for me," Massimo ordered, and then: "Do you have a torch?"

The pilot sat back and rummaged for cigarettes in his jacket pocket. "Yes. And I might allow you to hire it, if you ask me nice."

It was not such a difficult cemetery to break into. Beyond the entry archway, the cloisters marked the beginning of the graveyard proper. But Massimo ignored it. Adelina might well have been buried here, but she was not here now. The island could not take bodies indefinitely. Having gorged on the dead for so long, it had reached bursting point. Now the bones of the resting were lifted every ten years or so for another final journey to an ossuary on the mainland, in order to make way for the next wave of cadavers. If Adelina's name was to be found here, it would be on a plaque, not a headstone. Massimo trained the feeble torchlight on the neatly arranged plinths, readying himself for a long night's hunt. At least they were easier to read than the weathered slabs.

The snow that had begun to fall on the heart of the city found its way out here after half an hour. Massimo blew on his hands to keep them warm and tried to ignore the impatient hoots from the *vaporetto* horn. The pilot was going nowhere; his pockets would remain empty if he did.

He covered the cemetery in a slow strafing movement, his hopes lifting with every plaque that did not bear her name. Perhaps, simply, he was going mad after all. When he did not find her here, he could return to the mainland and find it had returned to normal. All he needed was this restorative jaunt to pick clean the tired crevices of his mind.

But then, of course, of course: *Adelina Gaggio, 1963-1973*. The characters were chiseled in marble as cleanly as if they had been formed that very afternoon.

He found himself back at the water's edge with no recollection of climbing over the monastery wall. The pilot had turned his back on him and was eyeing the wink of lights across the Venice coastline. It was a pale comfort to Massimo, but the longer he stared at his home, the more he wanted to be back there. He would turn himself in and try to help the police as best he could, even if it meant being charged for obstruction, or worse.

"Start the engine, friend," he said, as he clambered on board. The pilot did not move. A white glove lay on one of the seats. Massimo struggled to piece together a sudden scattering of jigsaw pieces in his thoughts, but none of the pieces would fit, they seemed to be from different puzzles and he knew they could not match the complete picture he was striving for.

"I don't—" he began, but his words were coated with too much breath, too much saliva to complete his sentence.

He touched the pilot and watched as he toppled back in his seat. Massimo recoiled as he saw the pilot grinning at him, but the grin was too low on his face, and too wide and wet.

The glove was nothing of the sort. Or rather, it could only have fitted the pilot's hand. It had been skinned with a surgeon's precision.

"It doesn't fit," she said. "None of them ever fit."

She solidified at his side, as if structuring herself from the particles of dark that helped to make up what the night was. Almost immediately it was as if she had always been there.

"Don't worry, Mass," she whispered. "When you called me, why, it wasn't you calling me at all. It was the hotel. It was the Europa, bringing me home. Our true resting place is never the final resting place, is it? It's where we drop. That's what takes our essence. The rug in the room you were so afraid of. That has the flavor of my final breath in its weave. It's an *always* place. More real, I suppose, than our city, trapped in a yesterday none of us believe in anymore. More real than I ever was."

He was paralyzed with fear and doubt.

He saw her hand come free of the glove, which she dropped over the side of the boat. What he thought at first to be tattoos of some kind, a weird graffiti that sprawled across her flesh, revealed itself to him as the veins and sinews of a severely damaged hand. The fingernails were warped with the aftershock of septicaemia. They looked as thick and twisted as ram's horn.

"They sliced my fingers as though they were bits of meat, Mass. They stuck splinters under my fingernails and set fire to my palm. They skinned me. For fun. For *fun*. And your father took money for it. Hush-hush money. He pocketed his bundle of notes and at the center of them was my pain, wrapped so very tightly."

Massimo was weeping now. "I didn't know," he said. "You were my friend. I didn't know."

She gently rubbed his neck with her grotesque claw. "You saw what was happening. But you forgot. I called to you. The men shouted at you to go away. And your father gave you money to forget. But you saw all right. Every cry for help since, haven't you chosen to ignore it? Haven't you always turned your back and thought, 'well, what can I do?' You're like this city, Mass. You close your eyes to ugliness. And the blood that runs through you is as cold as the water in those canals."

He had slumped against her. So exhausted was he, and enchanted by the Venetian lights, that he failed to notice what her hand was doing until it was withdrawing.

She said, "Your hand, when you held mine, Mass, didn't they fit together so perfectly?"

His flailing mind saw that her hand, with its five gnarled horns, was sheathed by a new glove. A really quite beautiful glove that waxed and waned in his eyes like the beat of water in the canals. It was a deep, glistening red. He was going to ask her what material produced such a fine color, but he was too tired to speak. The last thing he saw before he became indivisible from the night was the flash of a cleaver as she pulled back the deep corners of her cloak. And even that was beautiful.

OTHER SKINS

Through my window at bedtime I'd watch the tree and the faces it made at me. When the streetlight next to it was working, soft shafts of orange thrust out of its clutch of leaves as though in a slow explosion. If my parents weren't arguing, its shushing was the last thing I heard every day.

Winter it would become just another famished thing, along with the exposed bones of more demolished houses on our dwindling street. The wrapping of night turned the diggers into still monsters cocking their heads for the slightest sound. These brittle days flogged the life from me. The tree was a dead thing—a totem which everything around tried to mirror. The ground turned black and white save for the people it cradled and quietly sucked the life from. My friends, my family, we were all gray things dying with the town. Skies at the year's arse-end were birdless and stained with the breath of the detergent factory. Any grass was bleached by exhaust fumes; any snow that might have prettified the place was streaked with filth. When we met by the tree—me, Rob and Dave—it was as if the lethargy of the wood had crept up through its roots into us. Our playtimes were morbid affairs. We dug in the soil for life and mashed or torched it. We threw stones at trains as they passed behind the hospital and pissed into empty crisp packets which we flung at pensioners by the bus stop. On the days we made it into school (of which we only had another six months till we left), we behaved so badly we were forced to stand in the corridor. Often we just buggered off home again.

It became so cold I had trouble sleeping. On nights like that I would look out for my dad returning from the pub at the end of our street. The murmuring wireless downstairs told me what Mum was doing. Sometimes, with a lull in the music, I'd hear the clack of needles as she knitted something she never seemed to finish. More often than not, when Dad appeared Mum would be in bed and he'd stroll down to the house with a woman linking him. The branches of the tree appeared to become more lively then, as though in welcome of someone it knew—a fantasy I liked to entertain. Standing beneath the tree, they'd smoke and chat and I'd sometimes see his face rippling beneath the tree's restless shadow. Their bodies might sag against each other and his eyes would roll till I saw whites embedded in the orange of his skin, his teeth clenched like a yellow bar as her hand briskly rubbed a dark area between them. After a while he'd kiss her goodbye, slipping into the house while I watched her lurch towards the main road, the tree's long black fingers falling upon her. I'd hear Dad getting into bed, Mum's laughter and the tired song of their mattress for a few minutes, till silence returned and I lay clenched in my blankets thinking of Dad's eyes rolling deep into his head beneath the tree.

Weekends, when he wasn't working, he spent at the allotments. Sometimes I went along to help. It was good to walk down there on my own. You could see the chimney (God's cigar, Rob called it) behind the hospital and the great blue gasometers on the horizon of roofs. I liked to look at huge buildings, they reminded me of pictures I'd seen of cities, of places that were away from here. I heard the men in the allotments before I saw them, shouting and laughing, or if it was too chilly for that, the gritty noise of spades as they broke through soil. Approaching from the top of the hill I'd see them hunched like black commas over cold, dull blades as they hacked at the earth, smoke rising from them like empty thought-bubbles. The sight both cheered and demoralized me. The allotments were nestled in a valley on the town's edge and winter frequently brought day-long mists, which, like batting, tucked itself into the gaps between thin garden sheds. More men would loom out of the white like ill-sketched figures or you could see pulses of orange as they tried to get warm with cigarettes or candles.

I'd help him turn the ground or plant seeds and he'd share his sandwich with me, let me have a swig from his bottle of brown ale. At times like those I felt a raw affinity with him, though I knew better than to assume the distance between us had been reduced. Had I asked him about the woman he'd have clocked me and sent me home. Later they'd have a fire at the center of the allotment and pass round a flask. All those pale eyes staring into the flame plucked at something within me and I watched their interest in this brief flicker of warmth and color as an almost holy thing. For a while the mist was pushed back and the black creases of their faces softened, let through moments, or at least memories, of innocence. All their poison: the hatred and resentment and frustration building up inside them was forgotten. The fire touched upon something ancient and pure, something unquestionably male. A community had brought them closer than any huddle could possibly manage. It was all there, in the spark of fire in their eyes. For my part, it rescued me from thoughts of the tree which, I then realized, I latched onto all the time. It was the bolt to which all my plans and actions were fastened. Still, I didn't perceive that as any great threat. Not then anyway.

Eventually, the frosts which trapped the rubble like fossils in amber melted, though the weather still contained enough of a pinch to bruise the skin blue. People died. Men and women I'd seen the previous week, or month, were gone. The coffins ferried through town worried me. I wanted to stop each one to check someone was inside, to reassure me that Mrs. Harris, Mr. Ollier and the rest of them hadn't just disappeared.

Thoughts of hollowness, of shells, haunted me. Every night for a week I watched the tree. In its sinuous tangle of arms I saw their faces. Sometimes I'd swear blind the tree was breathing. Its bark writhed as though it wanted shed it like a coat. My dreams were filled with glistening flashes of what moved underneath, but, thank God, I forgot upon waking. The knowledge that a tree can look healthy while its insides spoiled and died from disease bothered me deeply. It was a symbol I could see everywhere.

Mum died, not from the cold but because of it; killed by a rogue patch of ice by the market. This time I got to see someone lying in a silk-lined box though it did nothing for my phobia. The cold seemed to have followed her to this final bed, whitening her cheeks. Though pallid, she looked perfect. Dad cuffed me when I kissed her waxen mouth; I cried even harder when he gathered me in his arms and whispered sorry.

I saw less and less of Rob and Dave; ironically, the absence of my mother proved more a check on my behavior. Perhaps a more acute guilt was involved. Anyway, I stopped playing cruel games and took to drawing the tree. From a new angle, looking at it with my back to the demolished terrace, it seemed fatter and its trunk was curved and knotted like a spine wrenched out of true. As much as I strived for a likeness, my tree didn't contain the faces I glimpsed in its bark or branches. Come spring, and its leaves, there would be even more.

The thought I'd be leaving Mum behind as we crossed the threshold of the coming New Year filled me with a profound despair that lasted for weeks. Christmas was an empty time—I was growing to see it as a tawdry bit of glitz meant to relieve winter of its dour persistence, but which was unable to pierce a cynical shell I was retreating into.

Towards the middle of February, Dad brought Helen into the house for the first time. He was spending every day in the pub (having lost his job on Twelfth Night). I didn't mind her being there but Dad felt he had to go overboard to make sure it was okay by me. As if that mattered. I started picking through the rubble. Here and there, shoots were pushing through the chaos of brick and plaster, cheering me. Of all the seasons, Mum liked spring best. It was easy to picture her smile; it was good to feel close to her in the sprouting of these bits of green.

On the night before the first warm sun of the year, a squall tore across the town as though angry that winter was over, or in preparation for milder days. For an instant, when I heard the laughter, the rhythm of their bed, I thought she was back, that winter had been a hoax played by my mind. The tree was a glossy piece of tar teased into a shock of lines. Its branches whipped and struggled with the wind as if it were a tangible stuff. Slates lifted from roofs and smashed silently on the ground. In the uppermost reaches of the tree—level with my window—I saw Mum's face. I thought it was a reflection in the glass but when I turned around only the tussle between light and shadow on the wall greeted me.

"You'll come visit me soon love?"

"Yes Mum," I said, natural as you like, looking back into the black core of the tree where darkness nested. Gradually the storm passed on, unlike my fear, which thickened as I brooded upon what I'd heard.

In the morning, leaves peeked from the swollen joints of the tree and the memory of Mum's voice was more a comfort than cause for panic.

Coming back from the allotments one afternoon in that week (the weather brightening every day; at one point I was able to dispense with my sweater as I troweled a shallow trench) I felt a compulsion to alter my route. By the time I reached the cemetery that need had dissolved into a warm band of rightness, of expediency. Rather than feeling honor bound to be near her, a gentler more natural yearning had taken me, for which I was glad. Immaculate as it was, I fussed her grave, briefly disturbed when I imagined that raised mound as a thick blanket stifling her. Of course I was tensed for her voice which didn't come and I don't know whether I was grateful or disappointed.

Maybe Dad noticed how subdued I'd become that evening because he slapped a little aftershave on my furring cheeks and took me down to the pub with him. It was a still night; the houses seemed coiled in expectation of some kind of event. Though the calm was a pleasant change it only made my nervousness more noticeable. I was grateful Dad didn't chide me about it. The pub was a mass of yellowed windows: my shadow cowered as Dad pushed open the door and people roared his name. We entered a fug of smoke and sweat. Women I didn't know ruffled my hair and winked at Dad while he bought drinks. Anonymous hands patted my backside. When Dad returned, pushing a big glass of foam into my chest, his forehead bore a brown lipstick smear. In the second before recognizing it as such it looked like he'd opened a third eye. I wondered what my dad's true constitution was like. It seemed as though I'd only ever seen him as this fleeting harlequin figure in guises of drunkenness and deceit. Beneath the cologne and bravado he was as much a stranger to me as the other faces in this bar. In that clenched knot of people I felt a moment of abject panic: the one genuine person I knew was gone, and I couldn't associate my own identity with anything more solid than the tree outside my window. In a slow, swooping vision I saw myself ten years on, resigned to the crude safety of parochial life and playing a rake's role within the beery cocoon of this pub.

Predictably, my pessimism faded as the bitter took hold and I was swept into the bawdy camaraderie of it all. Comments that I was "the spit" of my dad made me feel proud, not threatened. A haze fell, when everybody's faces melted into gently shaded rumors and I couldn't distinguish between one person and another. I slurred my goodnights and barged my way outside, vaguely registering a volley of protests at my departure. The soapy air dilated the disharmony in my head so that the lights became great glassy shards I couldn't see beyond.

"It's this way, lover," came the voice at my ear and what I'd assumed to be the bloated sensation in my guts proved to be the arms of a girl encircling me from behind. She frogmarched me home; I could just make out the tree, jarred with each footstep into a dim beast, arms outstretched to greet me, its many faces lost in the blaze of orange flame. I began to flay my arms when she maneuvered me into its shadow as though I was a sacrifice but she spun me around just as I saw its brackish maw become discernible in the pattern of bark. Pressed up against me, her mouth trying to draw some kind of orderly movement from my own, I felt the runnels at my back squirm, as though, like a slowly feeding thing, it was trying to subsume me. Trapped, I rolled my eyes in desperation, struggling to voice my distress, and, seeing my vacant window, understanding what I was becoming, struck out against the girl who was working her leg between mine. Off balance, she fell on her backside; I couldn't decode the babble of filth she spat at me: my mind wasn't working that quickly. As she hobbled away, I let myself into the house, imagining the tree straining against its concrete base to recapture my warmth, to suck me into itself. I slept shallowly, dreaming of disease. I imagined pink, smiling faces collapsing from corruption, eating people inside out. When I woke up, my head thudding, I was afraid to move lest parts of me caved in. I lay still for hours that day, smelling the grimy sky drift though our house, listening to the hushing outside.

These things I remember well.

And here I stand again, on the street I finally managed to escape so long ago. The pub's still standing though it doesn't look as busy as it once was. All the houses are new: our terrace must have been knocked down shortly after I left. Dad's well and still living in the area. I'll visit him in a while. The tree. I can see the tree. I'm brave enough to touch it—

momentarily it feels as spongy as skin, but that's just moss on the bark. "Hug a tree," my old English teacher used to say. "They're extraordinary things, beautiful things. Show you appreciate them."

It's with some surprise that I realize I never climbed the tree or tied a rope to its branches and swung like a monkey. Why was that? I'm asking though I know full well.

With my penknife I carve the first letter of Mum's name but it's too much like cutting myself. I have to turn away, to go *now*, before I see the sap: I'm not sure it will be the color I expect.

God, the way you whisper to me as I hurry down the street. And were I to take one last look back, at the faces shifting in your branches, might I see my own somewhere?

THE WINDMILL

As they drove past the gutted skeleton of the Escort, Claire tensed.

"What's wrong?" asked Jonathan, easing off the accelerator.

"There was someone in that," she said, twisting against his seat belt to look out of the back window. "Stop. Go back."

He shook his head. "Will you stop messing about Claire? I can never tell when you're being truthful. You should have been an actress."

The car diminished. It was standing on its hubs, the tires having melted, in a pool of oil. Claire squinted at the driver's side: a black shape was bolt upright in what remained of the seat.

She turned around.

Jonathan was fiddling with the tuner, trying to find some music. The only station that cropped up on the automatic search was a thin grainy hiss, punctuated by a slow "whump… whump" sound.

"Welcome to Radio Norfolk," said Claire, trying to forget. *He'd had no lips. Just a gritted sheet of white. His fat had oozed through the black shell of his skin and hung in yellowish loops, like cheap pizza cheese.*

The Fens reached out beyond the hedgerows muscling against the car, green fields splashed with red poppies and sprigs of purple lavender. Claire wound down the window and breathed deeply, trying to unwind. This was meant to be a relaxing weekend but already she felt that she'd made errors. And that riled her.

"*Norfolk?* Why are you going to *Norfolk?*" they'd asked her back at the office. She'd felt the need to defend the place, even though the nearest she'd ever been to the county was a day trip to Mablethorpe as a child.

"There's lots of unspoilt coastline," she said. "I want long, windswept beaches to walk along. And there's a stack of wildlife. Apparently."

"You should try Suffolk instead," a colleague, Gill, had said, almost desperately, while her deputy looked at her with an expression approaching pity.

Jonathan had suggested they go to Paris but she quashed that idea because she didn't want to spend too much money. And anyway, what was the point of going away for a weekend to another busy, polluted city? But that wasn't strictly true. Her negativity had more to do with the fact that the break was Claire's baby: she wanted to come up with the plan. Now, as they swept through mile after mile of flat, sunbleached land, she was beginning to wish that she'd thought of Paris first. And she was also thinking of Jonathan's disappointment and the "told you so" triumphs of her workmates once she got back.

Jonathan was aware of her frustration. He rubbed her leg. "We'll stop for a drink, hey?" he said. "Next pub we come to. We'll try some good old local brew."

"There was someone in that fucking car," she snapped.

"Fine," he said, braking hard. "Get out and go and save him."

They sat in silence, the heat building. Claire strained for some sound to massage the barrier loose between them but none was forthcoming. They hadn't seen a car, a moving car, for an hour or so. The buildings they'd passed were gutted and crippled, the life seemingly sucked from their stone into the sallow pastures that supported them.

"I'm sorry," she said. "I just—it's work, you know? It's been getting me down. I just want this weekend to be perfect. I need this break and maybe… maybe I haven't realized that you need it just as much. You've driven all the way from London and…" she trailed off, lamely. Work excuses were crap, she knew that and so did he.

Jonathan didn't say anything. He started the car and moved off.

"Put a tape on then," he said. "Anything. I'm getting antsy with all this bloody quiet."

She dug for a cassette from the pile on the back seat. Most were hers although there were one or two tapes from his past, recorded on blanks by ex-girlfriends and scribbled over with red kisses. Alexander O'Neal. Luther Vandross. He had some new stuff, Fugees and Skunk Anansie but she couldn't get the irritation out of her where those older albums were concerned. It wasn't so much the music—it was shite, that went without saying—it was thoughts of what he'd been up to while she listened to it. Why would you play Luther Vandross if you weren't doing what he was singing about?

Her fingers settled on a Pavement album they both liked. The tension between them relaxed a little but Claire was glad to be able to point out a pub—it would be good to get out of the car and make the distance between them an optional thing.

"Where are we, navigator?" Jonathan asked, parking the car in the gravel forecourt. Behind them, a stone building with no discernible purpose was the only other sign of life around.

"Um, Cockley Cley. Just south of Swaffham."

"Right. Let's get re-fueled. Hungry?"

A man wearing sunglasses and a padded Parka uncoiled from the corner of a bench outside the pub, where he had been sunning himself. He snaked out a hand to the adjoining picnic table and withdrew a pallid sandwich from a paper bag. His flask was attached to a sling around his shoulder. Jonathan nodded as they walked by but if the man reacted, Claire didn't see it.

Inside, three men were hunched over their meals, whispering conspiratorially. A cold meat buffet under hot lights reminded Claire of a Pantone chart of grays. To their left, the lounge was empty: two men were sitting at the bar, exchanging lowing, long-voweled words. Claire wanted to leave.

"Jonathan—"

The man facing her wore a shirt opened to his navel. His gut lolled there, a strip of sweat banding his sternum. His nose was a sickening chunk of discolored flesh, bulbous and misshapen, hanging down almost to his top lip. She watched, fascinated and repulsed, as he dragged a handkerchief across it, threatening to smear it even further. It looked as though it was melting. His companion was dressed in a cheap suit with a purple shirt. His hair was greased back, one blade of it swung menacingly in front of his eyes. His grin was loose and slick with spit. She could see his dentures, behind the pitted white flaps of his lips, clacking loosely around his mouth.

She edged towards her boyfriend as the landlord appeared from behind a gingham curtain. She was conscious of movement behind his arm: a swift descent of something silver, a hacking noise. She backed into a chair and sat down.

"Pint of Flowers. And, er—" Jonathan looked at her and she saw a little boy lost. The men eating their dinner had looked up at his softly blunted northern tones. They looked confused, as if they ought to act upon this invasion but didn't know what course to take.

"Glass of fresh orange," she said, her voice too loud.

The landlord poured their drinks and took Jonathan's money. He had the look of a pathologically strict Sergeant-Major. His moustache and his accent were violently clipped. His eyes were unpleasantly blue.

They took their drinks outside and sat on the bench adjacent to the man with the flask. He was still eating his sandwiches. He gave them a cursory once over and zipped his Parka closer to his throat.

"Jesus," whispered Jonathan, downing half of his drink. "Jesusing Christing piss."

"Did you see that man's *nose*?" hissed Claire, fidgety with nervous excitement. She was close to guffawing. "What do you think it was? Syphilis? Cancer?"

Jonathan polished off his pint. "Demonic possession," he said, standing. "Drink that, bring it or leave it. We've been here seven minutes too long."

They spewed gravel getting out of the car park. Claire looked back and saw the Sergeant-Major step out of the door, his hand raised, a stricken look on his face.

Neither of them said anything until they hit the relative bustle of Swaffham. Even then, their relief could only manifest itself in gusts of laughter.

"I love you," she said, surprising herself. It seemed easy to say after the minor trauma of the pub. It was a comfort.

"I love you, too," he replied, although she hadn't meant it as a cue. "I thought we were goners. I thought we were going to end up as part of a very disappointing Scotch egg."

She laughed again and then suddenly felt like crying. Her upset was nebulous, there was no real reason for it, no rational reason. They'd just been people, strange only because they were slightly more different to her than she was used to. Must be exhaustion. She closed her eyes and through the reddish dark of that unshareable interior, she immediately saw the measured sweep of a deeper blackness across her vision. She opened her eyes but there weren't any boringly equidistant trees to cast their shadows, no houses since Swaffham now lay behind them. She shut out the light again and yes, here it was, a slow black glide from the top of her eyes to the bottom. And again. And again. Again.

Her heartbeat then, she reasoned, not without some discomfort. But before she could offer any satisfying alternative, she was asleep.

She swam out of the dark, panicking that she wouldn't grasp Jonathan's question and be able to answer it before he lost patience with her. But it wasn't a question, he was merely talking to himself, loud enough for her to infer that he was pissed off with her sleeping while he did all the work.

"Sea view, they said. A sea view at the hotel. Oh yes, certainly, if you've brought the Hubble telescope along with you." He looked at her and she could tell why; both to check she was awake and that she appreciated his joke. God, he really could be a minor irritant sometimes. "Wells-Next-The-Sea, they call this place," he continued. "Mmm, and my name's Jonathan-Two-Dicks-Chettle."

"We're here then?" Claire stretched in her seat, and blinked against the late morning sunshine. A clutch of beached boats seemed to cling to each other in the distance. Well beyond them, a silvery gray line—like a mirror seen edge on—marked the leading strip of the tide.

"Yes, arrival can usually be said to be on the cards when the driver is in parking mode. And hey! We're in a car park. Well done. Super."

"Oh shut up, Jon," Claire sneered. Twin glints of light drew her gaze towards a range of thin trees forming a paltry windbreak against the sea's muscle. Someone was looking in their direction with a pair of binoculars.

"Birdwatchers," Jonathan said, with a mock shudder. "This place'll be crawling with them. Come on, let's go and christen our room."

They checked into the B&B and were led up a grand staircase past mounted blunderbusses and badly stuffed seabirds. Their room looked out on the car park but was only slightly higher up, giving a better view of the acres between the hotel and the sea. Jonathan pressed up against her while she took in the tangy air. She let him peel down her jeans and panties, take her from behind even though she was dry. His pleasure, transmitted into grunts and selfish stabs, did nothing for her, but it was better than arguing about sex. She wondered why she had suggested this holiday as he withdrew and came on her buttocks. She wondered if, as he wiped himself against her, it was to prove to herself that she didn't want him anymore.

"Quick walk before dinner?" he said, tucking himself away and kissing the back of her head. "I'll wait downstairs. See if they can recommend some good restaurants."

She masturbated herself to a swift, shallow orgasm, then cleaned herself up and pulled on a pair of shorts. Jonathan was leaning against the door outside, absently sniffing his fingers. He looked at her, obviously irritated that he'd had to wait so long, then motioned with his head and set off for the road before she'd reached him. They followed its uneven surface towards the boats then struck out across the fields, past dun-colored cows. Thick reeds nestled in a gulley off the track, hissing.

The quick, unexpected smell of camomile pleased her, a scent she'd always associated with long summer walks as a child with Dad through the woods behind their house. She'd ask him where they were going and he'd reply: "The land of far beyond." They never arrived, though she'd soon lose her excitement of that unseen place in favor of his soft words as he told her about the plants and the buildings and the animals they saw. More often than not, she'd end up in his arms, too tired to walk, as twilight drew around them.

"What are you smiling at?" Jonathan asked.

"Sorry," she said, reluctant to share her memory. He'd probably only scoff. "I thought this was a holiday. I thought I'd be able to smile without being invited."

"Do you have to be such a snidey bitch all the time?"

"Only when I'm with you, lover."

Violently quiet, they approached an expanse of mud. Riven with trenches and pits, its scarred surface stretched out towards the sea. At this landlocked end, dry, stunted plants sprouted from its surface sheen. The acrid smell of salt was accompanied by something cloacal: oil bound up in its organic processes, farting silently through moist fissures.

"Jesus," said Claire. "Fucked if I'm wading through *that*."

"This holiday was your idea, kid," Jonathan sang. "We could have been sipping *serré* outside Café de la Mairie by now."

It took the best part of an hour to cross the mud, by which time they were hot and cross with the way the mud sucked their feet in easily enough but was reluctant to give them back without a fight. Eventually the land solidified and gave itself over to a tract of well-packed sand. They squelched towards a band of shallow water and rinsed their feet. At the other side, they headed towards the boats, parallel to the path they'd taken. Two hundred yards away, a man collecting shellfish in a carrier bag cast featureless glances at them while a dog scampered at his feet.

The journey back seemed free of obstacles and they were able to relax and enjoy the walk. The sea breeze flirted gently with them, taming the sun's heat. Claire was able to laugh at one point, at some lame crack or other that Jonathan came out with. She didn't care. The water that they'd crossed had broadened and it soon became apparent they'd have to re-cross it to get back to their hotel. It seemed much deeper, with a fast running spine.

"Shit," Jonathan spat. "We could swim it."

"I'm not swimming anything. I've got my sunglasses on and money in my pockets. And my watch isn't waterproof."

"And God fucking forbid you should smudge your fucking make-up!"

Claire flinched from his rage and inwardly threatened herself not to cry. She wouldn't do that in front of him again. She wasn't happy with her silence—a mute response might only goad Jonathan further—but if she opened her mouth she'd start bawling. She couldn't remember how their relationship had started. It was as passionless and inexorable as a driver grudgingly picking up a hitch-hiker on the road.

While he judged the depth and keenness of the water, she watched the tide in the distance, creaming against the slate-colored sand at a tempo to match the beat of her resentment towards him.

"I'm going to try this, try walking across. To show you. Then you'll be safe."

Do I hate him? she thought, bitter with her redundancy in this situation and angry that he should be illustrating her uselessness by making such a sacrifice. My hero. Suddenly, she didn't care if he disappeared into the sand and drowned. She wouldn't dive in to help him, she wouldn't scream for assistance. She might just sit down on the sand here for a while and count the bubbles.

"Nah," he said, waist-high in water. "Sand's giving way. Too dangerous for you."

She gritted her teeth and looked back along the course of the water. She saw a place where the water chuckled and frothed and padded over to it.

Shallow land. She'd skipped across to the other side while Jonathan was still struggling to free himself of the beach's suck. She had to turn away from him to conceal her laughter. He caught up to her, red and soaking.

"You might have told me, you twisted little cunt," he hissed into her ear, and strode off.

Yes I do, she thought.

Shocked and hurt by his attack on her, more than she wanted to admit, Claire rinsed her feet in the sink while Jonathan languished in the bath. It seemed his good mood had revived somewhat. His hand was gripping the head of his straining cock.

"Hey, baby," he said, in a mock cowboy voice. "Why don'cha mosey on over here 'n' milk my love udder."

"Fuck off," she muttered, leaving him to it.

She dressed and went downstairs. Ordered a drink from the bar. An hour later, Jonathan was with her. His distress was a palpable thing, spinning out from him like hooks on umbilici to become embedded in her flesh. She felt subsumed by his personality, as if he were trying to ingest her. Maybe it was the drink, but she was convinced his feelings for her were as shy of respect and concern as she'd suddenly come to realize for him.

"Sorry about that whole 'cunt' thing. Bit strong. You know I love you. What shall we have for dinner?"

She picked at a chicken and apricot pie while he polished off a bowl of mussels. "Christ," he said. "This sea air! I'm knackered!" He looked at her hopefully.

"I'll stay down here for a while," she said. "I'm not ready for bed yet."

He saluted and trotted upstairs. She swallowed hard. It seemed an age ago that she'd been able to think of him as attractive and warm. As—God, had she *really?*—a potential life-partner.

She took a drink with some of the other tourists, middle-aged women in oatmeal coir jumpers and Rowan bags. They tolerated her presence although she could tell she unnerved them for some reason. The hotel owner came in and lit the fire, asking everyone if they wanted brandy and she was going to start a game of whist if anyone was interested.

Claire bid everybody goodnight and went up to her room, the skin of her nape tightening when she heard the word "blood" mentioned behind her, by one of the women. *Did you smell the strength of her blood?* She thought maybe that was what she'd said.

Jonathan was snoring heavily. The TV was on, a late-night film starring Stacy Keach. She switched it off and went to the bathroom where she undressed quietly. And stopped.

Her period had begun.

Did you smell the strength of her blood?

"Oh," she said, feeling dizzy. "Okay." She cleaned herself up and slipped into a pair of pajamas. Stealthily, praying she wouldn't wake Jonathan, who'd read her clumsiness as a prompt for sex—or an argument—she climbed into bed and willed sleep into her bones before her mind could start mulling over the steady, sour creep of their relationship. She failed. She was awake as the full moon swung its mocking face into view, arcing a sorry path across the sky that might well have been an illustration of her own trajectory through darkness. Jonathan's ragged breathing ebbed and flowed in time with the tide of disaffection insistently eroding her from within.

As dawn broke, she managed to find sleep, although it was fragmented, filled with moments of savagery and violence that were instantly forgettable even as they unfolded shockingly before her.

Gulls shrieking as they wheeled above the hotel woke her. Jonathan had left a note on the pillow:

Didn't want to wake you for breakfast—you were well out of it. Nipped out for a newspaper. Enjoy your toast. Love, J.

He'd wrapped two pieces of wholemeal toast and marmalade in a napkin and left them by her bed. The gesture almost brought her back from the brink but she guessed he considered it a chore. *If he mentions it to me later,* she thought, *I'll know he's after a reward, a pat on the back. I'll know it's over.* She giggled a little when she thought the death of their relationship should come down to a few slices of Hovis but that wasn't really the case; it was just a tidy way to cap it all, a banal necessity to make the enormity of her realization more manageable.

An hour later, they were piling along the A149 coastal road, Jonathan singing loudly to a Placebo song. The sea swung in and away from them, lost to bluffs and mudflats before surprising Claire with its proximity once more. She didn't like the sea here. It appeared lifeless and sly. Where it touched land, gray borders of scum had formed. It simply sat there, like a dull extension of the Norfolk coastline.

They pulled off the road for a cup of tea at a small café. While Jonathan argued with the proprietor, who was loath to accept a check under five pounds, Claire watched an old woman attempting to eat her Sunday lunch. Her hands shook so badly that she couldn't cut her meat; her cutlery spanked against the side of her plate like an alarm. The winding blades of an old-fashioned fan swooped above them all. Something about its movement unsettled Claire.

"Come on," said Jonathan, imperiously. "We'll have a drink when we get to Cley." He turned to the café owner, who was now flanked by her waitresses, alerted by the fuss.

"Suck my dick, Fatso," Jonathan said, and hurried away. Claire raised a placatory hand but the proprietor only looked saddened. The woman raised her jerking head and showed Claire what she was chewing.

"Jon! How could you say that? How could you embarrass me like that?"

"Us Chettles don't suffer fools lightly, Claire. I'm not about to start now."

She wanted to leave him, to just go home, but it was his car and she didn't know where the nearest railway station was. Sheringham, probably, a good twenty miles away. She hadn't seen a bus or taxi since they were in Ely the day before yesterday.

"I don't feel as though I'm on holiday, Jon. I haven't been able to relax. All we've done is drive and argue. And I really needed this break."

"Hey, it was your choice."

"Oh, like it would have been different if we were in Paris?"

He was nodding. "Paris is the city of romance. It's impossible to have an argument there."

She snorted. "There's a word for people like you. Dumbfuck, I think it is."

He let that one go, but she could see his jaw clenching, his knuckles whitening on the wheel.

She saw the windmill first. It rose up from a coppice beyond a low range of roofs, its naked, motionless blades seeming to pin the sky into position. She pointed it out and Jonathan nodded, turning the car on to a gravel track. They crested a small humpback bridge over a stream choked by rushes. The windmill was white, tall and solid. Some of its windows were open; lace curtain wagged in the breeze.

Jonathan parked the car and got out without looking at Claire. He walked through the heavy wooden door at the windmill's base. Claire collected the bags and stood for a while, looking out towards the dunes. On the path, a cluster of birdspotters in brightly colored windcheaters alternated their focus between her and a clump of gorse. Occasionally, one of them would raise their sunglasses and favor her with a brilliant stare. One of them trotted further down the path and the others followed. Claire laughed. They looked intense and foolish.

At the door, she paused. She couldn't see anybody inside.

"Jon?"

There was a visitors' book open on a bureau next to a coffee cup. A small jar of lollipops on the windowsill had been discolored by the sunlight. "Hello?"

She left the bags by the door and headed towards the room to her left. The door was ajar; an old woman was turning back the covers on the bed.

"Oh, hello?" said Claire, raising her hand. The woman looked up and smiled.

"Hang on dear," she said, fiddling with her ear. Claire saw she was wearing a hearing aid. "I keep it turned off when I work. Nice to have silence every now and again."

"My name's Claire? Claire Osman? I booked a double room for tonight."

She moved past Claire and checked her name in the ledger. "Yes. Room for two. Where's your partner?"

"He went in ahead of me."

The old woman gave her an askance look before shuffling towards the other end of the room. She twisted the handle on the door at the end but it was securely locked.

"Nobody came in here, my love. Are you sure?"

"I'm certain!" Claire blurted. "I saw him come in before me. He must have gone through that door."

"Aye, if he was a spirit. That's the door to the windmill. It's always locked unless we have a party of schoolkids come round, or enthusiasts, you know."

"The other guest room then. He must be joking with us."

"There's someone already in that, my love."

"He *must* be in there." Claire felt sick. She'd have been happy to see the back of Jonathan in any other circumstances but this was just too weird. Suddenly too final.

She pressed up close against the old woman's back when she disturbed the other guests, who were sorry they couldn't help, but no, they hadn't seen a soul in the past half hour. Claire felt her head filling with gray. She smelled Trebor mints and Lapsang Souchong on the woman's cardigan. The next thing she was aware of, she was sitting on a high-backed wooden chair in the dining room, her eyes fixed on a cut glass bowl filled with boxes of Kellogg's Variety. The old woman had her hand between hers. The other guests—a woman in a pair of khaki shorts and a fleece; a willowy woman in a track suit sucking vampirically at a cigarette—watched, concerned, from the corner of the room.

She introduced herself as Karen and looked as though she'd smoked herself thin. The type of woman who hurried a meal, picked at it really, just so that she could have the cigarette afterwards. Claire wondered if that was the way she had sex too. She drew the smoke so deeply into her lungs that it was almost without color when it returned.

Her partner, Brenda, offered to call the police and look around the dunes outside. "The tide here is pretty innocuous but, you know, water is water."

Claire sat in the room, looking at Jonathan's travel bag. It hadn't been zipped up properly; a corner of his Bolton Wanderers flannel was sticking out of it. Two WPCs arrived. She told them what she knew, which was nothing.

They made notes anyway. Checked the car. Told her to relax and there'd be someone to talk to her in the morning. Best not to go anywhere tonight. In case Jonathan should return.

"He's got the car keys anyway," she said. The policewomen laughed, although she hadn't meant it as a joke.

She watched them go back to their car. They talked to the old woman for a while, one of the policewomen turning to look at her through the window for a few seconds.

She ate with the other couple at the ridiculously large dining table, Brenda quick to let her know what a sacrifice this was as they'd aimed to go to The Red Lion in Upper Sheringham for food. Karen puffed before and after courses and during mouthfuls. Her cheeks seemed permanently hollowed.

"Has he ever done this before?" she asked.

Claire started to cry through her food, something she hadn't done since her childhood. She'd forgotten how hard it was to eat and cry at the same time. It was quite interesting to try, really.

"I can't talk. I'm sorry." She left them and went to her room. She drew a hot bath and soaked for twenty minutes, tensed for his knock at the door and his impatient, stabbing voice. She never realized she'd miss him so much.

Later, she watched the dark creep into the sky. Mars clung, a diamond barnacle, to the underside of a raft of cloud. The birdspotters were still out there, a mass of colored Kangol clothing and Zeiss lenses. There was even a tripod. Cows stood in a far off field like plastic toys.

Pale light went on outside. A soft-looking young girl carrying a hose slowly drifted around the perimeter of the windmill's grounds wetting the plants and the lawn. An overweight dog ambled alongside her. Claire listened to the fizz of electricity until it calmed to a dull murmur and then went to bed.

Sleep claimed her quickly, despite her loneliness and the alien posture of the low-slung room. Her dreams were edgy, filled with savage angles and lurid colors, as though she were a film director trying too hard. She was in a car too big for the road, plowing through a village where there were no men. She was heading towards a windmill in the distance that didn't seem to get any closer. Occasionally she'd drive over some indistinct shape in her path. Before long, the roadkill became larger. Some of it wore clothes. It didn't impede her progress; she drove straight over it.

whump... whump... whump

Shanks of flesh squirted up on to the windscreen. The engine whined as it bounded through the bodies.

whump... whump... whump

Awake. Grainy blackness separated into the lumpen shapes of furniture and pictures on the wall. Imperfect light kissed at the curtains, turning them into powdery tablets of neon.

"Jonathan," she whispered, softly, hopefully.

whump… whump

A deep creaking noise punctuated that heavy sound. The window filled with black, then cleared again after an age. Blackness once more. Then soft light.

She opened the curtain. A blade of the windmill swung past her, trailing ragged edges of its sail. Down towards the end of the lawn, a huddle of people sat, a pinkish mass in the gloaming. Were they having a midnight party? Why hadn't she been invited? Maybe they wanted to leave her to her grief.

She shrugged herself into her toweling robe and picked her way through the shadows to the main door. The air was sharp with salt and still warm. She followed the path round to the garden, stepping through an arch crowded with roses. The windmill creaked and thudded, underlit by strange, granular arcs from lamps buried in the soil.

She was halfway across the lawn when she saw they were naked. They were surrounding something, dipping towards it and moving away. She recognized the young girl who'd watered the lawn, the old woman and Karen, who was lying back, cigarette in one hand, Brenda's thigh in the other. Brenda was talking to some other women. Claire realized she hadn't seen a man since the pub in Cockley Cley. The Sergeant-Major bustling out of the door. Holding up his hand. Mouthing something.

whump… whump.

The windmill hadn't born sails when they arrived that morning. She took another, hesitant step forward when she was spotted. One of the policewomen pointed at her. They all turned to look, peeling away from the dark, wet core of their interest. She saw their bodies were painted with blood. The old woman wore feral slashes of deep red across her forehead and neck.

Claire felt a thick, hot release against her thigh as she turned to look at the blades of the windmill, wrapped in the still wet hide of her boyfriend.

She turned back to the women, who were advancing towards her now. She reached beneath the folds of her robe, smudged her fingers in her own blood and began to paint.

WIRE

I send sweets to my mother at the weekend.

She's fond of buttery caramels, or éclairs, or mint lumps that take forever to tame with the teeth. In this way I think I prove my love for her, more so than what a letter or a phone call might achieve. I remember the flare of joy I felt in childhood when she came home from her shift at the hospital and planted a white paper bag in my hands, a kiss on my forehead. I spent so much time sitting on our peeling wooden gate waiting for her that my dad swore he could see grooves developing in my backside.

Mum was easy to spot. She'd round the corner in those late summer evenings—a tall, broad-shouldered woman with wheat-blonde hair and big eyes—and my jaws would squirt with the thought of aniseed and sherbet and toffee. Mum's neck was soft, a heaven of smells. Sometimes, before I grew too big, she'd whisk me off the gate and ask me how I was; what I'd done that day. She listened to me even though her eyes ached for sleep.

Our ritual: I loosen the twists in the bag. I peek to see what she's bought me. Always, I offer the first one to her.

These days I live by the sea. Nothing grand. Just a pleasant terraced house that takes a battering every once in a while by arctic winds channeling down through the North Sea. This town is a winding-down town. Old people come here to die. I'm maybe a third of the age of some of the characters who drift and stagger through these streets. Sometimes, on the beach, you'll see them moving across the sand, mouths agape, limbs wheeling as they take in the sea view for what might be the last time. Seeing so many of the old struggling like this, it seems to congeal the air with pain. They're like solid ghosts, infected by the gray of the ocean. Slowing down. Seizing up. I look at the horizon and see great swathes of black cloud closing in and it's hard not to believe that the dying aren't contributing to the confusion up there, even just a little bit.

There's a sense of waiting among them. It's as though something is gravitating towards this town. Coming home.

But not just them. No, not just them.

When I was young, we lived in a police house that backed onto a school field full of bent and broken goal posts. Dad had been in the police force for fifteen years and bought the house when I was one year old. Back then, police houses could be acquired through the constabulary; Dad had applied and won the right to purchase it. Twelve Lodge Lane. It had a pleasant sound about it. Police houses are no different from ordinary houses, really. Apart from an extension at the front, which served as an office, in lieu of a proper station. Such offices were now defunct. There weren't the resources.

It was nice to live so close to a school. When I was old enough to attend, I used to roll out of bed at ten to nine and be first in to the classroom for registration on the hour. But by then I was suffering from stomachaches. And I had a stammer. I could hardly speak sometimes. Drawing in a sketch book helped relax me, when I felt myself tying up in knots. I drew feverishly, layering bits of memory upon fragments of observed shapes, upon the form that I imagined my parents' speech might take if it could be turned into a visual thing. All sorts of things, really. I never finished anything, it simply tailed off, or formed the basis for something else. I had pages that, to the untutored eye, showed little more than a frenzied scrawl. But to me, each page was like a series of cells from an animation, albeit compiled arbitrarily. It was similar to staring at the branches of a winter tree, or the shapes in a fire; before long, order would suggest itself. You might see faces in there. You might see anything you wanted, or dreaded, to see.

I loved drawing. It was a place for me to retreat to when my inarticulateness threatened to render me insubstantial; I felt as though I were shrinking from sight, as though my stammering was a bubble of invisibility being blown from my lips, encompassing me. I couldn't understand how the things I wanted to say, that formed so clearly in my mind, were being translated to gibberish by my mouth. I kissed my mum and dad with that mouth; I smiled at them with it. How could it not allow me to tell them that I loved them?

When I didn't have any paper, I drew on the walls. When my pencils or crayons ran out, I scratched patterns on the pavement with a piece of stone. The pictures in my head flew from me in this way. If they hadn't, I think my head might well have burst apart.

I wish I could say that my unhappiness as a child was down to bullying, or night terrors or even an allergy to food. We weren't well-off financially, as I understand it now, but both my mum and dad worked and they were climbing out of debt; they were getting there. I loved my parents and I believe they loved me. I was unhappy. Maybe that's all there is to it. Don't you always need a reason to be happy too?

It's November 12th, 1977. I'm not well, I'm never well. It's Dad's birthday. He's out at the pub with his friends. Mum's looking after me. We're sitting on our PVC sofa in front of the TV. It's dark outside. There are small explosions of rain on the window, like someone scattering shot against the glass. I'm eight years old. I want to be sick but it won't come. I love sitting next to Mum. She has a comfortable way about her that is infectious. She sits with her legs tucked under her, one hand in her hair, twirling it through her fingers. I do this for her too. She smells like... well, like Mum, a secret scent that mums are no doubt provided with when they are young and being taught the intricacies of what it means to be a mother. It's a smell to make you dizzy with love.

On the screen: *NEWS FLASH.*

A body has been found on the embankment under the train line that connects Liverpool to all points east. Mum leaps in her chair, knocking the bottle of juice out of my mouth. She swears and I laugh because I've never heard Mum bark like that. She swears again and now she's crying. I pull her hair gently. Her big, hazel eyes are wet through.

"What's up?"

She hugs me for an age, until the television reverts to a game show. Questions and answers and audience applause. Everyone's face looks rubberized. As though you could pick it away with your nails and there wouldn't be anything underneath but rotten air.

I fell asleep, I remember. Then Mum's renewed sobbing wakened me, what, a minute, an hour, a night-time later? Dad was back. I could smell him on the tails of the air that he pushed into the house ahead of him: alcohol, smoke, fried food. I heard his mackintosh crumpling as he embraced my mum.

I got out of bed and crept downstairs to the landing, making a cartoonish step over the riser that creaked when you trod on it. From here I sometimes watched television when Mum and Dad thought I was in bed. Late night films in black and white. Women with immaculate hair. Men who smoked and hunkered in the shadows wearing hats and raincoats.

Mum and Dad were in the kitchen. I saw their shadows on the wall as they talked in murmurs over cups of coffee. I heard words I didn't understand but which sounded awful. *Murder... ripped... stabbed...*

gutted…
"In our town," my mum kept saying. "In our town."

Johnny Roughsedge was my best friend. He lived at 63 Lodge Lane. He came round to play the next morning, a Saturday. Sitting in the garden, chewing bubble gum, flipping through our collections of football cards, we talked about what we had both learned since last night, which was probably more than my mum and dad knew by then. Apparently, a woman's body had been found by a bunch of kids playing knick-knack. One of them was Johnny's cousin. They had knocked on someone's front door and legged it into the mound of vegetation that separated the main road from the steep mass of land leading up to the railway tracks. A lad bringing up the rear had tripped over something that felt too spongy to be bindweed or brambles.

"All of her tits were scooped out," Johnny said, eyes as big as the jawbreakers with which we were ruining our teeth. "And she was so jammed up with little pieces of glass, she lit up when they put a torch on her, just like a Christmas tree. Every hole in her was filled with ash. Imagine that. Eye sockets, filled with ash. Her mouth. Her bloody mouth!"

Dad was coming home late from work. He was helping out with the enquiries, going door-to-door, asking people what and where and when. It was getting cold. Our town, a northern town, was nestled in a little bowl of land between the Irish Sea on one side and the Pennines on the other. We were visited by all kinds of weather, in any and every shade of bad. Dad's face turned weird. It had this blustery redness about it, spanked alive by the chill winds, but shivering underneath the color was a permanent mask, in pale cement. It was lean and hard. It was as though he had two faces. I never knew which one of them he wore when he looked at me. But then, at that time, he rarely looked at me. He was either looking out of the window or staring into a small, chunky glass filled with whisky. Mum too.

It got so that Mum was scared to walk home. She worked all hours at the geriatric ward of the hospital. It was ten minutes away. But to get home, she had to walk under the railway bridge. Nettles and broad dock leaves grew wild up the sides of the bridge and threatened the gravel stretch of the railway. Four o'clock in the afternoon, it was already dark. The streetlamps had been bricked out by kids. Mist often hung about the roads here, ghosting in from the canal. There wasn't enough money for her to take a taxi and she always turned down lifts from the other members of staff.

"You just don't know, do you?" she said. "How can you tell?"
The body was that of a hairdresser called Elaine Dicker. She had gone

to the secondary school for which my primary was a feeder; she had been one of the prefects. Elaine had cut Mum's hair. Elaine had stopped some bullies from pushing in front of me at the queue for ice cream. She had gently impinged upon any number of lives in the neighborhood. The ordinariness of her and the extraordinary manner of her death plunged the town into a torpor. There wasn't so much panic in the streets, as a slow kind of awe that shifted through them.

Women gathered on the pavements to talk about the murder. I watched them from my parents' bedroom. Some appeared to revel in the fact that a killer had come to our town. There was the hushed admiration of celebrity in it. They used his shadow as they might currency, handing over a few coins of gossip, snapping their lips shut on suspicions of his identity like the cruel clasps of an ancient purse. As the daylight slunk away, so did they, seeking the sanctity of a locked door, a roof.

I continued to sit on the gate, waiting for Mum to come home. She took to taking the bus, which meant she couldn't stop by at the sweet shop for a quarter of something for me. No kola kubes or midget gems. No peanut brittle. No raspberry laces. No fudge. Her face was drawn when I rushed to greet her, stepping from the bus with her uniform in a Co-op carrier bag. I saw in her features how death might one day settle in them. I was afraid for her and saddened by my disappointment in her fragility. When I hugged her she seemed thinner and she smelled of disinfectant. I did not know it then, but to be surrounded by the dying at work and to be shadowed too on her way home by death's specter took a lot out of her. Her little boy wasn't enough to reset the balance.

Things didn't get any better for her. She was assaulted by a drunk one night who tried to put his hand up her skirt while she waited at the bus stop. From then on, she resolutely marched home, willing to take her chances. Only later in my life did I realize how brave she was. And how foolhardy.

One night I thought I would help Mum. I left our house at four a.m. while Dad was slumped against his desk, and walked Lodge Lane to the traffic lights at the top of the road. It wasn't so cold that night, but moisture hung in the air, teasing out the bulbs of the red, amber and green lights so that they resembled miniature explosions. In my front pocket I carried my penknife. I also had my catapult in my back pocket and a length of string, to tie the murderer up with. I had dressed in black clothes and rubbed black boot polish into my face to camouflage me against the night. I was a wraith. Nobody saw me as I drifted through the streets. I even moved like a commando. Johnny had told me that soldiers marched for twenty paces and jogged for twenty paces. In this way you could cover enormous distances quickly without ever becoming tired. Whenever I jogged, my voice kept time with this mantra: *I will kill you mis-ter mur-der-er/I will chop your bloo-dy head off/I will kill you mis-ter mur-der-er/I will chop your bloo-dy head off....*

On Lovely Lane, I tried not to falter as I approached the railway bridge over the road, but I had to stop. There was a figure standing underneath it, spoiling the geometric pattern of the bridge's shadow with his hunched shoulders and bobbing head as he stalked around, the cleats on his heels skittering and scratching against the concrete.

I argued with myself. He couldn't be the murderer. Murderers hid in the dark waiting for someone to walk past. This man was openly showing himself to the world. But what if he was the murderer and he was simply pretending to be normal? The police, I knew, were having difficulty trying to find any clues to make their job of narrowing their search easier. The killer was a clever man.

I nipped across the road and down a side street that would bring me onto the cobbled alleyway near Toucher's bowling club, a drinking den that seemed to have been constructed for the sole use of fat men with mutton-chop whiskers and their wives, who sported tall nests of hair and left glossy, plum-red lip-prints on their cigarette ends.

The alleyway was jammed with Ford Cortinas and Austin Allegros in various shades of beige. A scabby sign above an archway read: *Franks Motor-Fix.* Through the archway, cairns of automobile parts gleamed. I hurried past, holding my nose against the soft breaths of burnt oil. Ahead, rising above a diamond link fence, lay the embankment. On the other side was the vast expanse of the hospital car park.

The fence was not as secure as it might be. I ripped and tore at a hole that had been begun by a dog or a rabbit and pushed my body through. I froze halfway up the embankment as the killer whispered to me.

"Shall I show you the shadows of the soul?" he hissed.

But it wasn't him. It was the tracks, spitting and sizzling with the promise of a train. I edged further up the embankment, thinking that I might beat the train and get to the other side before it chuntered past; it would be slowing by now anyway, the station was only a quarter of a mile further along. At the top, I could just see the soft lights on the platform stuttering in the mist. Behind me, however, the train was already upon me. I slunk back into the shadows as it clattered by, lifting the hair off my scalp and farting diesel fumes. I saw my face, a gray orb, in the dirtied steel of its flank, warped, streaming into a featureless smear by the speed of the engine and the tears filling my eyes.

The taste of the scorched diesel stuck in my throat, I palmed away the grit from my face and hurried over the sleepers, careful not to make too much noise in the gravel bed of the track, even though the thunder of the engine would no doubt be sufficient to mask any sound that I made. The car park was white with frost. Black rectangles hinted at recently departed vehicles. From here, they resembled freshly dug graves awaiting the coffin. I slithered down the other side of the embankment in time to see Mum striding across the road, her head down, a plastic bag shining under the lights of a florist's. I started running towards her and glanced to my right, at the railway bridge. The man was gone.

I saw Mum falter as she approached the span across the road. At the last moment, she stopped and turned back, disappearing down a side street running parallel to the track. I called to her, but my voice was small in the whipping wind. I still had some grit in my eyes. I hoped that the shadow that bobbed and jerked after her was her own, but surely it must have been too long.

I ran after her, my legs failing to cover the ground as quickly as I would have liked, and plunged into the sidestreet after her. Terraced houses rose above me on either side, leeched of color by the poor street lighting. I could hear the click of Mum's heels and the clip of something sharper. The echo, I hoped, although my doubts were growing. I saw shadows leap and shudder on the wall of the end house of a lane adjoining this street. By the time I reached the same spot, I was breathing hard and little black spots were exploding behind my eyes. The cold had sealed my lips shut. An intense stitch had replaced my heart.

At the foot of the street, a car park stretched into darkness. Garages lolled like a row of rotten Hollywood façades. There was an industrial skip brimming with timber and rusted scaffolding, a tarpaulin cover failing to protect the contents from the inquisitive wind. It flapped and fluttered like the wings of some crippled prehistoric bird. To the right, another railway arch created a dreadful frame for the school field and the sky beyond. I saw how Mum was thinking. If she took the route that was too obviously a dangerous route, how could the murderer possibly be lying in wait for her? Nobody would be stupid enough to take this path with a killer at large.

I watched her move through the arch, her head still bowed as if in deference to the enormity of the silence, the almost religious blackness of the place. I tried to keep pace with her, but she was hurrying now and I was very tired, my arms and legs filling with cold. The wind was enjoying its directionless game and ripped at me from all sides. I staggered across the fields in the direction that I hoped was my home. The thought of my bed and the hot water bottle, Mum bringing me some warm milk and shutting the curtains made my stomach lurch.

A woman screamed. I don't know where the scream originated from but at once it seemed as though her voice was assailing me from all angles. I continued to run, sobbing now, certain that I would trip on the steaming shell of my mother's remains. But it didn't happen. I found the path alongside the school and followed it to the end where our house stood. In the upstairs window, I saw Dad with his hands resting on the sill, looking out at the night. I didn't see much else until I got inside. I was crying hard. It had been the first time I had been outside and separated from my mother. Though she had not heard or seen me, it felt terribly as though she had abandoned me.

They called him The Breakfast Man.

Both Elaine Dicker and Hannah Childs, the second victim, were killed at around 5 a.m., a time, in our town, when the hardcore workers turned out of bed to scrape a wedge for the family and the roof that sheltered them. Wire was our key industry back then; the town was noted for it. If you were up early enough, you could watch scores of men in black donkey jackets warming their fingers on the nipped coals of roll-ups, or hunched over the handlebars of their sit-up-and-beg bicycles. They drifted towards the wire factory like fleshed out Lowry sketches. None of them had any straightness in them; they looked defeated, primitive. Yet they moved resolutely through the dawn mist as though sucked in by the opening of the factory gates.

The police believed The Breakfast Man was one of these workers. Someone with a grudge, someone whose frustrations and failure had manifested themselves in brutal violence.

Dad said: "Five'll give you ten the killer was divorced in the last six months." He said: "The killer lives alone and he can't cope. With anything."

I didn't know Hannah Childs, but plenty did. They pulled her broken body off the mangled wood and iron teeth of the skip I had scurried past that morning. I didn't tell anyone where I had been. I didn't tell anyone about the scream. I didn't need to: they had found the body anyway.

Hannah worked at the hospital too. She was a clerical assistant. In her spare time she showed pedigree dogs at competitions across the north-west. She had a prize cocker spaniel. Its name was Skip.

A week later. Mum told her superiors at the hospital that she would no longer work the graveyard shift. If she can't work afternoons, she told them, she won't work at all. Goodbye, they told her. There were plenty of women who weren't as knocked back by the deaths as much as Mum. Plenty of hungry women in our town.

Dad's bottle was half-empty. He was snoring slightly in his chair, an envelope in his hands. He had taken to falling asleep in the office during the evenings and those days when he wasn't required at the station. Photographs fanned from the envelope's mouth but I couldn't make out what they depicted. When I disturbed him, he opened a drawer and dropped the envelope into it. Then he lifted me on to his lap and hugged me. He smelled sour and sickly. He smelled of sleeplessness.

"Danny," he said. "What are your five most favorite places in the whole world?"

"Here," I said. "The field and the sandpit. Nana's place. And in my head."

"In your head?" Dad mulled this over, his eyebrows raised, before nodding slowly. "I know what you mean. Good answer. As good a place to be as any."

"Safe," I said.

Me and Johnny could no longer go out to play on the field at the back of our house. The weather was deteriorating rapidly. Five or six days out of the week, there'd be a caul of frost on the grass, or fog loitered among the goal posts, turning them into exposed bones on a fossil dig. But on the first day of December, a hole appeared in the sky and through it came a few weak, watery rays of late afternoon sunshine.

Coincidentally, my stomachaches retreated. I felt better than I had for a long time. I badgered my mother for an hour's play on the field and although she did not relent, she agreed to let me go up there, as long as she could come too. We collected Johnny and set off through Tower's Court, a little maze of houses that abutted the field.

The cricket pavilion was the first thing I saw, picked out by the sunlight. A fence had been erected around it because it was rotting and in need of demolition. That didn't stop kids from climbing over and using it for a den. Walking by it now, we saw a boy and a girl kissing in the shadows, their faces moving in a way that reminded me of how a dog watches a washing machine work. Another boy was spray-painting his name in red on the boarded windows.

Johnny had brought his ball and we kicked it about in the mud. Mum looked better in the sunlight. She laughed at us as we slid about in the dirt. I let the ball bounce on my head and shrieked when about half a ton of slime spattered my face. Mum had brought a few pieces of lardy cake with her. And some Tizer. We ate and drank. Johnny showed us how he could gargle the first verse of the National Anthem without stopping but it went wrong and he ended up snorting pop through his nose. Mum and me laughed till I wet myself. I think Mum wet herself too, just a little bit. It was a good day.

The next morning, the milkman found Mum nailed to a lamp-post with a cat's head stuffed so hard into her mouth that the surgeons had to break the lower jaw to get it out. I couldn't get through to Dad for days. Even with the light on, he seemed to attract darkness to his face. He didn't reflect any light at all, he absorbed it. He was dark matter. He was a black hole.

One thing my dad said that I remember, when he wasn't drunk or unconscious:

"It's as if she willed it upon herself. She was convinced she was on his unwritten list. She was a line and his arc bisected it."

At least she survived. Dad thought it would have been better if she had not.

Mum came home from the hospital a few days before New Year. Christmas might as well have never happened at all in our house. There were no presents or cards, no decorations. A cake, awaiting its toppings of marzipan and icing, sat in the kitchen, the only signifier.

Early in the morning, Mum had been disturbed by the sound of a cat yowling in the street. She went outside and saw a thickset tabby with its back arched, its tail swollen to the size of a draught excluder. She had tried to comfort the cat and was looking into the street to see what had frightened it when The Breakfast Man attacked her from behind. Knocking her out, he pinned her to the lamp-post and did for the cat. He was readying to chisel Mum open when the chink of bottles and the whine of the little electric engine on the milk float sent him running for cover.

The police wanted to know what he looked like. Mum couldn't remember. He wore one of those snorkel jackets, with the hood pulled up over his face. She said he was probably wearing a stocking over his head too; she just couldn't see anything behind the oval of grainy darkness that contained his face. She remembered how he smelled of lead, like rusty pipes, she said. His breath was like rusty pipes.

How could we expect her to revert to her normal ways after that? She grew distant and yet, to me, she seemed closer than ever. Perhaps it was because she was inhabiting the same regions of isolation that I had been traveling for so long. We understood each other's dislocation. Precious little connected with us; people seemed to operate on a different level, as though something fundamental had been omitted from our make-up, a vital element of the human blueprint that was out of stock at the moment we were rammed into being.

That said, Mum recoiled from me, whenever I came into the bedroom to be near her. Her eyes flitted around, seeing things that weren't there, or that were there and she had been granted the privilege of witnessing them.

It's okay, Mum, I wanted to tell her. *I see them too. You won't be harmed.* But I couldn't say it and even if I could, she wouldn't have heard me. In me, she had focused all of her fears and apprehensions. I hoped that it was coincidence. That it was as likely she zeroed in on a bunch of flowers or an old slipper to help pin down her neuroses, but I couldn't help feeling that her resentment of me had long been there, buried within her, and now, as her health gradually declined and she became less linked with what was real, she could give it full rein without remorse or self-consciousness.

Dad too was diminishing, a kite whose guy had broken free. His drinking had increased; he was getting through a bottle and a half of whisky every day. I remember how he used to wince when he gulped it. Now he was swigging away as though it were water.

His superiors had allowed him unlimited compassionate leave but he spent most of his time in the study working anyway. He had built up a deep folder of newspaper cuttings. Whenever I went to see if he wanted to kick a ball around in the garden with me, he would stare at me with his bruised eyes as if I were a stranger who had wandered into his house. Then some ember of recognition would pulse deep within and he might try on a smile, or ruffle my hair. But it was to his dossiers that he then turned; never to the comics, or the Meccano, or *The Three Stooges*, stuff that we had huddled over together in the past.

He didn't tell me what to do anymore, or how to behave. He let me play out with Johnny pretty much when and where I liked. Most of the time we wandered down to the canal which ran along the end of our road. Its towpath led to a stile at the mouth of a dense wood. Not too far in was a mulchy clearing dominated by a tree trunk felled either by lightning or the rot that had consumed much of it. Mum and Dad used to come here, when I was a toddler. I'd play near the tree while they filled a wheelbarrow with leaf mold for our garden. In October, we'd visit with black refuse sacks stuffed into our coat pockets. There was a clutch of chestnut trees at the wood's eastern edge. If you timed it right, you could arrive with the sound of chestnuts falling to earth like strange rain. The vibrations went through your wellington boots and you'd have to shield your head to make sure the spiny cases didn't clout you. We'd eat as many as we picked, it seemed. Under the pith, the chestnuts were pale and creamy with a crunch and a sweet taste far more enticing than that to be found when they were roasted. I write that with a jolt of surprise; I have yet to eat a roasted chestnut. I trusted my dad when he told me they were inferior.

Johnny and me, ghosting through the silver birch, the copper beech. We didn't have any jam jars with us to go sticklebacking. It was too late for chestnuts. We walked. Johnny apologized for the description of Elaine Dicker's mutilated body, in the light of what had happened to Mum.

"How d-d-did you know abuh-about her in-injuries?" I asked. In my pocket, my fingers rubbed against one of the textured pages in my sketch-book. I had a brand-new, freshly sharpened Lakeland by Cumberland 3B pencil behind my ear. I was aching to use it.

"I made it up," Johnny said, sheepishly. "Well, I didn't exactly. Not on my own. Dave Cathersides made most of it up. Him and Callum Fisher. It was just a laugh."

I saw tangles in everything I looked at; in the pattern of the leaves against the sky, in the fruiting loam, in the collapsed cobwebs depending from the massed ranks of rhododendron. There were signs in the spiral wormcasts, messages in the glittering frogspit wadded in the exposed roots of the hawthorn bushes. Even on Johnny. I peered at him, the whorls of fair hair under his ears, the minuscule patchwork of diamonds that made up the skin on his face, the pores ranged across his chin, gleaming in the wintry sunshine. What was so different from him, from all of this, to the stuff I created in my drawing pads? Just a nudging towards convention, a fluke of geometry.

I didn't say anything. We dug around in the humus and tossed pine cones at each other. Johnny spotted a fox. We watched it jogging through the undergrowth like magical fire, coloring in the uniform gray and black of its surroundings. The vortices it created in the mist dragged more through the boughs until it wreathed our legs. We couldn't see our feet. We pretended that we were blinded by the mist, and ranged around in the undergrowth, arms outstretched, eyes closed. Every time we bumped into a tree, we apologized profusely. I was in tears, laughing.

When I opened my eyes, the mist had risen to my throat and I jerked my head up reflexively, as though if I didn't, I might drown. I couldn't see Johnny, but I could hear him, still excusing himself and laughing, mad as a satchel of badgers. Looking up at the canopy, I managed to pick a way through the trees towards Johnny's laughter. Suddenly I saw him. The mist had somehow caused him to look elongated. It was like viewing someone from afar on a hot day, an instance of *fata morgana*; Johnny's head appeared as two or three disconnected bands linked tenuously to an etiolated body. He moved ponderously. You might believe that the mist had infected him and the dampness in his bones was now grinding him to a halt.

I took out my sketch pad and translated the shocking sight into my comfortable scrawl. Then I remembered the way a teacher had lost her temper and screamed at somebody to be quiet and the sketch took off in a new direction. And again: the train on the tracks and my face staring back at me without any eyes. And again: Dad's lips pressing together on another mouthful of pain relief. And. And. And....

Johnny found me a little later slumped on the ground, my head ricked back against a tree, spittle oozing from the corner of my mouth. My eyes had rolled back into their sockets and I had gone into spasm.

My hand moved independently of the body's trauma, filling the page with graphite jags and curlicues and cross-hatchings.

The following morning, a woman was discovered face down in a water barrel. He had tried to peel her skin off in one piece, as one might do with an apple, but had given up on the task and split her in half, vertically, instead with a series of heavy blows with an axe they found wrapped in newspaper and dumped in a litter bin. Her name was Michelle Paget, a nineteen-year-old veterinarian's assistant.

She was the last of The Breakfast Man's victims.

I still have those old sketch books with me now.

This morning, I flicked through them, trying to pinpoint some madness in the method. I suppose I was hoping such a study would prevent me thinking about what came next. But of course, rather than distract me, the sketches, ostensibly vague, served only to crystallize that time in my thoughts.

I took the sketch books with me down to the beach. It's a nice beach, if a little exposed. Raw winds tear into the coast during winter. There's a good mix of pebbles and sand and, if you know what you're looking for, you can find little nuggets of amber among the stones.

There was a shag on one of the outermost groynes, wings outstretched, bill agape. An old couple walking a dog far in the distance. And the waves, sprinting in to shore, their tops disintegrating to mist as they met the ferocious winds.

The sketches seem to have been imbued with fresh meaning. It was a bit like looking at one of those 3-D pictures that were popular a couple of years ago. The ones where you have to stare *beyond* the hectic patterns until something solid pops into view so forcefully, you wonder how you could not have seen it immediately.

I saw things I don't want to talk about. I saw suggestions in the confusion. I saw faces that are no longer around.

Dad committed suicide. I found him slumped across his desk. He had a tumbler next to him, but it hadn't seen any whisky at all. I guess he used it to trick himself into believing his drinking remained civilized; he was necking the Scotch straight from the bottle. There were pills. White dust clung to his lips.

I reached across him, my arm brushing against his cold forehead, and pulled open the top drawer. The envelope was still there, with its glossy, awful cargo.

And all I could think, as I shuffled through this unconscionable deck, was how alike The Breakfast Man and I were. Only, his canvases were flesh, his pencil a 15-inch boning knife.

The police closed the case. They believed my dad was the killer. Mum made half-hearted protests from her bed in the psychiatric ward at Winwick hospital. But the police were vindicated. There were no further deaths. I wonder... I half-wonder whether my mum suspected Dad. I quarter wonder.

I went to stay with Nana until she died and then for years I was volleyed around the care system. I lost my appetite for sketching. I lost my appetite for everything. In my teenage years I got into trouble with the police for fighting, shoplifting, drunk and disorderly. I didn't see Mum in all that time. Then they told me she had had a stroke and would not live for much longer. That was ten years ago. I tried to end my life that night. I hanged myself with an old school tie from the lamp flex in my bedroom, but the light was frail and half the ceiling fell to the floor along with me.

"Want one?" A nurse who smelled of Daz and nutmeg offered me a bag of caramels. She couldn't understand why I collapsed in tears.

I burned all of the sketches under the pier. I might have been kidding myself but the smoke smelled, I'm sure of it, of growing up. Of Johnny's bubblegum and Mum's warm neck and Dad's cardigan when he pulled me in close for a hug or a wrestle. The last sketch in the batch I couldn't fathom for a long time, but then I saw how the swirls parted and allowed me to see myself. A vague profile. I think I'm smiling. But not for much longer. I think after tonight, the police might re-open their files on The Breakfast Man.

A last wrap of sweets for my mother, then. I love the way the shopkeeper will lick his thumb and rub away a white paper bag from the sheaf hanging from a piece of string on the wall. How he flaps it open and pours in the quarter measure of boiled sugar from the deep metal dish on the scales. Taking the ends, he twists the bag shut with a few flurries of movement.

I wish I could do the same with my own thoughts. Twist them shut, seal them in. Offer them to no one.

THE BURN

He flinched in the darkness when she reached for him; he could hear her feet scuffling beneath the sheets, smell perfume rising from her hair.

Adam switched on the light and stared down at the empty, creased mass of bedclothes. He fancied he could still hear the ghost of her breathing but when he laid his hand on the mattress, it was cold. The illusion had seemed stronger this night, like a developing photograph in stages of clarity. Previously he'd sensed only a suggestion of movement, never smells or the rumor of warmth reaching towards him.

Downstairs he made hot chocolate, looking out of a kitchen window that, in daylight, afforded him a view of school fields and a forest clinging to the horizon like storm clouds. The fields had been bleached by fierce August afternoons, the hot, sweet smell of their burned grass filling his room at night. Though he couldn't yet see these things Adam stared anyway, as if the blackness might calm him. Certainly, by the time he finished his drink, the light panic he had experienced in the bedroom had lifted and sleep was hovering, ready to fill the vacuum. Confronted with the prospect of returning upstairs he moved to his living room, nudging Sumo awake as he switched on the fire. The cat mewed a reproach and slunk away.

Adam rubbed at his palms as the flames grew. It reminded him of the weather these past few months: his shoulders had blistered and his fringe had been scorched blond by the sun. Kids played with molten tar in the streets, pulling it into loops like warm treacle toffee. Adam imagined what sudden rain might do to baked pavements.

A crisp tide of static burst from the radio as he plugged it in, drowning a voice that had murmured the last syllable of his name. He reduced its volume but the voice must have come from the stereo for only silence rushed to him from the house save for the odd tick as the fire became hotter. Though he preferred classical music he now steered clear of the stations which broadcast it, selecting instead a program full of chat hosted by some smoky-voiced woman to give him company until dawn came. Gladdened by her presence he relaxed, his eyes fastening on a sliver of blue between the curtains.

He thought of Monk and Debs at the office, how they'd protest when he rang in sick later. It wasn't something he particularly wanted to do but the close weather and his current insomnia had conspired to bring him headaches, one of which he could now feel building down the left side of his face. His eye would be covered by a red net by lunchtime, the pain's pulse so pronounced that he'd see it translated to ripples in the mug of coffee he held. The dreams, or remnants of dreams—for he could never remember their content—compounded his discomfort. Each night for a week Adam had wakened in his bed, sleepily satisfied as his wife stretched beside him until the vague echoes of his dream caught up with him. It was only then that he remembered he was a bachelor. Why he should be indulging in wishful thinking he couldn't fathom. He had never judged himself lonely—alone yes, but not isolated, brooding. His circle of friends was wide—he never wanted for company—but his celibacy was of his own choosing; it had nothing to do with being incompatible. Perhaps his partnered dreams were filled with arguments, moments of spite dredged from the deep waters of his youth.

Those times had been tear-filled for him, listening from the half-mask of his blanket as his parents' voices lashed each other. He'd known a burning knot that grew in his stomach, tightening with each muffled scream of hate, each curse. Once there'd even been a slap and an ensuing silence that did more for his dread than any amount of invective. He'd promised himself a life without wives, growing to believe that being born alone was the sign—for anyone willing to recognize it—that life was meant to continue so. No matter how sweet the fruit of love might initially be, ripening and decay must follow.

He washed down a couple of pills and dressed in his running gear hoping a little fresh air might cleanse him. Outside, the night's color was weakening, with dawn already an ochre stain threatening the rooftops. He'd be back before its promise of light was fully realized. He set off at a swift pace to get his blood keen before settling into a measured stride that took him down by the allotments at the foot of his road. To his left, beyond rows of frazzled cabbage, the woods stole back their shape from the night, ready for another onslaught from the sun. Light skirls of dust twisted between stunted vegetables like ghosts dancing on graves. Despite the cool morning air, Adam's mouth became rapidly spitless, perhaps because of the sight of so much parched land. It was as if the color green had never existed. The people he saw were mostly silhouettes in windows, backlit by fires or lamps though he jogged past one man clenching a plastic bag between his feet. The man watched him from behind a caul of orange. It took a moment for him to realize the man was raising a flame to his cigarette but by that time Adam had rounded a corner and was heading towards Dallam, its houses bunched between tracts of land that on one side cradled the brook and, on the other, the gasworks. Beyond that lay the dual carriageway connecting the motorway to town.

Adam hoped that by the time he returned he would be whipped enough to catch up on some sleep, though the pain killers had yet to make in-roads to his headache. If anything, the pain had intensified, now lacing his hairline and jaw, pummeling an eyeball as effectively as a hastily swallowed cold drink. Trying to ignore the discomfort, Adam turned his mind to Carol who had been his last girlfriend.

Curiously, she appeared as a series of snapshots clipped from memory—none of them impressing him with importance, which made him feel guilty. They had gone together for two years; it seemed selfish that all he could muster were a few petty images of their shared time— she pulling off her sweater and getting an earring caught in the wool; running after an old man who'd dropped his wallet; catching fruit Polos tossed to her open mouth from across the room. Unremarkable all, leading him to think their relationship had been foolish and wasted. The one crucial memory had been of their last exchange when he told her he didn't want to live with her. She'd assumed too much; assumptions ought never to be made, he thought, as he chased the night sky, a stitch beginning to contest the throb in his head.

Once home, he slouched over his front gate sucking air into his lungs. He looked up and saw a light go off in his bedroom though he didn't recall leaving it on. He let himself into the house, moving slowly in the dark, listening for footsteps. None of the rooms showed any sign of intruders yet the light bulb by his bed felt warm. He switched it back on to prove it hadn't died, then perched on his bed wondering if the electricity flow in the house was faulty.

Adam took a long shower and, as the water drained him of tension, his mind relaxed, offering further rationale for what had happened. His fingers had been chilled by the run—that's why the bulb felt recently used. Also, his headache might have fashioned popping lights in his skull; one of which he could have mistaken for something more sinister. Or it could have been a doused light from over the road reflected in his window.

The rash that had arrived on his palms last week was developing, becoming more distinct every day. Now there were soft weals traveling the pads of flesh on a parallel with his life lines. If he put his hands together, miming an open book, the weals made a V shape across them. He dried himself carefully and splashed disinfectant on his hands, wincing at how raw they felt.

He tried to recollect how the contagion had found him. There had been no nettles he could think of, or scratches that might have caused infection. And unless he had suddenly become allergic to Sumo, no reasonable cause occurred to him. When first he had visited the surgery, the doctor had guessed at prickly heat; certainly the weather encouraged it, and Adam had gone away reassured. But surely that didn't involve swellings of this kind? If they failed to improve by tomorrow he would seek a second opinion.

He dressed the weals lightly, flexing his hands to ensure some give in the bandages. The pain surprised him; hadn't he made a drink this morning without its distraction?

Minutes before nine he called the office. Debs answered around a mouthful of toast, cheering him instantly. Though he now had a bona fide excuse for absence, he wondered if being at work might bring the tonic he needed.

"It's Adam," he said. "Guess what."

"Monk's going to go up the wall you know."

"I know, but he can cope. I've a bad head and my hands look like they've been washed in acid."

He heard her swallow before taking another bite of breakfast. "Will you be in tomorrow? It's stock-taking, don't forget, and there's no way we'll get it done on our own."

"Promise. Even if my hands fall off in the night."

She sighed. "Okay, but don't blame me if you get an earful from Monk later on."

He hung up and silence fell, wreathing him like smoke. The thought of spending his day in the house made him uncomfortable though he'd done it often before. He could measure the increasing heat outside as it increased purely by watching the people that walked by the windows. Early morning had produced a light sweater, a cardigan, even a man in a coat. Now, approaching eleven, boys in shorts, girls wearing halter tops and cut-offs were the order of the day. The heat was accumulating inside too until by noon, it settled over him, stealing the air from his lungs and gluing his fringe to his forehead. Eyes closed, he drifted in and out of sleep, the tattoo of pain in head and hands keeping perfect time. The dryness in his throat became so acute that he began to gag, though the sound seemed dissociated from him. When he came to, the proximity of the walls sprang back as though startled by his eyes. The sounds continued, clearly not his own. They were coming from upstairs. It sounded as though someone were strangling.

He took the stairs two at a time, pausing on the landing as Sumo strolled out of the bedroom. They looked at each other as the cat casually licked at a paw. The sounds had stopped.

"Fur balls again, Sumo?" Adam asked, crouching. The cat ignored him. "Go on, cough again. Show Daddy." Sumo yawned and collapsed on his back, offering a white tummy which Adam stroked.

He made lunch for them both but the heat had spoiled their appetites. Ensuring Sumo's water bowl was full, Adam pocketed his keys and went out, heartened to find it was slightly cooler than indoors. By the time he had reached the park, a film of sweat covered him, painting a patch on the chest of his T-shirt.

The park wasn't as full as he had expected. He felt as though he'd brought part of the house with him; its mood, its claustrophobia. Where he believed he'd find freshness, he'd stumbled on more still, stale land. The houses across from him shimmered in bands of molten brick. A brown smell of canal. Horns bleated on distant roads as drivers were poached in their cars. Everywhere: the sun. It shone so intensely in the blanched sky that Adam couldn't even begin to guess where it might be. An impure heat it shed, drenching him as eagerly as rain. Licking his lips Adam could taste the air's heavy flavor as well as his own salt.

Further along the path, where greensward swept down to a rapidly dwindling pond, benches were clustered beneath trees. He perched on an iron armrest and looked down to the water. A figure strolled its perimeter, plucked by haze to nonsense: an elongated blur of white and pink. He sought an expression in the blonde curve of hair but ripples from the pond had infected her substance. The lower half of her body was sucked into a seamless metallic union with the water. The subsequent impression he gathered was that she glided rather than stepped, an illusion furthered by heat vapors that clung to her, softening her body's angularity to an extent that she resembled liquid. Slowly, her shape diminished as she moved away from the pond's farthest bank. She seemed to be sinking into the gray strips of mirage and Adam was reminded of carnival mirrors chopping sections from his body until he was a face with feet. Threatening to vanish completely, the girl turned his way, the pink suggestion of her face eliciting his gasp. He made to call the name that had pricked some dim part of his memory yet he'd forgotten it just as swiftly. By the time he reached the pond she'd gone.

Back home, he prepared vegetables for that evening's meal, trying to come to terms with what he had seen. Glasses of red wine helped, assuaging his headache and offering a comfortably softened point of focus— something medicine had not been able to do. He guessed the suspicion that he knew her had arisen from a projection on the woman from a part of his past, though he couldn't imagine why he had reacted that way. He felt he knew her. He also felt she was completely alien to him. The unease created a chill pocket that enclosed him, manifesting itself in the flashback of waking moments when his dreams lay restless beside him.

Pans filled, he took the bottle to his living room where he dug out some old photograph albums to satisfy his maudlin pangs. Since moving from his parents' house some years before, Adam turned frequently to these pictures, searching for some aspect of family that might cheer him. There was no doubt he got on better with his mother and father now he no longer lived in the same building but his link with them felt weakened. Visiting them was like visiting friends. He would now sit in the living room and discuss the economy where once he would have snatched crusts of bread from the kitchen and go up to play records in his bedroom. Those things he missed. Trivialities like mum calling him in for dinner—he doubted he'd hear that again. The photographs helped rekindle the better moods of those times, helped to camouflage the nasty truth. His parents would love to see him married, despite their own failure, yet Adam thought it would distance them even further from him for then, though he would still be their son, he would be somebody else's primary responsibility. Growing up, he thought, flicking the pages, was all about wrenching yourself away from people who would die for you.

He turned a page and happened upon a picture of himself, perhaps six months old, gazing dozily from his mother's arms. His eyes were blue then—weren't all babies' eyes blue? His grandmother was fond of saying that the color you were born with belonged to the body you owned in a previous incarnation. It would fade as your new body forgot about its past. Adam's eyes were hazel now.

The house closed in around him.

Even with the television on, Adam couldn't shake off the heaviness of the air. It felt gravid with meaning, like skies primed for a snowfall. When the night came, offering another stifling layer, Adam closed the curtains and switched on all the lights. He stared at the food waiting to be cooked. Rather than inspire his appetite, the wine had dulled it. He climbed stairs into an area of palpable cold. Presumably the landing had been protected from the afternoon's heat.

In the sanctity of his room, he peeled the stained bandages gingerly from his hands. The swellings had lessened, though now the weals had grown a pattern, a series of raised obliques, as though a length of hemp had bitten into his flesh. He dabbed ointment, bitterly relishing the bright sting. His grandmother had always said that if a cut stopped hurting, you should worry.

He left the blinds raised and opened a window to combat his room's humidity. Pulling back the sheets, the moment of shock he felt as the darkness came for him fretted his heart. He listened to its rush as the moon made a negative of the rooftop view.

He drifted, thinking of rain and the walk he would take in it as it washed the world. Outside, a hum rose into the sky as if the buildings were relaxing in the brief respite from summer. The lazy blink of Adam's eyes became more pronounced; his dreams hovered, sensing his arrival. He felt the duvet twitch beside him as a frost spread across the window rapid as breath. On the cusp of sleep, he saw the beautiful woman by the pond look at him, her head tilted to one side. The tilt did not seem natural. Next to him, someone started to breathe. It sounded strained, hoarse. He saw the glitter of her eyes, the pattern at her throat which matched that on his hands. As he felt her cold body move over him, he wondered if he might once have been married after all, many years ago.

THE OWL

Walk continuously around a tree with an owl in it: the owl will keep its eye on you until it has wrenched off its own head.

He couldn't remember where the words had come from, but he knew they were old and the last time he had heard them he could have been little more than five years of age.

Luc, the estate agent, turned the stiff corpse of the barn owl over with his foot so that they could all get a better view. *"Hibou,"* he said, and smiled, almost apologetically. "This place, they have lots of owl."

"One less, now," Ian said.

"Yes, well," Molly said, giving him a look. "No need to go stating the obvious, is there? Poor thing. It's beautiful."

"It won't be for long," Ian said, and wished he'd kept his mouth shut. She was right: the bird *was* beautiful. He had never been this close to an owl before, and was struck by the size of its head, how round it was. Luc shuffled, clearly indicating that they should move on. There was much more of the house to see and dusk was pouring oil over the garden; soon it would be too dark to see anything.

"I forget my torch," he said, and shrugged. "This house has good electric. But not switched on at present. Come."

They proceeded up a makeshift wooden staircase that would not be safe for too much longer; tiny holes were scattered across the grain, fresh frass on the floorboards. Ian felt his wallet wince. He plucked at Molly's sleeve. "This whole house... you know, we're going to have to get it *all* treated for woodworm."

She moved away from him, clearly annoyed by his pettifogging. "I'll wait here. I'm not going up there, not in my condition."

Ian followed Luc up into the attic. He couldn't speak much French, beyond *Bonjour, ça va? Au revoir,* so the atmosphere grew slightly strained, despite his liking the estate agent. Luc was pointing at the curious circular windows low on the wall, a peculiarity of the Charente region. *"Très jolie,*

111

non?"

"Like portholes," Ian said.

Luc smiled, frowned, shook his head.

"Never mind."

There wasn't much else to see in the attic, except for the awkward, low beams and a few rotting *batons* that would need to be tackled quickly if they weren't to deteriorate further over the coming winter.

"Good space for children," Ian said to Molly as he carefully returned down the stairs. He pressed his hand against the firm swell of her belly, and kissed her cheek.

The storms in the Charente were spectacular affairs, Ian had been promised. He had always fancied himself as a stormchaser, and harbored a wish to one day visit Tornado Alley, go in search for some big game like the guys he saw on the Discovery Channel. There was something about lightning and the brightness in the sky turned right down that appealed to a raw and ancient part of him. The lowing of thunder, miles away, getting closer. The air pressure, grinding down on you.

In the Charente, the flat countryside offered nothing upon which the storms might spend themselves. They drifted away but then they might come back again. On very rare occasions, two storms might gather in the same area, and revolve around each other. One of these broke the first night they spent in the house, after the contracts had been signed in the presence of the solicitor in Matha, the nearest town to their little village.

"It's a double-yolker," Ian said, face pressed against the window of what they had chosen for their bedroom, a ridiculously large room that could have easily accommodated a walk-in wardrobe and an en suite bathroom and still left them with more space than they had known in their one-bedroom flat in London. "Listen to that thunder. It's practically on top of us."

Molly was lying on the inflatable bed, watching the steam rise from her mug of raspberry leaf tea. She was trying to read a book about herbal remedies especially aimed at pregnant women but the candle light was too faint, or too agitated for her to concentrate properly, because she gave up after only a short while, tossing the book to the side of the bed. She ran a hand through her hair. The fingers of her other hand were absently toying with her belly button, which had recently become convex. Ian had altered the depth of his focus so that he could watch her reflection in the window, her transparent face blitzed by raindrops. He liked the way she always seemed to be able to find the most comfortable position with apparently minimum effort. In this way, she reminded him of a cat. She could fall asleep anywhere. There was a photograph of her as a young girl, half hanging out of a wicker chair, her head almost touching the floor, as content in sleep as she might have been in a deluxe bed.

They had met on Brighton beach, a little over two years previously. She had been kneeling on the shingle in such a bizarre way—her almost supernaturally long legs somehow splayed out and tucked beneath each other—that it seemed more like a torture than a position of rest. The first time they made love, she had hooked her legs over his shoulders and then, hushing his protests, detached herself from him, lifted herself up on her neck muscles alone, twisted around and lowered herself slowly into a new position, presenting her rear to him, laughing deeply in the dark. She seemed double-jointed, treble-jointed. She folded herself around him like strange origami.

"I love you," he said, the words falling out of him, coming from somewhere beyond his control, fuelled by the sentiment in his memories. Rain, like buckshot, scattered across the glass. The sky was so alive with pulses of lightning now, constant, random, that it could pass for day.

Molly laughed and reached out her hand to him. He could not remember the last time he had told her he loved her and didn't know whether that was a good thing. He joined her on the inflatable bed and she pressed his hand against her stomach, the skin as tight as that on a drum. "Say hello to the baby," she whispered. He did so, touching his lips to that warm curve, passing on a message of love, of hope.

"Hello baby… Daddy here…."

Molly moved against the tickle of his mouth, gently touching his face with her fingers, nudging him lower.

Some time later, the storm having finally tired itself out, they lay awake, listening to each other breathing in the dark, and the beat of water as it leaked from the roof onto the attic floor above them.

"I wonder if all the houses, even the ones in good order, have leaks?" Ian said.

"This house *is* in good order," Molly said. "Or it will be soon. There's a lot of work needs doing, but we knew that at the start, when we first talked about this, remember?"

He remembered, but their moving here seemed to have come around so quickly. Too quickly, for him. He had been happy in their one bedroom flat, even though the space seemed to shrink around them by the day. "I'm a DIY dunce, Mol," he said. "I see a claw hammer, I don't know if I should hit something with it, or pick my teeth."

"So you keep saying. But nobody is born with that kind of knowledge. You'll learn. You'll have to. *We'll* have to."

Sleep drew them down. Ian was on the edge of it, his thoughts deepening, fracturing into nonsense, into dreams, when the shriek slapped them both awake.

"What in Christ...."

Molly was already up, standing at the window. Her naked body didn't appear pregnant from behind. *A boy, that means,* she had said. *A bulge out in front, that's a boy.* Light from the floods trained on the church outlined her. From where he lay, perched on one elbow, he could see a great sweep of stars spraying out across the sky, like spilled sugar on a dark tablecloth.

"Bats?" Ian asked.

"Maybe. Maybe owls."

"Owls make that kind of noise? I thought they hooted. It sounds like someone being torn apart."

He saw her shrug. "Maybe it was. I'm no wildlife expert. Maybe it was a rabbit or a mouse being killed. Maybe it was the local cat being fucked. Maybe it was somebody's hinges need oiling."

He could never tell, when Molly was in this mood, whether she was merely teasing him or being more aggressively dismissive. He was aware that his questions tended to be on the pointless side, begging, for the most part, confirmation of something already said. It needled him that, two years on—married, with a kid on the way—he still did not know his wife as well as he felt he ought to.

The noise came again, a truly creepy rasp vented somewhere from the lime trees that shivered outside their window, and Ian saw how it could not possibly belong to an animal being hunted. It was a predator's cry. It was what bloodlust sounded like.

"Come back to bed," he said.

He dreamed of climbing the church tower from within. It was an old building—thirteenth century—and the interior stone, though initially pale and attractive, was, up close, failing rapidly. A wooden staircase took him only so far. He had to ascend the remaining darkness by a rickety ladder, some of the rungs of which had rotted away and been replaced by lengths of rusting iron, or sawn-off shafts of broom handles. The smell of bird shit was intense, it burned his nostrils. The netting, hung over the open arches to prevent the belltower from being invaded by wildlife, had decayed badly. It flapped ineffectually in the breeze. Night shifted beyond it like something that could be touched. As he reached the landing, a group of pigeons leapt nervously away from him, heads cocked, eyeing him with suspicion. He paused for a moment, the shape of the great bell within arm's reach. Its stillness was all wrong. Its size and silence seemed to go in direct contradiction of all that was meant for it. As if in acknowledgment of his thoughts, the bell began to move. Slowly at first, the sound of the cord as it was tugged fizzed lightly against the chamfered apertures of the landing. The bell tipped this way and that, gathering pace, and fear tipped with it, filling the gaps in his body with cold until his temperature had dropped so drastically it seemed he could be nothing but vacuum. He didn't want the bell to swing so violently. Not because of the immense sound that it would generate, but because it would mean he would be able to see through to the other side of the landing, and what waited there for him. He could not escape quickly enough. The pendulous slices showed him a scattering of picked corpses. The owl moved out of the shadows. It carried a dead rat in its beak. The owl's eyes held Ian like the headlights of a car will trap a rabbit. With a claw, the bird raked open the rat's stomach and half a dozen hairless, blind babies spilled from it.

Ian's laboring breath wakened him, more so than the dream. He lay listening to Molly sleep and tried to unpick the dream of its threat before his discomfort grew to the extent that he would have to get up, switch on some lights, make tea.

Owl's don't leave bodies lying around like that. And not so big, either. The bones of their prey were evacuated in their spoors. Owl shit wasn't scary. Christ, *owls* weren't scary.

Before breakfast, still feeling jittery but much happier now that the night was over, Ian spent some time in the garden, acquainting himself with the flowers and shrubs as they solidified in the early morning mist. The field across the way was a featureless gray screen. The church tower was soft, like something captured out of focus on a camera. He paid it scant attention.

The hibiscus, the geranium, the hazel tree were known to him; pretty much everything else was not. Ivy scarred the walls and inserted damaging fingers under the pan tiles that protected them. The ground was covered with what seemed like thick grass, but it came away in great swatches when he pulled at it, like hair from the head of a person suffering from alopecia. The soil was stony, uncooperative. A tree had collapsed, possibly during one of the great storms, and a riot of ivy and convolvulus had knotted around it, anchoring it to the ground. The only tool he owned was a rusty scythe he had found lying in the grass. His own teeth were sharper. There was so much work, everywhere he looked, that it appeared insurmountable. He didn't know where to begin.

And then Molly was at the window, pushing back the shutters, smiling down at him above that splendidly proud stomach, and he realized that it didn't matter where he began. They had all the time in the world.

"What does a sodding starter motor look like, anyway?" he said, leaning over the Xantia's engine, trying to find some sense in its weird steel and plastic codes. "Have a look at the manual."

By the time they fired the engine up it was gone ten and the pleasant morning they had envisaged pottering around the market stalls of Saintes was steadily being eaten away. The N10, usually so quiet, a pleasure to drive along, was congested with great lorries. Added to that, the radio was asking him to input the security code and neither of them had noted down what it was when they picked the car up from the garage in Oxford.

"The guy who sold us this *Shitroën*, I'm taking a contract out on the bastard."

Molly ignored him. She was leafing through a baby catalogue, marking items they needed with a red highlighter pen. More money they didn't have. It didn't seem to make things any better to consider these things essentials: a car seat, a travel cot, changing mats; at least he hadn't yet bothered to work out how to convert Euros to Sterling. This way, the total would just be so many figures that he didn't understand; it might make the pain of unfolding his wallet that bit more bearable.

They arrived in Saintes as the stallholders were in the process of packing away their produce. Hastily, Molly hurried to buy vegetables and a few cuts of meat for that evening's meal, her easy way with the language never failing to impress Ian.

"Look at the cheeses," he said. "My God. Look at what we've missed."

"We can come again," Molly said. "There's always the market in Cognac we can go to. There's even one in Matha, although I'll have to find out when it's on."

The baby shop was on the other side of the market, on a one-way street. They passed the remaining few stalls, and their owners, who were hosing down their pitches and loading the last trays and cartons into their vans. A butcher wiped down his chopping blocks. Steel glinted. A pile of skinned rabbits gritted their teeth at Ian as they were tipped into a thick polythene bag. Their eyes seemed too big for the heads that contained them. Molly was hurrying on, aiming for a gap in the traffic. In the instant that Ian's attention swung back to his wife, he saw another pile of peeled bodies being swept into storage. When he checked himself and stepped back to have another look, to confirm they were what he thought they were, the butcher flipped the latch off the awning and drew it across the service hatch.

By the time he opened the baby shop door, and navigated a path through the prams and buggies, Molly had already gathered a number of items under her arm that hadn't been on the original list.

"What, do you want the baby to have nothing?" she asked, when he pointed out that their budget might not be sturdy enough to factor in these items.

"I didn't say that," he said. "But come on. Toys, nightlights. A bean bag. Hardly essentials, are they?"

She dropped the things at his feet. "You sort it out, then," she said.

He shrugged at the shop assistant as Molly slammed her way out of the shop. *"Je suis desolée,"* he said, haltingly, and then paid for everything.

He found her sitting outside a café on the Cours Reverseaux. She was sipping a latté and flicking through a magazine at speed. Not reading anything, hardly looking at the pictures, just needing something to do with her fingers to deal with her anger. Her left foot bounced against her right. He watched it. He watched the sun glinting on the silver ring that encircled her little toe, a present he had given her on their honeymoon in Bali.

"I'm sorry," he said, but he had uttered the words too often for it to have any meaning.

She thawed a little, on the way back. It helped that he had bought something that wasn't on the list either: a small toy owl. It had seemed fitting, somehow. A tribute to the dead creature.

The traffic had dispersed for the legendary French lunch; they made good time going back, and could enjoy more of the scenery now that there were no tailgating Renault drivers, or swerving HGVs to keep an eye on. Crumbling farmhouses; fields freshly opened by the tractors, the soil dark and dense, brown as wet leather; long gray roads. They turned on to one now, flanked by elm trees, an object lesson in perspective.

"Now there's pretty for you," Molly said.

"There are moves to pull trees like that down," Ian said, and then mentally kicked himself for once again putting a downer on things. Why couldn't he just agree occasionally? It was what she wanted to hear.

"Why?"

"Too dangerous. They hide the junctions joining the main road. So if a car comes out and you swerve so as not to hit it, there's a tree waiting for you to wrap yourself around."

Silence.

"But you're right. Pretty. Reminds me of the opening titles to *Secret Army.*"

Molly returned to her baby magazines and her yoga manuals. Ian switched on the radio. Normally he could not stomach the inane Europop that tumbled from the speakers, but anything was better than this atmosphere. But then, a few minutes later, the signal faded, replaced by a wall of static so dense that Ian had to lash out at the volume control.

"Jesus," Molly said. "Do you mind?"

"It wasn't my fault," he said, but she had blanked him again. Ian swallowed against his rising anger—he didn't want to get into a fight with Molly in her state—and tried tuning the radio to a different station. Static followed him, wherever he sent the dial.

"This bastard car," he said. When he returned his full attention to the road, snapping off the radio with a curse, he flinched. A shaded figure was standing inches away from the Tarmac, a red fracture splitting his head. The fact that it was only a cardboard cut-out was no relief.

"Did you see that?" Ian asked. "Look, there's some more."

Single black figures, or pairs, were positioned by the road; they marched off into the distance, provocative, ineluctable, all of them with the same crude head injuries. Molly seemed unimpressed.

"They're *fantômes*," she said. "They're a warning to drivers. They signify that there have been deaths on these roads. Violent deaths. So slow down and watch what you're doing."

Ian said nothing more on the drive home. He stopped off in Matha and bought an English newspaper, then popped into the local *Bricomarché* and bought a garden fork, a spade, some secateurs, a machete and a pair of gloves.

"Ian," Molly said, as he got back behind the wheel, "look, I know we're not going through the best of patches at the moment, but things will get better. What might help is if you lay off buying things that we don't need."

"The garden is in a mess, Molly. We need gardening equipment. What do you expect me to do? Kick the weeds into submission? Talk to them in a stern manner?"

"Darling, there's no need to be facetious. The garden can wait. We need to sort out a room for the baby."

"Which will be done."

"I know it will, but not if you're out in the garden all day."

He swallowed, counted to ten. There was no question of him returning the gardening tools. Just let her have her moment. *Let it slide over you.*

"And those newspapers. They're so expensive for what they are. Why don't you just check out the Beeb's website?"

Back home, he unloaded the car and made tea for them both. Molly watched him and then said she didn't want any tea when he handed her a cup. Ian stared at her, but kept his mouth shut. He emptied the cup, rinsed it, grabbed his paper and his own tea, and headed for the door.

"Where are you going?" she asked.

"I'm going for a shit. Is that okay with you?"

There were a couple of owl droppings on the cement floor of the *hangar*, he saw, as he was returning from the outhouse. He poked at them with his boot and they disintegrated: a tiny mandible, ribs like fishbones, half a skull, the size of a pistachio nut. Above him, a beam was spattered with white bird shit, like pointless graffiti. He suddenly found himself thinking of his child, safe and warm inside Molly. It had been this size once, smaller, even, and just as fragile. Its own bones as thin as an eyelash. A heart beating, the size of a pinhead. He entered the house determined to make things better. Molly was in the room they had chosen for the baby, chosen for its lack of a window, painting the roughly plastered walls.

"You shouldn't be doing that," Ian said. "The fumes. Here, let me—"

"Get away from me!" Molly's eyes, in the gloom, glinted like scratched coal. The paint brush had become a weapon she held out in front of her. "Just leave me alone. I'll have the baby without you, if that's what it takes to be happy. I'm sick of doing everything around here while you swan off buying garden tools. I'm the only one preparing for this child. You haven't even talked to me about what names you like."

He was too taken aback to retaliate, or to reason with her. He moved away from her as she returned to the wall, streaking the plaster with fiercely applied strokes.

Crazed thoughts descended on him as he stepped into the garden, like the leaves that spiraled down from the disrobing trees. *Leave now. Take the car and go. Fuck it. But the baby. The baby. Fuck it. She'll leave you in the end and take the baby with her. Stick around for the birth and it will only be worse. It will be impossible to leave once you've held the child in your arms. Leave. Leave now.*

An agonized cry caught in his throat. Tears of impotent rage made further nonsense of the wild garden. He stalked to the barn where he had stored his equipment and rammed his fingers into the gloves. He took the machete and walked around the house to the fallen bough. She couldn't let go anything he said; nothing he could do was good enough. Even this, trying to clear the garden of obstacles, she'd criticize. *I'm stuck here toiling and you're outside doing all the lovely creative stuff. Great. Thanks.*

He attacked the naked limbs of the tree almost in a panic, shaking from the absurd interior arguments he was fashioning. Jesus, she wasn't even around and he could get into a row with her. What did that mean? Nothing good, nothing good. The virgin blade chewed into the damp wood, squealing as he recovered it. The shocks that flew up his arm were welcome distractions. After a couple of minutes of senseless hewing, he stopped, exhausted. Despite the cold, sweat coated his forehead and steam was rising from his muscles.

At the point where the tree had split from its roots, a great mass of stinging nettles had sprouted. Thick climbers and thorny vines moved through it, reminding him of Walt Disney scenes of enchanted castles guarded by menacing flora. He snorted and lifted the blade again. *And they lived happily ever after.* This time he worked more systematically, lopping off the branches close to the trunk and stacking them in a pile to be either burnt on the spot once it had dried, or to be stored as kindling. He thrashed at the nettles until enough of the climbers and vines had been exposed to be able to get at them. After half an hour he had cleared a goodly portion of the tangle and the underlying shape of the garden was coming through.

He felt calmer, and was beginning to enjoy himself, the sense of achievement as it grew, but the air was changing, deteriorating. The sky to the east was leaden, sucking all of the light into it. The hairs on Ian's arms shifted slowly, like the legs of a cautious spider making itself known to something it hasn't yet recognized on the web. A rumble shifted across the horizon.

The engine fired first time, thank God. He didn't relish the prospect of asking Molly to help him start the car, and the inevitable queries. He didn't bother closing the gates in case she was already on her way down to see where he was going. The country lane to the main road was less than a mile long; by the time he had covered it, rain was spitting against the windscreen. There was nothing else on the road. The countryside opened up around him. A village a couple of miles to his left was painted momentarily with gold through a rent in the black sheet. Rain hung like fishermen's nets, trawling the skies in great swathes. It must be ten miles across. Beyond it, or within it—Ian couldn't tell—a sudden trigger of lightning burnt everything onto his retina. It was followed almost immediately by the crash of thunder, so close it seemed it must split the sky above him. Ian heard it despite the protesting engine.

He pushed the car hard, hoping to intercept the storm as it passed over the N939. If he missed it, it would mean a pursuit along the smaller country thoroughfares, which would be impossible, especially if he had to slow down to fifty kph every time he hit a village. He wound down the window and was assaulted by the chill wind, the almost horizontal slanting of rain.

"Come on!" he screamed. "Come on!"

He took the car off the road at the top of a slight rise and parked without caring if he had spoiled the plowed patterns of the field, or whether he would be able to drive out of the mud when his adventure was over. He stumbled out of the car, unconsciously stooped because of the closeness of the sky. The darkness was alive. At its edges it trembled, where real light still existed, somehow compacted and intensified at the horizon, as if the pressure of the storm was affecting it. He could still make out the soft, black ribbons of rain as they approached, before they engulfed him and he became a part of their pattern. The howling of the wind went away as the storm's heart settled over him and for a moment he could hear nothing, except for the beating in his own chest. It felt as though something invisible was being drawn up from the ground. He felt his testicles contract; the hairs on his nape standing to attention. He felt as if the sky was breathing him in. And then the sky opened under a brilliant slash of a knife that drove the grim colors away for a beat. Thunder collapsed around him, shaking him. Again he screamed, as hard as he could, but the sound was lost; his was a tiny voice, an insignificance. He slumped back against the car as the storm left him, now one, now three, now five kilometres further west, still violent, but already sounding weak to Ian's ears. Rain continued to batter down, but he barely felt it. The sharp, almost sour taste of ozone flooded him. He felt alive for the first time in his thirty-odd years. He felt, somehow, defined. He watched the storm recede until it disappeared, and yet he stayed on, willing it to return, until the darkness around him no longer had anything to do with the weather.

When he arrived at the house, he found he could not remember his return journey. Maybe the electrical play had done something to his mind, short-circuited him, thrown a few switches. Maybe pure elation had wiped a little bit of him out. The clock on the dashboard read a quarter to midnight. He eased himself out of the car and trudged in the dark around to the front of the house. What he'd give for a hot, deep bath now, instead of the cold shower that was their only means of keeping clean. A cognac then, and a piece of last year's Christmas cake. He'd take some tea up to Molly and tell her about the storm. He would apologize, and promise to make things right between them. The storm had scored a line beneath him. Things could change. He wanted the best possible start for their baby.

His clothes were strewn about the garden like the remains of bodies that had decomposed into the grass. The photograph of him and Molly on their wedding day was hidden behind a white star in the glass. His love letters to her were torn and discarded, fluttering at his feet. The front door was locked. He rapped on it, but Molly was either asleep, or ignoring him. He moved back from the door and looked up at the bedroom window. The shutters had been closed.

"Molly? Molly, please?" he hated the wheedling tone that edged his voice. But she wasn't giving way this time.

Ian picked up his sopping clothes and the disintegrating cards and notes and dumped them in the outbuilding they were using for storage. He briefly considered spending the night in there, but it was cold, and there was an unpleasant smell of bleach from a sink where they washed their clothes. He went back to the car, shivering now. The storm had scoured the sky and it was eerily clean; there seemed to be more stars than the space they were studded into. Cold filled the gaps. Inside the car he started the engine and turned on the heating. It didn't take long to warm up. He dragged a blanket from the boot through the access hatch in the back seat and wrapped it around him. He tried the radio. No static this time. There was a faint classical music station and he felt himself drifting as a soft, soothing piece played. He wondered vaguely who might have composed it and what had driven him to do so.

As sleep came, he recalled the tableau from the road as the lightning's flash photography trapped it in his mind. The village, the black wet strip of Tarmac, the sheets of rain, the trees like shocked things staggering back from the ghastly breath of the weather. There was something else there, something, in his excitement, that he had missed the first time. A fat cuneiform shape, arresting itself against the thermals, talons outstretched in a classic pose of predation.

A shriek startled him out of a dream that he could not fully recall, other than it involved the machete, and dark parts of the garden that became more, not less, tangled as he scythed through to them. He moved in the seat and pain ricocheted through him like a hard steel ball in a game of bagatelle. His arms felt as if they had been wrenched into impossible positions, forced to do things beyond what human physicality ought to be able to achieve. They felt tenderized. His hands were raw and itchy, as they were when he washed lots of dishes in detergent without moisturizing them afterwards. Gingerly, he straightened and his gaze fell upon the rear-view mirror. In it he saw three figures reduced by the night to faceless mannequins: two close to the rear of the car, one further behind, almost at the great arched gate. All of them approached stiffly, incrementally, their outlines filled in with a black that was deeper than their surroundings. They seemed, somehow, *damaged*. The click that jerked him from his paralysis was his throat reacting as he tried to swallow.

He got out of the car. He got out of the car and he did not look back because to do that was to confirm his own madness. He would not allow that. There was nobody else in the grounds of his house. Ian stood by the car long enough for them to be able to touch him, if that was what they wanted, and then, feeling vindicated, walked to the front of the house. Dawn light had set fire to the lowest edge of the gloom, but it was damp and it burned slowly, coming on with the same terrible slowness as the figures he had seen. Thought he had seen. He tried the door and felt a bitter victory to find that it was unlocked. Molly had capitulated. He was being offered an unspoken invitation to return to the fold.

He passed through the kitchen, which smelled faintly of the previous night's casserole and he broke off a piece of stale baguette to take the edge from his enormous hunger. Food could wait. At the top of the stairs he smelled the fresh paint in the nursery and felt cold fingers of rooms seldom used reaching out to him. In the bedroom he switched on the light and was greeted by an empty bed, the covers torn away from it, lying in a pile in the middle of the floor.

"Molly," he said, and his voice fell flat. Had she gone into labor while he was sleeping? Why didn't she come to him in the car? Surely her troubles with him could be forgotten if their baby were on the way. She wouldn't go to a neighbor for help instead, would she? Their first baby. How could she not want him with her?

He hurried downstairs, feverishly patting his pockets for the car keys. Presumably she would have been taken to Saintes to give birth. He ought to ring ahead, but he didn't have the number, and anyway, he was reluctant to talk to a voice that couldn't understand his urgency, and time was precious to him now.

All that was forgotten when he stepped into the cold mist of morning and saw the figures again, shifting slowly around the corner of the house—two walking abreast, the other still lagging behind—the jagged wounds in their heads clearly visible, shining wetly in the embryonic light.

He stepped away from them, into the shade thrown by the canopy of trees. He heard the ticking of long gone rain on a carpet of dead leaves as the branches gave up the water they had gathered the previous night. The owl landed on the wall and began to clean its bloodied beak.

The light's slow accretion, so subtle that it couldn't be measured.

Ian turned to look up at the crooks of the branches and waited for her wrenched shape to assume there, and that of the strange pendulum that swung bloodily from her guts. He retrieved his machete from the foot of the tree at the same moment that the third figure joined its companions. Ian rejoined his own moments later.

THE NIGHT BEFORE

Mrs. Janner came out with another plate of salad. I said I couldn't eat another thing. She said it wasn't for me.

"Who's it for then?" Norman asked, leaning back on the bench and patting his waistline. The bottle of beer in his other hand was sweating hard. Norman was, *is*, Julianna's father. Julianna is, or was about to become, my best friend's wife. My best friend is Oliver. It was his mum, Shirley, with the salad. Also there were Frank, (Shirley's husband) Geoff, (their other son) and Julianna's mother, Lucy. Julianna was there too. And so, while we're at it, was I, having flown to Perth a week previously at the behest of Oli who wanted me to be his best man. I was getting drunker by the minute.

"It's for me and Lucy. We've got figures to think about."

Norman shook his head and leered at me. "Don't talk to me about figures," he said. "Who do you think is paying for this bloody wedding anyway?"

I don't think there was another soul within five miles of us. Mr. and Mrs. Janner had been invited by the McRaes to stay at their house for the week. A few days after they had settled in, there had been a spectacular storm. At the bottom of the slope, the creek emerged through the treeline. According to Frank, it had reached much higher.

"We were thinking of leaving," he said, in thick Geordie. In Australia, the accent seemed ridiculously out of place, like seeing a snow leopard foraging in a London bin. A crumb of sausage had stuck to his beard. Nobody was saying a word. Geoff had started a sweepstake to see how long it would take to fall off. "It was water up as far as that tractor there."

The tractor was an old, rusting wreck, about a hundred yards down the slope. Geoff was smacking old golf balls with a seven iron off a piece of carpet, trying to hit it. If Frank wasn't exaggerating, then the creek must have been cradling the canopy.

Every time the cicadas ceased their deafening rhythms, it would jolt us to discover how loud we had all been speaking. Into the endangered silence, one of us would remark about the barbecue, or the impending wedding, or the stars.

I had never seen so many stars. In some places, they were massed so thickly it was hard to discern any night between them. Fix your eye in one place for a few seconds and meteors would slash across your line of sight, like self-erasing scratches of chalk on a blackboard. There were other, slower moving stars that didn't make so much fuss, just moved smoothly along their trajectory.

"Satellites," Norman said, imperiously, as if he had personally launched them. There were dozens. It was better than TV.

I was standing next to Geoff, my neck craning. Geoff said, "I reckon it won't fall off all night. I'll put a tenner on it." He sliced a golf ball into the next field. I looked around for Julianna but she was as elusive as the last pickle in the jar. I turned to Geoff as he was teeing up another shot. He wore a vest that revealed his well-toned arms. On the biceps of his left arm was a tattoo: *vice addict.* "Do you think Oli is all right?" I asked.

"Of course he isn't all right," he snapped. "He's getting married tomorrow. He will be tossing all of his "all rightness" down the bog, I would imagine."

"Julianna seems fine." I caught a glimpse of her sitting on the blind side of her mother, raising a flute of champagne. The slow, sodium light chanced across her lips and teeth.

"Yeah, well," Geoff said, flatly, letting fly again. "Hooked it. Tits!" He stepped back off the carpet, his eyes fast on the gloaming. "Thing with Julianna," he said, "is that she has got balls and a half. Nothing fazes her. Oli told me that the first time he met her, she was getting rottweilered by her boss for something. I don't know what. But she was standing there calm as coma, while she got her hair dried by this dingbat. She's a robot, that one. Nice with it, though."

I don't know what I was hoping that Geoff might come out with. I knew that Julianna could be distant, but I wanted to know if there was a reason for it. Strangely, she seemed to be most distant with Oli, but that might just have been wishful thinking.

Last night she said goodbye without looking at me. But she had been wearing the most beautiful smile. Now Lucy, her mother, was similarly aloof, wrapped inside a thin cardigan, a glass of chardonnay, a cigarette, watching everyone but rarely speaking. At the same time she exuded a warmth that seemed to transcend what was human. She and Julianna, perversely, came across as the people everyone gravitated towards. They were like Sirens.

I took my beer to the hammock and surreptitiously climbed in as Oli returned from the toilet looking like Stunt Zombie # 1. From here I had a better view of Julianna, but only momentarily, as she moved to make space for her husband-to-be who obscured her, but for her legs sweeping out from the hem of a flimsy summer dress, the languid spread of her tiny hand on Oli's shoulder.

"Isn't it bad luck to see the bride on the eve of a wedding?" I asked, a little too gruffly.

Everyone turned my way. Julianna's hand retreated and she stood up. She leaned towards her mother and said something; a fan of gold hair dropped across her profile. Frank had come up with some retort that only he found funny. I didn't bother asking him to repeat it. Julianna crossed the porch and disappeared into the house. Was that my cue?

Despite a swim on Cottesloe beach that afternoon, and a long, hot shower, I could still smell perfume on my fingers. I wanted to go to her, but if I fell out of the hammock now, it would all be too obvious.

"Anyone for more beer?" I called out. I'd had more than enough, but what else could I do?

Geoff called yes, but I could no longer see him; there was just the occasional, punctuative *thwack* as he sent another golf ball down to the creek. I was shifting to comply when Norman stood up. "Don't worry about it, Patrick," he said. "I'll go. You want another?"

I stayed where I was and watched the swirl of cosmic dust, trying to quell my panic. She had put her hand over my mouth when it seemed I might say something that would damage the situation more than what we were doing. The only words she said, when we were both on the cusp of losing ourselves to the soft, soundless sway of our bodies: "My love." Her eyes were closed, her head back so that all I could see was the soft, inverted V of her jaw. Her breasts soaked up the light from the candles until they seemed to glow from within.

"My love. My love."

They came outside together. They were laughing, carrying bottles.

"Hello."

The voice behind me made me twist so violently that my balance went and I lurched out of the hammock to more laughter from the porch. At the fence, a girl of about fifteen was watching me. Behind her, almost lost to the night's color, a black colt waited patiently for her. The girl was smiling. Everyone was smiling tonight.

"They're getting married tomorrow, that's right isn't it?"

"Yes," I said, blinking stupidly at her. I was starting to feel ill.

She said, "Julianna used to babysit for me."

"*For* you?"

She put a hand to her mouth and giggled. "You know what I mean.

When I was a baby. Me."

She was loose-limbed, but losing some of the gawkiness of adolescence. Her tummy glinted in the light where a navel ring trapped it. She wore very tight, very short shorts. She understood, whether consciously or not, what poise meant. I wish I did.

"Interesting," I said. "Do you remember when she babysat you?"

"A little. I'm Rachel, by the way. And this is Gus."

The horse moved closer and harrumphed, in recognition of its name. Rachel's hair was cropped close. She had soft, friendly brown eyes. She reached out a hand and Gus pressed his muzzle into it.

"Nice to meet you, Gus," I slurred, and put out my hand for him to shake it. Rachel laughed. "We can high five if you prefer, Gus. Or hoof five."

Gus moved away, bored.

"I have that effect on women," I said. Behind me, Geoff called out: "Stop worrying the wildlife, Pat."

I winked at Rachel. "Don't mind him. He's my pet idiot."

Rachel laughed again and stepped up on to the fence. She leaned over and brushed some grass from my hair. "Are you from England?" she asked.

"Can't you tell?"

"Well, yeah. Which part?"

"All of me," I said.

She was shaking her head. "You're weird."

"I know. London, anyway. I'm from London. I'm Patrick."

She told me how Julianna used to sing her songs while she was in bed. And how once, when she had been ill, she stroked the back of her neck for hours until she went to sleep.

"Look," she said, and turned around. "See?"

On her neck, there was a birthmark. "It's in the shape of an angel. Can you see? She put it there with her fingers."

"I can believe it," I said and took a swig of beer. It tasted sour. Enough. Rachel said, "You love her don't you?"

I looked at her, feeling more sober than I had done all night. "Don't we all?" My voice was anything but glib. She reached into her pocket. "Give her this. A wedding present. You don't have to say that it's from me."

She blew me a kiss and sank into the dark. I heard her and the horse moving through the grass until I was no longer sure that it was them who were making the sound, or the breeze.

The others were taking their glasses inside. The temperature had dropped and the insects were gathering in greater numbers.

The only seat available indoors was a small stool in the corner of the room. Julianna was sitting on Oli's knee. Her body had folded against his,

an arm curling around his chest hid her face. I was beginning to forget
what she had looked like, or, more specifically, my mind could only deal
with one detail of her face at a time, as though complete, it would be too
much to cope with.

Lucy poured gluey liqueurs. Mosquitoes and moths crowded at the
window, drinking in the light. "Look at them!"

"Like a plague of locusts," Frank said.

Shirley laughed. "The gods are angry."

"So are Dad's Y-fronts," said Geoff. "Too much salsa on his sausages."

Everyone whooped as Norman mock cuffed his son's ear.

Talk turned to the wedding. I felt something stiffen inside me.

"Is Rachel one of the bridesmaids?" I asked.

Oli shifted his weight to look at me over the top of his spectacles.
"Who's Rachel?"

"Your next door neighbor. I mean, Mr. and Mrs. McRae's next door
neighbor."

Lucy looked uncomfortable. "Mick and Liz Beswick live next door.
They don't have any kids."

"I was talking to this girl at the fence—"

Geoff snorted. "You were talking to a horse, alcohol boy."

"—and she told me Julianna used to babysit for her when she was a
child."

The mood had turned. Norman was making tiny "cut" motions with
the flat of his hand. Lucy was close to tears. She gathered the hem of her
cardigan into her fist.

"Have I said something I shouldn't?" I asked.

Julianna sat up. She stared at the floor. "How do you know about
Rachel? Were you going through my photograph albums?" She added,
quickly: "I don't mind if you were, just tell me, and we'll forget it as a bad
joke, okay?"

"I didn't—"

Norman said, "Rachel used to live next door. She drowned in the creek
last year. We don't talk about it. We were close."

"You're a little pickled, aren't you lad?" said Frank. And then, to Lucy:
"He must have wandered in earlier and seen something. Now he's
forgotten. He's a good lad. He doesn't mean any harm."

"Look—" I protested.

"No more," Frank said, more firmly now.

"But look!" I took the gift that Rachel had given me from my pocket.
It was a small, sculpted piece of steel that made the infinity sign.

Julianna loosed a small cry and buried her face in Oli's shirt. Oli was
looking at me as though I had just been demoted to worst man.

"What is it?" asked Geoff.

Lucy pressed her lips together and took the ornament from me. "It was Rachel's. It was her favorite thing. She took it everywhere." Her eyes flashed at me. "Where did you find this? In the field?"

"She gave it to me."

Frank gave me a look. "He must have found it, Lucy. You've got so much land here…"

The atmosphere leavened, thanks to Shirley telling everyone about the time she took Geoff to the circus when he could have been no more than five or six. "The ticket girl took my money and said, 'It's all right, madam. No charge for the boy.'" And little Geoff got all indignant. Puffed his cheeks out, he did. Close to tears. 'But I *want* to be charged!' It was so funny. The poor ticket girl was in stitches. We had to pretend to pay for him in the end."

Geoff was rolling his eyes, but clearly loved the attention. The warmth that had tied itself into a little knot between Oli and Julianna was slowly spinning out and affecting everyone in the room. Shirley leaned into Frank and kissed his cheek. Geoff poked his mum in the arm and then held her hand. Norman worked Lucy's hand until it loosened and he peppered the top of her head with soft kisses. Lucy regarded me sadly but managed to smile. I just sat there quietly, gripping the neck of an empty beer bottle.

"We should go," Shirley said after a while.

Everyone said goodbye in that protracted manner that takes in promises of visits to come, jokes about Frank's cookery skills, wishes for good weather in the morning. Norman was dropping Julianna off at her sister's before taking me and Oli back to Oli's flat. I shook every hand that was proffered and kissed every cheek apart from Julianna's who appeared to be blocked from me when we might naturally have come together. I apologized quietly to Lucy, who hugged me and said it was okay.

And I realized not once, all through the evening, not once had Julianna met my gaze.

As we were leaving to go, I touched Julianna on the arm. Still she did not look at me. Her head twitched my way. I saw a hint of a smile. "I think you've left something behind," I said.

As she moved past me, back into the house, her hand brushed against my fingers and held one, just for a moment.

The following day, for the wedding, I dressed in black.

EDGE

Quietly obscene, the taking of E here, where old women walk three-legged dogs along Loch Broom and you can order your fish dinner from the restaurant before it's even been caught. As if the mountains could fragment, the Loch boil with the indignation of spurning their natural high for a chunk of synthetic. Pippa's eyes bloat black. Blemishes are sucked into the TV color of her skin. We talk too quickly, trying to keep a grasp of the mundane but even discussions of moored boats and gliding lights in the distance spawn gentle leaps into the fantastic. It begins. As does the rain, flecking her Goretex and disappointing us with its intrusion. No soft-nosed needles bursting sub-apocalyptically on our flesh here: just rain.

Earlier, over open prawn sandwiches and beer at the Ferry Boat Inn on Shore Street (served by a tough, likeable ball of flab, hair like a razed band between tracts of Scots fir. The prawns had a glaze not unlike that of his right eye—which was glass), we wrote postcards home. Pippa's fingers dabbed at the McCoy's. My backside was blockish and numb from driving—we hadn't stopped since leaving Dunvegan that morning. Loch Broom flat and dull as a blade. A boat, permanently tethered, cringed in the expanse upon which it was resting, its rust-orange hull gathering fire as the sun spent itself on a rind of mountain.

Hello Mum and Dad—Driving like idiots. Warrington to Oban in a day! And then on to Skye where we walked a beach of black sand.

"Here?" she said. "Shall we do it here? I reckon we should because if we leave it till tomorrow we'll be fucked for the drive back."

"But Durness," I urged. "The North Sea. Fuck off waves. Imagine that."

Pippa flipped the last corner of her ham sandwich onto the plate. Dug for a cig. Which pissed me off. Kissing her after she's been kissing the filter of a Marlboro Light is like frenching an ashtray. Sometimes I wonder if she eats just so she can have a cigarette afterwards.

"Yes, chicken. Very romantic. But be practical. We have to be back in London in two days' time. A long way. And I don't want to be driving whilst wazzed."

Eaten a full fry-up every day. I'm beginning to resemble a fried egg. I'll try porridge tomorrow—as long as they don't put any salt in it!

"All right," I conceded. I felt on edge. "Not too bad here, I suppose."

"It's beautiful."

"I love you," I said, for want of a better.

She smoked like a novice, watching the coal as it frenzied, the gust of blue as she exhaled. I suddenly meant what I said. In that green, waterproof huddle she looked so damned vulnerable and soft—as if the ruthless career Dalek she became back in the Smoke had been smothered. Her breasts were under there somewhere, sweating up: dough introduced to an oven.

"I've got a hard on."

Durness tomorrow, then back home via Inverness. Pippa is desperate for a fresh fish dinner and I'm going to make sure she gets it. See you soon....

"Do you reckon I could get both your bollocks into my mouth at the same time?" Another drag on the weed. Quite sexy, come to think of it. Bacall-ish. "I've never met anyone whose cock was so greedy before. You'd get a hard on at the drop of a hat. You'd get a hard on if I said 'Bangladesh'."

"Ooh, you sleazy minx. Take me now."

"Finish your beer. We've got bags of time." She gives me one of those smirks that brought me to my knees right at the start. Somewhere between a smile and a purse and a lippy shrug. Almost the kind of indulgent moue you'd give a child. I'm not entirely sure I know what I'm on about, but I can't describe it. She has these moments when she is utterly, incontrovertibly, fucking gorgeous. Nobody can hold a flame to her. When she's tired or angry or bored, she looks as compelling as an oatmeal cardigan. Spinning between these two poles, like a magnet torn, I'm kept on my toes.

Back at her Micra, we unload the bags. My briefcase looks conspicuous, absurd, but it's got a combination lock on it. While Pippa goes through the pleasantries with the woman in the B&B, I dump our stuff and pootle down to the Post Office with the cards. Pippa's handwriting is an object lesson in efficiency. Some of her letters are improbably joined due to a short cut she's found over years of writing essays and exams. Her energy expenditure is minimal. Thankfully, none of these cost-cutting practices have found their way into our bed. If she ever down-sized her double-handed Turbowank into some streamlined, eco-friendly two-fingered jig I'd be more than a little miffed.

M + D. Ullapool beautiful. North tomorrow. Speak to you Monday pm. P.

But for the cheap W.H. Smith turquoise ink, her only indulgence, it's brutal and lizard-cold. That's it with Pippa. She's got something of the robot, the replicant about her. On the way back, I toyed with the idea of asking if she's ever seen *Demon Seed* but I didn't think she'd appreciate the joke.

In our room. She's propped up against the pillows. One breast is free of her halter top. Her legs are in a loose pincer shape, feet almost touching each other. One hand is sprawled over her mons, middle and index fingers spreading herself so I can see flashes of her liquefying cunt, like moments in a zoetrope, as her other hand blurs over her clitoris. Slowly she arches, her left foot twitching, mouth folding from stiff oval to flat, thin line and back. Eyes disappear to black slots. On the cusp, her features slacken to something like surprise, to the kind of surprise characters in films adopt when they've been shot or stabbed without warning.

"Some welcome back," I say, homing in.

And now.

I can feel the lobes of my brain fizzing. Every breath becomes cleaner, colder, more congealed, as if soon I might be able to chew on the air. We've had a Dove each. I want to go and run up Ben Eilideach—all 1800 feet of the fucker. It's like a huge, beautiful dick. A dick tenting a bed sheet. And the sky is the mother of all cunts. A wraparound cunt mocking the cock with teasing, unattainable distance. I tell Pippa this and she falls about.

"How do you feel?" I say, through clenched teeth.

"Absolutely wazzed."

We leg up and down the loch front like we're trying to plow a furrow. But no matter how ripped off my face I might feel, I'm buggered if I'm walking to the end of the terrace. Something is rustling there and it isn't an empty bag of Golden Wonder.

"Look, chicken!"

I heard it before I saw it. The schuss of waves and a backbeat throb of engine. Then rounding the crown of land came the ferry, its lights pearlescent, like underlit smoke in the windows. If there wasn't a figure at the prow of the boat, twisting himself in and out of extravagant knots, slithering like oil along the railings, expanding like a blot of ink on bandage, there ought to have been: it was a gorgeous sight. Just the night though, no doubt, wanking with my mind. The night and the pill.

The rain on Pippa's face was a thin matting, like hoar frost. She was so still, my heart spasmed as if she'd died on me, while I was chuntering on about bush shapes lunging for me like servants carrying trays of food that they were zealously getting me to sample. Then she moved, holding my hand and pulling me towards the B&B. Inside, we held each other so tightly, it seemed I'd just open up and fold around her. The heat coming from her settled, a layer against my skin. She made glottal noises and shuddered occasionally. Her jaw spasmed against my cheek. She was off somewhere I couldn't yet know, despite the almost unbearable rise of the drug: a balloon inflating in my head and threatening to take off with or without me. I licked her gullet. I pulled her head down and kissed her. The kiss developed rhythms independent of us. Mouths melded, it felt as if I could slowly melt into her, without pain, until my mouth quested from the back of her head. I tasted, very acutely, her black stream of words which squirted onto my tongue.

We shall go to the very edge together.

"What do you mean?" I said, breaking away: a thin rope bridge of saliva looping between us.

"I didn't say anything."

We'd reached our ceiling. A few minutes later, I was reluctantly controlling things, even though great pollen-like clouds of wow were still softly exploding. We walked back to the pub and sipped beer by the fire. I couldn't look into the flame: it was too much like staring at ripped flesh.

I drove the next day, knowing that Pippa was always drubbed out after a trip. We made excellent time, bisecting the mountains while the tape looped The Breeders' "Hag" over and over till we got tired of it and played Radiohead instead. Pippa read out loud to me: Steve Erickson or Joel Lane or Patrick McGrath. She told me what she'd do to me once we arrived in Durness. We watched the fighters make languid arcs over Kinloss and Lossiemouth.

Traveling north seemed to be cleansing us of all the city dirt and impatience. Pippa looked more relaxed than I'd seen her for weeks, the lines and shadows around her mouth gone, a rose to cheeks which had been waxen and livid for too long. We hadn't discussed work (or in my case, the lack of it) since the first ten miles of our holiday. Her irritability where I was concerned had been sucked back into its shell.

It seemed almost feasible that we'd spend the rest of our lives together.

On the final stretch of road, a stream at the bottom of a glacial valley beneath us caught a lozenge of sunlight which chased the car: a blip on an ECG. A T-junction loomed; beyond was a bluff of land and little else, save for the ocean which unfurled towards a whitish, ill-defined horizon.

"Welcome to Durness," said Pippa. "End of the line."

We parked by the information center, which was closed for the winter. Luckily, the souvenir shop opposite was open and while I picked out a pair of gloves, Pippa asked about likely accommodation. Outside, she took on a grotesque approximation of the shopkeeper's accent and repeated to me what she'd heard, dressing it up and sounding more like a hysterical Frazer from "Dad's Army" the more she progressed. "Och, ye might try the Smoo Cave Hotelllll the noo. Mind how ye gooo."

"Ayyyyyyye," I got in on the act. "You'll nae be stayin' looong in our neck of the woods, I'll be bound. D'ye hear what they say aboot the people who dare to stay in the old Smoo Cave Hotel?"

"Ye might gae in," mugged Pippa, turning on me with a leer. "But ye shooor as heeell won't come oooot!"

I creased up, trying to steer the car up a sheer portion of road which ran along the perimeter of the beach. It took but a single slow pass along the front of the Smoo Cave Hotel for us to sober up, ruffled by how accurate our badinage had proved. The hotel was little more than a single story B&B, scabrous and shallow as a Hollywood façade. There was even a door that wasn't shut properly, slamming to and fro in the wind.

"You go," I dared.

"My arse," Pippa said. "Let's see if there's anywhere else."

Small place, Durness, but we found a farmhouse advertising bed and board as soon as we U-turned out of the grounds of Castle Grim. A pleasant, open-faced girl of my age answered our knock and I thought, yes, this'll do. Olivia led us to a room upstairs—a bit pokey—but I was so jiggered that a kennel would have sufficed. Pippa handed me a temazepam and I necked it with a glass of peaty water, watching her do likewise. We kissed and snuffled around each other for a while, until things became more serious, perhaps encouraged by the warm spread as the jellies kicked in. We undressed each other, reveling in the comfort of blankets which would have been starchy but for the downers.

She took me into her mouth, sucking just the head of my cock, her tongue lolling against it, eyes sexdrunk slits. Her hand worked me furiously. Occasionally, I'd slip from her lips with a *Schpluh!* before she plugged me back in. Reaching round, I felt for her sodden cleft and strummed gently at her from top to tail till she was trying to back up and swallow my fingers. I was losing myself, all of my feeling and heat racing to the purplish bulb which was being roiled around the delicious vacuum of Pippa's mouth. She sensed the twitch and, in extremis, moved her head away, replacing it with her left breast, which was slick with my spit, pulling on my cock till I gouted a great jet of come over her chest. I pushed her back and chased the pearly glut around against her nipple with my tongue before turning her over and moving into her.

I fucked her with her head into the pillow. She yowled but I was past the point of caring whether it was pleasure or pain. She was too, her hips bucking, hands clawing the mattress till it tore. The edges of the bedsheet curled back like a smile and showed me a black hole beneath that appeared so deep as to have no end. I felt myself being gulped into it, as slickly and effortlessly as into Pippa. A vertiginous rush eclipsed the core of my pleasure and I thought I was going to lose my balance. It suddenly seemed important that I be able to see what was watching us through the window: it felt as though I was out there, looking in. When I came again, thrashing to free myself rather than out of any recourse to pleasure, my head was totally banded by darkness and I felt, with the conviction that only dreams can muster, that I was dead, or close to death, and I would never see Pippa again. On the edge of my dissolution, however, the night dissipated and Pippa was stroking my backside, asking me what I thought of Flann O'Brien's *The Poor Mouth*. The window was misted: sex ghosts. Something hulked beyond. I walked the three paces and placed my hand against the glass. A deeper mist sprang from the edges of my skin. When I removed it, I saw, through the black star that remained, an ancient man, hair rioting in the wind. His eyes were wetted black grapes thumbed deep into the dry dough of his head. Through the slit of his mouth, his tongue jutted a moment. He said something. I read the movement of his lips: *Walk with me.*

"Wassup chicken?" Pippa's voice syrupy with sleep and trancs.

"Nothing." I went back to her. I wasn't afraid. Sex worked its palliative magic, working at the knots in my muscles, freeing my brain of worry, of 9 to 5 and getting my invoices in on time. But I couldn't sleep. Pushing through the comfort and the warmth was the cold prickle of something not right. I could sense something brewing inside Pippa. I wanted to unhinge the top of her head and peer beneath the lid.

Persistent, murmuring voices in the room abutting this one I used as the reason for my insomnia. At one point they became heated, although I couldn't make out what was being said, so muffled was their anger. I slipped from bed, but Pippa was too dead to the world to notice. Opening the door a crack, I spied a shiver of light bleeding through the bottom of the door next to ours. Pacing shadows disturbed it: a man and a woman. Something terrible in their voices, not so much anger as misdirected passion which twisted them into gross human spoofs. Yet there was something in their spiteful gainsaying which made something in me feel liberated. I don't know what it was. I could hear only fragments of argument: plosive words such as *betrayed* and *bitch* and *kill* from him and blistered reason from her: *on the cards*, I heard. And, in a moment of clarity: *don't be such a fucking stupid childish bastard.*

I left them to it, hoping it would blow itself out before any of their dark promises were kept.

Sometime after midnight. Me, eyes wide as peeled eggs. Pippa says, in a voice thick with desire: "Oh, Jeff. Suck it. Come on."

"What are you having for breakfast, chicken?" she said. "How about my tits on toast, hmm?"

I slid away from her yawning legs and ducked my head under the tap, blasted my tired, tired face with cold reality. She didn't notice my standoffishness and that suited me fine, because I wasn't ready to talk about it. I didn't know how to talk about it. Or whether I should talk about it at all—it was just, apparently, a dream. But that specific name. Jeff. Fucking Jeff. Jeff-rey. I hated the cunt. And I didn't even know anyone called Jeff-bastard-rey.

Olivia was preparing toast when we came downstairs. "No breakfast for us," I muttered.

"Great," she returned. "I suppose I'll just eat all this by myself."

"Give it to the folks in the room next door. They wasted enough energy bawling at each other last night. They'll need a good breakfast."

Her frown disarmed me and I hoped I hadn't heard her properly as I hurriedly shepherded Pippa outside: *There are no other guests.*

Despite being wrapped in thermals we kept banging our heads against a wall of frigid air built by the seafront. Huge boulders in the sand provided enough shelter for my ears and from prying eyes while Pippa lit a huge spliff. Her hair was savagely drawn back from her scalp, tamed by a simple green hairband made of elasticated fabric.

She took a few tokes and passed the J to me. I shook my head. Soft gray shapes emerged on the horizon, like thawing fossils from ice. Oil tankers probably. Pippa took a last drag and stuffed the roach into a crack in the boulder.

"Let's go and check out the cave," I said. A figure had breasted the prow of land to our left, next to the shell of a burned-out Allegro. He was looking towards us, hands deep in the pockets of a mackintosh, hair like a wreath of white smoke. Even from here I could see him hook his index finger. Beckon me. On his wrists, a curve of green. The detail made me wonder for a minute if there were still traces of MDMA sprinting around my brain but then I heard Pippa's measured tread on the stone steps down to the beach and I dismissed the thought.

There are eighty-eight steps down to the shingle beach which provides access to the cave. I counted them to give me a distraction: black words were ganging up in my head. I didn't want to unleash them before she had a chance to defend herself against my initial question, which I asked as we reached a rusted winch, bolted into the ground like a sculpture. A few sheep watched us from the hillside upon which rocks had been placed to make messages. "LIAM LOVS LUCY" I read. "KOL + FIONA DID IT HERE."

"Jeff?" she said. "I don't know—"

She's a fucking abysmal liar. I just looked at her. Her face changed, losing its expression of doughy victimization and finding instead a resilience. *Okay*, it seemed to say, *let's thrash this out then. I'm probably more fucking ready than you are.*

"Jeff's someone I met at a conference in Brighton. We meet sometimes. We go to bed. That's it."

"That's it? As if there's nothing wrong in what you're doing?"

"What's wrong? I fancy him. He fancies me. We fuck each other. Big deal."

"So why pretend you don't know him?" My hands were fisting like I was testing someone's blood pressure.

"Because I knew you wouldn't be able to handle it."

"You're fucking right I can't fucking handle it. You've been coming home to me, filled to the fucking brim with some other fucker's seed?"

"Oh, come on," she said, using the Grade A patronizing tone a teacher will reserve for a dimwit child. "Jeff and I obviously use a condom."

"Jeff and I..." I mimicked, not giving a shit if I was being cruel or puerile. "And I was speaking figuratively, anyway."

The cave seemed to deepen as we breached the lip; a muscled gullet distending as it drew us in. Our voices bloated and took on an echo to make it seem no pause for digestion had followed any sentence. Behind it all, a frenzy of water helped keep my adrenaline pumping.

"So where does that leave us?"

She shrugged, made a bow of her lips and looked at me with a kind of pleading scrutiny as if trying to both examine my feelings and get me to draw my own conclusions. When I simply stood there, like all the pathetic pieces of shit in the world stuck together, she shrugged again and took a Marlboro Light from her pocket.

"Is this it?" I finally snapped. "Are you finishing it?"

"I think so. Yes. I am."

"How can you do this? How can you betray me like this and then act as if it was such a fucking drag, a real bore for you?" Funny how, despite the beefy acoustics, my voice sounded wheedling.

Another shrug; another suck on her stupid little tube of grass. "Dunno."

"So are you going to go with this Jeff?"

Shrug. Suck. "Might."

"Aw, you bitch," I spat. "You miserable, heartless bitch. I should fucking kill you for what you've done to me." I went into the cave, relishing the cold that swarmed at my shoulders. A small bridge led to the waterfall which was causing such a racket. I walked it, squeezing past a tethered dinghy. Wondering what the hell use that was in a little pond like this, I didn't hear her step up beside me.

"It was on the cards, honey," she said. Soothing sentiment but it might have been Davros delivering it. I watched the water till its constant motion seemed so unchanged that it froze: wax ropes. I backed away, not least because I saw, filling the hole in the ceiling of the cave, his head as he leaned over to watch us.

Green lamps bolted into the heights painted the limestone an eerie hue. A boom, like thunder, filled the cave and I ran, not caring if Pippa was anywhere near me. I kicked at the stone messages as I climbed the incline. Sheep, tolerant to the point of boredom with humans, moved desultorily out of the way. Another boom, echoed moments later by a larger, nearer explosion.

The sea's limit hove into view above the severed foreground of land. I rushed to meet it, enjoying bitterly Pippa's beseeching yells. I stopped at the crumbling edge of the cliff and turned round. The Smoo Cave Hotel's doors clapped as if part of a participating audience. The old man had moved away from the hole and was drifting down the steps to the winch, his face turned up to mine. Any shiver he might have generated in me was lost to the general discomfort of cold.

"What are you doing?" she asked, in a wavering voice filled with either panic or ire. I couldn't guess which and I couldn't give a monkey's uncle.

"I'm going to toss myself off, if you know what I mean."

"Oh don't talk cock," she said. "Don't be such a fucking stupid childish bastard."

Another boom. Those gray shapes had found their form: battleships on training, firing shells into Cape Wrath. Dangerous Area. Keep Out. War Games.

She reached out to me and clasped my hand. "Okay then," I whispered. Turned. Grabbed her throat and her hair. Swung her over. Let her drop. She didn't make a sound. Her hairband came off in my hand: I let it slip over my fingers. Something to remember her by.

"Suck on that, Jeff," I said, and sent an unexpected, fiery jet of vomit after her.

Trudging back, through the tears of my nausea, I saw him moving up the incline towards me. He paled as we neared each other, misting before my eyes so that, as we softly collided, the weight of his arrival became nothing but a sigh, settling against me. We went for a walk.

A long walk.

MacCreadle's Bike

Delicate Freddy shifted in bed; last night's letter spiraled to the floor.

He wanted to go to Pris, tell her things he'd scribbled in lager havoc but prose was awkward on his tongue; speaking love, a stuttering habit.

The walk took him ten minutes. Every morning the same, the only route. Its habitude had driven him to daydreams. Here's The Rope—where last New Year he was groped by a middle-aged woman reeking of Pernod. He'd been sickeningly aroused and at the smell of aniseed he was wont to switch off and reminisce. Pepper, Rifle and Sawdust knelt like buddhists at his approach.

"Delicate, we beseech thee, give us a sign of your immortality." Rifle's eyes exploded, his lenses making graceful arcs before raining on the window.

"Bad mood rising," quipped Pepper, hitching his jeans up around his hips. "Pris awaits apologies galore."

I will not cry…. Delicate even managed to smile when the top of Pepper's head sheafed to flame, crisping him black.

Dare you? he glared at Sawdust, but he was leading the others into Rifle's house, hungry for the kitchen.

Delicate aped their casual swagger, that looping of the shoulders, the slow puncture of cheeks as they sucked in sensually. They were razor adverts: clean panther sleek. Their clothes hung massively—beneath waxed barbell bodies. Delicate moved like starched shirts—pin-filled and cardboard-collared. He gave up the pretence when they reached the fridge. They were chugging Holsten and though he hated lager, he chugged too, lanced by bubble tears.

Seven Arches awaited them this evening. They'd take a case of Holsten, get wasted while oily walls swarmed around them. Sometimes, after the pubs shut, the girls came down to talk and help with the lager. Feeling amorous, Rifle usually took Della on to the embankment, returning awhile later hot and red, zipping himself up. Delicate thought Della extremely

141

beautiful save for the ragged scar encircling her throat like strange jewelry. Delicate, Pepper, Rifle and Sawdust were banned from all the pubs.

Twilight encroaching, they set off across the field. Pepper was singing "Purple Haze." Rifle and Sawdust walked shoulder to shoulder discussing breasts while Delicate traipsed in their Siamese shadow, watching the long grass pulverized beneath his feet. Maybe Pris would come down tonight and he'd hold her awkwardly while they watched the Liverpool-Manchester trains clatter by. She always ignored the others and talked to him. Once she'd even laughed at a joke he'd told her—about copper wire being invented by skinflints wrestling over a penny.

Through broken school goalposts the Arches came into view. A brook ran beneath one; sometimes they threw stones at moorhens and swans. Rifle had once puked on a mallard.

Sometimes, in the winter months, used syringes could be found by the piss-stained weeds. But this was summer and, oddly, the junkies' tools were out of season; now only lager cans marked out territory.

Sawdust struck a match to the grainy light, his face glittered and spun. "Delicate, you look delish in the dark. Love to love you baby." Laughter.

Delicate fished for a riposte, could only muster "Suck my dick," which he spoke halfheartedly, hoping they wouldn't hear. But they were already necking their beers. Delicate necked too. Soon, throats loosened by luke-warm Pils turned to safe ground: football, women, blackouts. Rifle leaned against the wall, told of his exploits with a vindaloo—how his arse had resembled the Japanese flag the day after. When they stopped laughing, all eyes fell to Delicate who was collecting hot wax on the ball of his thumb.

"So tell us about Pris, Freddy. What's got you on your knees beggin' forgiveness?"

Delicate leapt forward and carpet-bombed Pepper's body with punches. Pepper dropped paralyzed. "Leave it out, Pep," he moaned, as Pepper glanced round, grinning, running his fingers through the gold black perfection of hair.

"Leave it out, Pep!" he mocked, falsetto. "You turd. Tell us. Couldn't get it up?"

"Couldn't get what up?" guffawed Rifle.

Sawdust snorted lager through his nose. "Noodle-dick!"

Delicate's face flared in the sputtering light. The others slumped, clutching hearts, throats. Within seconds they were dead; minutes, they were rotting.

Rifle burped apocalyptically.

" 'Kay," said Delicate. "I'll tell you… she doesn't want to see me again."

"Well pass the fuckin' Kleenex."

"No... well," and here he thought his ruthlessness might gain currency. "I told her to eat shit an' die."

"You told Pris to... fuck that's cruel, Freddy. Better watch her old man doesn't find out. He'll beat shit out of you." Rifle looked disgusted. He cracked open another can of Holsten by way of consolation.

"You wanted to know." But he sounded pathetic, hurt.

"Yeah, well we got more important things to drink about. Y'better apologize. Pris is a lovely bitch." Sawdust turned his back on him.

Delicate drank deeply, reached the weak, watery depths of his can before groping for another. Oblivion would be a good state in which to confront Pris if she turned up.

In the distance, a motorbike roared at speed.

"Listen to that, Rifle," said Pepper, fingers hitched in his belt-loops, unconsciously adopting the coolest pose should the girls arrive. "Some thunder on the road tonight. What y'reckon? BMW?"

Rifle hissed his contempt. "Harley... Jeez, what a sweet, sweet sound. Lust for some wheels like that. I'd have two legends between my legs. Sweet."

Came the rustle of bushes and a drunken giggle. The girls arrived, looking for drinks and fumblings in the dark. Over the rim of his can, Delicate espied Pris moving with cautious grace by the flames, weaving slightly. She really killed those halves of Dry Blackthorn when she got going. She made a point of shunning Delicate; perched herself on Pepper's knee, laid her head against his neck. When she drank from his can, Delicate looked away, sought Della's grotesque beauty. She was French kissing Rifle already, pressed up against him like a layer of clothing. Her hand fluttered at his groin and Delicate felt a heat inside him; he wished he had Rifle's cocky finesse, his danger.

Della caught him watching, winked, licked her lips and whispered in Rifle's ear. They laughed and strolled away to the embankment. The other girls—Simone, and a girl Delicate didn't know—were writhing over Sawdust who trilled "Rock an' Roll" at the walls.

A candle went out. A train rumbled overhead, brakes squealing as it slowed for Warrington Central.

" 'Lo Freddy," whispered Pris.

To hide his tears he buried his face in the smoky warmth of her jacket. "Sorry Pris." Scrawled pledges danced at his eyes. "I didn't mean to speak to you like that. I... love you like there's no tomorrow."

Pris held him. "Hush m'baby. Give us a kiss."

Rifle came galloping in, his belt buckle jangling like a metal heartbeat. He was breathless. "MacCreadle's out!" he was shouting. Della came into the candle's shimmering light stuffing a breast into her bra. She was clearly angry that their games had been interrupted.

"Hey, Delicate! Stop maulin' Pris. D'you hear what I fuckin' said? I said MacCreadle's out!"

Delicate watched as the tunnel collapsed on Rifle's head... but he was tired of making them die. After all, they were the only friends he had. "Makes you say that?" His skin was drenched in Pris' perfume. He felt wonderful.

Rifle's eyes like golf balls. "Can't you hear? Listen."

It drifted to them like slow mist: the throaty growl of the Harley.

"Could be anyone, mate," said Pepper, his fingers shuffling under Simone's sweater.

"That's MacCreadle's bike, man. Swear. He's done his time. He's out!" Rifle took off towards the headlight stitching darkness.

"Who's MacCreadle?" asked Pris, but Delicate was shivering. He'd been just ten when they put MacCreadle away for some diabolical crime. His mother used to scare him by saying MacCreadle would come to slice him while he slept.

The motorbike was getting impossibly loud. When the headlight exploded across the walls like a strobe, Delicate's heart lurched. The engine's scream was cut leaving its cooling tick and Rifle whooping in the distance as he ran to catch up.

"MacCreadle," said Pepper.

"How goes it, Pep?" came a low, smooth voice. His face, heavily bearded, looked like ice in the candlelight. Pale, pale.

"When did you get out, Mac?" asked Sawdust, running a trembling hand over the motorbike's bulk. It seemed to glow.

"Mornin'. Seen much of Patti?"

"Patti went down to the Smoke last August, Mac," gasped Rifle, jogging into the tunnel.

MacCreadle grunted, then gestured at Delicate. "Fuck's that?"

"That's Delicate Freddy. He's okay. Bit of a geek, no harm." Pepper sounded apologetic.

"Delicate? Jesus. Looks the type of goon everybody rips the piss out of. That right?"

Delicate rose, trying—God, trying—to be cool. "Nah. The guys muck about with me. S'all fun." He tried to swagger but stopped when MacCreadle got off his bike. He was huge—a mass of branch limbs wrapped in denim and leather. The girls eyed him.

"Like you, man. Y'got balls to stick around." He sized him up for a while, nodding. His eyes were like hot tar, swooning in the flame.

"Ever ride a bike, Delicate?"

"Sure. I've ridden bikes."

"No." He placed spade hands on Delicate's shoulders, gently massaged.

His breath was Juicy Fruit. "I mean, have you ever ridden a bike?"

Delicate's eyes flashed to the Harley and MacCreadle smiled.

"N-no."

Delicate was led to the edge of the tunnel where they looked out at the night. He felt big, cocooned by power; their eyes were on him, awed and envious.

"You know, ridin' a Harley D is better than ridin' any woman. Any woman. You 'member that."

The keys felt like cold silver in his palm.

They watched Delicate mount up, disengage the stand and rest his foot on the kick start. Only MacCreadle and Pris were smiling. The others were a blur of open mouths. Then loudly, beautifully, Rifle yelled: "Go for it, Freddy!"

Delicate kicked down on the pedal and was astride a beast itching to bolt.

"Goose it, man," mouthed MacCreadle and Delicate obliged, filling the air with demons. In a slow arc, he rolled the Harley outside. King of the Road, Man of the Moment. I'll show them. He tore about the field, churning grass to pulp and hurtled to a skidding stop in front of them. But the bronco bucked and he found himself on his back looking at the stars. The laughter, like stilettos, pierced him to the core.

"…fuckin' nancy…."

"…like a granma…."

"…pussy rider, haw! haw!…."

MacCreadle picked him up. "Show 'er some respect, man. Don't treat her like a toy—she'll kill you."

Delicate saw MacCreadle mashed beneath a car… but no. He couldn't see it. Not this one. Not MacCreadle.

He clambered back on the bike, hating the tears and laughter; opened the throttle, scrambled up the embankment to the train tracks.

"Watch me now!" he screeched, blasting between rails, juddering like a tangled puppet.

The tracks hissed and sang with arrivals. Delicate closed his eyes to the night, felt only the lunatic rush of air in his face, the hellish thunder of MacCreadle's bike. Sirens and screams heralded respect. *Watch me now.*

KNOWN

Povey watched white paint unfurl in chains along riveted steel shanks bordering the tracks. The Network South-East from Lee had been late again this morning and there had been no unoccupied seats. He'd stood hunched against the door, slow fire moving through his back, looking out at a colorless skyline as veils of rain hung motionless against the thin wash of buildings.

One word—*KNOWN*—endlessly repeated, blurred by broken obliques of moisture on the windows. The capital letters formed harsh angles which bracketed the soft middle "O." He couldn't decide whether it was the result of a brainless ego, or an attempt to impart something more significant. Whatever, he felt drawn to the uniformity of the letters as they dogged the train across Hungerford Bridge.

Only since leaving the center of London in favor of commuting in from the limbo of its outer districts had Povey begun to appreciate the ingenuity of its engineers and construction workers. Any available space was filled in with new flats, shops, entertainment arcades. Staying with his uncle, in a grim conurbation on the South Circular, he yearned to be in the heart of the city once more, to feel its pulse through his feet. He was looking forward to viewing the flat that evening. It seemed to call at him from over the rooftops, across the miles, like a desperate request from a distant lover.

Povey walked the Strand to Aldwych where he turned left. He liked the rain, the way it cleansed the buildings and turned them into glittering spires and domes. He imagined the city's detritus being washed into the Thames. The rats drowning, the pissy alleyways and door recesses polished. All those channels and creases scrubbed clean.

But not the graffiti. Somehow it clung, tenacious as tattoos. Even in this fresh, burnished light, the crude slogans and signatures looked vital and new.

At work, the feeling fell away from him, as if this office was somehow insulated against the banal miracles of the city. He discussed layouts with Lynn and blithely complimented every letters page and fashion spread she showed him. He wondered if his apathy shone through. Lynn was the editor of a "secret" magazine project. She had contacted Povey via a chief sub-editor from the parent company. He had done some work for her last summer and even though it was interminably dull—subbing real-life tragedy stories offset by "humorous" articles and tips to make household chores that much bearable—it paid well. He'd leapt at the chance of five weeks' employment, an opportunity to be nestled in London's center, even though Lynn's overtures to him on the phone prior to his first day were almost comical.

"So can we book you until the end of March?" she had asked, having explained that this was all hush-hush and that he would need to sign a document guaranteeing his lips to be sealed.

"Certainly," he had said, "what will I be doing?"

"Can't tell you," she had replied, "it's a secret."

It turned out the magazine was a downmarket version of their market leader. Called *Chinwag,* it was aimed at a teenage readership, hence the appearance of words such as "shag" and "willy" and "cum." The problem pages were a lifesaver amid grim copy-proofing and fact-checking. *MEN ONLY* screamed the banner in 108pt Soupbone. *My little man bends the wrong way… am I abnormal?* And the Top Tips: *Clean venetian blinds with L-shaped pieces of crusty bread.*

They were based at the top of a building in Holborn, in an office big enough to host a game of five-a-side. Golf. Along with Jill and Lynn, there was Yvonne, on features, and Sally and Fran designing the pages. Friday lunch times they nipped down to the Sun Tavern on Long Acre and talked about dreadful magazines they had worked on in the past. All the same as this one, save the name.

An hour or so into his work, Povey received a phone call from Sutton, his best friend. He was in the Smoke for a few days, visiting from the southwest, but he sounded strangely on edge and asked Povey if he could meet him that evening—he'd be in the pub from about three-thirty. By four o'clock, the skittish nature of Sutton's call had infected him and, in a mild panic, he went to the toilet, affecting a pained look and rubbing his stomach. In the mirror, he was surprised to find that he did not look well. The color had fled from his cheeks, giving him a greasy complexion. His eyes seemed to have sunk away from the flesh of their sockets: red filled in the gaps. He felt as though the real version of him hadn't caught up yet, that he was just a ghost, a sliver of the real Clive Povey. The real Clive Povey was stuck on a train staring at the codes and tag-lines sprayed on the portals to the capital.

"Lynn?" he said, cracking his voice just right. Jill, the assistant editor looked up too, which was fine by Povey. He knew she liked him and the concern that darkened her face told him that he'd pitched this correctly, even though he was only partly acting. "I'm going to have to go home. Sorry. I feel dreadful."

Lynn looked aggrieved that she was losing him, clearly of the opinion that freelances sold their souls when they agreed to work and had to sit at their desks even if they were to suffer an arterial bleed.

"Okay," she sighed, finally. And then: "Hope you feel better, tomorrow," with a smile that didn't reach her eyes. Hardly reached her lips either.

Povey limped back to his workstation and closed the file he had been using before copying it back onto the server from his hard drive. The dummy lay-outs he returned to their trays.

"See you tomorrow," he said. Sally looked at him acidly as if he had just stolen her plan for the day.

In the lift, Povey felt stitches of guilt about bunking off early and stared at the graffiti on the doors. He hadn't taken his lunch hour, so that supported him in mitigation but didn't stop him feeling like a school truant. They needed him; there was no need to worry about being sacked.

He seemed to descend too far, further than usual, but when the doors opened, there was the sliding glass entrance and beyond, Kingsway's mad rush. Although it was barely half past four, the sky had blackened and the rain angling in over the forbidding roofs showed no sign of stopping. Bruised light loitered behind the thinnest junctions between clouds; the streetlamps were off and the cars on the road drove blind.

He plugged his ears with a pair of headphones and depressed the play button on his Walkman. A grim and epic loop of sound instantly drew something immanent from the deflated sky, the constant traffic. Holborn Tube was closed off; a huge scrum of commuters stood with their backs to him, staring bovinely at the concertina gates and the ticket barrier beyond. Two fire engines ticked over in the center of Kingsway, lights flashing.

Povey made a series of turns into ever-diminishing streets—High Holborn, Southampton Place, Bloomsbury Way, Bury Street, Little Russell Street, Streatham Street—until the traffic's voice was toned down to an asthmatic gurgle. A crocodile of diners spilled out of Wagamama, thickening his sense of claustrophobia. Snazzy fucks in soft leather pants and white tee-shirts and linen jackets. Fifty-pound haircuts. A woman fingering her pearl necklace while talking to some pin-striped goatee who made expansive gestures with his Nokia. Everyone seemed to be traveling somewhere and never arriving. He brushed past and ghosts followed: CKOne, Fahrenheit, Dolce & Gabbana. Stuff he recognized from the peel-off strips in his magazines.

He caught the Tube at Tottenham Court Road and traveled north, imagining his colleagues belittling him behind his back. His lack of spine. Such an insular man, a cold man. He bristled, imagining them, and jolted the arm of a woman reading a newspaper. She clucked her tongue and rattled the pages. He remembered acutely the embarrassment he'd known as a child when everyone's attention had been reluctantly drawn to him. He pressed himself against the seat, reining in his claustrophobia as it tried to deal with their distance underground, the way the train was just big enough for the tunnel, the optimum exploitation of space.

At Kentish Town he surfaced, gulping air. At the Tube exit he watched the rain splinter the white and red exchange of car lights as people trundled home. A bus crawled by, its windows misted with condensation. Dark lumps filled every square of light. Each seat taken, every foot of Tarmac used, shoes secured pavement slabs as far as he could see.

The nest of lights on the underbelly of a jet shone through the barrier of cloud; through his feet he felt the chunter of trains worming north and south. By the time he crashed through the doors of the Academy Rooms, a hundred feet away, he was exhausted. It was as though there was no space for him to move. Every umbrella had wanted to do for his eyes; every briefcase clouted his knees.

He found Sutton squeezed onto a settee near the pool tables. He signaled a pint. Povey bought drinks and moved unsteadily towards his friend, casting a glance at the pool tables where a woman was playing a leather-clad boyfriend. Behind them, a huge screen formed a backdrop: footballers glistening under floodlights in a derby match.

"Hello Frank," said Povey, "have a drink."

Conversation tumbled around them. Povey perched on the edge of a stool that was being used as a footrest by a heavy piece of beef wearing sunglasses and combat fatigues. He heard the word "known" used twice in quick succession by different people, and tried not to let his anxiety show.

The girl at the pool table pirouetted around her opponent, tipping him over with her thigh as he lined up his shot.

"You sounded a little bit wired when you called me this morning," said Povey. "What's up?"

Sutton flattened his lips together and shrugged. "I'm having a bad time of it, Clive. I needed to see someone I know. Someone who would look *at* me instead of *through* me. Jesus, one of those days I've had, when everyone tries to walk over you like you're not there." He took a long swig of his pint. Povey wasn't sure how many of the empty glasses arranged around him were his, but he bet it was a fair few.

"Another thing," said his friend, staring blearily at the football match. "Perhaps the main thing. I tried to do a few things yesterday—simple things," he huffed what might have been sour laughter. "Sort myself a loan and find out why I wasn't sent a voting form for the local by-election. Same response on both occasions. Didn't know anything about me, couldn't track down anything to do with my history. They were very apologetic but it sounded like they were talking to someone who wasn't there. Who didn't exist." Sutton leaned over and whispered the last three words conspiratorially.

"Come on, Frank, you're just having a shit day. I'll send you an application form to join the club. You might have to hang on a while though, there's a fuck of a long waiting list."

Sutton was shaking his head now. "No, Clive," he slurred, "you are not yet in full possession of the facts. Today I opened the newspaper and found this bastard."

He passed Povey a crumpled copy of that day's *Guardian*. Sutton had ringed a section and Povey had to put his glass down before he poured it into his lap. Below the strapline *Death Notices* he read:

SUTTON, Frank Stanley died sadly on 31st March 19— aged 34. Fondly remembered by many friends and family. Beloved father of Gillian. Funeral at Broadclyst Parish Church, Exeter, 24th April, 2 p.m. Family, flowers.

"My God, Frank. But this is a joke, surely?"

"Yeah, I'm splitting my sides over it."

"This is awful," Povey said. "I'm really sorry. What are you going to do? I mean, you must go to the funeral, sort this out. Imagine their faces!"

Sutton seemed to have withdrawn from the animation of the crowd and Povey blinked to bring his edges back into focus. Too much smoke and heat. He watched the girl playing pool as she appraised the table. Standing over her shot, bouclée grip, her right breast collapsed around her cue like the slow unhinging of a snake's jaws as it envelops a rabbit's hip. She looked up at him through a dirty blonde fringe and took her tongue for a trip around the waxed O of her mouth. Flecks of white ringed her jumper sleeve.

"Not sure if that's a good idea, Clive," mused Frank. "I might turn up and spoil everyone's day. But I suppose there are some advantages. If I don't exist, I can't be harmed can I?"

Povey smiled. "I suppose you're right. Strangest thing I've ever seen though."

"Right." He drifted into his own thoughts and Povey had to reach out to steady him when it seemed he was about to lean back against a couple reading *Time Out*.

"I don't know how you stick it in this place, Clive, I really don't. Everyone I see here looks pasty and frightened. They look like… you know those transfers we had as kids? You rubbed them with a pencil and they came off the tracing paper? Well it's like that. People having their essence crushed out of them as they enter the capital so that all that remains are features, the husk."

"Yes, Frank," Povey smiled, patting his hand. "Have another drink, won't you? I have to go and view a flat." Povey tried to affect nonchalance as he waved goodbye to his friend and forced his way into the teeming night but his hands were shaking. *I know what you mean*, he should have said. But he was worried that Frank's left-field logic might insinuate itself. He felt vulnerable and unsupported. He didn't like the drifting aspect to his life, the way he could sometimes believe he was a ghost trapped on the conditioning thermals of a dull prior existence, doomed to live every day as an exact replica of the one that went before. Commuting now took up so much of his time that his life seemed to be truncating. Every day was like standing on a succession of edges. His nerves were permanently tensed and shrieking: a slew of violins in a Bernard Herrmann score.

It was happening to everyone around him, this thing they labeled routine but which deserved a less innocent name.

Rain had slapped the city awake. It pinched her cheeks and cleared snot from her nostrils; showered the rheum from tired eyes, rouged her cheeks. London in a night-black cocktail dress: sleek and sexy and switched on. Eschewing the bus, Povey walked up Fortess Road past tired shops flagged with hopeful FOR SALE signs. Accommodation blocks sat squat in the misting rain; pale squares of light played hopscotch into the sky. Ceaselessly motile, the traffic zipped closed the tracts of the road, barring his view of the opposite pavement. He wondered if he should have asked Sutton to come with him.

Povey had received the details of the property—a converted one-bedroom flat—on Crayford Road that morning. The thought of moving back to north London spurred him on, despite his fatigue and the prospect of an awkward trip back to Lewisham. He paced the orange-blue street to Tufnell Park Tube where he turned onto its namesake road leading down to Holloway. The fifth turning on the right, according to the estate agent, was Anson Road. First left off that was Crayford Road. He wished he'd remembered to bring his *A-Z*.

The neon streetlamps fizzed, teasing his shadow. Broad streets spliced with the arterial road; Povey counted them off. It took longer than he'd anticipated, the blocks of houses between each turn-off proving to be substantial. Maybe he'd miscounted because this, the fifth, was Carleton Road, not Anson. He spent the next twenty minutes trying his luck down various side streets until, by chance, he found Anson Road. But the first turning on the left was not Crayford, it was Dalmeny Avenue. The first left at the other end of Anson, just in case he'd got it arse about tit, was Melvyn Close.

Okay, he calmed himself, *you're late now. Stop panicking and just ask someone.*

But there was nobody to ask. Povey found his way back to the main road, intending to hail the first taxi he saw when he spotted an old man with a carrier bag walking on the other side of the street.

"Excuse me!" Povey called, trotting across the road. The man lowered his head, bringing the rim of his hat across his face, and hurried away.

Another man came out of his front door, saw Povey and hesitated, as if caught red-handed.

"Do you know where Crayford Road is?" asked Povey, before the man could retreat.

"No, sorry," he said, "I don't know this area." He slipped back behind the door.

Povey stared after him, confounded by what was happening. He returned along Anson Road, hoping he'd made a mistake and Crayford Road would reveal itself to him although he was late for the viewing now and the occupants might have gone out for the evening.

He rejoined Carleton Road and asked a woman wearing earphones if she could help. She seemed affronted, as if the earphones were a signal not to be disturbed, but waved vaguely in the direction of Tufnell Park Road with an umbrella speckled with white. Without bothering to thank her, Povey stalked away. It was as if he'd failed some test that prospective home-owners had to take before being accepted into the neighborhood.

Now he could see how the estate agents had got it wrong. They had mistaken Anson Road as the junction road with the main drag, when in fact it forked off Carleton. The fools. Here was Crayford Road, first turning off Carleton Road. *Carleton.* He dug in his bag, which was beginning to put a strain on his shoulder, and pulled out the property details. He underscored their false directions savagely. If he lost this flat it would be down to them. Should he hurry, he might catch the incumbent residents before they went out.

Povey ran past an estate on his right, all low, red-brick balconies and strip lighting. There was a figure moving slowly in the stairwell's dark pools. Povey glimpsed a whitish inverted cone flicker past the frosted glass where a head ought to be. Then it was forgotten as he reached the row of Victorian houses where he might set up and be happy. The light was on; his hopes soared. A woman's voice crackled over the intercom when he rang the bell. He tried to apologize when the buzzing of the lock drowned him out.

On the second floor he smoothed his hair and was attempting to dry his face with the sodden sleeve of his mac when the door opened.

"I'm glad to catch you in," he said. "My name's Clive Povey. I'm sorry I'm late."

The woman blocking the wedge of light stepped back, although her eyes seemed to be fixed on a spot behind him. As he stepped through, her face set in a basic mode of recognition.

"Sorry," she said, "the stairwell is so dark. I didn't see you for a second." She led him into the living room where a swarthy man was drinking from a huge mug. Povey raised a hand and the man swiveled his eyes just as steam from his drink clouded the lenses of his spectacles.

"As you can see," said the woman, who, Povey now saw, was heavily pregnant, "it's quite small."

I wouldn't say that, he suddenly wanted to blurt, and clamped his teeth against a shock of laughter. It was very hot in the room; every bar of an electric fire glared. On a stuttering television, a news reader told of a Royal visit to Kuala Lumpur. It must be the faded screen that caused the cuffs of the waving Prince to appear stained white.

"Through here," said the woman, "is the kitchen, which as you can see, is a bit tired but there's a surprising amount of storage space. The bathroom's just next door. Don't worry about the cracks, they're superficial. Nothing a dab of Polyfilla can't handle. And here," she gestured with her hand; the other rested against her tummy, "is the bedroom."

Giddy with the warp and tilt of the flat, Povey ducked into a bizarre room that seemed to taper away from him in terms of height and width; not so much the Cabinet as the Cubby-hole of Dr. Caligari. The far end was little more than a sharply-angled recess. To sleep in this room, it would be necessary to quickly evolve a needle-shaped head. He tried to mask his disappointment and mumbled something about being in touch. The television mumbled something about "suicide" and "train delays" as the door snicked shut on him.

Outside, the rain was muscling more intensely against the houses. It stung his face as he returned to the main road. The figure in the stairwell was across the street from him now, the cone shape revealing itself as the peaked hood of a gray track suit. He was spraying white paint from an aerosol onto the side of a black van and had got as far as the middle 'O' before stopping, his head twitching at the sound of Povey's gritting footsteps. Povey felt breath snatched from his lungs as the figure began to turn. He did not want to hang around to see the vandal's face. He sprinted towards the road, trying to ignore the tattoo of following feet.

"Taxi!" he yelled, hurtling into the path of a black cab. The driver seemed to take an eternity to set off for Charing Cross once Povey had blundered into the back seat. As soon as they were away, he chanced a look behind him but the drenched street had diffused the light spilling from the lamps to such an extent that the entire avenue was concealed by a core of liquid fire.

He lay in bed listening to the uncertain squish of valves in his chest. It was hard to believe there was any blood in his veins for the coldness, the enervation he felt. He was scared to close his eyes in case he faded completely away. At least while he was awake he exerted some kind of physicality, despite the illusion of the blankets reducing his body to two dimensions.

His uncle was in the bedroom next to him; a muffled radio play moved through the wall by Povey's ear. Over dinner his uncle had twice looked up startled, as if surprised to see his nephew sitting across from him. His uncle told him, as Povey had flapped his way out of his soaked clothes in the bathroom, that a body had been found by the deltoid spread of tracks leading into the depot at King's Cross. There had been some consternation when the authorities had been unable to find its head, his uncle explained, somewhat tactlessly Povey thought. Initially, they believed it to be a murder. But then someone had discovered the head rammed deep inside the chest cavity, which suggested that the victim had been kneeling on all fours, facing the oncoming train. A witness had since confirmed this theory.

Povey slept fitfully until his uncle brought a cup of tea in for him at 7 a.m. He had already decided not to go in to work. Rather than wait until Lynn was in the office, he rang and left a message on the answerphone. If they wanted to find someone else to do the work, he couldn't lose any more sleep over it than he was already.

After breakfast, tired of his uncle's gory speculation as he scanned the newspapers and watched the morning news, Povey opted to go for a walk. He negotiated the lethal rush of traffic on the South Circular and headed north, the wink of Canary Wharf like a beacon ahead of him, pulling him into the heart of the city.

He reached Blackheath half an hour later and wandered without much conviction among the shops and across the fields where, even in the rain, kite enthusiasts attempted to launch their vivid array of wings, boxes and scimitars. At least here there was space to think. On three occasions he caught sight of that simple, wise word: an expression of vigilance or the boast of an omniscient entity. He saw it sprayed on the coping stones of a bridge wall, on the back of a road sign, a bench. Almost everyone he saw was streaked with white. What was going on? Was it paint? Those that weren't daubed seemed to be like windmills without sails; all purpose drained from them. He saw faces in windows gazing at the totemic needle of Canary Wharf, flesh etiolated by a lack of association. Povey sat on a bench, numb to the seepage of rain through his trousers, and tried to remember what the word "community" meant. Terrible thoughts were gravitating towards him since he'd heard about the suicide. He had once believed that the culmination of all his love and ambition would manifest itself in his nurturing of a child. But the compulsion behind this need had mutated recently. It might be because he had failed to establish any precious links with the women he met, but he suspected it was more a crisis of identity. The fear that he might look into the mirror one day and not recognize the face staring out came from the same black source as the voice persuading him that giving birth was nothing more than the laying down of an eventual death sentence.

The rain had stopped. He watched the band of mist retreat across the greensward and tear the wrapper of shade from the towers ranged across the capital. His jacket smelled musty and his shoes rested in a thin gruel of pigeon droppings. Maybe he would feel better if he took a long bath and rang some more estate agents. Invigorated with a plan, he caught the bus back to his uncle's flat. There, he took the local paper and had a long soak, ringing possible flats with a red pen.

By the time his uncle returned from market, Povey was clean-shaven and dressed in a fresh suit, a list of addresses and accompanying times clasped in his hand. At the top, enclosed in a box, he'd written: *Clive Povey—potential accommodation.*

"I'm off flat-hunting," he said, as his uncle pushed by, dropping an *Evening Standard* on his armchair. Povey saw the words: "TRAGEDY OF LOST SOUL."

"Right you are, lad," his uncle said, picking at a blotch of white on his coat. "Although, by the look of you, you might as well be off courting Royalty." He laughed thickly and set about making a pot of tea.

Povey was tempted to read the lead story in the newspaper, but he would be late for his first appointment. He trotted to the station and made the platform just as the train pulled up. At this time of day it was empty and Povey enjoyed the luxury of sitting wherever he pleased. In the aisle, the pattern of cleats from a pair of trainers took a journey in white paint towards the front carriage.

Soon, he was spotting fresh instances of the graffito. Now it was in black paint, now red. Sometimes it appeared with a suffix: a colon or an arrow flying away from the final 'N' as though an urgency had developed in the author's craftsmanship, a need to convey the promise of something to follow.

It lifted Povey. His reading of the signs came as an epiphany, much like the sudden break in the weather. For the first time in weeks, his flesh seemed to sing and his nerves were attuned to every twitch of his clothes, each minute change of tack in the breezes that swept through the window vents.

Approaching London Bridge, he saw, plastered against the brickwork of a defunct printers, Known's acme of achievement. An oblique of lemon-lime letters, each a foot high, parallel to the fire escape's slant. The evidence of such industry seemed to match the sprawl of the city and the commitment to obliterate the concept of space. Povey had to believe that the word existed elsewhere in the country, and for many other people, not just the glut of girders and bridge panels here or the isolated jottings north and south of the city center. He wasn't sure he could cope with the possibility that the word was for his benefit alone.

At the terminus he passed through to the station concourse and checked the clock against his watch. He had half an hour to get to Finsbury Park. There wasn't much of a wait for a northbound train. Quick change at Warren Street for the Victoria Line and he'd be at the first address on his list with time to kill.

He sat opposite a man in orange tartan bondage pants and wrapa-round shades. He was reading the *Standard* and Povey stared for a long time at the photograph on the front page. It showed, beneath the same headline he'd read at his uncle's flat, a picture of railway lines. To the right was a cluster of policemen and railway staff in reflective clothing. To the left, stark and arresting, a white blanket failed to cover a body: its left arm poked out from beneath, the hand upturned and relaxed. It wasn't this that shocked Povey, nor was it the faint but legible word punctuating the containers on a goods train as it traveled out of the borders of the shot. It was the inset picture of Sutton.

Povey couldn't move his eyes from the page. When finally, the man folded his newspaper and stood up, Povey was left with the negative flare of the words on his retina, a red shriek of truth to jolt him from the black-and-white sobriety of the newsprint. A streak of white paint flashed before him as the train slowed for the platform; he'd overshot. This was Camden Town.

In no mood for the task he'd set out to achieve, Povey took the escalator, barely feeling the other passengers as they barged past him. On Camden High Street he was sandwiched by two men running to catch the same bus. His notes were knocked from his hand into a puddle. He watched as his name was washed away before moving off towards the Lock. Dusk was mottling the sky over the canal. He plodded down to the towpath, ignoring the street vendors as they plied him with stained glass light bulbs and kaleidoscopic knitwear. The buildings hunched their shoulders against him. Blocks of life piled on top of each other. No space left on the ground, take to the skies. High-rise and basement, purpose-built and luxury, maisonette and houseboat. Real-life soap in length and width and depth. If Povey had deviated by half a dozen steps from any roads he'd walked upon today he'd have ended up on somebody else's property.

Further along the towpath, where the bridge on Oval Road passed over the canal, a hushed gathering moved against each other like a knot of snakes. He saw a gray hood slipping swiftly in between the limbs, keeping the crowd's energy motivated. As he approached, he heard the people hissing, as though condemning a theatrical villain. But then he realized what it really was. He truffled around the drifts of litter at the towpath's edge and grasped a thick blade of broken glass, in case he needed to defend himself. He moved forward and prepared himself for a battle against the tangle of bodies as they vied for position in front of the wall; there wasn't much virgin space left on the brickwork. But as he tensed himself to enter the fray, the limbs unlocked and moved away from him, allowing him passage. Eyes assessed him, gracing him with a respectful nod to his physicality. His foot kicked against an aerosol and he bent to pick it up. For the first time in what seemed like weeks, he felt his mouth trying on a smile. Was there real blood surging through his veins after all? Might there be a portion of this tired, knowing city that could be his?

He clenched the glass and readied himself with the aerosol as white palms fed him to the wall. One way or the other, by God, he would reaffirm himself.

THE SUICIDE PIT

Fullbrook closed the door behind him and let out a rattling breath to compete with the rush of hailstones in the street. He had tried to get home without looking up too often, afraid of what—or rather, who—he might see.

He eased off his greatcoat and poured a large slug of vodka from the bottle on his fridge, took it through to the living room where he lit the gas fire and tried to lose himself in its warmth for a while. Even here, in the sanctity of his own flat, with its trifles and fripperies and baubles—all designed to comfort and relax—he could not escape the suffocating conviction that something was coming for him, eager to sniff him out and snuff him out. Dying in this flat, he realized in a surge of panic, would most likely mean a week or two would go by before he was missed. His time at work was so lacking in structure that his colleagues would not query his absence, unless an emergency occurred, and the Corpse—as the Subterra staff liked to call the rail network—had not seen any unpleasant action for some months now. The knowledge chilled him but he had been alone for long enough that such fears did not sadden him.

Fullbrook ran himself a bath and managed to cook a little something to eat although he was not very hungry. In the swirls of hot water, the sauce for his chicken, the edges of his mind drew him towards the persistent, grueling urban memories of recent nights, when his feet plashed through puddles stained with fuel, or brushed through frozen verges where a cross section of old snow might tell the story of a town's pollution in its grimy striations. It was on one of these unvarying streets, these interminable walks to or from work that he had hooked into a portion of madness that he could not let go.

It had been a foul night. Rain seemed to hang like a net, coating him rather than assaulting him. Haloes of streetlamps collapsed against the friable borders of concrete flanking the roads that snaked towards the city center creating a light that was mistrustful and edgy. Fullbrook's was a route he followed often, one that was packed with traffic and people at all hours of the day. Sometimes he would start, believing he had seen someone he recognized further along the street or crossing the road to catch a bus, but then the feeling would recede, especially when it dawned on him that the people he thought he saw—Mr. Wheaton from the council tax office, for example; or Mrs. Willoughby, a lollipop lady— had been dead for a number of years. But these impossible coincidences persisted, involving living people too, who, because of absence from the country or incapacitation, were no more likely to be traipsing the streets than their dead counterparts. Eventually, like the lack of pity he afforded himself over his marital status, his observations failed to impinge upon him. He explained such episodes away, one way or another: The nature of his job fueled his visions: he was tired; the light was too unreliable.

And then, one day last week, he saw himself.

He had been on a bus heading home from the shops in the midst of another soggy December evening. The park was a low sweep of straining black wetness and the pavement shifted constantly with water and light. Up ahead, through a little circle of relief in the condensation masking the window, Fullbrook spotted his own jacket—a dark red corduroy affair (the very one he was wearing now!) moving beneath the streetlamps, its wearer drawn into it, hunched against the foul weather as he strode north. He turned violently in his seat as the bus pulled level, causing an old black woman to cluck as her bags were jostled, but Fullbrook was too rapt to notice. He smeared a sleeve across the glass, which served only to render his view more confusing, but he managed to make out the soft brown briefcase slung over the shoulder, the mad froth of black hair.

Fullbrook had bounded down the stairs, bellowing for the driver to let him off, which he did at the next stop, some two hundred yards further along the road. Leaning into the lashing rain, unconsciously drawing himself into a mirror image of his doppelgänger, Fullbrook shambled back in the direction he had come. He saw his double fade against the rain like hot breath into a cold morning until, with about fifty yards between them, Fullbrook found himself bearing down on an empty pavement.

His walk to work in the mornings ended at the point where most began their journeys. Fullbrook was a death monitor for the Blue Vein and had wangled a small office at the station nearest his home. It was not work that he enjoyed but it meant that he was left alone most of the time— unless there was an accident. Most days he spent transferring old, typed records onto the computer archive. The lion's share of accidents he had to report on involved what the platform announcers politely referred to as "passengers on the track." Fullbrook would have to travel to the station in question, ensuring the platform was evacuated so that the emergency services could do their thing. He had been briefed by his bosses that part of his work ought to involve recording the incidents and so he ported an old Canon around with him and a battered Metz flash.

Now, as he breached the turnstiles at the station's entrance, he nodded at Haslam and Liptrott and hurried into his office. There was a phone message from his superior—Tate—asking why his weekly report was late; and a purple fax curling from its machine like a strangled tongue. It bore statistics on the tunnels outside his jurisdiction—all of them boasting better records than his own. Someone had switched on his coffee pot, for which he was grateful, although he always felt uneasy, soiled even, when he knew other people had been in his office before him.

Fullbrook booted up the ageing Apple Mac on his desk and accessed the hard drive. For the next hour he scanned in and subbed handwritten statements or carbon copies of typed reports. He absorbed the dry reportage without a quake of emotion, the monotony of work taking him out of himself to the extent that the lines about decapitations, arterial bleeds, eviscerated torsos became nothing but words massaged by technology into a refined form of chain gang toil.

Just before lunch, a warning light at Jute Street flashed on the wall map. Six stops from here. Fullbrook acknowledged the alarm and headed for the lift to the sister tube—an access tunnel closed to the public that would deliver him alongside the emergency site in minutes. On the way, he checked his camera was loaded and tested the flash, ignoring Henna, one of the ticket officers who never failed to give him a look that was all: *You sick fuck.*

The single carriage transports ran without a driver, launched when the doors were closed from the inside. Fullbrook took his seat as the train jerked away from the platform, successfully quelling the familiar swell of claustrophobia in his chest by focusing on what might be in store for him. It could not be any worse than what he had been keying into his Mac all morning, of that he was certain.

He was wrong.

The job over, he sought refuge from the rain in the library, loath to go back to his flat where every drawer and cupboard might spill a spur to his remembering the last few hours. Fullbrook ducked past the queue of members waiting to register their books, averting his eyes from the doughy rank of features floating by him. *Every face tells a story,* he thought, ensconcing himself in a corner. *Never judge a book by its cover.*

The camera in his lap burned with the dark secrets its eye had recorded. He doubted he would ever be able to develop this film.

There had been two policemen on the platform. One of them had been sick into his helmet and was sitting on a bench sipping tea. There was a host of paramedics, some standing by the platform entrance—barred by criss-cross lengths of yellow police tape—some down on the track in front of the grime-streaked snout of the train. Its driver was still in the cab, hands covering his face. A policewoman sat next to him, coaxing information.

Fullbrook had unsheathed his camera and plugged in the flash before dropping onto the track, safe in the knowledge that the live rail would have been switched off as soon as the accident occurred. But from that point on, things didn't follow the script. The guy in front of the train, for example, was still alive when he clearly had no right to be.

Fullbrook took a few pictures, used now to the withering glances of the uniforms. The flash popped and made a thin, frying sound as the tubes regenerated. Every time the flash was triggered, shadows scampered into the scarred arc of the ceiling and the eyelids of the man on the track flickered as though irritated. Something was wrong but Fullbrook couldn't work out what it was.

"What happened?" Fullbrook asked one of the paramedics who was busy drawing morphine into a syringe. A big syringe.

"Daft bastard," he spat, skimming Fullbrook's ID tag before returning to his task. "Jumped in front of the train, wouldn't you know. Only, the driver's a bit tasty in the reflex department. Slams on, bloke gets hit but not enough to pull his plug out. And now he's in one sod of a mess."

"Oh shit," hissed Fullbrook, finally noticing. The victim's legs had become trapped in the deep nearside gulley between the rails—the suicide pit—and at the moment of impact, the top half of his body had been twisted round while his legs stayed put. If he looked down, Fullbrook realized, faint-headed, he would be able to contemplate his own arse. "And he's alive," he managed.

"Not for long," the medic muttered. "All his internal organs are twisted and mushed to fuck. The moment that pressure is released, he'll bleed to death internally. Drown in his own blood. Tasty, hey? But we've got to try. What else do you do?"

The victim had revived somewhat; another paramedic was hunched over him, presumably trying to explain his plight. While he talked, the man waggled his head, tongue lolling as he tried to mouth some words. His eyes were fixed on Fullbrook's all the while.

Fullbrook took pictures of the train, the track; made notes of distances and times. He asked the policewoman for the bare bones of her interview with the driver. Throughout, his mind was on the victim who he could hear gently gargling through the Morphean haze that had been pumped into him. The way his body was wrenched at its center. Oh God. His spinal cord must surely have been severed; that must account for the lack of screaming. He felt no pain but he knew he was going to die.

Squeezing off a few more shots, Fullbrook edged closer to the man, who ignored the medics crowded around him and seemed more eager than ever to speak to the photographer, to impart some wisdom before he died. The medics began to lever him free. Just as was predicted, the moment he was loose, a great glut of blood fled from his mouth. Fullbrook turned away, trying to allow him a shred of dignity, and heard the words, bubbling through the rush of his life's liquid.

"I saw myself. You know it. You—"

"—wouldn't happen to have the right time, would you?"

He emerged from the shield of his book to find her barely able to meet his gaze; a slight woman in a black leather jacket, scuffed by time and overuse. She seemed to recoil when he put his book down, then she said: "Forget it, it doesn't matter."

He watched her move away, pretending to be interested in a row of crime novels, fingers slithering across their spines, but then she abruptly strode towards the exit and, beyond the growing queue of people, he heard her boots ring out on the tile floor as she ran for the door. Something in her controlled desperation found a resonance with his own. He followed her.

Late afternoon. The pavements rain-glossed and painted sodium orange. Her hair was blonde but it had darkened where it was plastered against her collar. She walked stiffly, her hands invisible, tucked into the sleeves of her jacket. Fullbrook watched only her, the nervous, jittery way she paused to look in shop windows or waited at junctions for the lights to change in her favor. She gave off an air of someone trying very hard to appear normal. People passed him by; featureless orbs of white and black and he was grateful for her uncertain target to draw his attention away from its usual sport.

She moved off the main road, angling down to the river where she unwrapped a packet of sandwiches, devouring them as she walked, her eyes fixed on the torpid ooze of water. There was a bridge up ahead and she walked that too, losing her shape a little to the fingers of mist reaching up from the river. At the other side, which marked the beginning of a less inviting portion of the city, she swept into an alleyway that brought her to a street market. He was convinced that were she able to get by without ever having to shop for provisions, she would, but she needed to stock up now. Fullbrook watched as she loaded brown paper parcels with fruit and exchanged a handful of coins for waxy wrappings of offal and fish. Quickly she carted this away in a box, choosing not to haggle like many of the shadows jostling with her for position beneath the market's mighty canopy.

She took off, heading deeper into the mire of ginnels and housing blocks. The streetlamps here were like teeth in an inner city mouth; one in every two or three was out. Wishing he had a hat, Fullbrook pulled the collars of his coat up around his ears and delved into the warren after her. Almost immediately, he was aware of a greater pressure of people although if anything, the streets here, though narrower, were less densely populated. He attributed this vertiginous quirk to his mild claustrophobia but then he sensed the figures move behind the plastic streamers of a shop's loading bay, or behind the smoky, greasy window of a hell-bitten drinking hole, or jinking behind ruined curtains in the estates and maisonettes that cluttered this quarter—and his fears were founded.

He caught up with her in a concrete clearing rescued visually by a solitary stunted tree and a child's scarf flapping on a roundabout that wouldn't still. She was crying, hunched over a concrete block that might or might not have been intended as a seat.

He approached quietly, lest he frighten her, his blood quick and fretful in his ears. She heard him nonetheless, snapping her head up like a startled deer. Her sobbing ceased. Into the silence that sprang from her like an assault, he said: "It's a quarter to seven."

In the following weeks they found strength in each other. Initially Sarah had been withdrawn and unforthcoming about her fears, but Fullbrook had guessed from her behavior that she shared common ground with him. She was seeing the same incongruities every day. It was good to know that he had an ally. The odds on them both being mad had assuaged his suspicion that he alone had entered lunacy.

"I saw my grandfather today," Fullbrook called as he opened the door to her flat—she had urged him to take her spare set of keys. A moment, while the streetlamp's bitter flood shifted through the steam from the bathroom and she coalesced, a tiny figure wrapped in toga and turban towels, skin pink from her recent dunking. He was put in mind of the way she had become fragmented on the bridge, the day he met her, losing her solidity to the mist like a thumb shifting a tablet out of true in a hand held puzzle. She moved through to the kitchen where she began making cups of coffee.

"He died twenty years ago," Fullbrook continued.

"Did you talk to him?"

"Hardly ever. I was only ten when he died and cripplingly shy—"

"No," she interrupted. "I mean, did you talk to him today?"

Fullbrook crumpled slightly, inside his greatcoat. He hadn't realized he was trying so hard to impress her. He shook his head. Although they had only become friends a few weeks ago, he could tell that she was disgruntled. Her shoulders, the set of her face carried a tension that the bath had been unable to relieve. "What is it?" he asked, taking a cup from her. "What's wrong?"

"You're no longer frightened," she said, accusingly. "Why is that? Just because you've found someone who can see the same way you do?"

Fullbrook shrugged and ducked his lip towards the rim of the cup, looking for a buffer. When she remained silent, expecting an answer, he said: "It helps."

"It helps me too," she soothed, unexpectedly tender now after the sting of her initial rebuke. "But it doesn't give me an answer. Why is this happening? Why are we seeing these... ghosts?"

"We all see them. Every one of us. It's just that, well, we happen to pay a bit more attention. We're sensitive, that's all."

"That's your theory is it?" she said.

"Part of it," Fullbrook replied, walking away from her into the living room. "These streets, they're filled with echoes of people who have gone before—and people who are still around but have left their mark on the area. Little samples and smears of humanity that won't erase, that keep retracing their steps. Like a double exposure on a photograph. Like going into an empty room and knowing that it's recently been packed with people."

She started getting dressed. He couldn't help but look, timidly at first, and excited, like a child witnessing something forbidden. But then, when he saw her scars, his survey deepened. The scars looped her body like the glistening routes carved by snails. Her breasts and groin were banded with broad, tight belts of livid tissue. He had to put his hand in his pocket to stop himself from reaching out to touch them.

"I'm not convinced," she said. "I feel threatened. I feel targeted. Why should that be if it's all as benign as you make out?"

"It's just an idea," said Fullbrook, wanting to ask about the scars. "I feel threatened too. I'm scared witless of dying alone. Of just dying, even."

A beat, then she said: "Where did your first sighting occur?"

He watched her fastening a denim shirt over the split-and-sealed gloss of her chest. The area behind her swarmed with shadow.

"Near the Corpse... the underground," he said. "I was working."

"Which one?"

"Loeb Gardens."

She swept hair from her face. She wore a challenging grin. "Show me."

They were about to leave her flat when he bit down on his shyness and gripped her arm. "Those scars, Sarah. How did you get them?"

Her face upturned, half hidden by the dark dropping on her from the landing. Her face, twisted into disbelief.

She said: "What scars?"

He felt stranger, traveling on the train, than he had in a long time. His head felt light and tickly, as though it were empty but for a feather floating around inside. Sarah sat opposite him, couched in her leather, her eyes softening when they met his, but finding some steel occasionally, maybe when she thought of his reference to scars.

The stations flew by: Obsidian Heights, Blue Street, The Herringbone, Glucose Walk, Monk Island. At Loeb Gardens, Fullbrook disembarked, Sarah pressed up close behind him, like a child who doesn't want to become separated from a parent. There were few passengers getting off here; there wasn't a connecting line and they had left the conurbation behind twenty or so minutes ago.

"You told me you were working," Sarah said. "What happened?"

Fullbrook turned around on the escalator. "I was up top, talking to a traffic policeman. It was raining—"

"It's always raining," smiled Sarah.

"—and it was dark, but there was plenty of light from the jets approaching the airstrip. Some woman had thrown herself in front of a train but had been kneeling in the road up here for a while. The traffic cop was just telling me what he'd seen."

They had breasted the ticket barriers now and they passed through onto a pale strip of road flanked by Gothic reaches of black stone: the financial outpost. A queue of airplanes were stacked up above Ochre Point airfield. Through the drizzle, the magic of perspective flung red points of traffic lights into a splintered retreat that reminded Fullbrook of the warning signs in emergency tunnels.

"It was just here. I saw my wife. She was walking along on the opposite pavement, carrying a net bag filled with oranges. She used to work here. I stopped what I was doing and called out to her, but she didn't look up. She just carried on walking and I was frozen here, a big lump in my throat because I hadn't seen her for years. Her hair was as I remembered it. This big, soft pile of blonde hair. I used to run my fingers through it when she was in bed. She was wearing her favorite leather jacket."

Fullbrook was aware of his own tears now, turned cold on his skin by the brisk wind. Sarah's hand had slipped inside his own.

"Then she just seemed to soften, as though she was dissolving into the air. And gone. And… gone."

He came to his senses and looked down, his eyes aching from the way he had been peering into the space across the street where his wife had been, as if she might reappear. Sarah was gone; he had been holding his own hand. But no, who was that, disappearing around the corner of the station? A whip of dirty blonde hair, a diminishing shadow.

"Sarah?"

He went after her. The buildings she was running past gradually lost the bullishness of their cousins on the main drag; soon, there was nothing but a track separating a few tired, punched-in huts. Up ahead, a heavy border of fencing closed the street from a large tract of greensward. A sign in red: GOVERNMENT PROPERTY—STAY OUT didn't dissuade her. Fullbrook watched as she squeezed through a gap beneath the fence where a groove had developed in the earth. Seconds later, he followed suit.

Over the rise of a hill, he saw the city swell beneath him, a mandala of light surrounded by barrage nets of rain. In the moment of his recognizing it, it somehow became alien to him too, a vertiginous dislocation that he hoped was merely due to a fresh point of view. Sarah had vanished; the only movement came from a row of starved, leafless trees.

Fullbrook moved down the hill, conscious now of a sharp smell. What he perceived as the light from the nearest portion of the city was too intense. He realized that it was coming from the hill itself. Four arc lights—little suns—crept above his immediate horizon and, as the wind changed, he became aware of a rank odor beneath the initial tang. That, and the sound of engines complaining.

He edged forward, using the paltry fingers of shadow from the trees as a shelter. The pit yawned before him, a great maw containing pale, gelid cargo. Tufts of black weed sprang from this strange mud and here and there, thin stiff outcrops broke the softly swelling topography. Occasional scars of red. It took a long time for him to accept what he was seeing, even when he had recognized the weed for hair, the outcrops as limbs yet to be digested by the lime now being voided from a funnel at the back of a lorry. At the opposite side, a JCB was shoveling bodies into the pit. Even from here, Fullbrook could see their thighs spoilt with large, black 'S' brandings. On an area of land to the right of the pit, body bags were being emptied by a team in surgeon green. Ghostly, gloved hands prepared the bodies for branding. Clothes and jewelry were bagged and marked. It was a smooth operation, despite the brutality of the location. No pristine units of stainless steel here. No heady smells of disinfectant.

Fullbrook watched—a lost, raw soul within several layers of shock—

as a fragile-looking woman was divested of her leather jacket, branded and slung into a scrum of corpses. He heard her skull connect with another's and the crack brought him out of his fugue.

He walked back up the hill, tasting the sourness of what saliva was left in his mouth. He flashed his credentials at the men working the ticket barriers at Loeb Gardens and passed into the lift that would take him to the emergency shuttle. He didn't want to be near anyone else.

In the creak of his door opening, he thought he heard her laughter. But the flat was empty. He moved through the rooms without conviction, picking up ornaments, feeling them, putting them back. A drink from the kitchen, a bar on the fire, a candle or two.

He unlocked the box under his desk after a few swigs of vodka. Jaws clenching, he riffled through the photographs, angry that after all these years he had still not become inured to the carnage.

He could not remember the last time he had done this but his reasons then must surely have been different. Perhaps a drunken need, in the darkest watches of the night, to reaffirm the reluctant beating of his heart, muffled for such a long time under the layers of grime from the Subterra lines, the crushed bones and flesh, the bilious smell of the paper on which he compiled his reports. These nights, all he ever seemed to picture as he closed his eyes was the marrow and pulp of something once human being scraped from the tracks. All he heard, the tools squealing as he fled another accident site with his bloody rolls of film. More than anything else—he believed, as he fanned a batch of photographs in his hand—the distorted ghost echo of the suicides' cries would follow him to the grave.

Pick a card, any card....

Usher Street, '87, Miss Danya Preece (read the camera print-out on the picture's reverse). Medics had collected the gray rope of her guts from the point of collision to the location where most of her ended up, seventy feet away.

Scissor Point West, '99, Mr. Robert Dendy. A week after he hurled himself in front of a train barreling into the station they had been picking fragments of his skull out of the ceiling arc.

Universe Curve, '70, Mrs. Bridie Bannermann. Spine concertina'ed to a fifth of its normal length...

Gannet Spires, '92, Mr. Jason Wade. Fullbrook had had to calm a woman reading her book on the platform who suddenly found his severed hand keeping her place....

There were hundreds of photographs here, measuring his span of work in so many different permutations of the same demise. His flat, like a crowd of ghouls pushing in for a look, closed around his shoulders. He continued to shuffle through the dense hand of photos, alighting on a face (where a face remained) that he recognized, or thought he recognized, when all the while he wished he didn't know any of them.

And then she magicked herself from the pile, as he had known and feared she would.

Howling Mile, '96, Mrs. Sarah Fullbrook. The photo showed three chunks of her body laid out neatly on a pink towel; a triptych that had his eyes sweeping back and forth like a reader of music. On the right, her legs and groin (one shoe still clinging to a foot). In the middle, her torso. On the left, her upper chest and head. The arms were still attached; she must have flung them out before her when she threw herself to the train. Whoever had laid out the body had stood this last portion upright. The head lolled against a shoulder. The eyes regarded the hands, which were folded like sleeping birds on the floor in front of her. It seemed as though she was sinking into, or about to climb out of, the platform. Behind her, the red-eye glare of a medic on the tracks, his hand over his mouth. Stifling bile. Or a yawn.

It was a pose Fullbrook suddenly found himself aping.

He was wakened simultaneously by a bleached trickle of sunshine through the curtains and the trill of the phone. Fullbrook let the answering service cut in. He was very late. It was Tate. Why wasn't he in his office yet? Who did he think was going to attend the emergency at Fahrenheit Steps? Where were his priorities these days? Who…. Why…. What?

Fullbrook pushed the sheaf of photographs away from him and rose, a morning chorus of crackles shifting through him like tensions finding equilibrium in a skin of ice. He splashed a little water on his face and brushed his teeth. The mirror offered him a cut-price, second-hand version of himself that made him wince.

"I wouldn't buy it," he sniffed dejectedly. "Wouldn't even rent it."

He slung his camera around his neck and shambled out under a sky that was glassy with light but threatened by an approaching armada of black clouds.

His office was empty but not for long. Liptrott and Haslam were quick to supplement his awareness of Tate's displeasure, commenting *sotto voce* that maybe it was time he was given a stint on the ticket barriers. Their smirks might not have been so obvious if they realized he would be happy to oblige.

Before they could suggest it, he loaded his camera with a fresh roll of film and jogged down to the emergency shaft. In the carriage he examined his feelings but, despite the proof about his history with Sarah in the stark block capitals of her surname, he could not eke out any shreds of grief. He didn't feel raw or exposed. He felt numb, more concerned with the flaws in his memory. *Why didn't I recognize her?* And, by extension: *Why didn't she recognize me?*

He disembarked at Fahrenheit Steps and was surprised to see that the platforms were still busy. He collared a guard with a blond spray of dreadlocks questing from a peaked cap. "Why hasn't the area been cordoned off?"

The guard looked at him as if he were a smear of something more unpleasant than shit on his shoe. "Cuz nuthinz appened yet, see."

Fullbrook explained who he was and why he was here; the guard's expression did not change. "Thez a guy down the end of the platform freatening to frow himself in front of a train, see. Burra currant give a monkey's uncle, see, cuz I is off dooty in four, nope, free minnitz. See?"

Fullbrook moved towards the platform. "Why is he doing this?" he called out over his shoulder.

"Owdeyell am I s'posed to know? Iz granny won't put out for him no more, I dunno. Your job, innit?"

"Help me?" asked Fullbrook, carving a path through the jostling horde.

"Am clockin' out, see. You be da hero, cameraman."

The LCD promised another train to End Of Steel in one minute. Heads lolled and jounced before him like strange fruit in a game of apple-bobbing. A pocket of calm existed at the opposite end. He cut through the bodies as a distant whisper breathed from the tunnel's throat. The coming tattoo of wheel against sleeper matched the thrashing of his heart so acutely that they cancelled each other out. All Fullbrook could hear was the mantra now rising from the figure at the end of the platform. His voice rose as blue light splashed the enamel tiles of the station entrance. "See me," he was yelling. "See me, see me, see me...."

It became harder to gain ground as more passengers retreated from the prowling, ranting figure, shoring up the path Fullbrook was attempting to beat.

A concussion of warm air as the squared off snout of the train shot out of the dark. In a split second, all of the sounds around him took off into a glissade from the banal mumbles of normality to something hysterical and exceptional. The squeal of brakes, the blast of static from a guard telling people to MIND THE GAP, the murmur of passengers—all of them contributed to a cacophony that suddenly cut out, providing a perfect pause, a stillpoint through which Fullbrook found he was able to move.

He stepped around figures frozen in a state of approach. Closer to the front of the train, however, he found people halted in displays of shock. A woman was recoiling, her eyes egg-large, mouth open, a single bar of saliva connecting one lip to its mate. A man whose face was contorted by horror and fascination had dropped his briefcase. It clung to mid-air. Others were similarly appalled and trying to back away from the sight before them.

Fullbrook approached himself, taking in the sinuous curve of his own body in the air. His twin had leapt backwards off the edge of the platform, arms outstretched. One knee was bent, his jeans were hiked up slightly, allowing a glimpse of gray sock. His eyes were cast back in their sockets, whites showing.

"Jesus God no," he managed, his hot and ragged words finding no comfortable egress from a mouth that felt as cold as ice. If he reached out, he could touch his own foot. If he reached out....

His hand closed around the suede shoe that his double was wearing. The eyes swiveled and fixed on him. As motion surged back along the platform, like blood pumped through a vein that has been temporarily clamped, Fullbrook felt himself diminish: people began to move through him. Their passage through his ethereal organs, his meat and bones was profoundly painful. He had been a ghost all along—he just hadn't realized it, hadn't been launched by his corporeal other. Those who took their own life couldn't be bothered with the kind of navel gazing in which Fullbrook had indulged on the event of seeing themselves. To witness oneself and carry on unaffected was beyond the crudities of real flesh.

His abject expression lasted for as long as it took for the train to shear it away from the boss of his skull.

Excuse the Unusual Approach

...the card had read. *I am looking for people who wish to add to their income.*

Gubb withdrew into his coat and hurried along the pavement, the reflection of his eyes snagging now and again on sleet-smeared panes as he cast glances back down the street. Nervousness rimed him; pulsed like the heat from an infected cut, but it was misplaced. It wasn't being generated by the punched and dazed thoroughfares he stalked, nor did it come from their inhabitants, who were less likely to harm him than he himself. The people—and the roofs that concealed them—served only to insulate the core of his unease, preventing its damping down. The threat of violence, to Gubb, was far more crippling than any act.

The cuffs of his flannel trousers ragged and damp, cold eating a route through the flimsy soles of his brogues, he clenched his hands and thrust them deeper into fraying pockets, as though making to clutch his last pound note, or a special key to warmth and comfort. In a way, he was, although he did not yet know what kind of door it might open for him.

A pub at the end of the street was a beacon in the gray. Floods of syrupy orange light poured from fogged windows. As he drew abreast of the main doors, the pub breathed on him: a mix of nicotine and souring grain. He recoiled from the scrum with its cluster-bomb retorts of laughter and invective. Snakes of unknowable conversation whispered after him as he sought the lane parallel to the canal. Spits of rain stained black the shoulders of his coat. How could they enjoy themselves like that when hundreds were dying on the front lines each day?

Contact Evelyn Orpen, telephone number 5612 (no investment required).

He remembered vividly the eyes of the person who had thrust the card into his hand on Sugar Street, possibly because eyes were all there was—the rest of the body was swaddled in deep folds of black waterproof fabric. A gray hat, far too large for the head upon which it rested, and a thick green scarf banded the face. The eyes were cross sections of an old, hard-boiled egg. Not a word had been proffered.

As soon as he could find a phone box that was neither vandalized nor occupied, Gubb rang the number and told the brittle voice at the other end of the line that he was interested in whatever it was they were doing. He realized too late how desperate he must sound but the voice seemed to pay no heed. Instead, it squawked at him to attend an interview the following day at an address in Gannet Spires.

"Do I need to bring anything?" Gubb had asked, writing the details on the back of his hand.

"Everything you require will be provided here at the de Fleche building." The line died.

Back home, while a can of soup heated on the burner, he idled over the single volume of photographs that he had hoarded since his youth. They were pictures he had found or bought or stolen over the years. Nobody he knew owned a camera; indeed, he had never even held one. There were pictures of them in some of the newspapers and magazines he had saved for the fire. Secret black boxes with capes to hide behind while you composed a portrait. Hand-held flashes that crackled and smoked when they were triggered. Gubb imagined what the smell would be like and wriggled excitedly in his armchair as the tiny squares of sepia offered their moments of truth.

His bedsit back at the high-rise provided its own little soundtrack for his viewing. A creak of waterlogged timbers in the attic for the boy at the turn of the century riding a bicycle past a shop selling signature rifles. The yawn of wind at the deep cracks of the bedroom window frames for the man in his waders casting for rare bream in a gravel pit filled with the corpses of executed criminals. The scrabbling of unseen vermin behind the walls for the giggling girls eating ice-cream while remote-controlled fighters turned the sky behind them into panels of liquid fire.

He remembered at school boys teasing him because he didn't know what a touch-tone phone was. He still wasn't sure. "I'm more interested in the now rather than the yesterday," he would tell them, while they hooted and spat. Girls thought him outlandish because he liked to wear tweed rather than the increasingly rare plasticized smart suits that molded to your body and changed color according to your body temperature.

Gubb ate his soup at the kitchen window, watching the city succumb to fatigue. Distant haloes of weak light from the gas-lamps pock-marked the black mist like *ignis fatuus*. He lit some candles and turned on the radio, listening to the hum as its valves gradually warmed. The signals were too weak these days to precipitate more than a few minutes listening at a time, but tonight he was lucky, hooking into an opera being broadcast from the New Continent. He spent a short time reading and then turned in, his mind already buzzing with the possibilities that the morning might bring. Just as he was about to douse the light, he spotted a corner of paper sticking under the door to his bedsit.

He opened the door and stepped into the corridor. Soft ochre light from gas lamps dotted along the walls failed to color the carpet. The stairwell was a black throat. Whoever had deposited the paper was long gone. He considered knocking on Mrs. Snelson's door but she would have him on the landing for an age, complaining about the broken lift or the smell of waste that drifted through the air vents on hot days.

He unfolded the tablet of paper on his way back to bed.

Don't do it.

No sooner had Gubb settled in his seat than the shadow of the conductor was upon him.

"Tickets," intoned the bored voice.

Gubb handed over a few pennies, mumbled: "Gannet Spires."

The conductor's brown, stubby fingers punched the fare into his ticket machine then blurred on the handle: a ticket ratcheted out. The paper felt coarse and damp in Gubb's fingers.

He sat back in his seat and watched the houses as they streamed by his window, looming out of and then sinking into the dawn smog. Pockets of the sky seemed to be on fire: gas lanterns struggling against the damp, smothering air.

He wondered about the war between the Bonnerists and Future Path, what it would feel like to die under a hail of shells or feel the wet fire of chlorine in his lungs. What would be preferable, the best way to die? Crushed beneath the caterpillar tracks of a tank? Bathed in a flamethrower's burst? Suffocating on Anthrax spores?

"Are you all right?"

At her voice he became aware of the greasy baubles of sweat on his temples and neck. He swabbed himself dry with his handkerchief and apologized without looking the other in the eye. He sought further distraction by running a comb through his oiled hair. He hadn't met an employer yet who didn't appreciate a sharp side-parting. His breathing back to normal, he tried to smile. "I'm all right," he said. "This confounded smog. We should be issued with masks."

"I won't disagree with you. Last week there were reports of TB in Troutbeck. Only a few miles north of us. We'll have the Black Plague back too before long."

"No doubt," Gubb said, wishing she would go away.

"My name's Elizabeth," she said. A gloved hand moved into his line of sight, making it impossible to ignore. "Elizabeth Hoyle. I've seen you about. You work in the factory over by the canal, don't you? *KK Korrection*. What is it they do there?"

"Raymond Gubb," he returned, shaking the hand and trying another smile. He lifted his wet eyes to hers and found the smile fit better for it. "We're a waste management firm. A troubleshooting outfit. We dismantle rogue computer systems, the networks that were infected by the Millennium Bug. We take away the dangers they might otherwise impose. We neutralize them. I say 'we' but I wouldn't know a microchip from a sausage bap. I work in the administration offices...." Gubb pressed his lips together; he was babbling. But she seemed to be interested.

"When you say dangers, what do you mean? That Millennium Bug nonsense was over fifty years ago."

"I really wouldn't know," Gubb replied. "I don't take as much interest in the company's doings as I probably should, to tell you the truth. It's something to do with a virus that caused something like 95 percent of the world's computers to either regress to little more than glorified abacuses or turn aggressive."

"Aggressive?"

Gubb held up a hand. "Not that they started eating people or anything like that. Aggressive in that the computers consumed their own data and whatever they were linked with. Not very healthy if you were, say, flying across the sea in a Behemoth at the time. Even the computers in domestic appliances: the irons, the fridges, the vacuum cleaners... they all went aggressive. There were deaths—"

"No!" Elizabeth's hand flew to her mouth. "I still have an iron—" She quietened immediately, realizing her gaffe.

Gubb frowned. "You really oughtn't. The amnesty twenty years ago... and the purges since... all computers should have been impounded by now." He looked about the bus. Spies were everywhere; he didn't want to find himself convicted of a crime by mere association.

Elizabeth clasped his hand momentarily. Despite the awkwardness of the situation, the contact seemed to reaffirm him, convince him of a physicality of which he was becoming increasingly unsure. On occasion, he had idled away an hour or two imagining himself thinning out to nothingness and becoming lost to the smog forever. He couldn't remember the last time he had touched someone; held someone.

"Will you come and check it for me?" Elizabeth asked.

"Ms. Hoyle. I am not qualified—"

"Well then, at least come and take it away for me. I didn't realize I was at risk. I wouldn't have kept it for so long had I known—"

Gubb considered. "I can't just now. I'm on my way to honor an appointment. And then I begin my shift at the factory this afternoon. I shan't be able to come till round midnight."

Elizabeth nodded. "That's settled then. I'll cook you a spot of something for your bother. You'll be hungry, I'll imagine."

She gave him her address and stepped off the bus as it became snarled in traffic by the markets of Jute Street. He watched her dawdle past the stalls, pausing to buy a bag of nuts and a pineapple, and then she was lost to the bargain hunters and the thieves.

Struggling through the carousel doors, Gubb found the lobby of the de Fleche building in Gannet Spires to be cool and dark. He walked the marble floor to a huge, curved oak desk that was so tall he could barely see the receptionist who sat behind it. Smothered sunlight breached the high tinted windows and made everything seem brown; it comforted him. He could hear the soft *tock-schuss* of shod feet climbing the stone stairway that curled away into the gloom above, but could not espy its author.

"Good morning," he said, to the purple hive that shivered beneath the counter.

It tilted backwards and a face emerged from the shadows, looking up at him. Purple too, was her eye, lip and nail make-up. Her suit followed suit, ditto her earrings. "I bet I can guess what color your shoes are," he said, but should have realized, before opening his mouth, that this was a face that didn't tolerate whimsy.

"You are?" she enquired, nasally.

"Gubb. Raymond Gubb."

"To see?"

"Umm, hold on...." he fished out the card he had been given. "Orpen. Evelyn Orpen."

"What time is your appointment?"

"Well I'm a little early. I didn't—"

"The time?"

"Ten."

"Seats are over there. You'll be called." The hive receded; he was dismissed.

There were two other people waiting, he saw, as he entered the dark pools where the seats had been provided. He positioned himself on a chair by a startled pot plant, straightened his tie and tried to relax. Opposite him, a woman carefully planted crisps between her heavily rouged lips and turned the pages of a wrestling magazine. The man sitting next to her steered a flat cap in his hands, watery eyes turned up to the balcony where murmurs and chuckles echoed like distant storms.

Who had planted the note? And what did it mean? Did it refer to his appointment at the de Fleche building? Gubb assumed it must, since there was nothing else in which he had recently become involved that would instigate such a demand. And why should it earn this attention? Did the person who wrote it have prior knowledge of the work he was applying for? Was it then less a demand and more a warning?

The questions snowballing, Gubb's head began to pound. He watched his companions as they were called for their interview; they didn't reappear. Maybe that meant they had been employed. He wondered if that meant he was not required; maybe it just meant there was a different exit.

"Raymond Gubb? This way." A woman wearing an expectant expression and holding a clipboard (from the voice, he guessed it was Evelyn Orpen) led him down a corridor to a chamber where three men and a woman were sitting in armchairs facing a single, uncomfortable-looking plastic seat. Here, Gubb deposited himself.

"Welcome to Reclaim, Mr Gubb. So. What is it about yourself that makes you special?" This from a man with a forehead so large it could have easily housed another face. The absence of preamble flustered Gubb. He gabbled some age-old cliché about honesty, diligence and loyalty that went down like an emetic.

"Stop right there," said the woman. "You don't have to toe that sad little line with us. Mr Hunny here is getting impatient, that's all. We've talked to twelve people this morning and none of them fit the bill."

"If I knew what bill it was I needed to, er, fit into... onto...." said Gubb, lamely.

Mr Hunny spread his hands. "Just talk to us about yourself, Mr Gubb. We'll give you the details later."

The woman, who introduced herself as Mrs. Flint (and also nominated Mr. Mannion and Mr. Kynaston), asked him where he worked. A tentative conversation began. Any initial hostility seemed to disperse. Tea was brought. A joke was cracked. Hunny, Flint, Mannion and Kynaston became Malcolm, Gloria, John and Brendan. When Gubb glanced at his watch, he saw an hour had passed in a trice. He still felt in the dark about their outfit.

"What is it you do, then, if you don't mind my asking?"

"We are—or rather, the people we employ are—hunters, after a fashion." This answer given, Brendan cast around for assent; this he received as a grunt, a nod of the head.

"Hunters?"

"Yes," said Gloria. "How best to describe this... Malcolm?"

Her colleague took up the baton without a pause. "Our city is dying.

You might very well have traveled through some of its sickest parts on your way to this meeting. Healthy-looking buildings and people are in fact rotting away from the inside. The fabric that binds us together, that forms society, is stained, torn and unraveling before our eyes. We want to halt that slide. We want to reclaim the fragmenting parts and make the city whole again."

Malcolm peppered his speech with expansive hand gestures. His lips grew wet with saliva. It was a magnetic performance. "Do you feel the same way? Do you understand the cancers that are invading our community?"

Gubb thought of the pub he had seen, its revelers ignorant of the bloodshed that was occurring just a few hundred miles north in the Galliope Steppes. He wondered if this was what Malcolm was angling towards.

"Yes," he said. "Yes I do."

On the way to the factory, his hand kept straying to the notebook and pencil they had issued to him, along with a tight roll of one pound notes. He had not counted them but he guessed there to be in the region of sixty or seventy. One of those a week, they had promised, for his information. You might wish to start at work, they had suggested. And where is it you work, by the by?

He was pleased that they were impressed by his occupation and sympathetic when he complained about the wage they were paying him. They had given him a few tests but it seemed they were going through the motions, a feeling confirmed when he saw Gloria penning a contract while he was still only halfway through the questionnaire.

"Are you based here?" he had asked. "I can contact you here?"

That wasn't possible. They didn't have a headquarters as such. *They* would contact *him*.

It was unorthodox, to say the least, but the money made it better.

"What, exactly, am I looking for?" he had asked, hoping not to sound too amateurish.

"You possess a skill, we can tell that," said John, shaking his hand and pressing him firmly in the direction of out. "You'll know what you're looking for when you find it."

Now, with twilight coming on apace, he looked for the wrought iron gates to the factory through the inky streets where the bus growled and sputtered. It had started to rain; large warm droplets that brought a patchwork of newspapers up to cover heads, along with ragged black umbrellas and Mackintosh collars. He stepped off the bus and followed his usual route through Herringbone Square to the gates where he showed his pass to Edward, the security guard.

Once inside, he hurried across the delivery bay to the administration office and unlocked the door with his key. He was alone tonight. Alice had taken a few days' leave to tend to her consumptive father and Eamonn was on a course in Lemon Beach.

Brushing the rain from his jacket, he placed a pan of water on the hob and turned to the mountain of filing on his desk, which had been little more than a molehill when he left it yesterday. He separated invoices from dockets from carbon copies and collected the staples and paper clips in a jar. Once the sub groups had been divided, he placed each in a folder, arranged by date, and slotted them in the filing cabinet. Next, he attended to the correspondence, typing out replies to queries, orders and job applications on his Remington Noiseless. These he placed in a tray for Mr Fenwick to sign in the morning.

By now it was gone eleven and throughout his labor he had thought of nothing but the roll of notes and the cryptic, though efficient, manner of his supplementary employers. He found the battered card in his coat pocket. *Excuse the Unusual Approach....* He noted the number and picked up the phone. Instead of the glassy voice that had greeted him previously, her was met by a flat, uninterrupted tone. He called the operator and explained the problem.

"That number does not exist, sir," she said.

"It did yesterday," he insisted, unhappy by the way he was being made to feel a liar.

"That's entirely possible, sir. But it does not any longer."

Gubb left work feeling unfulfilled. How would they be able to top up his wages if they were acting like ghosts? Was this all an elaborate joke played on him by his absent colleagues? He would have to call their bluff by going through with his part of the contract; after all, their cash was in his pocket, warming his thigh. If they didn't contact him again, it would be their loss.

He resisted the urge to return to the de Fleche building; there would be nobody to listen to his complaints anyway, bar the nightwatchman. Instead, he made his way to Elizabeth's home, angry with himself at agreeing to check out her silly little appliance. No doubt it would be a long defunct thing, a collection of spent circuitry.

She was waiting when he trudged up to her door. A warm smell of food sank into him as she let him past. "I was starting to worry," she said. "It was getting on."

She fed him a stew that refreshed his good nature but picked holes in his reserve.

"Did you post me a note, Elizabeth? Last night, under my door?"

She was busy with a mouthful of wine. "I didn't." Now the words were out and the wine stomached, she was able to display some confusion. "I only met you today. I don't even know where you live."

"There is that, I suppose. I'm sorry. I'm being irrational."

"What did the note say?"

Now that he had established she was not the culprit, he didn't want to reveal the truth. But he felt relaxed, and now she was away from the smoke and bluster of traffic, attracted to her. She drew him out of himself in the best way.

"It said: *Don't do it.*"

"Don't do what?"

He shrugged. "I imagine it had something to do with my applying for a new job. That was where I was going when I made your acquaintance."

"Do you think it might have been a threat from your employers?"

"But nobody could have known, other than me. I didn't discuss it with anyone."

"Then presumably, it has nothing to do with it."

"You're right, of course. Anyway, it doesn't matter. It's forgotten. Where's this iron of yours?"

Elizabeth led him to the kitchen, waggled her hands at a lump of iron and plastic on the sideboard.

Gubb picked it up by the flex and snorted. "Elizabeth, this thing has a plug! It's ancient. The most technological aspect about it is that it has a nozzle for extra steam."

"So I'm safe, then?"

"Quite, quite safe." Gubb replaced the iron and rubbed his hands together, as if ridding them of the feel of this relic and the irritation it had mustered. "If the national grid were up to it, you might be able to use it too."

"I knew it was safe," she said, in a small voice. "I—I just had to see you." Now the secret was out her voice gathered pace, as though trying to explain everything at once might help matters. She told him she had seen him often on his travels and grown to like him. He looked like a kind man, someone good to know. "It's so hard in the city, don't you think? Meeting new people?"

He agreed, but he was flustered. He didn't know what to say.

"I'm sorry," she offered.

"Please, don't—"

She had been watching him all this time, he noticed, scrutinizing him for a reaction, gauging him. He imagined he must have looked passive, inviting even, for her to muster the courage to approach him and enfold her arms about his neck. Within the circle she had created, he found himself kissing her without meaning to, crushing her against him as his body yearned to rediscover the meaning of proximity after so many years without.

He left at dawn, exhausted, exhilarated. Their lovemaking had consisted of nothing but strokes through clothing and murmurs of approval. At one point they found themselves laughing about the iron and now his mouth ached from the demands happiness had made upon it.

"This new job of yours," she whispered. "What is it?"

"I'm not at liberty to say," he jawed gently into her throat, trying to turn his deflection of her question into a joke. She sounded almost sad when she replied: "Ah well, don't we all have our secrets?"

At home he showered and changed, drank a cup of tea over the morning headlines while absently noting how improved everything seemed. The pages of his newspaper were whiter, crisper; the birdsong was spirited; even the smog carried a rosy hue in its belly.

He checked his suit in the mirror and selected a blue knitted tie to set it off. Cigarettes, comb, pencil and notebook. He slipped a couple of pound notes off the roll in his sock drawer and, pocketing his keys, nipped into the bathroom once more to tend to his hair. The steam from his shower still hung about the place like a fresher cousin of the foulness outside. On the mirror, picked out by the mist, a fingered demand: *DON'T.*

The sweat, smoke and bile of The Stolen Ukulele, even at this early hour, was at fever pitch. Across a swilling counter, Gubb asked the barmaid for a pint of bitter and eventually managed to carve a route through his steaming company to a relative stillpoint by the toilet doors. A deep swallow for his nerves, which jangled on from his recent shock, and a swallow too in preparation for his first foray into this covert work. *Look for grainy patches in the fabric of our lives,* John had told him. *Look for blackspots, vacuums, areas of negativity… don't worry, if you look for them, they'll reveal themselves to you.*

Gubb wasn't so sure about that. It all sounded a bit vague; he liked his world full of concrete things. To consider the shadows was to turn his judgment outwards for once. He felt uncomfortable training the glare of his scrutiny on others when so much of himself was engrained in darkness. Maybe this would be his moment of redemption; following a trail of sleaze to his own front door and offering himself as the principle flaw in society's warp and weft.

He forced such thoughts out of him with a snort; was the drink affecting him so soon? He cast around for a place to start, assessing the knots of conversation. Perhaps he would pick up a clue here amid so many wagging tongues. It was inevitable that he should find himself dragged into an argument, buzzing on the periphery of so many bunches. He was asked his opinion on the war effort and he dredged up some morsel of commentary from the newspapers, about how Future Path were contradicting their policies by entering into conventional warfare: a step back into old ways that was entirely at odds with their revisionist approach. "They should pack away their arms and argue their case by illustration," he continued. "Here are the computers—they failed us. Here is the technology—it promised us the stars and very nearly put us in the ground. They won't win playing Bonner's game."

It was not designed to provoke, but a woman wearing a green bandanna and ridiculously large hooped earrings took umbrage.

"You're a Futurist, friend?" (Gubb shook his head, but she was having none of it.) "Your kind sickens me to the back teeth. Lionel Bonner wants nothing more than to allow people the right to choose their own way. People like looking to the past for their inspiration; it's how we've always got on. Knowable routines passed on through secure family units; self-help and cooperation; playing by the rules... these are the tropes that have sustained us for centuries."

Gubb was making placatory gestures and about to agree when another stranger—clad in black and hunched on a stool like a sullen rook—chipped in. "Sheep," he spat.

One of the woman's companions ducked into his pint and murmured something about this not being a public debate.

"That's where you're wrong, sir," said the figure, straightening. Something about the man excited Gubb and he sidled towards him. Some forbidding glint in his eye; the stone in his voice or set of his shoulders. There's a history to him, Gubb thought. And danger too.

"We're in a public saloon and you're talking about something that affects us all. The war is drifting south. By the end of the week we could be snagged up in it. And what use will your rhetoric and polemic be then as you die twitching with bayonets up your arses?"

"What kind of talk is that?" demanded the woman, stridently. "Just whose side are you on? And give us a name so we might know who it is scaremongering all over the shop."

"My side," he quipped. "And the name's Stephen Dendy. There's enough mischief going on in this town to have all those soldiers scratching their heads and wondering what all the rumpus was in aid of, if only their shellshocked chiefs would stop pushing toy tanks over the maps and consider their own doorsteps."

"You're a moralist?" Gubb asked, this time hoping to elicit a reaction.

"Not at all, as it happens I favor the realpolitik, but you have to lay foundations before you can build. And the shower of filth fighting each other in the slate deserts of Troutbeck seem to be intent on knocking down structures that haven't even been planned yet. I tell you, I've seen things here that would flick the safety catch on anybody's gun."

The hubbub gradually deteriorated into volleys of one-word dismissals. Dendy evidently tired of the sniping, sinking his pint and moving towards the door as another chorus of "rubbish," "nonsense" and "lies" lifted from the group. Gubb followed him, tasting decadence on his wake. Here was his passage to the blackspots John had hinted at, stalking into the cobbled alleys by the canal.

Gubb flew after his shadow, eager not to lose him in the smog, or the darkness from which he had borrowed some color. As if in tribute to his speech earlier, a splinter bomb whistled through the sky, surely no further than fifty miles away. The scattered retort of its explosion was like fat spitting on a fire. Grains of light on the horizon gave its position away. Saliva squirted into Gubb's mouth as he considered the prospect of trying to live through battles pitched in his back garden. Unbidden, an image of Elizabeth finding succor in the crook of his arm while he failed to staunch the bleeding from a dozen wounds in her chest and throat meant he almost missed Dendy's latest route change. Gubb checked himself and slipped into this fresh slipstream, which took him across a weed-filled wasteground flanked by listing razorwire fences. Another half hour passed with Gubb concentrating solely on the eddies in the smog Dendy was creating.

Presently he heard horses nearby, prior to observing them hobble out of the mist, stirred by his approach. Starved, pock-marked creatures they were, their breath labored and wet. Gubb hurried on; the houses became hunched, dark and crippled. They were stabbed through with holes. Glistening black bin sacks slumped against each other in pathways and front yards, perishing, yielding their innards.

A footstep gritted on grains of broken glass; Gubb melted into the shade, wishing he were with Elizabeth, almost wishing he were hip-deep in dockets and export notices. He felt tremors pass through his chest; deep vibrations of fear. Dendy was still afoot, but he was doubling back. Perhaps he suspected a shadow. Gubb hung back until Dendy was almost invisible—a watermark on paper—and then refreshed his pursuit. This place, though on its knees, did not correspond with the targets outlined, however sketchily, in his remit; a feeling augmented by the sudden appearance of two children in a bedroom window, holding candles and teddy bears, waving at him, pink-skinned and beaming. There was happiness here: hungry and bruised, but happiness all the same.

After another twenty minutes of scurrying and scuffing after Dendy's scent, Gubb was ready to call it a day. He felt faintly foolish and green as they come; surely John's assurance that he had a talent was naught but a lure designed to hook him. Otherwise concerned, the fact that Dendy had landed was lost on him, as was the irony of his destination. This was Howling Mile, one of the most prosperous areas of the city. Once Gubb came to his senses and realized that Dendy was no more than eight feet from him, speaking into an intercom at the mouth of a glittering skyscraper of glass and light, he felt worms of unease nibbling in his gut. Once more he faded into the darkness, able, in this pocket of calm, to hear Dendy's words as they fell from his mouth, dulled by the smog.

"Nile Delta," said Dendy. A door breathed open and he stepped inside a glass lift which took him fifteen stories into the sky. At the same moment, from the lift's twin on the far side, a hollow-eyed woman slumped into the street, tugging a scarf around the bottom half of her face. She was carrying a large canvas bag with a perished strap strengthened by parcel tape. Her heels dragged on the pavement, underscoring her misery. Gubb almost went after her to find out what had influenced her funk but he held back, reluctant to provide any warnings of what he might be bringing. The thought out, he tried to answer it himself. Was he a harbinger? If so, what might these pale streets be in for, pending his report? He felt death here, a tiny aperture in the fruit of hope, readying itself to spread and consume from within until everything was black and rotten.

The gunshot provided an apt exclamation mark for his study. A pane of glass on the fifteenth floor blew out of the building like surprised birds.

He had to act. The war was like a great curtain, freed from its tieback and slowly falling across the light. He realized the tremors he had felt earlier were not of his own making but shockwaves from bombs falling ever closer to the city. These streets needed to be made doughty, beyond suspicion if they were to be able to withstand invasion. He believed Reclaim was dedicated to such work. And he believed Dendy was a source of the city's decay. He must be stopped. His resolve freshened, Gubb scampered towards the building and, mimicking Dendy's voice, spoke what he hoped were the code words for access. Moments later, he was rising above the city, and where the smog was thinnest, he was able to see its ungainly sprawl: a befouled picnic cloth unfurled in readiness for a rank repast. On the near horizon, smoke helixed into the sky, underlit by smudges of orange. He tried to understand the impetus for the war and, in microcosm, the impetus for his own behavior—but the octopus would not remain still enough to allow scrutiny. "None of us know anything," he muttered, as the glide of the lift retarded and the doors hissed open on an abattoir.

This evening, he thought wildly as he bent to inspect Dendy's sucking chest wound, *I was validating an order from Hungley Manor for two dozen valves.*

Seconds before Dendy died, he opened his eyes and smiled at Gubb.

Haltingly, Gubb searched the rest of the floor but there was nobody present. There was a large open-plan office containing a triptych portrait of an army general morphing into a slavering, wild-eyed beast. A few opalized pot-plants. Nothing else. He was turning to go when he discovered, peripherally, another message, smeared in Dendy's blood, on the wall. He didn't even have to look directly at it to know what it read.

He rode home on the bus, dozing a little under the thrum of the engine as it struggled in the damp air. He watched himself following Dendy and pulling back into the sky to see another figure following him and so on until countless shadowy people created a circumference of pursued pursuers reaching around the globe.

"Raymond? Oh Raymond, I was worried for you. The bombs...."

Gubb fell across the threshold and leeched some warmth and comfort from her embrace.

"Oh God," he said, close to tears. He slouched away from her and tugged the folded wad of notes from his pocket. He regarded them for a moment before opening the window and casting them into the canal that ran by the rear of Elizabeth's house.

"Raymond!"

"This job...." he said. "This job...." It was all he was able to say until she had brought him a chipped mug half-filled with vodka.

"I can't do this," he said. "I don't want to do this. It was wrong of me."

She looked at him for a long time before finding some cast of determination. "Come on," she said. "We're going away from the city. But we have to be quick, before it gets light."

"But the war," he said. "The border patrols...."

"I know a way through."

Elizabeth led him across the road and down an alleyway that fell away to the canal. Its treacly waters winked at him as she struggled with a padlock on a garage, the door to which was so black it seemed it couldn't be there.

"Where are we going?" he asked, as she finally sprang the lock and ushered him inside.

"I'm not telling you," she said. "And you have to wear this."

"Do you not trust me?" he grumbled, taking the proffered blindfold.

"Just put it on."

The Hillman Imp started first time, but complained a lot. Angry at the way he was being made to comply with her petty secrets, Gubb simmered in his seat, feeling the road change as time passed, from cobbles to Tarmac to something softer as morning light penetrated the black in front of his eyes. Sounds, too, altered. The rumble of bombs gave way to rushing air filled with sweet smells of foliage. By the time he heard the sea's crash he was in gay spirits and was prepared to overlook Elizabeth's conditions of travel. It helped that she was talking.

"The war…." she began, a prefix that he had heard many times before being followed by something not necessarily connected to it. It was a tool to help explain a pain, a free-floating anxiety. It was a way in to the thoughts you might never normally have wished to consider. "You know, it's wrong when people say that history is dead. When I was young I thought it was one of the truest things I had heard. But as you grow, you realize that the past is where we all wish to be. We exist in the present but we live in the past. The now and the next is too frightening to imagine. Everything is dead or dying now. Everything."

Before long Elizabeth brought the car round in a large arc and braked. When the engine died, he heard a door creak open and slam; he lifted his head in her direction. "Can I take this off?" he asked.

There was no answer. His annoyance returning, he flung back the blindfold and blinked at the dashboard, quickly trying to accustom himself to the explosion of light. Elizabeth had left the car. They were on top of a cliff, the flat blue limit of the sea stretching around him. He called her name; the wind gusted back something—an echo maybe. She had left no footprints though the ground was soft enough. Then he saw that she had left her shoes by the car. He ducked back into the car as his panic swelled. The keys were gone from the fascia. And there was a note tucked into the sunscreen. He unfolded it.

Don't.

"Don't what?" he screamed. A gull aped him, hanging in the air as though attached to a kite string. Under the back seat he found a black book containing a series of names: his was one of them; Dendy's was another. All but his had been scratched out with red ink. In the boot he found a canvas bag filled with documents that he didn't understand, pertaining to government buildings; defense figures; blueprints and maps. There were photographs too. In one, a man who looked the spit of Gubb was caught shooting a manacled man in the back of the head.

Dread sucked at his footfalls as he approached the edge of the cliff so that by the time he was able to look down to the splash of her color on the rocks below, he was almost going backwards.

He was retreating from the crash of the sea when he felt a presence at his shoulder. Recognizing his employers from Reclaim was difficult now that they had cast off their sharp suits in favor of jumpers and jeans. John had grown a beard. A gold ring glinted in Malcolm's nose.

"What?" asked Gubb, the question lowing bovinely from his lips. Had he managed to tell Elizabeth that he loved her, even while he was drunk?

"We apologize for your entrapment, Mr. Gubb," said Gloria, busy tying her hair back with a rubber band. That task completed, she pulled a snub-nosed pistol from her pocket and began to screw a silencer onto the muzzle.

"I don't understand," said Gubb, realizing how foolish he must seem, slouched over with a canvas bag in his hands, looking as blank as a cow in a field.

"Reclaim exists," said John, "but it's people we're interested in, not property, not terrain."

"Elizabeth was a top agent. She opened the lid on a can of nasty worms. It's a pity she's gone."

"She loved me," Gubb whimpered.

"Possibly," said Gloria, loading a single bullet into the chamber. "But that's in the past now."

They told him Elizabeth had planted a card on him and when he asked why they told him that he was a sleeper introduced by the warmongers, an assassin of great repute. He had been brainwashed and inserted into the city with a view to being reactivated once war had fragmented the country. They needed people like him to mop up.

"I don't believe you. I've been framed."

"You've been framed by the photographer a few times," said Brendan, nodding at the photographs scattered on the floor. They laughed.

As Gloria moved in, cocking the pistol, Gubb tried to get a grip on what was happening and, more importantly, what had already happened to him. "Wait," he said. "Wait."

But Gloria was impatient. She thrust the gun into his jaw and spat a single world: "Kneel."

He did so. *That's all in the past*, Gloria had said. He held on to that and wondered again who had written the notes. It must have been him, Gubb, but whether they were intended for Elizabeth, himself or were a general entreaty he could not be sure. It didn't matter. He could almost smell her perfume and feel the thrum of possibilities in her throat as his present, his future collided; scorched a brilliant path through his thoughts.

NEARLY PEOPLE
(For Rhonda)

part one: the dancer

I thought I saw someone I knew today—Mellish—but it couldn't have been because the teeth were all wrong. Mellish had a strange kind of third incisor that grew down over the normal two. This skull's dental cast was conventional. Still, I couldn't get the feeling of recognition from my bones. Maybe I had come to recognize something else, more subtle than any connection with a fellow Miler. Maybe I was just going mad.

That morning had begun for me as any other day. I bathed Jake and dressed his lesions and buboes. He was tired, which exaggerated his apraxia, but managed a smile though it did little for his face beyond emphasizing the deep lines that were worming into it. Just before I left, he made a sound and gave me a look. There was concern in his eyes, mixed with fear. Fear for himself if I didn't come back more than fear for my safety. It was the same every day.

"I won't be long," I said to him. I hardly ever was. Most people in the Mile spent a good day and sometimes part of the night on the hunt for meat but I believed that minimum exposure on the streets meant minimum chance of coming to grief. Simple maths. You wouldn't catch me on, say, Fahrenheit Steps after dark. Okay, the stuff I procured was hardly prime cuts, but we survived. Jake never complained. The dying seldom do.

The door double-locked itself behind me. My tummy writhed. The Corridor was freezing, as usual, but unpopulated at this hour. A bright splash of blood had decorated the far wall and bisected the drab gray paint on the door opposite mine. The blood looked fresh. Around seventy-five percent of attacks occurred in the Corridors. Not the Tar Babies, who stole the lungs of smokers to process into fuel for their motorbikes, or Mowers—they haunted the Outermost, picking off for food the ones who cracked and tried to escape—but domestics, like myself, who had been a part of Howling Mile since the Iridia Wave brought about its enclosure, a generation ago. Hunger makes you desperate. Real hunger

189

will drive away frivolities such as taste and texture. It's all about filling your belly. Shut your eyes. You don't want to see what it is you're eating.

I checked the knife was strapped to my thigh, drew my leather jacket more tightly around me, positioned myself beneath the arch of nozzles and waited for the red light to change to green.

As ever, the application of the coating from the nozzles was unnoticeable, apart from a faint detergent whiff. When the light eventually changed, I pressed a gel-filled capsule out of its blister pack and snapped it in half, drawing the vaporizing liquids into my nostrils. It had a strangely comforting but astringent effect on the septum and would act as a primary alert—the canary in the cage—should I wander into one of the city's HotZones, by making my nose bleed. Checking the gauge on my wrist— I had twelve hours until I had to return or refresh the coating—I hurried down the Corridor and stepped out into the winter morning. This is Howling Mile. This is home. Whether I like it or not.

2 hunt

Carrier didn't like it, but what was she to do? Month after month it seemed the Bordertypes increased in numbers and had actually begun roaming the interior, selecting likely escapees at face value alone and frogmarching them away. Last week, Rindt had vanished from her Corridor and had not returned. The week before it had been Vengox. If your face didn't fit, you were removed. If it did fit—if it were suitably inscrutable—you remained, and the likelihood was that a Mower would rip it off for you.

Other disappearances were being discussed in the alleyways and stairwells across Howling Mile. Panic was infecting everyone, alongside the fallout from the Wave. A petition to the Core had been repulsed with gunfire. Perimeter sniper steeples had begun to be adorned with flowers and picketed by women who sang ancient songs about love. A maverick graffiti artist was daubing slogans on the walls after dark. His, or her, ubiquitous statement, "Eternity," along with the tagline, "Rip," had appeared as far north as the horse hospitals and as far south as Obsidian Heights, where the city gave way to a desert of powdered glass. Nobody knew what it meant, but many had taken it on as a buzzword of defiance anyway. Astonishingly, the message had appeared three stories up the Core, giving rise to the rumor that its author was a renegade Bordertype. But any hope it inspired was false. Despite the protests, nothing changed. If anything, security was tighter.

Security.

Carrier ground her teeth at the irony. Howling Mile might be secure in terms of its relation to the rest of the country, but its citizens were anything but.

She walked swiftly to Blue Street, wishing she had put on thicker trousers to combat the chill; cold air knifed her legs and stiffened the knee that she had damaged while stretching in her sleeping quarters. You had to keep fit.

Her gut felt greasy after a view of the blood. She concentrated on exorcising her discomfort. Kicking at the bloated rats piled at the side of the road, she breathed through her mouth to lessen the impact of the smell. Come summer she would need a canoe to go hunting.

Howling Mile rose around her like the jags of mountains. It always looked unfinished from this perspective; maybe it was. Sheer faces of black steel and glass took what light existed and sent it back as something oiled and filthy. Rain in the night had turned the roads and pavements into a stew of shit and grime. The city's foul juices sluiced along the Tarmac like blood on an abattoir floor.

Carrier paused by the corner of Blue Street and peered into its depths. The boarded windows and steel shutters of long-dead shops would not allow any ingress should she need a swift getaway. Most of the fire escapes that clung to the sides of the buildings did so reluctantly. There were plenty of manholes, but nobody dared to descend into them to find out where their tunnels led.

Unfastening her knife, but leaving it sheathed, Carrier ducked into the street expecting the worst. It made for a depressing life, but it meant that shock and disappointment were feelings she rarely encountered.

She saw Kram as she emerged on to The Herringbone, a spine of cracked road that fed a grid of narrow ginnels once populated by the city's poorest folk. Freshly dead, he had been stripped and bolted to the wall. His chest proscribed the usual sag where the Tar Babies had snipped out the ribs in order to get at his lungs. The crudely stitched flaps of skin failed to conceal the brutality of the surgery. Carrier gave him the once over to check that they hadn't started filching the corpses for new delicacies and moved swiftly on.

On these trips, Carrier kept a look out for bonesmiths. It was rare to find one, but she knew they lived here in the city. She didn't understand the nature of Jake's illness, other than its connection with the flood of toxicity the Mile had suffered, but presumably there were drugs to counter the symptoms, if not cure them completely. Bonesmiths could sometimes be discerned by the cut of their clothes, which were usually a little less threadbare than most people's, and by the rude color of their flesh. Good meat and fruit would pay for treatments. They weren't hard to spot.

Food, however, was. Carrier had not yet stooped so low as to scavenge carrion from her dead neighbors, but she knew plenty who did. She wondered, as she examined the loose spoors of a dog on the curb, how long it would be before she succumbed. Meat was meat. Meat was life. What did it matter the form it came in? Close your eyes and it all tasted the same. The source meant nothing once it was in the belly.

The stool was fresh; she darted looks in all directions, hoping to see its author. Ahead, the canal was a grim brown split separating the north of the city from the south. Beyond it lay the boroughs of Mango, Bliss Key and Loeb Gardens. Some nights at Gannet Spires, beyond the northernmost reach of the city, you could see aircraft taking off from Ochre Point airfield, just outside the perimeter. Their lights winked red and white in the sky, but never followed a trajectory that brought them over the city. Everything that took off from Ochre Point was heading in the general direction of away. Watching them was a tantalizing hint of life beyond Howling Mile, a way of keeping a grip on what could be. One day.

Streetlamps struggled to penetrate the pall of smog over the canal but here and there they did at least manage to cast weak, wintry color onto the water. A Bordertype barge chugged by, gun turrets swiveling from the bleak, blocky Hub skyline to the sandbagged bank that introduced the Outermost. There were a few animal bodies, pale, bloated gas-sacs that were beyond her identification skills, lolling on the edge of the oily currents.

Movement.

The knife became a part of Carrier's hand so quickly it was as if it had always been there. She pressed herself back into the scabrous doorway of a defunct pickle shop and watched as a shadow lengthened on a bridge across the filthy water. What she saw next was so unexpected that she almost dropped her weapon. She could not stay her jaw, though.

It was a man, in brilliant white clothes, leaping and spinning barefoot as he reached the apex of the hump-back bridge. His hair was long and black, tied back in a pony-tail. He was smiling as he moved; at one point, the sheer exhilaration of his performance drew a bark of laughter from deep inside him. Then a motor cut through the silence and he was off, scampering down the banks of the canal and disappearing beneath the bridge. A bike roared past, two dogs—already skinned—hanging limply from the belt of its rider. The smell of the fuel as it farted from the exhaust could not conceal the aroma of raw meat. Carrier's mouth filled with drool. The Dancer was forgotten.

A promising day ended poorly. Carrier was able to catch only two pigeons, a pair of denuded, probably diseased critters, but they would bulk out a pot of vegetables and broth. She had been gone longer than she intended, but took her time heading back, checking and re-checking the route for street pirates. Manky though the meat was, it was good enough to be mugged for. Telling her what she already knew, the gauge on her wrist piped up. In an hour, the microbes that were crawling all over her skin would start making her feel very bad, very quickly. Jake was relying on her. What good would she be to anyone if she became what he was becoming?

The same sour smell of death, of dying, assaulted her nostrils as she passed through the decontamination arches and into the apartment. She locked and sealed the door behind her and entered the flat proper through a second door. She dropped the birds into the sink and went to see how her friend was doing.

"Gone a long time," he said.

"Don't start getting brattish, Jake," she admonished. "Pickings weren't exactly easy today."

"There are ways around it, you know. Not everyone goes out to hunt. There are alternatives."

She regarded him from the doorway. He was mashed into the corner of his bed with an ashtray full of cold butts and glistening twists of toilet tissue. His nose was a red bulb. His eyes had sunk so far into his head he should be able to see his skull. Carrier's heart went to him, despite the harsh code he was dealing her.

"There's no need for that. And I won't do it, even if there is," she said.

"You might live to regret it," he snapped, the words failing as he creased up under another barrage of coughs.

"I might," she said. "I'm going to take a bath. Then I'll make us some supper."

They weren't lovers. Not anymore. It had started that way, an easy, comfortable need that they could fulfill in each other. It was a way of finding humanity where precious little prevailed. Over the years, as the seal around the city was put in place, and fortifications were applied to the perimeter, strengthening it, so its captives weakened. Jake had been a tanner working in the east of the city, near Vermilion Hill. Carrier had taught underprivileged children at a makeshift school in Scissor Point West. They met during a rally in Sprint Gardens, just outside the Core. What began as a peaceful protest quickly degenerated into a brawl as the banner-wavers stormed the phalanx of troops guarding the Core. Many were shot dead. Tanks were driven through the square, dispersing the protesters. Water-cannon and tear gas were used. Over the noise and the mayhem, a calm, female voice was repeating rules that the citizens of Howling Mile must observe.

"Study the demarcation lines well, those trying to breach them will be liquefied.... May your death be swift and dignified.... Anyone found on the streets during curfew hours will be liquefied.... May your death be swift and dignified.... Howling Mile is an officially recognized plague area and has been contained indefinitely.... May your death...."

Jake had been involved in a running battle along one of the main streets radiating out from the Core when he was shot at point blank range with a rubber bullet. At the same time, Carrier had been clipped on the leg by the water cannon and was tossed into the road, slithering along on her backside as the jet sought to punish her further. She was brought to a stop by a lamp post that clouted her half-senseless. She lay on her side, staring dazed at the other figures around her, specifically this one, who was opening and closing his mouth like a beached fish, his face turning blue.

She struggled over to him and loosened his clothing, managed to relax him and encourage him to breathe. Miraculously, neither of them were arrested while she fought to revive him. It helped that one of the protesters, having wrapped himself in the national flag, set fire to his fuel-drenched body on the Core steps. He blazed so fiercely that the paint on an army vehicle six feet away began to blister.

Somehow, Carrier helped to drag Jake the half mile to the hospital while the skirmishes went on around them. He recovered quickly enough so that, a few hours later, he was able to watch the fires burning in the streets from a treatment window. She pulled him away and the movement turned into a kiss, so quickly that she had no idea how it could have happened. She took him back to her flat.

They made love while the city rioted.

The next day, the troops carried the corpses out of Sprint Garden and dumped them in the canal. Two days after that, the first of the helicopter patrols began; heavy-duty choppers armed with thermal-imaging cameras and flamethrowers blatted and thrummed low through the off-limit streets.

A week later, sores began to develop on Jake's legs.

"See any Mowers?"

Carrier shook her head. It was the first thing either had said since they started their meal. Jake had picked at his soup as usual. "I saw Kram," she said. "The Tar Babies had got to him."

"Jesus."

Carrier nodded. "That's the third this month. Before, they never took anyone within The Hub."

"It's a worry," agreed Jake, as a tidal wave of coughing creased him.

His chest simmered moistly once it had died down. "Did you find a bonesmith?"

Carrier said, "No. I was preoccupied with finding the food that you aren't eating."

"Don't, please," Jake said. "I'm trying. I just don't seem able...." He trailed off and regarded the gray broth miserably. "I found more blood today. In my piss."

Carrier didn't say anything. She collected the dishes together and withdrew to the kitchen where she cried hard and quietly, a storm that was over in seconds.

"Are you going out again tonight?" Jake called.

Carrier made an affirmatory noise as she scrabbled to dry her face.

"Extra care, then," he warned. "It isn't just the uniforms we need to watch out for anymore."

Jake's sores migrated. His back was ravaged by broad, purpuric sweeps of hot color. He complained of silvery stools. The whites of his eyes would redden under the slightest strain. Any light, even the dull, refracted mudshine that squeezed through the polyethylene roof, hurt his eyes. He took to his bed and there he stayed, seeming to sink further into it as his spine crumbled and drew his body into itself.

"I'm dying," he said, a year after they met. It had been such a statement of the obvious, something he could have uttered six months previously, that Carrier found herself laughing out loud. Perhaps he was too surprised by the reaction, and infected by a moment of hilarity that was all too rare in the Mile, that he could not complain. Instead he laughed too, until his frothing lungs arrested them both.

Now Jake wore his headphones, trawling the airwaves for radio stations that didn't exist, whenever Carrier went on a hunt, or, like tonight, when she slipped out on one of her illegal travels.

3 lifeline

>>> hi carrier. the sea has a strange look to it today. v calm, v blue, but wind qt powerful. not enough to make choppy, but odd vibrations on surface. looks like netting, as if someone had caught the sea on a fishing trip!

Carrier could not remember the last time she had visited the coast. It must have been as a child. Enderby had this infuriating quality, an ability to draw out the most recalcitrant of memories by simply dropping into their missives what were little more than diary entries.

She replied:

>>> e. wish as awlays i could be there to see for myself. maybe one day??? :-)

It took an age to type. The keyboard was old, the keys were either missing or stuck when depressed, and the screen was split by a feathered crack, the picture fading and flickering. Carrier invariably returned home from such evenings with pounding headaches and knuckledusters of pain.

>>> j. is in bad way. no med. end not long away i fear. any way you can get med? smugle it in? i'd pay.

Wind fluted through the stone stairwell, rattling the doors to the hospital. Here, on the fourth floor of a fire-ravaged building in The Hub, she made weekly pilgrimages to draw a bead on her sanity and remind herself that there was more to the world than the mange-ridden rat-runs of the Mile. How had she found this place? She struggled to remember. Tiredness, lack of good food, fear, all of that was conspiring to subtract from her what she needed to make herself feel real. She used to have a good brain, before the Wave. She was bright and quick, quicker than the sparks she used to teach under those tarps on the embankment in Scissor Point West. She and those children would clap their hands over their ears as the big, lumbering freight trains chuntered overhead, carrying weapons, or fuel from the mines in Kobi-Finn. She would pretend to carry on the lessons and the children would squeal and yell: *We can't hear you!*

Kram. That was it. Kram had told her about the building. It had been a small hospital, a cancer ward for children and little else. It had been consumed by a fire some years ago, at around the same time as Enclosure. Nothing had been done with it since. Even the squatters had not colonized it, perhaps in deference to the babies that had died there. Kram had sought her out, though. He was canny, Kram. He knew people and understood their cravings—or he did, before the Tar Babies had their way with him. For a few nuggets of wisdom about this and that, for a few tokens of her appreciation, he had given her an address where, he said, "You can fly for a while," his goatee beard dancing around excitedly on his chin as he spoke.

She had paid him without checking first what he was tantalizing her with. Trust was not something that existed among Milers any more, but certain individuals inspired a little of whatever had taken its place. Or maybe it had been that she was so desperate for a glimpse of something new that she risked his duping her.

Carrier had broken into the hospital that same evening, the first time she had deliberately violated the curfew. Somehow she quelled her panic as she climbed the stairs in the dark, her boots crushing the carapaces of unseen insects or kicking against some fleshy deadweight. Swing doors of partially molten plastic, smeared with grease and old blood gave in on a room full of tiny, carbon-scored metal cots. Cartoon characters tacked to a wall had survived the blaze. Carrier did not care to scrutinize what remained in the cots. She was grateful for the shadows that night fed through the windows. She tripped against a metal notice that had fallen from one of the cots. *DNR*, it read, and nothing else. A notice board filled with dozens of photographs of toddlers was a semi-charred tableau that, luckily, she did not need to study; what awaited her was in the adjoining room.

She could not believe that the computer was still working, less that its modem functioned properly—albeit slowly. The email folder listed correspondence only from an entity called Enderby. The author at this end had been a Dr. Geeson. The final few emails from Enderby, dated three years previously, had all been requests to reply as soon as possible. *Why won't you reply?* and *Have I said something I shouldn't?* and *To hell with you then!*

It had been too much to expect that Enderby would still be at the end of the line, wherever that was, waiting for a missive from an old friend, but....

>>> damn right u'd pay!!! but serious - how would i get it 2 u? just as hard and dangerous to break in as is to out?!? know it's hard 2 take, carrier, but listen. j is going to die. you have 2 deal with it. sorry sorry sorry. im here for anything u need, u know it, so long as it's just words.

Of course, he was right. Perhaps it was what she wanted to hear; she had been angling for exactly that response. In Howling Mile, you never knew what was right, only what was wrong. Enderby had aired what, deep inside, Carrier knew to be true.

>>> dont mean to bug you, e. just get a bit desprate sometimes. this place... hey - guess what i saw today?

>>> a shoulder of ham performing a shakespeherian rag?

>>> ??? silly. no, i saw the strangest person.

>>> a strange person? in the mile? get away!

>>> stop it. in the hub. i was hunting. and theres this man comes

leaping over a bridge! he was dre

Noise. New noise. Not the skirl of wind in the chimneypots or the occasional distant volley of rotor beats as choppers made their patrols.

The *schuss* of a foot on a riser.

Head craned hard to the right, Carrier strained to hear more, to hear *confirmation*. She heard nothing else, but a whiff of cigarette smoke was being pushed by something on the stairwell.

>>> z

Silently, she pulled the hard drive out of the tower and pocketed it. 'z' was a code she had agreed with Enderby early on in their correspondence. It meant she had to sign off immediately but would contact him as soon as she safely could. Eyes fixed on the door to the ward and its filthy, opaque windows, Carrier backed away. At her back, a glassless frame that she had covered with a blanket to hide her subterfuge from the choppers. The fire escape nudged up against it. She had never left the building this way, but had always considered that fire escapes might be an enforced option one day. Now her mistrust of them was about to be tested.

A wind had risen in the night, channeling through the narrow streets of The Hub, a foul breath of Outermost air that reeked of shallow graves and polluted lakes. Carrier swung a leg out of the window and hung against the wall, watching the doors. She heard the fire escape three feet beneath her, squealing lightly as it rocked in the wind.

A shadow moved across the plastic window in the door. A bloody hand obscured it, pushing a way forward into the room.

4 descent

How can he smoke if he has no lungs?

What was louder? Her feet clanging on the textured metal staircase or the thrum of blood in her ears? The zig-zag of black iron dipped and lurched sickeningly, a rending noise canceling everything else out as the pins connecting it to this rotten brick worked loose. She had to stop and scrunch herself into a corner of the stairwell as a helicopter chattered past; fortunately, its cameras were trained on a different area of the street.

Carrier glanced upwards, at the window she had vacated. A figure was hunched over the frame, looking across the city, a pall of blue smoke wreathing its head.

She continued down the fire escape. *Not right. Not right. Not right.*

The words fit the rhythm of her feet on the risers. It helped her to put one foot in front of another, so she went on. *Not right. Not right.*

It had been Kram she had seen bolted and splayed to the wall. Hadn't it? She forced her mind to return to that bloody spectacle, but it would only offload flashes of memory, as if the entire sequence were too much to relive again.

Kram riveted to the wall.

Kram's slack face, a pink froth of saliva dried to a glaze on his lips.

His eyes. His eyes.

It was Kram. His chest had been vacuumed clean and sealed shut with rough sutures. Broad black bruises spoilt his torso where the Tar Babies had performed their thoracic evacuation on him. Tar Babies invariably used tin snips, or some similar tool, to get at that sopping cargo.

It had been Kram. No question. She imagined those cold blue lips now, curling softly as he loosed his intoxicating promise into her ear... *somewhere you can fly....*

So what the hell was he doing stealing around the burned hospital? And after curfew?

Carrier snorted laughter and had to put a hand to her face to stifle any more. Rain had turned the street to a glassy film of blue orange. Studs of sodium light fizzed in the walls; blades of soft color pushed through the dark, at times dazzling her. For a moment, she was disoriented. The black claws of buildings were like beggars' hands beseeching passersby for coppers. Something with more death than dog in it worried a cluster of ancient refuse bins. Tin cans clattered and spun on the pavements. Someone screamed somewhere far away.

Pressing her hand against the drive in her pocket, Carrier struck out west, hugging the backstreets, keeping the knife loose in her hand, its blade coated with grease to kill its propensity to flash.

She noticed the moon, warped and muddied through the filthy synthetic enclosure, some three miles above the city. For a while, she watched it waxing and waning through the impurities in the domed roof, until a raft of high cloud smothered it. Now she moved again, more confident in this fresh darkness. She made a series of turns into crannies and nooks so narrow they hardly deserved a name, but their labels glowed in the mouth of every turning: Wasp Way, Priest Niche, Spinney Street, Hatchet Rise. She was making good progress, and was soon across the canal—a mere ten minutes from home—when, turning into Godless Arch, she was brought up sharp by a Mower eating its supper.

Oh... shit.... Dead soft, the words sucked back into her lungs, on a carpet of frigid air. The Mower was trying to empty the contents of a human head onto the road. Mouthless, it pressed its food against its throat, where teeth were ranged horizontally, peeking out of the flesh. It was necessary to fling its head right back in order to expose as much of its throat as possible during meals. Its eyes were visible at these moments: dull, ochre orbs writhing with tics. Its face was dead flat; nothing so grand as a nose provided relief, just a few strings of wet flesh, guarding a supersensitive membrane, like bars. Carrier hoped that her scent would be overpowered by the gobbets upon which the Mower was gorging itself.

Retreating slowly, she circled back, retracing her steps to the canal, where she selected a different route. The alert on her wrist began squawking at her. Time turning against her, she ran.

Jake was asleep when she returned. The flesh of his exposed chest was thin and febrile to the touch. She drew the blanket up around his ears and stroked his hair. It was the only thing about him that had retained any depth, any strength. She had left it mighty close tonight. The alarm had died—signaling the cessation of cover—twenty feet from the Corridor. She had got herself under the nozzles and doused her body with disinfectants, but there was still a thin chance she had been poisoned. Part of her hoped that maybe this time she had. She had not sprinted as fast as she could. Maybe, deep inside, she was sick of running and just wanted to be sick, like Jake. Wanted to slough off the heavy topcoat of expectation and reliability; to give herself to disease and death so that she wouldn't have to continue with what was no more an existence than that forged by the rats on the canal bank.

She crawled into bed and listened as the ticking of her watch met the slowing beat of her heart. By the time the two had found an equilibrium of sorts, she was asleep.

5 divertissement

Dawn in Howling Mile. How the city wakes:

On Blue Loop, the timber-logged circuit around Emulsion Ponds, Rijker and his brothers, Shane and Nathan, hunt for silverlings. An exposed section of the city, far from the glut of vertiginous buildings, and highly toxic, Blue Loop is a popular haven for these silver-furred mammals, who nest in a collapsed forest and find protection in the high levels of radiation seething off the milky surface of the Ponds. Good prices can be paid for the entrapment of silverlings. Hardly anything on the animal is wasted. Their pelts and teeth—prized as good luck charms—fetch top dollar outside the city. Rijker has a contact, one of the Bordertypes, who ensures his protection in return for titbits off the animals he slaughters. This morning, Rijker has a brace of creatures and is coming around the north end of the Loop when he notices Shaun pocketing a jawbone that he has torn from another silverling caught in a trap they set the previous night. Rijker hasn't been feeling too well of late. He shoots a harpoon through Shaun's shoulder. Though the blow isn't enough to kill him, his protective suit is breached. He's rushed to hospital but Shaun will come down with Iridia within 24 hours. He'll be dead within a week, his skin flashing with patches of slow decay, like meat on the turn.

Fallow lives on her own by Stone Tree Wood near Universe Curve. It might have been a prettier place before the Wave, though it still affords an excellent view of the skies thanks to a unique sheltered aspect provided on one side by a shoulder of land that cuts out the glare from the city and, on the other, a great swathe of petrified trees. Fallow is a quadriplegic mother. This morning she wakens early and waits for the locks to spring, alerting her to the arrival of her sister and full-time assistant, Suke. Last night, however, Suke was attacked in Jute Street. She was blinded by acid flung at her by a rogue Mower who had come in from The Outermost to hunt in The Hub. She escaped, but the acid eating into her flesh did not subside and she died by the canal. Scavengers quartered her body and stole away with it before the sun had chance to warm it again. Her screams had been heard all around the Mile; Fallow heard them too, in sleep, and called out to her sister. She remembered nothing on waking.

Now Fallow hears another cry, that of her child. She cannot move from her bed. It will be two days before the crying stops. Fallow will still be alive when, in a week, the smells of decay reach out to her from the nursery. Able to shift her head only slightly, Fallow will commit suicide by gnawing into the meat of her shoulder, a major blood vessel parting like perished elastic between her teeth. Neither of the bodies will be discovered for six years.

In Fahrenheit Steps, a group of dissidents, pitifully undersubscribed, put into operation a plan that has taken eight months to bring to fruition. A home-made bomb—a perilous undertaking, considering that the Bordertypes boast a state-of-the-art munitions detection system—has been passed from rebel to rebel, concealed during its construction over the months in places as varied and colorful as a toilet cistern, a graveyard for televisions and the chest cavity of a cadaver.

A distraction is underway as the first chapped fingers of sunlight reach across the sky. Three of the dissidents have started a fire in the street, an hour before curfew is over, igniting a desiccated pyre of dead dogs, ancient newspapers and torn, obsolete standards. They're all screaming themselves sick. Every morning for the last year or so, a single chopper peopled by three Bordertypes has patrolled this quadrant. A mate will rejoin the chopper as it heads out towards the Chabazite Stretch. It needs to work now. Heat is getting to the group. The bomb will be sniffed out sooner rather than later. A few of the dissidents are unhappy with the apparent languor of some of their colleagues. The raw materials for another bomb are unlikely ever to materialize again; the contacts for the last one have been arrested and, most probably, executed without trial.

A figure watches proceedings from a fourth floor window in a broken building. Having masterminded the strategy, he nervously chews his nails in the hope that they might succeed. Failure will mean removal from his current position.

Low strums of sound feather out from a gulley between distant buildings. An arc light punches its way out of the congestion of concrete and steel, shivers against the polyethylene roof and darts in their direction. The rotor's roar quickens.

Didn't their plan hinge on the usual approach of the Bordertypes? One warning, then woe betide? The leader motions to his colleague in the shadows. *They're coming.*

The chopper tips into the street, its beam homing in on the three arsonists. An insectile rasp from the onboard loudspeakers: "On the floor, face down, or be liquefied."

The dissidents hurriedly concur. They know what is coming.

The Bordertypes bring the chopper in to a shallow hover, flamethrowers trained on the dissidents. A figure races from the building, hunched against the beat of the rotors, and flings himself at the gunman, sitting side-saddle on the lip of the chopper's entrance. Before he can swing the gun to neutralize the threat, the gunman is trapped in a bear hug. Realizing that they are in danger, the pilot begins to steer the helicopter clear of the street before any more dissidents can storm the craft. The helicopter is at seventy feet and rising when the bomb, strapped to the chest of the dissident, detonates. A great arc of flame from a broken fuel line engulfs the dissidents on the ground. The leader of the group manages to escape the room that has been his observation post for the past few hours just before the chopper slams into the building, taking out the first two floors and causing the rest of the building to implode. Within seconds, the only sound is the fire as it spreads. The sun has climbed over the horizon and now adds color to the rest of the street. In the honeyed light, it looks almost pretty.

6 contact

Carrier came out of sleep at speed, convinced for a split second that her face was a bullet fired from a gun. Her body was fooled sufficiently to be unable to pull in breath, so fast did she believe she was traveling.

Something was different. She rose quickly, adding a pair of combat trousers to the black vest and pants in which she liked to sleep. She quashed as stupid the sudden conviction that Jake had died during the night but she went to check on him anyway. He was sleeping, shallowly, but at least he was resting. Too many recent nights had been filled with his coughs and splutters. She was tired of hearing him rage quietly at the moon. "Still alive, you bastard! Still breathing!" He didn't seem to possess enough energy to look for the moon now, let alone curse it.

Carrier went to the window and looked out at Madman's Square. More bad weather was ganging up on the Mile: hammerheads of cloud reared up in the south. She watched the road coalesce out of the hazy dawn. A helix of black smoke rose angrily from the rooftops; whatever had created the column was presumably what had wakened her. Checking on Jake again, and leaving a bottle of water by his side for when he stirred, she took a brief prophylactic shower beneath the Corridor nozzles and stepped outside.

Almost immediately she saw The Dancer.

He was moving east, beneath the verandah of what had once been a huge meat market but which was now a blasted edifice of bullet-studded concrete. His gait was loose, he didn't so much walk as bounce on the balls of his feet, and she liked the way his hair hung around his shoulders, unlike yesterday when it had been contained in a knot. He was carrying a flower. No flowers existed in the Mile anymore. Carrier was certain. She had only ever seen flowers on the color plates in whatever ravaged books she sometimes came across at the children's hospital. Her heart raced at the simple punch of violet that dangled from his fingers. She wanted to call out to him but her mouth was dry; she feared he might run away, like some startled rabbit.

She followed him instead.

He didn't move fast, but he was agile and, to Carrier, had made a turn without his body giving the least clue that it was about to. Sometimes it seemed as though he left a stain of himself on the air as he redirected, as if some ghost of himself was fading into the route he might otherwise have pursued. Carrier found herself hastening after these phantoms before realizing she was chasing air. Then she would have to retrace her steps, finding a narrow alleyway that she had bypassed and into which he had jinked. It was as though he knew he was being followed and was attempting to lose his tail. At one point, laughter burst from her. The freedom, the suppleness of The Dancer's limbs mocked the tension in hers. She was delighted with his fluidity. She grew suspicious of her awareness; perhaps she was still asleep and The Dancer was only a figment intruding into it.

The dreamlike quality to her pursuit of him increased as the rain began to fall. By the time the prints his feet had made in the mud were found by her own, they were already ruined by the water. He seemed able to erase himself in the very same moment that he so explicitly, yet subtly, made a statement of physicality. He walked without apparent caution. The rogue Mower that had panicked many of the streets in The Hub didn't seem to faze him; neither did the threat of Bordertypes enforcing the curfew, which they were still in defiance of. Whenever the sound of a helicopter bore down on them, he melted into the shadows and Carrier would have to react quickly, or risk stumbling upon him as well as giving herself away to the authorities.

Another turn, another check of her movements, another shift into a deeper part of the city. This thoroughfare was blocked by the roasted skeleton of a Bordertype chopper. Still smoking, the cockpit had been expunged, like the confused pulp pressed from a pomegranate. The only way onward was via the melted innards of the craft. Its portside guns had bowed before the ferocity of the fire, the sliding doors warped on their runners. Carrier counted four carbonized figures sitting inside the helicopter. The two pilots had drawn themselves into a fetal position at time of death. Bizarrely, the other two were bound in a tight hug. Parts of them had been blown off. Other parts, notably their ribcages, had been melded together by the intense temperatures at the height of the inferno.

She was still aware of her surroundings, still certain that they were south of the canal yet north of the Core. A few more turns however, all of them right, had her doubting her sanity. By rights, they should have been back where they started, or at least, tighter within a spiral of the immediate area. Instead, she found her feet treading on greensward. A hill swept away to her right, where previously she'd have sworn there had been a heap of slag and a conspiracy of rusting, collapsed cranes. The forbidding arches that sluiced you away into runnels connecting with The Outermost had been replaced by a fan of trees. The sounds were not those of a hot, slowly imploding and corroding city but the *shush* of dry grasses.

"Different, isn't it?"

Carrier flinched at the voice by her ear but when she turned, The Dancer was some ten feet away, twisting the stem of the flower through his fingers. He was not looking at her. Instead, his attention was commanded by a flock of Shelduck arrowing over a distant, misty wood.

"I didn't—" Carrier began, but her words drifted off lamely. What was she going to tell him that he didn't already know? *follow you? expect this?*

"No," The Dancer said, easily. "You didn't." Now he looked directly at her and even at this distance, she could see gray flaws, like miniature galaxies, in the brilliant apple green universe of his eyes. He smiled at her and moved away. "Come on," he called.

Who are you? Carrier wanted to ask him, but perhaps not as much as *Why are you?* She followed, keeping distance between them, silently marveling at the way he walked ridges and lips and dips in the earth as though they weren't there. His feet were amazing. He kept his rhythm no matter what, while she buckled and lurched in his wake.

"Where are we going?" she mumbled at last, the insanity of her surroundings anaesthetizing her to the adventure.

"Just up here," he said. His voice was nothing spectacular. It didn't shimmer and prance with extraordinary promise, like the smooth mash of muscles in his shoulders and back.

"Where are you from?" she asked.

"Back there," he said, gesturing with the flower.

She persisted. "Are you a Miler?"

"Are you?"

"I live there. So yes, I suppose I am." She looked around. So many trees. The only green she knew about was in the lymph that drizzled from Jake's ulcers. "But I've never seen this place before. Did we come through a checkpoint by mistake?"

"What do you think?"

"I think I'm dreaming," she said slowly. She remembered Kram at the window and shivered. "Or going mad."

"There's a lot going on in Howling Mile," he said. "A lot you know about, but a lot you won't have heard a squeak about."

"Why tell me?"

"You have gifts. You noticed me."

"You kind of stand out."

Another smile. White. Even, tiny teeth. Lots of pink gum. "I can assure you, I do not."

Carrier said, "You're like a beacon, believe me."

"Maybe I am," he said. "But it's of my own choosing, and I signal only those that interest me."

"Really?" Doubt needled her. She wasn't sure she liked the idea that it was she who had been stalked and prepared, like an animal enticed into a trap.

"We could be of use to each other."

Guardedly, she asked him what he meant.

"Moves are afoot," he said. She almost laughed. He had such an odd, old-fashioned way of putting things. "I'm talking not of the disorganized, tokenistic order of dissent here. This is something subtler."

"Why do you need any dissent at all if you have a link to this place?"

The Dancer bowed his lips dismissively. "This place? This place is a part of the subtlety. Let me clear something up for you."

He held the flower up between them. The petals were full and ruddy, a rash of moisture coating each one. With his forefinger and thumb, he plucked one of the petals from the stalk. She felt a similar action at the back of her head, where it curved to meet her neck. It was as though he had reached inside her brain and snapped something off. She felt woozy, and a little sick, but the fragmentation of the scene in front of her kept her focused. Everything beyond the frond in his hands was failing. His smiling face was melting, blending with the fleshy tones of the sky. His white clothes grew soiled, mixing in with the grit of a muddy pavement. His eyes became the punched-in windows of a crack den filled with nervous squatters, watching this mad witch as she fell apart on the street. The green turned to dust. Ash that had been his soft cape of hair blew in her eyes, and stung her face.

Carrier staggered away, seeking refuge beneath the sodden tarpaulin covering the face of a museum. She heard whoops and hollers shiver down the back streets towards her. Code. There were Tar Babies nearby.

One of the boards over the museum windows was loose. She tore her nails loosening it further and squeezed inside as the first of the bikes scorched onto the main road. She watched them as they cut up the muddy road with a series of violent skids and wheelies. The air was soon black with exhaust fumes. She sank back into the shadows and sought refuge beneath a marble angel whose wings had been ripped off. *Cast Out* read the legend on the base. A chink of light allowed Carrier a look at its face. Looking skyward, there was still joy in its eyes, even as it cowered beneath the very figure that had destroyed it. Crushed beneath a welter of feelings, fears and a twisted sense of hope, Carrier slept. She did not wake up for seventeen hours.

part two: la grande jetée
7 vantage

Carrier was shivering and didn't know where she was when her eyes cracked open. Vague mounds stole back their shape from the darkness. Soon she was able to discern that she was in a gallery full of vandalized paintings and statues. The angel was the only piece that had remained untouched, perhaps because it appeared to be damaged already.

For some inexplicable reason, she felt threatened. It was pitch black outside; far off she could hear the labored whine of motorbikes. She didn't want to leave the building now, despite her previous flouting of the curfew; she knew it would be only a matter of time before she was caught. Moreover, she didn't want to leave this room with its fallen angel. She felt safe in its presence, even though the vandalism around her proved that her safety was not impregnable. Curiosity won out.

A cold, stone stairway swept in a spiral up to a first floor, the windows of which were covered with great cuts of heavy cloth. Here, more paintings were slashed or daubed with paint, and a small fire in the corner had apparently consumed other canvases. All of the glass cabinets that had once housed ancient trinkets had been looted.

Carrier climbed to a second floor, and then a third. By accident, she found a small door behind another huge square of intricately patterned carpet—what she had assumed was a display—yet she felt a draft on her ankles from beneath it. The door opened on a wooden stepladder fixed to the wall. At the top of that, a hinged flap allowed her onto a long, flat roof. Amazingly, there was no evidence of life here. Clearly, the havoc-makers had missed the secret passage. Knowing that, she felt safer about inspecting the city from here. Beneath a caul of drizzle, Howling Mile was hangdog and feverish tonight. Carrier thought of how much fight the city had taken out of her; how tired she felt sometimes. How close to insanity. She thought of what she had seen—or thought she had seen—these past few days and, in her mind, she tried to back away from what it must mean. If you weren't prepared to bare your teeth at the city sometimes, it would consume you. There was plenty to worry about in that neat, exploding mandala of surprisingly well-lit streets. The Tar Babies. The Mowers. Carrier had been biting back for so long, she had lost any sense of what was good anymore. Even Jake was dragging her down. She felt bad about thinking that about him, but there it was.

She had a clear view of the Core from here. Pale, pulsing aircraft warning lights at its summit were just visible in the smudges of cloud that smothered it. The building was like a bolt pinning the city to the ground for fear it might otherwise succumb to the spin of the planet, peel itself free and fly off.

She watched a gang of youths closing in on a woman who was trying to carry a sack of grain home on her back. She wasn't aware of them; they glided down vein-thin alleyways, joining or splitting up depending on the route of their quarry. It was like watching quicksilver. Carrier tried calling to the woman, but her shouts were whipped to nothing by the rain and the distance. She turned away as the gang closed in, and went to the other side of the roof. No matter how she strained, she could see no evidence of the countryside that The Dancer had shown her yesterday. It must have been some kind of elaborate trick. Maybe he had drugged her somehow; that would explain the strange traces of him she had seen unraveling in the air. The sudden thought of him excited her; she marveled at the fact that he had been out of her thoughts even this long.

She watched the slow coming of dawn and the weird reflections it cast on the perspex roof of the city. She dozed a little while, feeling safe under the rim of the parapet, and dreamed of Jake. In the dream, he was bulkier than she knew him to be, with fresh color in his cheeks and eyes. He smiled a lot.

She wakened as the curfew alarm pulsed through the city. Her eyes were wet.

8 bonesmith

Tweeds and a tightly rolled umbrella. What else could he be? Carrier checked and doubled back. He was squealing before she had got within thirty feet of him.

"I haven't got any money! Look at me! Do I look like I have any money? And I'd be bad for eating. You'll catch something evil. Stay clear! Stay clear!" He had an unpleasantly nasal voice and an ill-fitting moustache which looked like something trying to escape his nose.

"Do you have any medicines on you? Anything?"

His panic subsided quickly. "You're a pillhead, are you? Well why not? What's your poison? Wax? Influence? I haven't any on me. You'll—"

"It's not for me. I have a sick friend."

"Right, yes. of course it is. Look, I haven't—"

Carrier touched his arm gently. "I'll pay."

"I have money. I don't need—"

Again she interrupted him. "I'll pay."

Blushing furiously, he checked and rechecked the watch that wasn't on his wrist. "This way," he said.

Mewling, he fucked her against the door in a small office above a decrepit fish-processing unit. Fat, dusty files sat on groaning shelves; copious notes formed unstable cairns on a desk cratered by coffee rings. The oily smell of ancient fish sweated out of the walls. She reasoned that, had he turned her around to face him, she might just have vomited; it would have all been too much. As it was, she kept her stomach in check until, with half a dozen grunts, he climaxed. She pushed away from him, careful not to glimpse what he had loaded the condom with; few people in the Mile escaped one kind of taint or another. She had helped Jake to masturbate on a couple of occasions, when he grew too weak to pleasure himself. His come had been marbled with bloody veins and stank like the morgue.

"Delicious," the bonesmith said. "I should introduce myself. I'm Doctor Smoker."

"Okay," Carrier said, hitching up her combats. Smoker had torn at her breasts; they were red and sore. She eased them back into her vest and swallowed hard against the heat and the smell of the office. "I need some stuff."

He filled paper spills with pills and powders. He gave her a clutch of smoky glass bottles filled with viscous liquid. "Not cures," he said, unexpectedly tender. "Palliatives. They'll see him through the pain."

"I don't think he has much time."

Smoker looked thoughtful. "Well then, when you think he's near the end, give him one of these." He unlocked a drawer in the desk and pulled out a fat, yellow pearl. It felt waxy in her palm. "It will end his suffering," he said. "And yours too, I suspect."

On her way back, she darted into the children's hospital and took the steps two at a time until she reached the final landing. Here she paused and listened carefully. She guessed that such a hiatus would mean it was safe to come back, but she didn't want to risk walking in on a new mass of squatters. She wished there was some other place where she could load her hard drive and contact Enderby.

A glimpse through the plastic windows told her it was safe, but also pointless to enter. The monitor's face had been smashed; the hard drive console was a jigsaw puzzle of plastic casing and circuit boards on the floor. She wondered why Kram had done this, if indeed he was the guilty party.

Carrier hurried home, again forced to take a frustratingly long detour when she came up against a patrol of Bordertypes. Ten people had been chainganged and shuffled along crocodile fashion; more unfortunates whose faces didn't fit the Mile. She didn't want to be the eleventh.

Jake was naked and had collapsed in the kitchen. She helped him up, shocked by how light he was. Memories invaded of an early night together, his body writhing and pressing against hers, such a welcome, warm bulk. A weight that wanted to join with hers. He had been crying; his cheeks were scored with wet tracks through the grime that was settling on him in the flat. He was like an unread book left to molder on a table.

She fed him capsules and dissolved the powders in water. She talked to him without ever mentioning Kram, The Dancer, Enderby or Dr. Smoker. Jake didn't ask where she had found the drugs, but there was a sadness in his eyes that she hadn't noticed before. She half-hoped it was because of the decay of his body rather than any deep-seated resentment towards her. What he said next ruined her optimism.

"You're never here anymore," he said. His voice seemed little more than a vessel to carry the wet noises from his chest. "I feel I don't know you. I hardly know you."

"People drift apart," she said, at a loss for how she could resurrect his spirits.

"They do when one of them is dying," he retorted.

"Don't be silly."

"It's true. You're behaving like I'm a dead man already."

"I can't live for two people, Jake. Not here."

He regarded her darkly. "Any booze?" he asked.

"Not with medication."

"What does it matter?"

"*Not* with medication. Hear me?" She moved to the door.

He said, "You're pushing your luck, you know that don't you?"

She acted as though she hadn't heard him.

"You go out a lot. Too much. And that means that the chances of you being taken by a Mower, or stripped open by a Tar Baby, or carted off by the Borders grows all the time."

Carrier drew the gel from the blister pack into her nostrils as it evaporated.

"Either that, or the sickness will get you. Carrier, it's only a matter of time before you hit a HotZone without the protection you need."

"Then I'll make hell a more comfortable place for your arrival."

9 maps

A sequence of saloons in Bleach Street gave up nothing but a few cadaverous absinthe sippers and silent landlords holding broken shotguns over heavily tattooed arms. Carrier hurried on. Some of the men in the bars tried to chase her. Some hurled their glasses at her as soon as she stepped across the threshold. In *The Gutted Mother* a scrap of flesh uncoiled from the sodden pools beneath the optics and tried to sell her some Wax. The dose disappeared up one of the user's veins even as he was making his pitch.

Do you know The Dancer? Do you know a man who dances?

Stone faces greeted her. Or abuse. One man parted nicotian lips to breathe sourly upon her: *No, but I know a man who fucks.* Tiny worms crawled on the head of what he proffered.

The saloons gave way to a dark restaurant with half a dozen winddried fists hanging in the window, and then a series of warehouses. Men in tight-fitting ganseys loaded ominous black packages into metal containers and transported them onto canal barges with a crane. One of the men lost a finger to Carrier's knife when he lunged at her. She was pursued half a mile into Whisper Street where they lost the taste of the chase and sank back into the shadows.

Sick with fear, and what she had been forced to go through, Carrier approached the fountain at the center of the square. It had dried up years ago, much like her. She sat on its concrete perimeter and stared at the battered faces of the concrete cherubs and fish. Air rushed at her through the spouts and sprinklers. She stood up and stepped back.

Gouts of dirty water rushed from the fountain. She was drenched in a second. The gurgle of the water in the sluices deafened her to the extent that she didn't hear him moving across the cobbles towards her. Later, she would suspect that even without any sound at all she'd never have been distracted by him.

"Catch," he said, at her ear. She turned, and he was fifty feet away, his hands behind his head, coming forward fast, releasing shards of silver that came straight for her face. Knives. They gleamed in the dull light. She yelled and put up her arms to absorb the blows, but instead, she felt a thousand kisses on her skin. She lifted her face into a cloud of butterflies. The Dancer had vanished once more.

"Where are you?" she called.

He replied, calling her name, and she spied him peeking at her through the metope of a Greek Doric order, one of a series of listing columns that had once been the proud face of the city hall.

"How did you get up there?" she laughed, thrilled but fearing for his safety. Fractures ruined the shafts; chunks of the cornice lay around the base. "You'll get yourself killed!"

Clouds shifted; sunlight dazzled her for a second. He was gone when the shade returned. She scanned the rest of the façade but he was nowhere to be seen.

"Did you think about what we discussed?" His voice was calm for a man who must have sprinted the hundred yards to be where he was now, sitting cross-legged by the fountain. The hairs on her neck lifted. Her breasts tingled, recovered from Smoker's clumsy hands.

"I want it," she breathed. "I want you to show me. I don't know how I could have hesitated."

"So," he said. And smiled.

The Dancer would not reveal his true name, or whether, in fact, he possessed a name at all. He took her to where he lived, but although she was certain she had paid special attention to the route, by the time they were inside, she had no idea where they were. The Dancer lit candles and the room's details shimmered into view.

It was spartan in the extreme. But for a wall-length mirror to which a *barre* was affixed, the room contained a wooden chair, a gramophone and a small ceramic vase replete with a single flower of the sort The Dancer had been carrying when she first talked to him.

"It's nice here," she said. Parallelograms of sunshine slid into the floorboards from half a dozen skylights. The motes that had risen from their entrance sifted through the air between them and the mirror. The Dancer seemed to fade somewhat, darkening as though a shadow had passed over the roof, but when she was able to focus on him again, he was at the other side of the room, while traces of him seemed to linger in the space a few inches to her left.

The Dancer leaned over the gramophone; a few seconds later it began to crackle warmly and the room was filled with old, wavering music, lots of violins.

"I haven't heard…." she began.

"Nobody has," he said. "The only music we hear now is during shows of military strength on the steps of the Core."

"It's lovely."

"It's very old," said The Dancer.

"I wish more things were."

The Dancer took her hand and led her to the *barre*. The mirror offered her a full-length view of herself. "I look like this?" Carrier asked, looking at herself. "How strange. I've never seen so much of myself before." She laughed, her eyes drinking in her image, and that of The Dancer moving close behind her. His reflected eyes never leaving her own, he drew her arms out until she made a T-shape.

"Concentrate on your fingers," he whispered, though she didn't see his lips move.

"Which hand?"

"Both," he said, simply.

"I can't. It's impossible."

"It's not impossible." The Dancer's own hands ran along the length of first Carrier's left hand, then her right. When he had completed these journeys, she found that she was taking in the movements of all her fingers while staring at her own eyes in the glass. Peripheral vision didn't even come into it. She found that, if she concentrated, she could stretch the limits of her vision so that, for one exhilarating moment before she fainted, she could see the back of her own head.

"I knew you were fast," he said, somewhere north of the fuzziness in her mind, but south of what felt real. She came to and vomited thinly.

"Sorry," she managed.

A glass of water was pressed into her hand. "There will be worse."

The words took an age to make their impact. "What do you mean?" she asked, finally.

"I mean that there is a price to pay for knowledge," he explained.

"Opening you up to fresh experiences, teaching your senses to read new lines… it doesn't come without a cost. But pain can have its benefits too."

"I don't think I like the sound of that. I'm not sure I want to get involved after all."

He smiled and held out his hand. Hesitantly, she took it. He said, "You already are involved."

It was hard work, not least because Carrier learned she was not the exclusive focus of his attention. There were others under his aegis. Rainy nights when the sky was too fragmented to see anything, he would take her to various safe houses around The Hub and introduce her to what he called his "friends."

Chamfer was almost as accomplished a dancer as the man himself. She had a hard body packed with muscles that writhed inside a packaging of white skin as she performed *entrechats* and *fouettés* and *jetées* in a relatively grassy park on Usher Street. Where the top of her left breast welled against the tight fabric that enclosed it, she wore a branding, a symbol that, she said, meant "eternity" in a language that was older than Howling Mile, or whatever country surrounded it. The anonymous graffiti artist had inspired her.

"How do you know it means 'eternity'?" Tusk had asked, giving Carrier a wink. "It might mean 'dogbreath.' Or 'dunderhead.' " Tusk was a squat, blind boy of about twelve or thirteen. His lips bore black nuggets, chancres that never seemed to heal. He had been ravaged by the Wave, but under The Dancer's tutelage, was learning how to fight the diseases that threatened him.

Mowse's family had been decimated by a Mower attack in which she was lucky to have lost only her right hand and right cheek. In dreams, she said, she saw the face of the Mower that attacked her dipping in low, its teeth strimming the air like rotors, designed to shave flesh from the bone in seconds. Its face had been a riot of ecstasy, eyes rolled back into its skull, blood slathering that awful, webbed mouth. She had managed to stab the Mower through the throat with a length of splintered wood but her parents and sister were already half consumed. She had had to leave them.

There was also a man called Phale who lived in a room that burned day and night with hundreds of candles. His pinprick pupils steeled out of eyes so pale it was as if they were devoid of irises. A prayer callous on his forehead matched the worn nub on a blue, hessian mat at the center of his room.

Breathing the scorched air with its waxy fumes, Carrier had asked to whom did he pray?

"Anything that will have me," Phale had replied. His pacific nature cut through the harsh vapors of his home and calmed her. He gave them strong, smoky tea and played music that sounded like white noise through a tape deck with huge buttons that clunked when they were depressed. He winked at her, nodding at The Dancer. "What do you think of him, hey? Our Dancer? Our *Maître de Ballet?*"

Carrier leafed through a binder of maps drawn on onionskin pages. She recognized none of the countries they depicted. That, ostensibly, they were unnamed territories confused her further. Footnotes and diagrams and mathematical equations formed dense, chaotic marginalia next to the simply drawn land masses. Beautifully solid, with their contour lines and railroads and blue shaded lakes, the maps nevertheless called at something inside her.

Later, when they were walking back to The Dancer's home, Carrier saw Kram in Scar Road. He was sitting with his back against the wall, blue smoke, as last time, banding his features. A cigarette burned in his fingers. Emboldened by The Dancer's presence, she breathed in to call him.

"No," said The Dancer.

"But I know him."

"Nobody knows anybody here. Something else you need to learn."

"Something's wrong with him though. I thought I saw him the other day. The Tar Babies…."

But he wasn't listening. He led her away from Scar Road down Sugar Street, which ran parallel to the canal. Occasional ripe blasts would channel down the side streets to them. In the dark, Carrier fumbled for The Dancer's hand. It was warm and smooth in her own. She could feel his pulse, a measured beat, and she suddenly felt like crying, presented with this simple testament to his mortality. He was as vulnerable as she was. She squeezed his hand harder and felt her own heartbeat slow down, find his rhythm. When they emerged into the light of Lithium Lane, he was twenty feet behind her and she was holding her own hand. His smile came out of the gloom before he did.

"Those maps. Those places. Where are they?"

"Hush," he said. "Concentrate." The *port de bras* he was teaching her had brought an elegance to her arm movements that she had never thought possible. It was as if, sometimes, her arms did not possess bones, so effortlessly was she able to move them. Her execution of the *plié* had also been mastered; now she was able to fully bend her legs without taking her heels off the floor or lose her balance.

"Dancing is not enough," he said. "It's the discipline behind the dancing that is the most important. In fact, it's crucial. More important than anything. The butterfly cannot go until its wings have strengthened. And so it is with you...."

She was so happy, being molded by his strong, gentle hands, she could not resist teasing him. "Am I your little butterfly?" she asked.

His hands on her. Coaxing a little more movement here; repressing there her reflex to compensate for it.

"Think about the way you lift your foot to climb a step. Change the foot. Change the way you fold your arms; put the other hand on top for a change. Understand how it alters the balance in your body. Learn it."

At one point his hand slid over her breast while he made minute revisions to her upper posture. At another, as he reached to press her tummy in during what seemed an impossible stretch, his mouth came within millimeters of her own. Light glanced off the wet edge of his tongue; she caught a smell of spice, of sweetness.

He said, "When you control the exterior, when you can channel the power of your body and make it shift in the way you wish it, then you will have control over your interior. The unknowable parts of you become as obvious as your face in the mirror."

"I know so little about everything," she said, closing her eyes to the fire in her muscles. "This place. You. Myself."

"Not for long," he said.

So it went on.

His ministrations, sometimes mild, sometimes forceful, helped her to find a new level of physicality that she hadn't believed existed. He would ask her questions about her past while, naked, she worked at plucking a strip of biltong from her sacrum with her teeth. Arms trembling as they supported her entire weight, her head would fold inward and travel down her body, past her breasts, and navel, past the fuzz of her sex.

"Reach," he would say, breaking off from the questioning. And then: "Tell me more about your mother."

Talking to him helped her to relax enough to allow her spine the elasticity it needed to enable her head to travel up between her thighs and give her a chance at the biltong. At times, the extremity of effort and the surprise of seeing her own buttocks quivering millimeters from her face caused collapse. But the harder she trained and the more committed she grew, the less extreme her self-absorption became and she was not distracted.

He said, "They are interior maps." He said, "To make sense of what you see around you, to become *you*, you have to learn to withdraw. Look inside yourself."

She would grasp for the ripples of color that hinted from these impossible regions. Her greed undid her. The drab grays and browns zipped themselves up over those brilliant fractures and she found herself looking at a perfectly sealed stretch of Howling Mile. More of the same. She had had no idea just how frustrating the colors of the city could be until presented with some unusual alternative.

Finding the patience to allow such secrets to hatch pained her. The Dancer would sit, inscrutable, on the edge of a step, drawing in the dust with a stick or watching the clouds roll over or under the perspex dome. Words of encouragement from him had dwindled; she knew what she had to do.

"It's like a muscle," he had said. "A new muscle. You have to work it, use it constantly. It will be weak for a while. It will hurt too. But eventually it will contain great strength."

She had found a level of concentration that staggered her. Just before these glamors revealed themselves to her, she would find herself so deep in meditation that she felt she could control the speed of her heart or, if she wished it, change the direction of the blood in her veins. But it also made her tired as well.

Sweat dripping from her as she stood, exhausted, in the street outside The Dancer's home, Carrier remembered that there were other things that helped to make her who she was.

"Hey," she said. "I need some help."

10 murdrum

Again, she tried.

>>> enderby? you reading this? reply. please reply. ***please***

Nothing. Her fingers on the keys sent tight little echoes into the heights. The library was constructed in a circle and spiraled away from her. All of the books had been blasted to smithereens or burnt into hard carapaces that could not be removed from their shelves. Rogue pages, millions of them, covered the floor. Now and again, little skirls of paper would eddy around her ankles as a breeze flitted through the cavernous rotunda.

It was like being in a crypt.

>>> e? come on. i'm desperate.

She wondered if she might meet Enderby one day. Was it too much to hope for that the border might disintegrate in the future? Or maybe, she fancied, as her eyes blurred, staring at the pixels on the screen, he belonged to the secret interstices that punctuated this world, the glittering corridors she had yet to tame and travel.

>>> i'm here, carrier. thought u were dead. where did u go?

Relieved to have re-established contact with her friend, Carrier typed for an hour, answering questions, telling Enderby about Jake's decline as well as the incident with Kram. She stopped herself from mentioning The Dancer. It was important, she felt, to keep a secret back for herself. Nevertheless, something seemed to cause Enderby a lot of concern all of a sudden.

>>> don't liek it, carrier. something not right asbout the whole thing. you should try 2 leave. when j goes. try 2 get out. it's possible. some have done it. but 4 now, b careful.

His words failed to hit home. A week, even a few days previously, she might have heeded his warning and thought about taking the chance, working an escape. But having met The Dancer, being so close to eliciting something magical from the doldrums of her life, how could she leave now? Howling Mile was about to give up its treasure. She wanted to weigh her pockets down with the stuff, whatever it might be. If it meant a better life here, then bring it on. If she could let Jake share in what might be its restorative energy, then how could she turn her back on everything?

0>>> understand your concern, e, but something special here. this place has secrets. i'm close. can't give up now. you know me... stubborn fool!!!

There was no reply from Enderby. Sometimes this happened. The server went down or one or other of the machines crashed. It was frustrating and Carrier hated ending a session without saying goodbye, but she appreciated that having access to mailing systems at all was a high privilege.

She logged out and disconnected the hard drive. Her boots in the chaos of paper made *hissing* noises that lifted like birds into the shadows of the dome. Outside, a raw wind had picked up and was sprinting down the streets, driving needles of icy rain before it.

On the way back to her flat she trapped a dog in a doorway and slit its throat before it could run away. It was woefully thin, but its bones would bolster one of her watery soups. The carcass slung over one shoulder, she grinned as she thought of Jake's face when she came to toss this beast into the pot. He liked dog marginally less than he liked pigeon.

Jake was grinning too, but Carrier quickly saw that he didn't really have much say in the matter. A knife had all but separated the top of his head from his lower jaw. Much of the soft tissue on his face was gone. Evidence of a scuffle manifested itself in a cracked mirror, a disturbed pile of cheerful, old photographs that Carrier had found at the children's hospital, Jake's torn shirt. His wounds were consistent with those inflicted in Mower attacks.

She cradled him, appalled at the amount of blood he had shed. "How could you be so thin," she whispered, "with all this life inside you?"

11 totem

The scabrous poster on the saloon wall blurred. A moment ago it had depicted a woman in a black bikini coiling a snake around her shoulders. Now it was impossible even to read her name. It was akin to viewing something through heat haze. She tried to remember what The Dancer had told her without losing her grip on the tear as it deepened. This time she was not distracted by the sequins of color beading the lips of the wound.

Her heartbeat was down to around twelve beats per minute.

She could see The Dancer behind her, stock still, his left ankle wrapped around his neck. He was facing east, waiting for the sun to rise. She wanted to call him, to show him what was happening, but the moment it occurred to her, the fracture failed slightly, its edges bruising as though she had injured it in some way. Perhaps she had.

Carrier pressed all peripheral distractions into a meaningless fuzz beyond the tunnel that contained the tear. Instantly, it blossomed again, widening, birthing its promise in a glut of sensory information that staggered her. It was as though the world was being sucked inside out. The more exposure, the less she had to concentrate. Beyond a certain point she could relax and watch it happen, this fantastic unraveling.

"Look," she murmured, but The Dancer was already staring at the spectacle. Parts of the Mile were being replaced by vibrant objects that bore a resemblance to their predecessors. This bowed, shattered streetlamp became the bough of a sapling; that giant pothole magicked itself into a pond; the scimitar crack in a black window sped into the sky as a bird on the wing.

"It's beautiful," she said.

He said, "It's you."

The Dancer refused to go with her when she expressed a desire to explore. Instead, he lay on the floor and closed his eyes. "I'll be here," he said. "I'll wait for you."

Disappointed, Carrier set off. She had wanted The Dancer to explain the topography as they walked it, but she quickly realized how she did not need a guide after all. This was her terrain. She no more needed a map for it than she did for her own flat. It was hard to believe that this was only the start of her revelations. *You have to know yourself before you can understand the secrets of the Mile*, he had told her. For her, though, this was enough. More than enough.

She suffered a mild twinge of regret when she thought of how she might have translated this knowledge into something that might have saved Jake, or at least salved his pain, but her upset threatened to draw a veil over her surroundings. A grainy aspect mottled Carrier country as though visited by twilight. Evicting Jake from her mind freshened the picture.

Gradually she learned how her mood could affect the landscape. She found too that certain regions corresponded with different parts of her anatomy. A range of stony hills caused her back to tingle when she traversed them. Paddling in a shoreline brought an ache to her eyeballs. Her kidneys shouted at her when she walked a path into a valley filled with tall grasses. And her heart raced as she came up against a totemic stack; a tall, sculpted piece of what seemed like bleached wood, but on closer inspection revealed itself as bone. It was so tall that its uppermost features were lost to thin rafts of cloud.

There were no buildings, as far as she could see, and no evidence of anyone having been there before.

"That's because it's your land," The Dancer explained, when she returned. "Nobody can make any changes to your land but you."

"Then what are you doing here?"

"You brought me with you," he said.

"Will this place be mapped by Phale?" she asked. "I'd like to see what it looks like on paper."

"If you ask him, I'm sure he'll oblige."

They stood together, The Dancer's hand lightly brushing against the hairs on her forearm. The wind was warm and gingered.

"I saw something. It was like a pole with faces carved into it. Very high."

The Dancer nodded.

"Do you know what it was? What it means?"

The Dancer shrugged.

"It's calm here," he said at last. "Some places... you wouldn't believe."

"What do we do now?" Carrier looked up at him. His skin looked so smooth it too might have been chipped away from a block of something beautiful and sanded to perfection.

"I think you're ready to try to leave the Mile," he said.

12 outermost

He was drilling her with information but now, after such a long period of concentration, all she could do was allow in whatever wanted to mess with her brain. Chief among the visiting flashes was Jake.

If you are shot at, I will leave you.

Things had gone so quickly she had found little time in which to consider what had happened and no time at all for the grief that was piling against her defenses.

If you get stuck at the Border, I will leave you.

Jake had been such a boon to her existence in Howling Mile, despite her curmudgeonly reaction to his depression. She missed him immensely. But there was nothing to keep her in the Mile now. She imagined—

Mower attacks, and there will be some, we can deal with, up to a point.

—tracking down Enderby and forging a new friendship. He would be her Dancer outside of the Mile, helping her to ease her way into a new way of life. Showing her how to cope with the lack of everyday challenges. She wondered if she might have problems with that. Did life become boring just because you weren't in fear of losing it anymore?

She said, "Why me?" She hadn't meant to say anything; the question blurted out of her.

The Dancer stopped packing his bag and gazed at her. "I already told you. You're special. You *spoke* to me."

"Yes, but what are you gaining from all this?"

"Plenty," he said, patiently.

"Yes, but what?"

He sighed and let his hands fall on to the bulging sack of food and clothing. No matter what posture he took, he looked ready for flight. Words such as "cumbersome" or "inelegant" could never be applied to him.

"Every time I help someone open up their own little world, my abilities improve, and my own land comes a little closer to me."

"You mean you've never visited your own country?"

"Correct."

"But you trained me. You're so in control."

The Dancer knotted the bag. "Maybe. But I'm no thaumaturge."

"But the first time. All that green."

"That wasn't me. That was you."

Carrier couldn't say anything for a moment. *"Me?"*

The Dancer nodded. "Amazing what the unconscious can achieve when it's coaxed along."

"So why can't *your* unconscious...."

"Look," The Dancer interjected, impatiently, "this isn't about me. It's about you. I chose you because I saw your potential. You are realizing that potential. You might see me as some kind of magus, some kind of freak, but you'd be mistaken. I haven't got half the strength you've got."

He plucked the bag off the ground and slung it across his shoulder.

"I'm sorry," she said. "I'm just confused. I don't even know what this is supposed to achieve."

"Know yourself and you'll know The Mile." He headed off, not looking to see if she was following him.

She attempted to put his words to the test as they made their way through the streets of The Hub. Behind them, the Core's tip pulsed like a smoldering cigar. She forced her concentration into each shadowed doorway and cobwebbed window. Nothing became illumined. No scales fell from her eyes. She wanted to ask The Dancer what he meant but she sensed she had already overstepped the mark. She also wanted to know why it was so imperative that she try to escape the city. If he thought she would come back if the experiment was a success, he would be waiting a long time.

They reached the canal without incident, but here their luck ran out. The Dancer motioned for her to stop. Ahead, a fat man in a gray apron patterned with the bloody handprints of children was shouting orders at a pair of heavily made-up women in red leather. On the towpath, two racks of carcasses, marbled with fat, swung gently on meat-hooks awaiting transport on one of the barges.

The Dancer assessed them and told her to follow him closely. "They don't look too dangerous," he said.

As soon as they reached the bridge across the water, the fat man pulled a cleaver out of his apron and called: "Oyst!"

Another man—Oyst, presumably—emerged from the barge carrying three chains, each of them tipped with more glittering hooks.

"Ah, Plessey, I see you've found us some more meat for the slab," he said. "Choice cuts."

"However," The Dancer said, giving Carrier a little smile, "looks can be deceiving. These men evidently are dangerous. But not where we're concerned."

She tried, in the hours that followed, to work out exactly how he managed to do it, but her brain would not allow her to linger on movement so swift or lethal that it defied logic, even though she herself had visited the extremities of what made sense not that long ago.

Was she a reliable witness? Did she really see The Dancer blur in the blink of an eye across the five meters to where Plessey stood? Could he have plucked the cleaver from his hand and *swick!* opened him neatly across the fattest part of his gut? Even as Plessey was only beginning to understand that death was upon him, his arms filling with steaming yards of himself, The Dancer leapt on to the deck of the barge and turned Oyst's head into fish food, swatting and hacking so swiftly that his hand disappeared in the air like a hummingbird's wing before Oyst had a chance to raise a fist in anger or defense.

The two women sent the meat crashing in their haste to be away. The Dancer let them go.

They had to hurry then; the meat on the racks and the fresh blood would have brought all kinds of unsavory types on to the streets. There was a danger too that the Mowers would venture in from the very area Carrier and The Dancer were about to cross into.

"It could work to our advantage," The Dancer offered. "The more Mowers tucking into a free dinner here means the fewer waiting in ambush in The Outermost."

The streets dwindled after another hour of walking and dodging patrols. Soon they were walking dust tracks through low tufts of scrub. Few dwellings remained; of those that did, every doorway was filled with the shadow of a figure holding a weapon waving in their direction until they had passed. Dunes of glossy black undulated into a distance filled with criss-cross beams of light; the perimeter, where sniper steeples would spot them a mile off and specially bred guard dogs with incurved fangs and electrifying speed who could sniff you out of an offal trough. Reaching the perimeter, let alone passing through it, seemed an impossible task. But The Dancer skipped on, regardless.

"I know a place where we can rest," he informed her. "A friend, Ana, has a shack about half an hour's walk away. She'll let us stay till dawn. Dawn is the best time for us."

Ana's shack was just visible when Carrier's alert kicked in, causing her to jump. "Does Ana have cleansers?" she asked, digging in her rucksack for a blister pack of nasal gel to refresh the dose she took that morning.

"Of course she does. Doesn't everyone?" He sounded irritated.

"How come you never take any preventatives?" she asked.

"What makes you think I don't?"

"I never see you applying anything."

He shook his head. In the gloaming, his eyes were shiny ball-bearings.

"You never see me at toilet either, but that doesn't mean I don't go."

With the gel inhaled, Carrier relaxed. "Fair point," she said. It was then that the Mower attacked.

It came at them fast from behind a termite mound, claws outstretched, raking through the air for the soft tissue on Carrier's face. She ducked and shifted her weight, somersaulting away from the danger, reaching for her knife in the same fluid motion. From the corner of her eye she saw The Dancer static, but poised, his body bouncing easily on flexed legs that would carry him away, or into the fight, in a trice. She didn't need him. Her body sang with liberty. The extent of her suppleness shocked her now it was called into action. The speed of her feints and dodges frustrated the Mower and his phlegmy, guttural cries grew ever more violent. A lunge made him overbalance; his back to her, Carrier slashed twice with the knife and as he arched with pain, she swept in close and rammed the knife into the back of his neck. The heel of her free hand met the butt of the weapon and she drove it home until it was flush with the meat. It was a superfluous action, but her instinct had told her to finish the job; if anything it would send a signal to other, unseen, Mowers that had observed the contest. She stood over the body. If anything, her breathing had slowed. Endorphines widened the blacks of her eyes and made her blood buzz. When The Dancer approached, her head flew up and he flinched. "It's me," he said, uncertainly. "It's finished. You killed him. Rein it in, Carrier. You did well."

A brilliant white flare arced up from Ana's shack and created false daylight all around. Shells followed, concussing in the air like the blows of a carpet-beater. Stitches of dirt skipped their way.

The flare died but the shots kept coming. Carrier felt The Dancer's hands pushing her out of the way, and suddenly she was on the floor. Warmth flooded her. She felt herself blushing; how stupid would she seem when he saw that she had wet herself? And then nothing but stars and the last thought as awareness faded: *How can I see stars if I'm face down in the gravel?*

13 ana

The sound of water. She had forgotten how beautiful it could be. Whispers overlaid it, turned it into something sinuous, something to be mistrusted. She opened her eyes and saw an old woman squeezing water from a flannel and frantically hissing at an unseen party—presumably The Dancer. Without looking her way, the woman dabbed the flannel across Carrier's forehead.

"How was I to know?" she heard. "I take action, then ask questions."

Carrier tried to speak but her throat was too dry. The croak that came from it, however, was enough to drag the old woman's attention her way.

"She's awake," the woman said, no longer needing to keep her voice down.

The Dancer emerged from a shadowy corner of the room. "Are you okay?" he asked.

"I don't know," said Carrier, feeling the first twinge of panic. "Am I?"

"Ana clipped you with a shell. Across the shoulder. She panicked. Didn't know what was—"

Ana interrupted him. "I didn't know who you were or what you wanted," she said. "My eyesight's all buggered to shittery. Don't blame me!"

Carrier closed her eyes. *That's me done, then*, she thought, more calmly than she'd have anticipated. She always suspected she would one day fall victim to the Wave, but never at the hands of a gun-happy old woman.

"How bad is it?" Carrier asked.

The Dancer shrugged. "You lost a bit of blood but it's nothing more than a flesh wound, really. Nothing you can't get over."

"Funny." She struggled upright with The Dancer's help. The room bulged and span away from her, but closing her eyes for a few seconds helped.

"What do you want me to do?" Ana was saying. "What do you want me to say? What do you want me to do? I could say I'm sorry but I wouldn't mean it. I'd do it again, I promise you that."

The Dancer gently led Ana away. Carrier eased the dressing from her skin and whistled softly. The scar would be ugly, but The Dancer was right. She'd live. For now.

"Hungry?"

"I can't see you," Carrier said. "Can you put on some lights?"

The Dancer prepared them some supper. At no point did he ask her if she was up to finishing her training. She was glad of that. As pointless as it might seem now, she wanted to succeed, to show him she could do it. Maybe if she got out, she would be able to find a doctor who would be able to cure her. She concentrated while pots and cutlery clattered in the background but could not yet feel any of the toxicity moving through her veins. Jake had sometimes talked of the languid shift of poison through him but she suspected he was always pulling her leg. Well, time would prove him right or wrong.

"Ana's sleeping," The Dancer said at last, as he set steaming plates down on the table. Carrier picked at her food. She was hungry enough, but the shock of being shot was starting to kick in. She felt queasy.

"How do you know her?"

The Dancer pushed his food around the plate but never brought any to his mouth. Maybe he wasn't hungry either. Maybe he was as nervous as she was.

"She brought me up," he said.

"She was a dancer too?"

"The best. She traveled the world dancing for kings and queens. She invented much of what you might call modern dance."

"And the other stuff. Did she teach you that as well?"

"To a certain extent."

Carrier's laugh turned into a grimace as pain shot through her shoulder. "What does that mean?"

"Ana never pushed herself. People with natural ability never have to. I was never as gifted as Ana so I had to work at dancing. Sometimes, when you push yourself to your limit, beyond your limit, you see things—"

Carrier wasn't going to argue. She knew what he was talking about. Never in her life had she forced her body through such a punishing schedule and just as it seemed she was going to black out or be sick, her body would give her a little more, and that was the point when the glamors revealed themselves.

"Will you make love to me?" she asked.

The Dancer regarded her for a long time. Then he silently stood up and took their plates away. His back to her, he said, "There are some painkillers here, if you need them in the night. Try to relax. We leave early morning."

14 threshold

But he came to her, and loved her, in her dreams. They lay on an outcrop of rock in Carrier country. The sun beat against the land and the wind took layers of dust and drew them up into the sky so that by the time the sunset came, it was a riot of oranges, violets and greens. They didn't move for hours, unless it was to change the position in which their bodies were yoked together, or to look into each other's eyes. She found flecks of gray in the green and a cobalt corona encircling the iris. If she concentrated, she thought she could see the topography of this place in its pattern, as though he had always carried its map, the map of her, within him. The color brightened and deepened as they lost themselves to the deliquescence that bound them together. When the color of his eyes was consumed by the palette of dying sunlight all around them, she woke up.

Her shoulder was stiff, but it didn't feel infected. Perhaps she was becoming paranoid. Ana had clearly cleaned the wound well. She had a brief vision of the arm growing black with sores, but managed to excise it before hysteria could take hold.

The Dancer was anxious to be off. Carrier found him on the porch working through a series of stretching exercises, while the distant clatter of helicopters told of another morning of nervy vigilance in Howling Mile.

"I'm sorry," she said. "I wasn't myself last night."

"It's forgotten," The Dancer said, flatly. "Are you ready?"

They made good time in the cool dawn. The ground here seemed purple; silver grains glittered in it like the flashes in coal. Twice they had to flatten themselves into the scrub when helicopter patrols returned from their morning duties, but they weren't spotted and reached a less exposed tract of land, dotted with the huge corpses of incinerated trees and the impressively broad banks of a dead river. From here they could see the sniper steeples, punctuating the perimeter fence every quarter of a mile or so. The steeples stretched off to the horizon in both directions. Her skin crawled, seeing so much determination to keep people hemmed in.

"How are we going to breach that?" she said, failing to keep her voice level.

"Maybe, if you have to ask the question, you aren't ready yet."

"Maybe you're right. I'm going to get myself killed here. Shot twice in twenty-four hours. Not bad for someone whose idea of a bad injury before today was stubbing a toe on the doorstep."

The Dancer looked away from her, assessing the steeples as one might take in an impressive mountain range. "If you do as I taught you, you'll be fine."

"Okay. I'll try. But how do we even get close? I can't see how there would be any blind spots."

The Dancer nodded. "I know what you mean. But there *are* blind spots. Just not how you'd imagine them to be. You're thinking in terms of what's here."

Carrier worked at getting her breathing down. Her heart was pecking away at her innards like a bird. "You mean I have to travel within me to get out of here?"

"Of course," he said. "What else?"

Something went wrong.

In her preparation for the escape, something happened. She wasn't sure what it was, but the closest she could come to rationalizing it was hearing two pirate radio broadcasts merge with each other until they became an inaudible howl of noise.

She didn't tell The Dancer. She didn't think it was too important. After all, the moment passed and she found herself settling into relaxation. To break off now would further delay their progress and she didn't want that. She stretched her body until parts of it burned and she felt they would separate from the rest of her. When the pain reached an unbearable level, she breathed deeply and stretched even further. At the same time, her heartbeat grew sluggish and her thoughts coalesced and sharpened, dismissing trivia, honing, paring down, until all she could see was the path she would take to the border. Even The Dancer was relegated to a soft white blur at the edge of her vision. He might as well have been a million miles away.

A gurney, rattling along cobbled streets awash with blood, a confusion of pale limbs loosely restrained, flopping and spasming with each jarring yard.

Her brow twitched at the invasion. But she was able to suppress it and return to the matter of slowing down. Here it came. The air rippled and peeled back reluctantly, displaying a hot red core that simmered like magma. It was as though she was slipping a key into the lock that would open her door.

Gunfire. Shells slamming into the walls of a hospital with ragged black flags flapping from the roof. The gurney threatening to topple. Screams joining the sounds of confusion. Bodies clawing at themselves while fire smoothed their features.

Gritting her teeth, Carrier repulsed the images. What were they, fragments from forgotten dreams? The slit in the air was threatening to suture itself shut. She would not allow Jake's death to be for nothing. She wouldn't fail his memory. Carrier imagined her heart in her hands, responding to her gentle touch as a sleepy pet might. It slowed further. Her breathing was almost non-existent. The slit became a gash became a flapping rent that lost itself to her desire for what lay within. Its edges weakened and flew apart, sending wisps of itself into the sky. Like a page catching fire from the inside out, soon there was nothing of what had existed before and Carrier was through. Alone.

The sniper steeples had resolved themselves into a rank of what appeared to be black churches with crooked spires. She found it fascinating that transitory items, such as the steeples, or a crack in glass, could mutate into a negative image in the interior. She wondered if she might appear differently to another observer, but then concluded that was unlikely. After all, this was her land. This was *her*. And The Dancer, when he had traveled with her the first time, was no different to the way she usually appreciated him.

Did the absence of any snipers mean that this would still be a dangerous task? The churches looked peaceful enough. A tiny wall enclosed them and wild grasses hid what might in another world be construed as a graveyard.

She approached cautiously, reaching for the knife in its hasp, but it wasn't there. Had she removed it and left it at Ana's house? Or was it usual that things became lost in the translation? Her control of her own environment must be such that she could neutralize any threat. But knowing how was one lesson The Dancer had failed to pass on.

Nothing moved here. The trees were still, as were the faded, blistered doors of the churches. She liked the way the air felt against her. It was hot and heavy, moving on her skin like layers of silk. In her mouth, the air was peppery, and imbued with an underlying sweetness. She wondered if it would be possible to stay here all the time.

Interference.

The gurney almost toppling over as it nudges aside a body in a dark corridor. Live? *comes an impatient, anxious voice.* Live, yes. Just. *A vague white smear solidifies out of the gloom. A man in cracked spectacles is standing by a stainless steel table that is anything but stainless. A rack of forbidding surgical instruments, like some hellish* batterie de cuisine, *flashes in the stuttering light from a dying neon tube. His mouth is covered by a surgical mask. He wears gloves that make his hands appear formed from wax.*

Put him on here. Make sure he does not wake up. Hear me?

The body is unceremoniously dumped onto the table. It displaces a puddle of serous fluids and a thick hank of hair.

He's out cold.

The lenses of the nurse's glasses capture two coins of light as he lifts a syringe in front of his face. Hard day, *he sighs.* Non-stop, this thankless job.

Forcing the air from the tip of the syringe until a squirt of liquid appears. Step back, friend. You don't want any of this juice on you…. Where did you pick him up?

Outside End of Steel. A Mower got to him.

Polite way of putting it. I'd say this chap is going to have a hard time of things without his lips. Poor thing. But he'll live. For a while anyway. End of Steel, you say? That's good. We haven't had a Steeler for a while now. This should warm things up for them out there.

The plunger depressed, the liquid released, the porter dismissed. Darkness fell.

Carrier's head could not deal with such a dichotomy of thought. Her surroundings were failing. It was akin to watching meat rot. The sky blackened and tiny rents made a leopard skin of the scenery. What did it mean? How could she have been invaded with such awful pictures? Was her concentration span really so poor?

Again she fought to keep a grip on Carrier country. Bit by bit, she sealed the slashes and wiped the granular sky clear. But things had changed. Now, where there had been silence, there was a dull, buzzing sound. She couldn't see what was producing it but it made her feel ill at ease. As she neared the closest of the black churches, the sound intensified but its source remained a mystery. A kissing gate allowed her into the church grounds. The grasses were so long and dense that she could not tell if they concealed any headstones. The spire reared up above her, a helter-skelter pattern biting into its matte black cone. She was glad she couldn't identify the gargoyles that gurned at her from the flying buttresses that surrounded it; the overwhelming conviction that she'd spot her own likeness up there made her feel sick.

It was obvious that the church door was not locked yet she had to press hard against it to gain access. Stale air puffed out at her; she reasoned that the church could never have been entered before. But then this was her world. Who else could visit it but her? Inside she sneezed twice in quick succession. Dust danced in a beam of light lancing in through a rent in the stonework. All of the pews had collapsed, as though pushed over in an act of sacrilege. There was no obvious effigy to suggest what kind of church this was. Nobody came to see who she was or what she wanted. The church was empty.

Outside again, the drone had become even louder. She was about to walk away from the church, in a direction that would put her on the non-Mile side of the border, when she saw what was creating the noise.

Insects.

Black wasps. As soon as she saw them, they charged her. Fear caused another partial disintegration of the immediate vicinity. But she knew that she mustn't lose control now, if what existed here became something else on the outside.

"Carrier!" The Dancer called to her. His voice was muffled, as though reaching her from a mouthful of cotton. "Come out! You have to come out!"

His voice ruptured things further. The sky became striped with decay. The first of the wasps resolved itself into a bullet that zinged past her face by inches. He would not stop calling her. But to come out now was to be torn in half by sniper shells.

"Carrier! Carrier! Come out of it!"

Running back to the church would be suicide if everything were to fail now. Making a break for what existed beyond the border was possible, but not at the rate of dissolution. They'd pick her off almost casually. She had to fight it. She closed her eyes and imagined the hospital. She wondered if Jake had ever been there and hoped that, wherever he was now, he was at peace. The drone lessened. The very fabric of what lay around her grew warped, as though it were collapsing in the face of great heat. Where the ripples ended, so something new was introduced. Gradually, the landscape became modified.

She thought, *It isn't working. I'm dead. I'm dead.*

But what crystallized around her was not Howling Mile, but another stretch of Carrier country. Caves punched holes into a hillside. Hard gusts of wind whipped up the dust here, making it hard to see detail, but she was able to pick out the black birds that fussed and fluttered at the entrance to one of those deep, shadowed entrances.

"What else could it be?" Her words startled her. At once, they sounded as much like her and as alien to her ears as any voice she had ever heard. She moved through the miniature sandstorm, guarding her eyes with her arm, and stood at the mouth to the cave. The birds clattered and cawed but did not move.

"Come on then," she whispered, and let her grip loosen. She shed the country as swiftly as a piece of clothing.

part three: the core
15 infected

Ragged black flags beat weakly on their poles, ranged above the entrance to the hospital. Inside, it became clear that it had been evacuated. Of the living, at least. Bodies were slumped in varying stages of decay along the route to the operating theatre. She saw one young man trying to move, his chest laboring as he tried to suck in breath, but when she bent to assist him, she saw it was other things, beneath the skin, that gave him the illusion of motor control.

Rattled, she stumbled into a staff room that was mercifully empty, and splashed cold water against her cheeks. Had she changed at all, inside? Knowing what she did now, having this special key to a new part of her, had it altered who she was? Of course it must, to some extent, but she could see nothing to indicate any maturity or wisdom in this foxed, flyblown mirror.

Recovered, she moved into the corridor once more, forcing herself not to study any of the wasted shapes that lay at her feet. The lighting overhead had been shot out; bullet holes dented the wall, augmented by the odd arterial spray or blot of jellied offal. Gurneys stood abandoned, wrapping anonymous bulges with blankets. A stretcher leaned vertically against a doorway, its occupant strapped in, looking down at his feet like an errant schoolboy being disciplined.

Carrier paused at the entrance to the operating theatre. Through a crack in the doors she saw the man with spectacles sitting on a stool, a startled expression on his face. His surgical mask had been removed and blood painted a line from his bottom lip to his chin. He seemed to be weeping blood, too. Surgical instruments and phials lay around him. Carrier's heart quickened at the sight of them.

The theatre smelled heavily of sour sweat. It was hot in here.

Behind the nurse's glasses, Carrier could see that his eyes had been stolen. His lips had been snipped off and one of his cheeks had been slashed open. Presumably the Mower had been interrupted during this operation, otherwise there surely would have been more pilfering of the nurse's body. The wounds were bloodless because they had been created post-mortem, and as such, they seemed unreal, faked. Carrier tried to swallow the jagged lump in her throat and concentrated instead on one of the phials. It was a dark bottle containing a syrupy liquid, its label bearing only a black spot.

Almost imperceptible: the hiss of a plastic door flapping open, then closing.

Another door in the operating theatre led deeper into the heart of the hospital. Carrier didn't wait behind it to see if what was coming down the corridor was the Mower, intent on finishing his grisly job, or a breath of wind. She stumbled through the semi-dark, appalled by the numbers of bodies piled up like dirty laundry. She seemed to run for an age until it dawned on her that there was an alternative way out. In full-flight, she sought the torpor that would rescue her. The vertiginous unfolding of new surfaces and sensations flummoxed her and she clouted herself half-senseless against the wall of the cave. An ecstasy of bats shrieked and shat and battered the air around her. She headed towards the light and emerged, barely holding the scream inside her that had wanted freedom since she had entered the hospital.

The sky darkening with bats, she looked down at the phial in her hand. It had transmogrified into a shriveled, embryonic heart.

She followed the cats to the fish processing unit. Long dead, the ghost of the sea still held sway over these starving scavengers. They swarmed around her ankles, drooling and miaowing, hoping that she might magic a titbit or two out of the marine cloud.

Instead, she pushed through the door that would take her up the stairwell to the offices above. Doctor Smoker was in. A woman around

Carrier's age was sitting on the edge of his desk with her top up. The doctor was prodding at her breasts with his stubby fingers.

"You should be struck off," Carrier said, as she forced her way into the tiny office.

The woman didn't flinch, didn't even adjust her clothing, but the doctor blustered around his desk, straightening papers as though the woman were not there.

"I thought our business was over," he said, without looking at her.

Carrier said, "Which one of us are you talking to?"

"That's all, Miss Lissey. Your chest is fine."

The woman got down off the desk and shrugged on her coat. "You forgot something," she said, archly.

The doctor withdrew a tightly folded envelope from his desk drawer. "Take twice a day, before meals," he ordered. The woman ignored him and shook her head as she pushed past Carrier, emptying the coins from the envelope into her hand.

The doctor looked mortified. Carrier couldn't help feeling sorry for him. His tweeds were getting grubby; the collar of his white shirt was as black as his shoes. He was starting to explain, but she held up her hand.

"I'm not interested," she said. The doctor's florid face relaxed into the welter of flesh that surrounded it. "All I want is for you to tell me what this is."

He took the phial from her and shook it, watched intently the oily droplets rilling across the inside of the glass. "Interesting," he muttered. "What does this black spot mean?"

"I don't know," Carrier said. "I thought you might recognize it."

The doctor shook his head. "Lab job," he said, grandly, winking at her. "Come on."

He led her through a narrow passageway from his office to a tiny door that he unlocked with a key selected from a huge collection attached to his waistband. Ushering her through, he worked his arms into a laboratory coat that was at least one size too small for him. He used a pipette to dribble a little of the liquid into a test tube which he stoppered and fixed to a centrifuge.

"This could take some time," he warned her. "Bed?" He gestured to an even tinier room off this one.

"No thanks."

"You want me to just identify this stuff and tell you out of the kindness of my heart, do you?"

Carrier unsheathed her knife. It was still encrusted with the blood of the Mower she had killed yesterday. She leaned over a sink and casually washed it off until the blade's grin was spotless.

"Yes," she said at last.

Dr Smoker couldn't take his eyes off the weapon. "Right you are."

16 kram

It took the best part of a day, dipping in and out of Carrier country, but she eventually found the library. She cursed herself for not taking note of the route when The Dancer had first led her here, but she had been so wound up in his theories and his oblique way of looking at things, that she had traveled here as though in her sleep. At least the journey had allowed her to polish her skills, dropping in and out of both terrains to a point where she could almost execute a crossover instantaneously.

The library was much as she had left it, a shambles. Luckily, the monitor was still in position, hidden by a sheaf of papers that she had put there. She slotted the hard drive into the console and booted up.

>>> enderby. it's carrier.

>>> thank god you're ok. i've been busy.

>>> me too, e. if you only knew!

>>> shut upp and lisen.

Carrier took her hands off the keyboard and sat back. The hard drive chuckled and chirred. Enderby had never been so direct with her before. Neither had he been so swift in responding. Sometimes she had to wait half an hour before he checked his in-box.

>>> ive been checking stuff out. nearly got myself killed th other day. snooping round th border, i bumped into this guy in a hat, tells me he escaped from th mile couple of years ago. tells me he waits in all weathers for his wife. she was sposed 2 follow him out. been waiting all this time, comes 2 th border every day 2 see if she's around. he used 2 work in th core. no shit. really worked there. nobody's seen/heard anybody from th core. showed me his id card. seems like

>>> there's no such thing as the wave?

>>> ....

>>> how did u know?

>>> i've been busy too, like I said. what does *xenopsylla cheopsis* mean to you?

>>> nothing. what is it?

>>> it's the bacterium passed on to human beings by plague carrying fleas. aka Iridia. I found some. in a hospital. *they're administering it

to people*. they're doing it to make people think there's infection everywhere, but there's not.

>>> I know. And I know why. they enclosed th mile not because of some awful epidemic that they were afraid would leak out, but because they wanted to keep something else in. there's someone they've been hunting for years, someone with th ability to bring the mile down. but they reckon they can use him, if they catch him, to extend th influence of th mile. turn it into some kind of supercity. put all th surrounding regions under its thumb.

>>> nice.

>>> this guy in th hat, he told me all about it. he talked about a dancer. said it was a dancer. a dancer! how mad is that?

>>> I know who it is! I've talked to him!

Pages swarmed into the library, pushed by a breeze. The soft moan of hinges oiled by nothing other than grit and the passing of years. Very distinctly, there was a single retort as a heel clipped the tiled entrance hall.

>>> carrier, be careful!

>>> z

Carrier killed the link and hauled out the hard drive. Her eyes never left the wedge of light allowed in by the door. She was being followed. Her flight at the hospital she had put down to paranoia, but not now. Not with the etiolated shadow of a figure reaching through the doorway like a surge of black oil, or blood.

She backed away. Behind her, the scorched shelves reached up to the domed ceiling, shiny as tar. Reading booths were ranged like love seats, alternatively hemmed in by a partition and free-backed. Carrier edged to one of them and ducked under so that she was hidden from view. The only way out was via the door that was now being slowly closed. The darkness grew deeper. As the door snicked shut, a soft, wet gargle reached out like an attempt at contact. Carrier closed her eyes. A Mower—the rogue Mower that was terrorizing the Hub—was in here with her.

Air dragged across the membranes in its face, creating horrid music. She heard the teeth in its throat chatter at the thought of a meal. There was no doubt that it could smell her in here. She inched to her left as her eyes grew accustomed to the gloom. The monitor was still on, a slow band of lilac light journeying repeatedly from the top to the bottom of the screen. It reflected off the Mower's crimson eyes which, thankfully, would be almost useless in this dark. They were as wide open as possible, like bloody yolks suspended above the moist grille that even now was rating her flavors. It made a few delicate trilling noises, totally at contrast with its brutal appearance, as if it were a lost pet tracking down its owner. But then Carrier saw the sheaths on its hands peel back to reveal razored claws and she knew she was right to feel afraid.

The two of them moved like scorpions in a tense dance, the Mower keeping itself between Carrier and the door. Carrier was trying to maintain her distance and at the same time gather herself for an attempt at crossing over into her own land. She didn't want to imagine what the Mower would become once she arrived there.

She found the tranquility she sought, but nothing was happening. There was no quivering air, no rents in the fabric of reality to spur her on. Just the Mower, killing the distance between them, its head swinging to and fro, a froth of hunger forming on its maw.

Carrier reached for her knife, but had a better idea. She reached behind her and felt along the rows of books until her fingers met a volume that wasn't so damaged she couldn't slide it off the shelf. She tested its weight and then stood up, hurling the book at the monitor. The Mower jerked its head her way and bared the glistening fangs in its throat. The book struck the monitor on the corner and sent it crashing to the floor. The Mower was distracted enough for Carrier to make a move for the door but then she noticed the tinder dry pages had caught and a fire sprang up, quicker than either of them. Luckily, it provided a wall that she was on the right side of. The light it afforded showed the Mower backing away, but not before Carrier caught sight of Kram's face dangling like a cheap mask from the Mower's chin. It had become rugose and discolored, but she clearly recognized the shape of the eyes and the tuft of beard favored by her former neighbor.

The fire caught rapidly. It was as though, Carrier thought, hurrying down the corridor to the exit, it was grateful for the chance to finish the job it had started at the library, many years ago.

17 closure

She walked newly sodden pathways, mindful of flash floods after a storm that had lasted a day and a half. Howling Mile's sewers and drains were not up to the task of sluicing the water away and, as a result, rats and refuse were heaping up on the pavements like some foul bunting in preparation for a street party.

After escaping the library, Carrier had gone home and slept solidly until the noise at the height of the storm wakened her. Around midnight she watched the play of the lightning over the rooftops, hoping that the rain might wash everything away and reveal the Mile at dawn as a clean city where all that had happened to her was nothing but the detritus of her dreams. And soon Jake would leer at her over a coffee cup and suggest they go back to bed and she would smile and kiss his nicely muscled, flawless chest and lose herself on top of him for a while.

But as the night wore on and daylight crept over the city, she saw how the streets churned with filth. The body of an old man swept by her window, face-down in the water and for an unforgivable instant, she wished that they could trade places.

Everything was collapsing around her. The Dancer had gone missing, there was no way of re-establishing contact with Enderby and her ability to travel in Carrier country had deserted her at a moment when she needed it the most. A helicopter fizzed past and the Bordertype stationed at the gunwhale looked directly at her. How might she warn The Dancer that he was being pursued? Perhaps he had already been captured. It was awful to think that his skills would be commandeered by the Core to reach beyond these confines and stain the rest of the country. Ultimately, after all the scaremongering, their ambition *was* a kind of infection.

A burst of gunfire turned her window into an opaque oblong of stars. Another sent it crashing in, but by then she was out of the door, ignoring the chitinous voice that buzzed from the helicopter's loudhailer, commanding her to not dodge the salvo.

She knew her backstreets better than any Bordertype. She fled through them now, jinking and ducking and doubling back. More shots brought her to a halt, but they were distant and she reasoned that they were fired in hope. Her blood was up, but not her panic. Pursuit, she decided as she cut down Incision Lane to the canal, became like a chore. It could even get boring.

After a while, she slowed to a walk. She remembered this part of the city. Didn't Phale have his living quarters around here? Almost as soon as she entertained the thought, she saw the door that he had opened for them. She wondered if his skill as a cartographer might help her regain the power to blend into her interior land again. Nobody answered her knock. She waited for a while, even shouting up to his window, but the grubby muslin did not shift to reveal his face.

The alleyway at the back of Phale's street was a mudchute. She picked her way along until she found the corresponding fire escape and climbed out of the morass. At the landing outside his floor, she smashed the window and let herself in. Mushrooms were growing on one patch of the carpet. His door was ajar; Carrier could smell the candles' acridity even from here. His tape deck was playing more of that harsh music.

Carrier advanced slowly, a melting feeling in her gut. She knew before she opened the door that she would find him dead. That he was not was a surprise, but she soon discovered that he would not be of any use to her. Clearly he had been suffocated, but whoever had smothered him had not completed the job. She hoped that was the case. The thought that whoever had done this had resuscitated Phale knowing he would be irreparably brain damaged was too shocking to entertain.

Carrier watched Phale gurgle and twitch, his eyes roiling as though without control. She slit his windpipe, checked through the maps and scrolls for any clue as to The Dancer's whereabouts, and hurried out, empty-handed. Clearly, whoever had done for Phale was also on The Dancer's trail. She only hoped she could get to him before the unknown assassin did.

They were all dead.

Chamfer and Tusk she found at the Usher Street park. They had been tied to a tree trunk and slashed open with knives like joints of meat ready for the oven. Chamfer's mouth had been crammed to bursting point with a canvas ballet shoe. Tusk looked to have been strangled with a tutu.

Mowse, then. Carrier had heard that she lived in a region where there had once been many mines. She had made a joke about it, on the only occasion they had met, referring to it as "the pits." The only place she knew was Kobi-Finn, which was in the western part of Howling Mile. She knew how to get there; the school in Scissor Point where she had taught all that time ago was on the way.

18 deceleration

Like everything else in Howling Mile, the mines at Kobi-Finn had been long closed. A treacherous place due to the proliferation of blind shafts, it was a district that could punish you if you did not know it well.

It was dark when she arrived. There was nothing to offer relief for the eye here. Just scarefied land. Rusting cranes thrust out of the smog like the skeletons of prehistoric beasts. The scars in the earth had been adapted by settlers. Carrier approached one now, hoping that she was not too late. If the lack of urban claustrophobia was a difference out here, the hostility she encountered was the same as that found deep within the city. Many refused to acknowledge her presence, let alone talk to her. But one woman pointed her in the direction of Mowse's living quarters before hurrying away into the dark.

It was a brightish domicile, at least compared to the sunken, defeated aspect of the others in the terrace. Faded pink curtains hung in the window and a dried flower had been pinned to the door. A mat in front of it bore a faded message: WE C ME. Carrier never made it as far as stepping on it. She heard a woman grunting, in pain, a sound that reached for her from an inky passage that led down the side of the house. The wind fluted through the arched tunnel as she crept into it, at times collapsing the sound, at others enhancing it, so that it sounded as though its purveyor was standing mere inches away.

An allotment of sorts stood at the end of the tunnel, accessible via a gate that offered only a rudimentary barrier to the stunted vegetables and convulvulus beyond. Carrier had a fright when she gingerly pushed through the wall of bindweed to find a dwarfish scarecrow staring up at her with clumsily stitched eyes and a mouth squirming with a nest of mice. Another muffled howl of pain drew her to the left. A trampled area lay ahead; at its center was an unlit bonfire. Mowse was tethered to the wood, her mouth wadded with cloth. A Mower was straining at a leash attached to a steel bolt in the ground, his gnashing throat just nipping at the flesh of Mowse's thigh. The sight and smell of the cuts was driving the Mower into a frenzy. Carrier ran back to the scarecrow and dragged out the stake that was allowing it to stand upright.

When Carrier entered the clearing, the Mower immediately turned its attention on her. The peg that arrested its approach twitched in the earth; it wasn't going to hold for long. Carrier doubted her weapon would have much effect on a Mower that was in such a rage. She was about to try to knock it out when The Dancer stumbled into the clearing.

"There you are!" Carrier exulted. "Quick, untie Mowse!"

The Dancer did nothing. "I thought you were dead," he said. And then she knew. She knew even before The Dancer went to the peg and lifted it out of the ground, releasing the Mower. It was upon her before she had a chance to swing the stake. She thought it was Mowse screaming until the blood in her mouth made her choke and the screaming stopped and she realized it was her, trying to plead for her own life.

Her fingers came away wet from her neck. She couldn't speak but there was nobody around so she didn't need to. The allotment had resolved itself as a plot of shallow graves. Bones jutted out of the earth like strange crops. The pyre had become a hill of skulls. Scarecrows were now awful inverted crucifixes stained with blood.

Had it always been her they had sought? Could she, in her days of ignorance before The Dancer enlightened her, still have posed a threat to the Core? She remembered how he had said, when they first made that fantastic journey into Carrier country, that it was she who had taken her there, when she had believed he was their navigator. Could nobody realize that it was The Dancer that was the most dangerous threat to the Mile's security? All she had wanted was to care for Jake and try to make her life in Howling Mile as comfortable as possible. Her ambitions were not so grand as to include bringing the city to its knees. But now she understood how that must happen if she, and the remainder of her people, were to be free. She only wished her epiphany had come sooner.

Mindful that The Dancer was the only other being she had seen in these lands, Carrier traveled cautiously. His threat was difficult to gauge. He was able to mesmerize the Mowers for his own ends, that was plain, but had he not shown her a modicum of tenderness during their time together? Had he not called the Mower off just as it seemed it would slake its thirst with her, allowing her to seep into her interior? She contended that he was not lost to the Core, that somehow she might turn him round and become the ally she had always believed him to be. He had shown mercy at the brink of death; what more proof did she need?

She walked her country, staggered by some of its beauty. She saw distant peaks wearing scarves of purple cloud. Forests hugged swelling valleys. A stream rushed by bearing ribbons of every kind of blue. She walked for a long time, until the light was failing.

The totem cast its shadow over her long before she reached its base. She peered at the faces, frustrated that she could not recognize any of them, but somehow certain that her own face was etched somewhere into its remarkable surface. She quelled the suspicion that she would not be strong enough to finish what she had unwittingly set in motion, but enough people over the years, including The Dancer, had lauded her strength, her determination. Carrier took Dr. Smoker's yellow pearl from her pocket and swallowed it. She pressed a hand against the smooth, cool skin of the totem and closed her eyes.

It wouldn't, it couldn't budge under the pressure from her arms but she tested her weight against it anyway. Now she thought of Jake and her parents as they had sheltered her from the worst of those early days of Enclosure. She remembered how she had wakened one morning to find them gone and the remains of a meal unfinished on the table.

Her heart slowed.

She clung to the kindness of Kram and the way his dignity had been raped. She imagined the horror of bearing children in this place. She thought of Enderby's voice keeping her sane for so long. She thought of the tender betrayal of The Dancer.

slowed

Cracks began to show in the totem. They crept through and up the column, responding to the intensity of her dismay. The false sky darkened and thunder thrummed deep beneath her feet. So deep was her reverie, so committed her will, she did not notice the figure approaching in the distance, banded by the wavering shadow of the monument, nimbly picking his way towards her.

slowed... slowed....

In Howling Mile, people stopped what they were doing and looked up at the sky. Another storm, they thought. But then they saw the Core was listing. Its lights fused in a spectacular spray. Chunks of masonry slid out of true with what had for so long been a pristine tower around which the squalor of the city revolved. The highest forty feet of the Core toppled off the rest of the needle and crashed to the ground. At the same time a giant fracture traveled across the concave innards of the perspex ceiling. Real twilight poured through the hatching shell, blinding the Milers who had poured onto the streets to watch their city die.

The Dancer sprinted and darted through the disintegration, leaping clear of the falling debris as it crushed or clouted his fellow citizens. He moved with the lissome abandon of a wild cat, his eyes full of prey.

At the shuddering foundations of the Core, he slowed. Troops were pouring from the building, cheering and firing their weapons into the sky. All around the Mile, the tanks would be deployed by now. A great phalanx of infantrymen ready to move out of the shattered border and re-establish themselves in a country stagnated by more than fifty years of enclosure imposed by the pacifists beyond these city's confines. They would show those lost people what guns were; remind them of the color of blood.

The Dancer, euphoric, found the statue of a broken woman reaching up towards the Core. Tears were in her eyes. He kissed her gently on the cheek as veins of dissolution spread across it. A soldier clapped him on the back. "Well done, Enderby," he yelled. "Well played!"

To Carrier, The Dancer said, "Thank you." And then: "I'm sorry."

... stopped....